Nick Wood was born on Christmas Day, 1943, and was a neighbour and childhood friend of John Lennon. In his varied life, he has studied composition at the Royal Northern College of Music, worked for the John Lewis Partnership and the civil service, been a Liberal member of Liverpool City Council, and opened an arts and crafts centre in an old fire station in Shropshire. He has also written for many different markets and published a fantasy novel, *Chiaricho* (Scotforth, 1993), as well as short stories. He and his partner of more than thirty years, David Reece, now live in Devon.

Light Out

NICK WOOD

First published 2003 by GMP (Gay Men's Press),
an imprint of Millivres Prowler Limited,
part of the Millivres Prowler Group,
Spectrum House, 32–34 Gordon House Road, London NW5 1LP

www.gaymenspress.co.uk

A CIP catalogue record for this book is available from the British Library

ISBN 1-902852-43-5

Printed and bound in Finland by WS Bookwell

Distributed in the UK and Europe by Airlift Book Company,
8 The Arena, Mollison Avenue,
Enfield, Middlesex EN3 7NJ
Telephone: 020 8804 0400
Distributed in North America by Consortium,
1045 Westgate Drive, St Paul, MN 55114-1065
Telephone: 1 800 283 3572
Distributed in Australia by Bulldog Books,
PO Box 300, Beaconsfield, NSW 2014

One

In everyone's life there are moments when they think: if so-and-so hadn't happened, this-and-that wouldn't have occurred either. Here is an axiom that defines Evolution, a cliché describing our very existence. So it was for the Timperleys. On the far side of the globe, and by the actions of total strangers, a pernicious virus was already beginning to contaminate their family. It would quickly change their lives so profoundly that, for years to come, the cry from their hearts would be: 'What if those two hadn't gone...?'

Carol indulged herself with a smile, one that her friends wouldn't have recognised. She knew it was a bit smug, but only she could see how it slightly distorted her normally amiable features. She again wiped condensation from the bathroom mirror.

Mike was up; she could hear their twenty-three-year-old getting breakfast ready downstairs. He was usually first. Besides, his father had spent much of last night helping a ewe whose lamb had turned badly. Mother and new-born were now doing well, though Brian would be sleeping in for an hour or so to compensate.

Making a clear patch on the squeaky window pane with the back of her hand, Carol could see by the slaty morning half-light those familiar sheep-dotted hillsides in their annual April colour coats. Most of the scantily clad lambs were under the lee of dry stone walls keeping close to their mothers' shaggy woollens for protection from the frosts that still beset these altitudes almost nightly. As soon as the expected sunshine warmed the air, the youngsters would resume the lively gambolling they'd left off yesterday. This is surely what family is all about: we cling to one another during the hard times, then let go when conditions are kinder and allow space where individuals can grow. It certainly works for us Timperleys, Carol congratulated herself.

Recollections of some of the bad and good times they had lived through – nine out of ten of them resulting from their own doings, or lack of them – were once more idling through her mind. There had been occasions when they'd wondered whether the continual struggle up here against the elements was worthwhile, then others had amply rewarded their doggedness in scores of ways.

Of those ups and downs most affecting the children, Carol was thinking of the time when Sarah had shut her little brother in the old shippon when he was four and she six and had come in to tea saying that Mike had run off and might she have his piece of chocolate cake? She naughtily refused to divulge his whereabouts. When the lad was eventually found unconscious, he had fallen from trying to reach a window opening, striking his head on the stone slabs of the floor and breaking his left wrist.

Although they locked the shippon after that until they brought it back into use some years later, no matter how hard the couple tried to avert them, there were still such a lot of immanent dangers to children at the farm that she and Brian had inherited from her uncle and on the fells it enclosed, so many temptations to lure the inquisitive offspring.

The most precocious of their brood was, of course, Richard. Little Rickie, as he was affectionately known to the hands. Couldn't call him that now! He had arrived three years before she had their second. He was into everything almost as soon as he could walk. The first challenge of competition in the shape of Sarah put his nose out of joint for only a few months. When she was barely past toddling, he would be observed by watchful adults leading her by the hand around all his favourite haunts. He knew, from the frequent scrapes he had got himself into, how to protect his sister from harm. Indeed, it was not until Rickie's attention was diverted by what he by then regarded as his job, being the eldest, of showing the world to Mike in his turn, that Sarah's adventures in this wonderland took her into realms where bruises and knee gashes became more commonplace.

In the days when matters not connected with survival were disregarded by sensible folk, this sturdy early 18th-century house was built, for wholly practical purposes, actually straddling the ancient county border. Its huge kitchen, the master bedroom and one of the dormer-windowed attic bedrooms were in Derbyshire; the rest comfortably deferred to Cheshire. Tor Farm was well inside the more recently designated Peak District National Park. It was also at the convergence of several sedimentary geological formations, which was why those who put up the house and its original outbuildings had been able to make quite decorative use of sandstone, associated gritstones and the grey-white limestone, all to be found hereabouts. The domed site was well drained and not prone to flooding from the numerous nearby courses of peat-reddened water, while those higher moorland hills surrounding it afforded some shelter from the winds which were an everyday feature of life in this broad landscape.

Each Timperley child went to primary school in the nearest village – in Derbyshire, but later on, their home's divided allegiance and split local council tax bill doubled the choice of schools available to them. In the event, they all completed their schooling in Macclesfield – Cheshire. One after the other, they had the usual problems and successes every caring parent knows about, but eventually they all acquitted themselves satisfactorily, qualifying for higher education places in the colleges of their aspirations.

Even when they were away from home, the family was constantly their centre of gravity. Well, aye, there had always been those petty, short-lived squabbles between them, but they remained close not only to their parents, but to each other, sharing together as much of their lives as they were able.

Sarah's wedding had gone off a treat last month. Pity it couldn't have been up here, but it would have been unfair to expect Peter's father to endure the journey from Essex so soon after his operation. Sarah had adamantly refused to be 'given away', so her father merely presented her at the chancel steps. Although Peter's Yugoslavian mother of the Orthodox persuasion didn't approve, Sarah was fully supported in her stand by the groom and her brothers. "Besides, Jon," Rick had quipped to his partner loudly enough for practically everyone at the reception to hear, "Sarah's hardly a free gift. Peter'll soon find that out if she gives up work. She'll cost him a bloody fortune!" That had elicited predictable reactions from the Happy Couple and laughter from the guests. Younger brother Mike could have taken someone with him, too, but he was incapable of choosing between the three girls he was currently running, so he latched on to Peter's sexy younger sister for the day.

In fact, Sarah and Peter had found themselves and each other in the same UNESCO team in Cambodia last year. They were part of the international effort helping that afflicted country to reconstruct itself. Straight after their fortnight's Hungarian honeymoon, Peter had to go back to the far east, but Sarah came home for a further two wonderful weeks, and had flown back only yesterday to rejoin her new husband.

Carol was proud of the way her children were turning out. Why shouldn't I feel a little smug? she thought, her mind not at all on the job as she finished towelling herself.

A light tap sounded at the bathroom door. Carol blinked out of her reverie.

"Mum?" came Mike's whispered voice. "Your egg's getting hard. Got a man in there, or something?"

"We'll be out of the shower in a few minutes, dear!" his mother played along. She began talcing her refreshed skin.

"All right. But he can cook his own breakfast!"

Mike ran fleetly downstairs.

Like so many of their generation, all three of them were tall, yet Carol had noticed how many teenagers beginning to come up behind were already showing signs that they were going to far outstrip those ten years older. Both of her boys were strongly framed, too. They had all started out with her fair hair, but the lads' had darkened tremendously as they grew up. Only Sarah's was now of a lighter brown – if she let it stay natural, which was rarely.

By the time Carol sat down at the big, well-scrubbed kitchen table to the kind of hefty breakfast they needed to keep them going for the day, Mike was up on the moor with two of the dogs, after once again passing an eye over his father's overnight ovine patients.

From his vantage position, he peered down towards the track leading from the Buxton road. Dead on time as usual, the bachelor brothers Luke and Paul were coming up in their red Ford van. In their mid-forties, they had been working for his parents for as long as he could remember.

Theirs was a situation not uncommon among country boys. They lived together contentedly enough on what had been their father's sizeable smallholding down behind the village. They worked up here for four days a week at this season of the year, the other three being spent on their own undivided land where they grew produce for the local markets. Not that they had celibate existences – if their reputed financial support of several local women was anything to go by. Quite a lot of children in the district were popularly thought to favour them. Probably an exaggeration, in truth. Apart from one or two churchy people, nobody really sat in judgement on their lifestyle. To have split the smallholding on their father's death would have made it uneconomic. Besides, they worked hard and did their duty, as they saw it, by their women.

Mike was well wrapped up against the wind as he went on his rounds of the walled fields. His canine companions trotted unhurriedly from sheep to sheep, helping him to make sure there were no problems with them. The new season's grass was coming through the old coarse stuff nicely, well in time for softer young mouths to tear at and chew. Down in a wooded clough a mile from the house, they found tell-tale traces of where a newly born lamb must have been taken in the night, probably by a dog fox feeding his vixen and her whelps.

Mike knew that if anything happened to his mother and father, his brother and sister would make no claim on Tor Farm. It had been willed to him because it was his livelihood. It was what he had worked for; academically qualified to achieve. A number of his acquired modern management techniques were in place even now. Rick and Sarah would inherit in other carefully thought-out ways, but all that was hopefully in the far distant future.

He was carrying out minor repairs to a red stone wall when his phone began chirping.

"Oh, hi, Rick. Where are you, mate?"

"I'm at home at the moment. You?"

Mike told him. "This is early for you. Jonny out on a call, or something?"

"No, he's just come back to bed."

Rick looked down at the blonde head of his sleep-starved partner. He had come in only half an hour ago after putting down a Friesian heifer which had strayed and blundered into half-pissed oncoming headlights – the downside of a vet's life. Rick had been about to get dressed to go to the agricultural college where he was a lecturer, when the bedside phone had rung for the second time since they'd come to bed last night. That was Rick's reason for calling his brother.

"Listen, Mike," said Rick urgently, "Peter Simpson rang just now."

"What, from Cambodia?"

"No, Bangkok. Look, Sarah's not turned up on the flight she left on."

"Not turned up? What do you mean?"

"I mean, Peter went to the airport to meet her – they had some Displaced Populations conference or something in Thailand, it seems.

But she didn't get off the plane. Peter checked with the airline, and they said that she boarded at Manchester – I watched her go into the Departures area myself, in any case – and remained with the flight after it put down at London Heathrow, its only other stop. The cabin crew checked everyone off on arrival, they told him, so he must have missed seeing her in the crowd."

"So did he? Miss seeing her, I mean." Mike sat down on some exposed bedrock colonised by lichens.

"No. He says they had a back-up arrangement whereby, in the unlikely event that they missed each other, they would rendezvous at this particular spot they both knew at the airport. Not that they really expected problems, like. After all, people don't normally get mislaid in airports. Their luggage quite often, but people, no."

Jon turned his head on his pillow and looked up at the anxiously pacing Rick. "Tell him about Customs," he murmured, twisting his body round to lie on his back. "That's even odder."

"Too right. When she still didn't appear," Rick went on to his brother, "he made straight for the Customs office. They examined their records. She and her bags had passed through all right. When the Thai officers were told that Peter, like Sarah herself, was a United Nations official, they even showed him her landing documents filled out in her own hand during the final hour of the flight.

"No doubt about it, according to the airline, the Customs and the airport authorities, our Sarah's in Bangkok. But of dear sister there's absolutely no fleshly sign. Poor old Peter's going off his nut with worry. He's back at the hotel where he'd already booked in. She's not shown up there, and she hasn't contacted the UN office either. Peter's been on to the police, but they say there's no evidence that she is involuntarily missing."

Rick turned the telephone volume higher so that Jon could hear Mike better.

"Meaning what?" said Mike caustically, "That she's taken a runner? She's disguised herself somehow so that not even Peter would recognise her? Anyhow, how could she do that and be allowed through Passport Control? Then there's why?" He covered his face with his hands, letting the phone slide partly from his ear. "What bloody reason could she have for wanting to disappear like that?" he groaned, and rubbed at his dark hair through the knitted navy cap he was wearing.

There was a pause.

Jon clasped his big hands under his head, elbows jutting on either side. "I don't suppose she was harbouring any secret regrets, was she?" he asked.

Rick frowned. "About what?"

"Hey, about marrying him. It's happened before, you know." Jon saw by Rick's expression that he was not best pleased with this notion. "Well, just thought it was a possibility," he repented lamely. "But I've only been acquainted with her for ten years or so. You and Mike know better than me how she ticks."

"What's that Jon's saying?" called Mike.

"He was only wondering whether Sarah's taken fright about getting married."

"Post-marital blues? Not Sarah! I've never seen her more sure of anything." Absently, Mike took off his cap and stuffed it into his parka pocket, letting the steady wind comb through the naturally wavy hair he had severely tousled. "So, what do we do now?"

"Peter says, if she doesn't turn up soon, the UN will be taking it up themselves," said Rick. "They don't like their people dematerialising. It can sort of lead to all kinds of sensitive international complications. They'll do a lot of the investigating, with the help of the police here as well as the Thai government. Mum and dad will have to be told. I thought it better for you to tell them rather than me over the phone or, even worse, the press, once they get wind of it."

"The press? Oh, yeah. Okay, Rick. Look, have you really any ideas why she might have disappeared? You don't think she could have been abducted, do you? To do with her job?"

"Does she have that kind of job?" considered Rick, sitting himself on the edge of his side of the bed. "As she describes it, it doesn't sound as if she gets mixed up with international spy rings or anything half as exotic as that!"

"Not intentionally, at least," Jon interpolated quietly. His father was, as Jon liked to express it, something unmentionable in the Civil Service. "People can get drawn in without realising it till it's too late. Not that I'm thinking that's what's happened to Sarah," he added quickly. "She'll arrive in the hotel lobby any time now, all flushed and with a perfectly rational explanation. You'll see." He squeezed Rick's arm.

Brian tried to comfort his shocked wife, but then he wasn't too steady himself. He looked across the room to where his younger son was standing, his powerful back to them blocking out some daylight, as he stared unseeing out of the kitchen window. Carol had such a strong personality, but here she was showing how vulnerable she really was. Like his own, her hair was growing a little greyer by the year and she looked all the more beautiful for it. He stroked it lovingly as he held her to him. She wasn't crying or anything like that, just shaking a bit, as he could feel himself doing.

Lifting her chin, he raised her head gently and saw her lovely green eyes glistening with the anxiety a mother feels when trouble threatens her family.

"We don't know she's come to any harm, my love," he softly reminded her. "Any minute now, the phone will ring, and it'll be them to say she's arrived safe and sound!"

By evening the phone had rung on numerous stomach-jolting occasions, but none was the message they most needed to hear. Helpless to move things on, they tried to sublimate their fears by concentrating their minds all the harder on their various customary tasks.

Even so, the day was unreal. It dragged on without ever touching their consciousness somehow, as in a dream. Brian and Mike never wandered far from Carol and the house, leaving the farm hands, Luke and Paul, to look after the further flung parts of the farm.

Coffee sustained them until Rick and Jon drove up at seven from their Knutsford home, the dogs welcoming them as enthusiastically as was their wont, but somehow vocally much subdued. Jon took one look at everyone and deduced that, if they were anything like Rick, the other Timperleys had not felt up to eating a decent meal. Saying not a word, he dived into the freezer and the potato store and set to with the Aga and the microwave to prepare proper food for them. Going without would only make the situation seem even worse than it was. Unconvincingly weak protestations from Carol that she had been just about to fix something merely provoked Jon's threats of force-feeding by veterinary methods if they wouldn't eat through choice.

There was still nothing they could do about Sarah, but they felt better being together this evening. They half watched tv before their self-appointed chef produced the first course. After they'd finished their meal with surprisingly little difficulty, they washed up and attempted to concentrate on a card game.

This time the call was from Peter. His new father-in-law answered it immediately. It was nearly midnight.

"Oh, Christ, Brian!" Peter sounded despairing. "Where the hell is she?"

"Still no news, then?"

"Not a whisper. Could she be on her way back to you, do you think? The airport records might all be wrong, and maybe she took the next flight straight back to England." There was still hope of sorts.

"Don't you think she'd have phoned by now, Peter?" Brian replied, labouring hard to keep impatience out of his voice. He took off the metal-framed glasses he sometimes wore, then drew the back of his hand across tightly closed eyes. It was no use taking his disappointment out on Peter. The lad was only clutching at what straws he could.

"What about my parents' home?" Peter wondered. "Perhaps she's developed some kind of amnesia; forgotten where she was going. She could be on her way there! God, first my sister's kids and now Sarah!"

Brian signed for Rick to come over to the phone. He covered the mouthpiece.

"Thinks Sarah's gone off her head or something," he told his son exasperatedly, "an's making for Colchester for some reason."

"Rick here, Peter." He took over the phone. "What makes you think Sarah's going to your parents'? Anyway, wouldn't she have got there hours ago?"

"She may be lost or... Oh, I don't know, Rick." The voice was striving not to sound tearful. "I'm just trying to think of something – anything which can make sense of this bloody stupid situation!" His tone softened. "You see, I love her so much," he explained simply.

"I know you do. We all love her. Tell you what: why don't you ring your folks and ask them to keep a look out for her in their area?" At least he'll feel that'll be something positive happening, Rick thought, even if it was stretching the bounds of credibility to think that Sarah might have flipped.

"Okay. I'll get on to them. Good idea. They could alert the local police, as well." Peter sounded a mite brighter at the prospect of actually having something to do. His shocked mind had been in such turmoil that, untypically, he hadn't been thinking straight enough to come up with practical ideas like that.

"When I took her to the airport, she was wearing that new blue outfit she bought in Kendals," Rick recalled. "White shoes, I think." His mother nodded. "Yes, white," he confirmed, "... and her handbag?" Again Carol agreed.

"Meanwhile," Rick went on, "I've arranged to see the airport authorities at Manchester first thing in the morning. To see if their security has come up with any clues at their end."

That was where the discussion with his brother-in-law was left.

Rick kept his airport appointment. Nothing had come up anywhere to suggest that any intending passenger had failed to board their aircraft. Both the security company and the police were as helpful as they could be. Rick was offered a viewing of videotapes routinely taken by cameras in the departure areas at about the time Sarah was there.

He sat in a side room off the main concourse with two DCs and a uniformed security official intently watching as thousands of travellers of two days ago entered the life of the tapes, lingered, then passed out of it again. Rick himself featured for a few moments as he kissed his sister goodbye just before she went through Passport Control. Later, she was seen sitting in the Departures Lounge reading a magazine she had just purchased. A woman in a pink coat sitting next to her engaged her in apparently casual conversation before Sarah, with a polite smile, left her and returned through the lounge to the duty-free shopping area, where she commenced to browse desultorily among its alluring displays. She had at least a further hour's wait before her flight would be called. Rick knew that she would not be interested in acquiring any of the merchandise she was looking at.

There was that pink coat again almost off screen. A woman of about Sarah's own age. Similar build. Fairer hair than Sarah currently had hers, it passed through Rick's mind; more like her natural colour.

"Can you freeze it there for a moment?"

"Seen something, Mr Timperley?" asked one of the detective constables.

"Can't be sure, yet. I just thought it might be worth our while observing that girl in the pink coat over there by the jewellery. See? She's not unlike our Sarah in some ways."

"Wasn't she the one talking to your sister before?" said the security officer.

Rick nodded. "Looked innocent enough, but you never know."

Closely regarded by all four men, the pink coat was approached by a portly, late-middle aged man dressed like a tourist in a brightly printed shirt and fawn slacks that emphasised his girth. An expression of surprise appeared on her not very distinct face and they embraced like old friends. Animated chatter ensued. Just one among the scores of other people moving around the shop, Sarah was minding her own business, oblivious to the pink coat and her new-found companion. The same encounter was watched from another camera's angle.

Eventually, the two went on their way towards the cafeteria, where she sat down at a free table near one of the entrances, while he went to the self-service counter and fetched tea and scones for them both. Meanwhile, Sarah left the duty-free and made for the ladies' room. When the man reached the table with his tray, his lady friend rose, excused herself with a little laugh and crossed in the direction of the ladies' room.

The men watching tensed, anticipating the obvious. However, after several minutes, they were given a long-distance view of Sarah coming out through the same doorway and returning to the seating area of the lounge, where she resumed reading her periodical. A short while after, the woman in pink emerged, gazed round as if looking for something, then slowly walked back to the cafeteria. When she made for the entrance farther from her table, the man stood up courteously to draw her attention and she stepped over to him.

She maybe looked more unhappy than hitherto. Sitting down again, she crossed her legs, revealing a glimpse of blue skirt as she opened her capacious black shoulder bag and took out a tissue to dab her eyes and nose. Yes, she was crying. Tears are often shed at airports and nobody in that crowded place took much notice of the female wearing a pale pink overcoat. Her companion patted her arm consolingly. The two took their refreshments in silence, then he said something and they rose to walk directly to a boarding gate. Evidently their flight had been called. Sarah sat on, reading. The pair passed in and out of range of successive cameras as they proceeded to their gate. Yet more partially shown cassettes were piling up alongside the video player.

"Hey, stop it there, will you," exclaimed Rick.

"Right," said the first DC. "What have you seen?"

"That girl's hair. Just take another squint at it," Rick cried excitedly.

"What, its colour, style or what?" asked the older security officer.

"Chiefly that white comb thing keeping it together at the back."

"Yes, I see," said the younger policeman.

"Now let's go back to that shot of Sarah going into the ladies'."

After a bit of hit and miss, the appropriate part of tape was fed through the machine, then, at Rick's behest, the pink woman entering soon after was re-screened.

"There!" said Rick triumphantly. "Did you notice that?"

They'd all noticed it this time. The girl in the coat was not wearing any ornament in her hair. On the other hand, Sarah going in before her was.

"Yes, I remember my sister was wearing that comb with the decoration of a spray of flowers on it. Now that other girl has it!"

The tape was run fast forward and paused at the point where Sarah came out of the ladies' again.

"Now look a bit closer," Rick went on. "And, by the way, Sarah's hair seems to have got several shades lighter. Am I imagining that?"

The others peered at the screen. One after the other, they slowly nodded their agreement.

"They've switched, by hell!" breathed the senior of the detectives. When the coated woman emerged sporting the hair comb, he added, "And that's your sister, if I'm not mistaken."

The girl now in pink needed to look for the cafeteria, then she went to the wrong entrance for her table and had to be put right by the fat man, whom she joined.

"Well, we seem to be getting somewhere," said the senior detective, "but I'm afraid I'm bound to say, sir, that your sister seems to be in on whatever's going on."

Rick said nothing at first. He was struggling with his own doubts, but they were only momentary.

His hazel eyes surveyed the others' studiedly doleful faces. Behind those masks of professional propriety they were thinking that this young man had just helped them to identify a potential crime and, in doing so, may have been the unwitting cause of implicating his own sister in the affair.

They were again seeing the unlikely couple on their way to the departure gate.

"D'you know the gent, Mr Timperley?" enquired the younger detective. "At least, have you ever seen him before?"

"I don't and I haven't. What's more, I don't think Sarah had until that scene in the duty-free that I think was put on not only to fool Security, but especially to show my sister the man she was expected to join up with later."

The two policemen were sceptical, but the security officer was more sympathetic to Rick's theory. He viewed their impassive faces with barely concealed amusement. Some of these rozzers didn't like members of the public out-sleuthing them and marked out anyone capable of thinking logically and easily through conundrums which they themselves had been intensively trained to solve, as some kind of trespassers upon their own private preserve.

"They're not very clever, though, are they?" he said, half-addressing Rick. "That hair slide was a dead give-away."

"Intentionally so, if you ask me," came Rick's reply. "I don't know how Sarah did it. Maybe she took it off when she went first into the loos so that the other woman would forget about it when they swapped clothing and things, then she put it back on after the woman had gone and before she herself came out wearing the overcoat."

"You think she was an unwilling accomplice, then?" asked the guard.

"Bloody certain she was," growled her loyal brother, in a tone that warned the others not even to hint otherwise unless they could well and truly justify themselves.

"Why?" The senior DC stared directly into Rick's face. "Why do you think she's got herself involved in something which, you must admit, looks very like a criminal conspiracy of some kind?"

"I've not the faintest idea," Rick confessed. "But it's obvious – isn't it? – that she was deeply upset by it all. She was sobbing her heart out when she joined that fat slob in the café. One minute she was happily looking forward to rejoining her new husband in a few hours, the next she was meekly allowing herself to be kidnapped; smuggled off to God-knows-where for Christ-knows-what purpose!"

Two

Ever since he first met Rick in Manchester when they were both eighteen, Jonathan Reynolds had been made welcome at Tor Farm. For eleven years that would be. Initially, they saw each other just sporadically. It was only after they went off to their respective universities that their hearts grew fonder of each other. They hadn't realised that either, to begin with. They were too busy living and learning. Well, as things turned out, it had been fundamental to the learning part, hadn't it? – that they had been in love all this time without really being aware of it. Occasional sexual trysts and short-term affairs with fellow students, though usually one hell of a buzz at the moment, never quite came up to expectations, not after having already 'spoilt' themselves with those far deeper experiences of someone they could never have borne to let slip from their growing funds of memories.

The deeply implanted need to have lots more of the same brought Jon and Rick together more and more often. At first, they would spend a week of their vacations youth hostelling at some caving or rock climbing resort or other, then it became a custom to pass a second week at Tor Farm or at Jon's mother's home near Chester or even at his father's large and opulent Hampstead flat. Jon's parents' marriage had fallen victim to his father's career ambitions when the boy was thirteen and his sister, Emma, fourteen, so his mother had come back up north with her children to her family's roots where, two years later, she remarried

– a professor of tropical medicine who was based at Liverpool. It was really that medical influence, combined with a more full appreciation of animals and things rural gained from his association with Rick's decidedly earthy background, that ultimately redirected Jon onto the path of veterinary science, albeit somewhat late in his academic life.

The only parent who had any difficulty in the beginning with their budding relationship was Deputy Commissioner of Police Rupert Reynolds, who intended to shed the first word of his job title at an early date. Having come up through the ranks of the Met during the sixties and seventies, he was unable to accept that any progeny of his – or even a more distant relative, come to that – was not designed to be fruitful and to multiply in accordance with the Biblical traditions he had been brought up to espouse. Consequently, whenever the three of them consorted socially, subjects touching on marriage and sex were assiduously avoided by unspoken mutual consent, so they all got on famously.

After the couple had been living together for nearly three years, and Jon's father had been transplanted to a small-but-special government department and immediately hitched up several grades, a knighthood came his way. He now held the small-but-special government department's top job equivalent to Permanent Under-Secretary, commanding the ear of both the Home Office and the Foreign Office. An evening post-investiture celebration party was given for him at Claridges by his former and present colleagues. Emma was there and Tim Calver, her husband of one year, as were Jon and his life partner, Rick. Amazingly, Sir Rupert introduced Rick as such to his cronies, and Jon was so enormously proud of them both.

Thus, as soon as Rick had recounted to him the events of this morning spent in the airport, it was to his father that Jon naturally turned for advice, even before Rick reported back to his own parents. So Rick was called upon to repeat over the phone to his father-out-of-law what the videotapes revealed about his sister's unaccountable behaviour before she absconded, or was abducted.

"Then which flight did Sarah take?" quizzed Sir Rupert, speaking at his Whitehall office.

"It was going to Chicago, Sir Rupert. ETA 19.40."

"Call me Rupert, Rick. No, better still: Emma's Tim calls me dad, so why should you not do likewise? If you want to, that is."

"I'd like to. Well, both, if that's okay, – dad."

Jon raised his eyebrows at this. Seated alongside him on their sitting room sofa, he ruffled Rick's thick hair and smiled his pleasure.

Rupert was continuing, "I dare say they had no information yet from Chicago's O'Hare Airport by the time you left Manchester – about what happened to your sister and her companion after they landed?"

"No. The police weren't even too keen to let on to me what they were going to do next. They seemed to clamp up once they smelled foul play."

"Yes, they would, of course. Right then, I'll get on to them pronto to tell them of my concern and that I want to see all the data they get hold of. This is a matter which may very well fall into my department's lap in due course, anyway, so there's no harm in our anticipating things, is there?"

Jon's father had taken a keen interest in the case. That was a hopeful footnote which Rick was able to add to his news update for his puzzled and distraught parents.

It was by now 3pm. Jon had a regular farm call to make, and Rick dashed off towards Nantwich to relieve the woman who had covered his tutorial for him while he was trying to sort out Sarah's disappearance. When he reached the Agricultural College, he was called in to the Principal's office to tell Tom what was happening.

Eyes open wide, Tom sat rigid in his chair while Rick conveyed his story to him omitting only sensitive details.

"Rick, this really is gobsmacking stuff. It must be awful for your family." A sympathetic smile crossed his bearded face. "We will be as supportive as we can to help you out, and I'll be as flexible as possible, just as you've often been when we've found ourselves under pressure here.

All I ask is that you give as much notice as you can over any necessary absences."

It was true that staffing levels had been below par until fairly recently, and Rick had been one of those who'd put in scores of extra hours – many unpaid – to ensure that gaps in teaching schedules were plugged. Not everyone was fortunate enough to have a boss like his who appreciated conscientious effort.

"At least that's one big weight off my mind. Thanks a lot, Tom," said Rick. "Though I fervently hope I'll not have to take you up on it."

Even while they were talking, things were evolving at a pace which prompted a call from brother-in-law Peter before Rick arrived home that evening. Jon passed on this latest as soon as Rick closed the front door behind him.

"Peter's heard that the woman who entered Bangkok Airport on Sarah's papers left Thailand on a flight to Vienna. She probably never even left the airport."

"Surprise, bloody surprise!" Rick stared at Jon. "So what's being done to intercept her at Vienna?"

"Too late, kiddo. The plane landed two hours before it was realised what she'd done. She could be anywhere by now. And, hey, Sarah's luggage was unclaimed at Bangkok, so Peter's got it now. It's been searched for explosives or contraband. No sign of her cases having been tampered with, though."

"Why the fuck didn't the airport authorities cue on to it in time: that a supposedly missing UN official was leaving by another flight?"

"I said that to Peter, sure, but he said that apparently she left on a pre-booked ticket. A different airline from the one she'd arrived on, of course, so the connection with her wasn't made until long after the woman had landed back in Europe."

"And was that seat booked in Sarah's name, or what?"

"Seems so. It had been paid for in cash and collected at the airline's agency in the city a week ago. The address given for her hasn't been checked yet."

Just after nine, Sir Rupert rang with his latest information. Much of it confirmed what they already knew.

"Obviously, Jon, this was a properly planned operation. We believe it's one of a number of international terrorist organisations. We're presently sorting through the mug shots of known members of such groups."

"But why would Sarah get herself mixed up with killers like that?" cried Rick, listening at Jon's shoulder. "It's a bloody ridiculous idea!"

"She may have had no choice," came the patient response. "It's far too early for us to know how deeply she's involved. We must assume that she went off to the US against her will." His way of putting this implied that his options were still open on that score – something not lost on Jon, who wisely forbore to press his father on his meaning.

"Dead right we must," Rick declared. "She was obviously broken hearted when she went to sit with that guy in the airport café. Yet I can tell you, Rupert, that when she was with me only an hour or so earlier, she was as happy as I've ever known her. After all, she was about to rejoin her new husband she loves, and the job she's devoted to."

Jon held Rick's hand. "Dad, is there anything we can be doing?"

Rupert grunted. "Nothing so far as I can see. We have Interpol, the United Nations and the security forces of eight countries working at it already."

"Hmm, impressive," Jon observed. "So you'll be getting some results soon, you think?"

"When I'm able to tell you anything, I'll do so, certainly. Meantime, the press will be speculating about the degree of Sarah's involvement. I advise you all to remain as aloof from them as you can. Tell them that you know absolutely nothing more than they do."

Sure enough, Tor Farm was soon under virtual siege from newspaper and broadcasting reporters with their camera teams. The reluctant local community was beset by them wanting to know everything about the Timperleys – their family history, their children, schools, even what kinds of livestock they kept. Where did they grow their wheat, barley and spuds? Why not? But cannabis hemp really was grown up here, wasn't it? The invasion spread to every square metre of the farm, making life hell for those already suffering more than enough anxiety before that flock of vultures swooped on them.

Mike's love life was thoroughly probed. Luke and Paul Platt were not spared the investigation either. When they obstinately refused to answer scandal-raking questions about the Timperleys, their own lifestyle came under scrutiny. Their punishment came in the form of titillating exposures, meanly identifying their womenfolk and their hapless children, in some of the Sundays. Not content with this, one popular daily rag went so far as to infer that surely an incestuous relationship bonded the bachelor brothers together – a libel the men stood no chance of refuting in costly court actions, as the perpetrators well knew.

Quickly ascertaining where Sarah's elder brother lived and worked, the pry-scribes started conjecturing afresh – about why Rick might be living in a joint-mortgage relationship with another young man in that modest, double-fronted Victorian detached house set well back from the Knutsford-to-Holmes Chapel road. Even so, most of the journalists treated the couple with some respect, but others, intent on confirming ancient prejudices, pretended to wonder whether this was a clue to the sister's 'defection', for everyone knew – didn't they? – that people like them tended to be disloyal to their country and were always a security risk, their oozing canker infecting their families and the community at large. That the United Nations was not an organ of the British government anyway was a detail conveniently ignored.

In such scrabbling haste were those reporters to get into print, that they had postponed going into Jon's background, which they hoped would prove a fathomless resource for some droolingly salacious copy in subsequent editions. In high dudgeon, Jon's background immediately revealed itself in the vengeful form of one of Britain's top security chiefs dropping heavily upon the necks of their shocked editors, eliciting from them prominent retractions in their next issues.

None of that filth journalism bore any true relevance to Sarah and her disappearance, in any event. Residents nearby resented this unwarranted intrusion from outside, and rallied to the support of its principal victims – a couple of unpretentious professional men they knew to be kind and helpful neighbours, and who were quite active in local affairs. A Liberal Democrat councillor got up a petition calling upon certain newspapers to lay off. It attracted nearly two thousand signatures inside the week. The town mayor remonstrated against blameworthy newspapers in a speech. All very heartening, but Sarah still had to found.

Peter, by this time, had taken matters into his own hands by flying off to Chicago. He phoned Rick from there for several days running, then went missing himself.

Jon fixed up an urgent meeting with his father at his Whitehall office.

In that huge complex which was 50 Queen Anne Place, Sir Rupert and his department enjoyed a prestigious suite of rooms on the first floor of the building they cohabited with the Home Office.

"He shouldn't have gone like that," Rupert complained, irritably twiddling one end of his grey military moustache with large fingers like those his son had inherited. "Stupid of him. Might have blown our whole investigation for all I know."

"We didn't know he'd gone, till he called us when he got there," Rick told him again. "He promised to phone us daily from then on, but he hasn't been in touch for four days now. I've asked Mike, my brother, to drive down and check our answerphone in case Peter does ring while we're up here in London."

"And my people have had all the major hospitals and police departments across the States alerted just in case he, or anyone answering to his description, turns up."

Jon asked, "And what if nothing comes up in spite of all that? We can't just keep waiting around for something to happen. We feel utterly pathetic, like Peter must have done; a pair of bloody wimps doing bugger-all to try to find Sarah – and now Peter himself. The only thing that's kept us sitting on our hands for so long is, as you say, the possibility that any clumsy intervention by us could make difficulties for the professional security services, and even make their jobs more dodgy."

Rupert eyed the two men, but said nothing.

"We've got to do everything we can to find them, Rupert. My sister was snatched away from us twelve days ago for no reason that we know of. We don't even know whether she's still alive, for God's sake!" Rick's handsome face contorted as more of those intractable thoughts about how Sarah might have been disposed of invaded his mind. "I know you have to keep pretty schtum about these things, but can't you sort of tell us more than you have? I mean, why? Why, Rupert?"

Surrounded by his bodyguards, the President of Bosnia emerged from the palace in Geneva at the end of a further fruitless day of peace talks, sponsored by the United Nations and the European Union hoping to end that internecine civil conflict which had burst out of the vacuum left by the implosion of the Yugoslavian state. He descended the great ceremonial flight of stone steps to where the world's press attended on what he had to say. The outcome of this latest session mattered little to the correspondents for, whatever happened, their own reports were assured of occupying prominent places in the next editions.

From behind the brick parapet of one of the mansions across the square, the muzzle of a powerful automatic rifle was being aimed at the President's heart. Through her electronic sights, the young woman had long since noted the positions of members of the security forces keeping watch over the comings and goings at the palace. She had selected her outlook point well.

The President began issuing his statement on the palace steps. A heavy crack was heard, and the President staggered. A short pause was succeeded by another shot, flooring the man instantly.

The intervening delay had enabled the security sharpshooters to pinpoint precisely where the second shot came from. A calculated risk. By the time their bullets started chipping at the protective wall in front of her and the enormous chimney stack sheltering her from the right, she had carefully slit her left arm whence she knew plenty of blood would flow, but which she could staunch whenever she wished. Lowering herself through the wooden shuttering of the roof service access, she rapidly contrived to lose herself among the building's tortuous corridors. Those arteries were soon splashed with her blood as though she'd been badly wounded by the security forces. She had spent the previous three days exploring these dim and dusty passages, planning her escape route.

When Sir Rupert put down the phone, which had interrupted his promising that there was nothing more he could yet tell his visitors, he sat silently facing them across his magnificent desk. His forehead furrowed as he assessed the import of this latest intelligence, then he made up his mind.

"This changes everything, boys," he articulated quietly. "It now looks as if Sarah's joined up with the terrorists after all. She's just shot the Bosnian President!"

Three

"They call themselves The Light of the World," Sir Rupert told them, his tone expressing the irony of it. "But they're not any old anarchist group: they are a well-trained international army of terrorists dedicated to destabilising authority of all kinds, who hire themselves out to any and every insurrectionary movement having the money to pay them handsomely, wherever they may be. They lend power to the elbow of incipient rebellions all over the world, helping them to set up just enough momentum to make lawful government impossible, then they fade out of the action with their coffers filled. Their mercenary fighters make a real killing in every sense.

"Needless to say, the backers of the organisation are extremely wealthy entrepreneurs whose financial interests are served by maintaining such pockets of instability on every continent. Their business is the supply of funds to users of the world's defence industries, at hugely inflated rates of interest. They thrive by the very fear they help to engender in the governments which buy their money."

The Head of Department took another sip of his lemon tea, and gazed pensively at the couple sitting in the heavy leather Chesterfield to one side of his desk. "So, The Light of the World pulls out of the conflicts it helps to create as soon as the rebels it has been sustaining seem close, by themselves, to replacing the government – or, indeed, whatever it is they are trying to overthrow. A government strapped for cash, it should be said, reneging on its business deals with the shadowy backers, will very quickly find itself overwhelmed by local forces controlled by The Light. Those taking over the government's role must then pay off the debts."

"So, heads the backers win; tails their customers lose, is that it?"

"Exactly, Rick. And we suspect that some of the biggest names in world finance must be involved in the loathsome business. But they are, of course, well concealed by layers of obscure front runners who carry out the transactions for them, without knowing the identity of those they're working for.

"That's another reason we are so tight-lipped about these operations. We just can't be sure how much of what we know might get back to the high-ups in the organisation. Their people are everywhere."

Jon stated the obvious. "Those top dogs must be pretty shady customers lurking behind the intense light they generate."

"What's your point, Jon?" asked his father.

Jon hesitated. He didn't really have one. "Well, I suppose... Hey, expose only one of those generators by hauling him or her out into the glare, and the resulting short circuits may cause the whole strobing gantry to collapse."

"Thank you, my son," came the caustic reply. "We'd never have thought of that without your help!" Those blue eyes twinkled. "You're wrong, in any case. That 'gantry', as you put it. There are scores of them, all self-determining units, or cells. One collapses; all the others still function."

Against his blond hair, Jon's blushes flamed like beacons of their own.

Rick managed a weak grin through his pain. "He's always doing it: thinking out loud like that! Just as well you didn't follow your father's profession, Jonny! Wouldn't last five minutes before you were hauled up before the beak for breaching the Official Secrets Act, or something just as bad."

"There is nothing as bad as that!" declared Rupert, with a tolerant smile.

"Still," Rick pressed on, "this surely isn't to suppose that Sarah's, like, really taken to assassinating politicians, is it? You don't believe that, Rupert, do you?"

Rupert shuffled uncomfortably in his chair. "Let me put it this way," he said. "I've only met your sister once, briefly. She happened to drop round to your house when I was visiting you a couple of years back. Otherwise, she's always been away whenever I've been up in your neck of the woods. The rest of your family, of course, I know and like very well." Rupert pushed his glass to one side.

"Factor number one." He counted off a finger. "If Sarah actually was abducted..."

"If?" protested Rick loudly.

Rupert raised a calming hand. "Bear with me for a moment, Rick. Please," he added firmly. "We must be thoroughly objective in these matters, surely you appreciate that."

Jon touched Rick's arm, and Rick nodded his reluctant acquiescence.

Even so, Rupert rephrased his remark. "Assuming that it is Sarah we see on the videotapes being abducted from Manchester Airport, she did fly to Chicago under the name of one Anna Reicke. Oh, and by the way, for what it's worth, she travelled alone Tourist Class, while he went in the First Class cabin.

"Factor two," another finger was counted, "that villain she met is a known lowlife, Umberto Ciampi, known to the FBI, that is, as a fairly obnoxious small-time crook who has dealings with the Mafiosi throughout the Midwest."

Rick drew a sharp breath through grimly clenched teeth. "That's great news, like, really great. That means she's been in the Mafia's clutches all this time?"

Rupert gave a little shrug. "Perhaps. Perhaps not. We can't really tell. Ciampi isn't of the Cosa Nostra himself, but he's certainly very beholden to them, one way or another. The days when gangsters openly controlled whole neighbourhoods as well as sectors of the government of Chicago are long since past but, as in most large cities, there are strong criminal elements there operating just beneath the surface.

"He owns a house and a small apartment block in Roosevelt Road in the area of the city known as Little Italy. Know of it? Oh, you've not been to Chicago. I see." Rupert paused only for a moment. "Anyway, we're told that his HQ is in a mostly derelict warehouse district of North Kingsbury Street, a couple of miles away."

"You wouldn't divulge any of this to us before, when I asked," Rick interjected. "But the data's suddenly coming in thick and fast now."

"Dad, why are you telling us all this? I mean, all this detail. Do we need to know it?"

Jon was interrupted by a deferential knock on the heavy oak-panelled door.

"Enter," called the denizen of this imposing room.

In came a short man bearing what might be a letter or memo of some sort. He would be thirty or so. His dark, scarcely receded hair was long enough to be sleekly tied back in a pony tail. Like every other male employed in this building, he wore a dark suit, though the raffish way he inhabited it with its sombre necktie broadcast his distaste for the outmoded custom and his own preference for more informal gear upon his unmistakably well-built body. Definitely a sporting type.

"Yes, Andy?" He turned to Jon and Rick, themselves dressed smartly casual. "This is Andy Gregson, the man leading the investigation for this department. Andy, this is my son, Jonathan and his life partner, Richard Timperley, who is also brother to Sarah Simpson. I told you they were coming to see me today."

"Sure. You did, Sir Rupert." He proffered a powerful-looking hand.

The two men rose and returned Andy's handshake equally firmly, then sat down again.

The newcomer seemed as though he wanted first to speak to them, but he turned instead to his boss.

"This has just come over from the Foreign Office, Sir Rupert." He handed his paper across the desk. "UNESCO delivered it to them by hand."

Rupert glanced at the sheet, and tensed as he read it. "Any other details?"

"Posted in Vienna two days ago, Wednesday."

Rupert moved the notepaper in Rick's direction. "You'd better see this," he said quietly.

Jon passed it on, and saw Rick's grip tighten and crush its margin while he read.

"Is that her writing?" enquired Andy.

Rick took a deep breath. "Yep. It looks like hers." His voice had grown hoarse. "Posted in Vienna, you say?" He relinquished the letter back to Jon.

"Naturally, UNESCO have repudiated its contents," Andy assured Sir Rupert, who merely went "Uh," absently at first, then he became more troubled.

"What for? Why was it necessary for her to send such a letter?" Rupert placed both arms on his desk and stared down at the ever-unused regulation blotting pad.

Jon read aloud: "'To, the Director of Operations, UNESCO, London. Dear – Mac', is that? Can't make it out. Anyway, 'Dear Whoever, Everything's going to plan. I am staying at the – Hapsburg? The gold arrived this morning. I'll be very glad when it's all over. Killing really isn't my line.'" Jon incredulously surveyed the faces round him. He returned to the page: "'Still, it'll be in a good cause if it stops the war. My disappearance must have caused my husband and family a lot of worry, so I can hardly wait to get back to them and put their minds at rest. Sarah Simpson.'

"Chr-rist!" groaned Jon vehemently. "I can't believe this, I really can't. Dad, why would anyone undertaking such a sensitive operation be so crass as to write a letter about it to their superior?"

"Just so. Even a phone call would be unsafe."

"Dynamite, actually," Andy joined in. "It's not even as though she's passed on any useful message or anything. This is just some idle chatter, really."

"Thank God the President was wearing a bullet-proof vest," said Rupert.

"And a carbon-fibre shield under his jacket," Andy added. "Stopped two heavy-calibre bullets. Bruises and a broken rib, that's all."

Rick had remained silent. He was examining the pale green wove paper of the letter. He held it up to the light pouring through the big leaded windows.

"Archery used to be one of Sarah's things," he said almost to himself. "School, yeah. Went to Buxton Tuesdays and Saturdays till she was, ooh, twenty. And it would come naturally to her to use 'gold' like that: the bull's-eye of an archery target." He stiffened and sat forward to the edge of the sofa, still peering intently at the paper. "Hey, wait a minute. What do you make of this?"

He stood up and gave the letter to Rupert. "Where do you think this may have come from? The watermark," he indicated.

Rupert followed Rick's example. "Hmm, well, it looks like an eagle. The Austrian eagle, I suppose – standard hotel continuation notepaper from the Hapsburg, where she says she is staying." He noticed Rick's disagreement. "Or is it?" He frowned a little as he tried to remember.

Andy took his turn. At length, measuring his words carefully, he dared to suggest, "Do you think perhaps it may be the American bald eagle, Sir Rupert? Is that what you thought, Mr Timperley?"

Rick nodded.

Jon was now staring at the watermark. "Nice one, Rickie lad," he whispered.

"Nice one, indeed," agreed Rupert, smiling approvingly. "One of my weaknesses, I'm afraid: differentiating between similar heraldic devices and such things. But I see what you mean now. It's quite different from the spread eagle designs more usual in central and northern Europe. I wonder what we might deduce from this?" he put as a question to his assistant, who was motioned to sit opposite him in the high-backed leather chair.

"Well, Sir Rupert, only that the paper was almost certainly made in the USA. We should be able to check that quite quickly, and we can extrapolate several scenarios from the fact, of course." He looked at the younger men. "To your knowledge, has Sarah been to the States lately?"

"A couple of years back, she went with some girlfriends to Washington DC, New York and one or two other places," Rick responded. "On vacation."

"You see," Andy cupped his chin, "I'm curious as to why she didn't use the hotel's address-headed version of the notepaper, as most people would – if only to save themselves the bother of writing the address. She chose only a continuation sheet, and even then didn't write a heading in."

"Do you think she may have had some notepaper with her from her American holiday?" Rupert asked him.

"Could be. But isn't it at least possible that she didn't write the thing in Vienna at all, even though it was posted to London from there? There's no knowing where it may have been before that."

"Like Chicago, for instance?" reasoned Jon.

"For instance," Andy said noncommittally.

"I don't suppose you can get the envelope it came in from the Foreign Office, Andy?"

"I can, and I have, Sir Rupert. It's with the Met's Forensic as we speak. If you agree, I'll have this letter sent across to them as well, now that you've seen it."

"Very good, Andy. Do you boys have to go back north today, or can you stay the weekend with me?"

"We'll stay and cramp your style," grinned Jon, "if that's okay, dad!"

"It'll take more than you two to do that," retorted Rupert. "Besides, there's a good play on at the Barbican, and I think I can get us some seats for tomorrow, if you'd like that."

Rick was for declining the invitation. "I don't know, Rupert," he said, "I'd never be able to concentrate on a play with all this going on."

"Nonsense, believe me. Help you to get your minds off your worries for a short while. Clear your heads for thinking. Any developments in this case, Andy, you know how to get me."

In that dark and hushed house, she knelt by the prone body of her knifed and dying husband, their children peering between the staircase banisters at that tragic scene below them. The only sounds were their pathetic sobs.

She tearfully, tenderly kissed his lips; a last, lingering goodbye... and the laden atmosphere was instantly shredded by the piercing bleeps of somebody's personal pager alarm. Three shamefaced men rose from their seats in the packed centre stalls, and pushed their way as hastily as they could crabwise, through a three-mile gauntlet of lowering disgruntlement, to the nearer gangway leading them to the comparative refuge of the theatre's distinctive foyer.

They found public phone booths. Responding to his pager's summons, Rupert had just commenced dialling the appropriate number when hundreds more of the first-night audience began streaming out at the end of the new play's second act, whose poignant dénouement had been wrecked by the disturbance. Some of the crowd glared balefully at the two men they recognised guarding the booth while the third party sedulously kept his back to them.

"If they try to lynch us," muttered Jon behind his hand, "just tell them it was all Dad's fault. If that fails, scream!"

The couple moved closer to Rupert when they heard him mention Andy Gregson's name. He listened for several minutes to what Andy had to tell him.

"Ah, now we're getting somewhere," Rupert was finally saying. "Very well, Andy. Come round to my place in the morning about eight and we'll talk about it some more. Good night. Oh, and find out about flight times, will you? Thank you."

Putting down the handset, he turned to his companions. "That notepaper Sarah's letter is written on is exclusive to the TransUnion

Inns group. Know of it? Yes, well, their hostelries are to be found all over North America, the USA and Canada."

Jon looked at Rick. "None in Europe, then? Right, so unless for some reason she picked up some of the paper when she was on holiday a couple of years back, and kept it –"

"As one does," Rick interpolated drily.

"That's so right. As hotel guests everywhere do – well..."

"Just stop there, Jon," his father broke in. "Andy says that a bright spark at TransUnion Inns told him that they customarily change the background colour schemes of their bedrooms at intervals of about two or three years. Personal accessories like towels, soaps and writing materials are also changed to co-ordinate. What this means is that they started using that particular avocado-green coloured notepaper only last July."

Instinctively, the men had strolled towards the nearest bar, which was by now crammed to the doors with noisily chattering amateur theatre critics, each vying with everyone else in authoritative praise of the play, its cast and the production. There was so much to get said during this mere twenty minutes' intermission.

The trio went instead to join the sober-sides in the coffee lounge, and mingled with those individuals mostly standing in groups contriving to hold cup-and-saucer and over-full sandwich plate, while eating finger salad and talking animatedly over each other at one and the same time. Aspiring performers all.

Jon eventually managed to order, adding his own style of acrobatics to those teetering around him as he threaded himself and his refreshments-for-three from the servery through the self-auditioning crowd, to where his father and Rick were so earnestly in conversation that they had forgotten to come and help him.

"Thanks a lot," he gasped sarcastically, while they relieved him of his marvellously balanced burden.

"Sorry, love," Rick said, "but your father's just been telling me that he's now sure that Sarah's still in the States."

"That she wrote that letter there," Rupert equivocated, toeing surreptitiously at a cocktail sausage roll that he'd accidentally dropped on the sensible, crumb-patterned carpet, until it reposed guiltily beneath the nearest stool, occupied by an elegant lady whose straight back was toward him.

"What's the point, dad? I mean, what are they trying to achieve with all these machinations of theirs?"

"Isn't it pretty obvious?" asserted Rupert. "Listen, this is a damned good play, but do we still want to see the last act?"

Rick gazed about him with a hunted expression. "After what happened when your bleeper went? Rupert, a crew of wild sailors couldn't drag me back in there!"

"He's exaggerating, of course," drawled Jon throwing him a wink, which brought Sir Rupert to a chuckle.

"So, what is it all about, dad?" Jon went on, returning to what most concerned them. "Do you know yet?"

Rupert set his plate on the narrow shelf wrapped around a shapely concrete pillar nearby, and reminded them, "Among all three belligerent factions in the Bosnian civil war – the ethnic Serbs and Croats and the Muslims – there are elements who want, above all, to discredit those sponsoring the peace talks currently in progress: the European Union and the United Nations.

"Today, the news media reported on the Bosnian President's attempted assassination. Tomorrow, the world will be told that those shots were fired by an employee of the United Nations, no less."

"Oh, Christ, no!" cried Rick, prompting the lady perched decorously above the rogue sausage roll to look askance at him for a moment. He lowered his tone. "Will Sarah's name be mentioned, do you think?"

"How can it not, since her name was practically stamped all over the scene of the incident?"

"It was what?" Jon almost shouted, turning more heads.

"Andy tells me that the security forces fired back at the would-be assassin. When they subsequently reached the spot where the marks –

marksperson, should I say? – had been, there was lots of blood to indicate that she or he had been wounded."

Despite himself, a chill passed through Rick's body. No, it couldn't have been our Sarah. But still...

"A trail of blood led the investigators to a pension not far away. There, in one of the bedrooms, they found some hurriedly abandoned personal effects of one Sarah Simpson – her passport, of course, a family photograph and some other pictures apparently taken in Hungary."

"Sarah's honeymoon photos," explained Rick, feeling physically sick. "She'd had them developed in Macclesfield, and was taking them with her to show Peter."

The resonant bong of a tubular bell started to chime at five-second intervals, warning of the impending resumption of the stage drama.

Rupert carried on with one of his own. "It seems that there were some other small items lying about which evidently also belonged to Sarah. Perhaps rather strangely, although the woman had already left the bedroom again by the time the security chaps entered it, there was no sign of any more blood showing where she had gone."

"Maybe she'd managed to stop the bleeding," suggested Jon helpfully.

"Or could be," Rick said, "that there were people waiting for her to come back, then they rushed her off for medical treatment." In some way, that thought made him feel better.

"Without making the slightest effort to conceal her identity, it should be noted," Rupert observed. "Not a little odd, do you think?"

Rick looked directly at him. "Hence your 'set-up' theory: they were not abducting Sarah's person from Manchester Airport so much as her identity. Hmm," he said thoughtfully, "well, yes, but doesn't it look, sort of, too obviously a scam?"

"People at war won't see it that way. Common sense and reason get fired out of the gun barrel with the first artillery shell."

That persistent bell was tolling every three seconds now, giving final notice especially to those not yet drifting out of the coffee lounge that the curtain would be going up in three minutes' time. A sedate urgency took hold. The neighbouring lady stood up and moved her stool, then quickly pushed it back again, trying and failing to hide from her two female friends the sausage roll gaffe she'd unknowingly committed. Jon and Rick mutely shot a rebuke at their elder role-model, who assumed an air of absolute remove from the red-faced woman's predicament, and carried on talking.

"People tend to believe instinctively what they think their eyes are seeing, unless they possess both the time and the inclination to rationalise about it; to see through to what may lie beyond the obvious. Populations engaged in brutal life and death struggles like the one going on in Bosnia enjoy neither of those luxuries, so they will naturally choose to accept what their own side in particular tells them. It's easier."

Jon said, "I doubt if any of the sides will exactly want to pass up an opportunity to rubbish the UN, will they? From what we hear, none of them is ready to quit where the battle lines are drawn at present."

"That's most of the trouble – there aren't many real battle lines," declared Rupert, putting down his cup alongside his companions'. "This is a situation guaranteed to raise the temperature and add months, if not years, to the conflict. Perhaps no amount of irrefutable proof that it was all a set-up will ever convince those who want to believe and spread the lie."

He turned to leave. "Shall we go?"

Dejected, the younger men trooped obediently after him through the foyer and into the street. They called a cab.

On reaching Rupert's apartment, Rick sat himself down in one of the capacious brocaded armchairs and rang his parents while the others were getting a bite of supper ready.

Just to be able to talk to Rick ought to have been enormous relief to his mother. What she'd been lately reading in the press and hearing on the news was bad enough, but now to be told what else was to come out tomorrow was horrifying.

"I thought you should hear it from me first, rather than learn it from the tv or something," he said. "It may even be out already on the late bulletins. I can't say too much over the phone, mum, just in case you-know-what."

Carol pulled distractedly at her hair, the tears rolling down her cheeks. "But it can't be true! None of it is true. She wouldn't do such a dreadful thing, would she? Sarah just couldn't!"

"Of course she couldn't," Rick's soothing voice assured her. "It's a conspiracy, that's all it is, mum, just to bring the UN into disrepute and so stop the peace talks, without blame for the failure being seen to fall upon any of the combatants."

"But that's terrible!" his mother wailed. "Using poor Sarah in such a wicked way! And what about the baby?"

"What baby?" demanded her son with a catch of breath.

"Sarah's nearly six weeks pregnant. Didn't you know? Oh, no, she was going to tell you all next time she was home. I don't know why not till then. It'd be obvious, anyhow." Her voice rose. "Oh, tell them, Rick. Tell them, for God's sake, that your sister is incapable of such a terrible deed! She'd never harm a hair of anybody's head!" She broke down. Brian gently took the phone off her and sat next to her on the sofa. She clung fiercely to her husband, burying her face in his sweater.

"Hello, Rick," said his father, his voice subdued and fearful, "your mother is taking your news badly, I'm afraid. Tell me what you've told her, will you?"

Ever since the road accident two years before, which had deprived him of the use of the lower part of his right leg, he and Carol had grown closer, if anything, than ever before. The physical injury had been a signal reminder of their mortality. It also meant that his wife and Mike had to be extra crutches for him on the farm. There were large tracts of land no longer easily accessible to him even in the converted Range Rover unless one of them, or possibly Paul or Luke Platt, accompanied him.

Truth of the matter was, he was no longer necessary. His youngest had, to all intents and purposes, taken charge of affairs. Of course, Mike generously pretended to defer to him in all major decision making. It was a bit of an unspoken game really. Brian went along with it because he knew that he shouldn't be seen to have given up. Yet what use was a bloody cripple on a rough moorland farm like this? And he was constantly needing to be reminded to take his medication to control high blood pressure. If anyone with his leg handicap had applied to him for a job in the past, he wouldn't have given them five minutes' consideration. So, in Mike's position, why should any preferential treatment be given to his father? I'm no good to anyone now, Brian sometimes thought bitterly when his depressions were at their worst. Oh, yes, he had all that experience. But then, so did Mike, who had a good degree and a diploma in farm management to boot, which was a lot more than Brian had ever felt able to aim at.

He loved his sons as he loved himself – better, these days. Nevertheless, Sarah was something special to him: so like her mother in many ways, more in manner than anything else. One of the brightest lights of his life. How could she ever have got herself into this mess?

As Brian began listening with crushing dismay to Rick's account of Sarah's situation, Mike entered the big farmhouse kitchen, taking off his wet boots. It was a filthy night. He'd driven down to Rick and Jon's empty house with his currently favourite girlfriend to check their ansaphone again for messages – there were no relevant ones. That this promiscuous young man hadn't been away long enough to have taken advantage of the seduction opportunities so offered was a mark of his anxiety for his sister. Mike kissed his tearful mother, then placed a protective arm across his father's hunched shoulders when he half knelt on the settee in order to hear what Rick had to say.

"Hi, Rickie," he at length announced himself into the mouthpiece. "What can we do about any of this, anyway? They'll say all this bullshit about Sarah, and we'll be left to carry the can, as always. You know the eager beavers have still got your place staked out?" So he and Figgie couldn't have tarried there anyway. "And I'm sure they've all got their rotten little gongoozling binoes trained on us, watching every friggin' move we make up here."

"I'll bet they have. No calls, then?"

"Nah, 'fraid not, mate."

"Are you coming back tomorrow?" asked their father.

"We're just going to have a talk here about what to do next, dad. If I don't go home, I'll jot you a line, or Jon will call on you if he goes back by himself. I only rang tonight to warn you, really, that things are going to hot up."

"Thanks, son," said Brian wearily.

The doorbell rang. Mike stood up, flicked aside a curtain of the nearest window and looked out. A small knot of sleet-sodden pressmen had converged on the house again. A camera flashed out of the darkness, and Mike quickly thrust the curtain back into place. He disconnected the doorbell, and peered over to his parents who had finished speaking with Rick.

"Cuppa?" he said practically, crossing briskly to the friendly kettle.

Four

"UNESCO have naturally rebutted all suggestions of their involvement, and so, by implication, Sarah's," Rupert reassured his guests, commenting on the 7am News broadcast, which had added nothing to its revelations of the night before about Sarah's attempt on the President of Bosnia's life, though it did elaborate on the earlier but generally unreported disappearance of her husband, another minor UN official. Protests had been lodged with the UN Secretary General by the Bosnian Government's delegation at the peace conference, while all the parties in the conflict were 'seriously reconsidering their positions'.

Rupert went to answer the security buzzer which had just sounded. "This'll be Andy Gregson, dead on time."

It was. He entered the room a couple of minutes later, having come up in the art deco, walnut-panelled lift. It being Sunday morning, he had taken the couple's lead by appearing more at ease in a blue, open-necked sweatshirt revealing the promise of a massively hairy chest, jeans that fitted him exactly and a black leather blouson jacket, which he hung on the back of his chair after gladly slapping upon a side table the hefty roll of Sunday newspapers he was carrying. They weren't left there for many moments.

Promptly offered coffee and breakfast, Andy declined the latter but slurped his drink with gusto while sitting at the family table briefing the small company.

Rupert had never before seen Andy so attired, and intuitively noted the other men's probably involuntary heightened interest in his assistant, whose attraction to members of the opposite sex was quite legendary in the office; seemingly to all of them, single or not, the most glamorous being inured to his charming advances, while the not so blessed affected to receive his solicitous attentions with varying degrees of good-natured fortitude. So far as his superior knew, however, the man didn't follow up his numerous emotional conquests by dating even the most nubile of them, careful to keep his office relationships and his private ones well apart. Wise, that was – a measure of his self-discipline, a quality essential in his professional work. Rupert had once overheard, while closeted in the gents, some of Andy's young male colleagues outside ribbing him half-admiringly to his face, calling him, among other colourful epithets, a clit-teasing wanker – an expression Rupert would find it hard to forget.

"There was a fire in one of Umberto Ciampi's warehouses on Thursday," Andy announced this morning, "soon after Peter Simpson also went missing."

Rupert glanced at him sharply. "Anything found by the Fire Department?"

"Our burrower in the FBI spoke to the CFD's fire chief last night – it was mid-afternoon in Chicago, of course," he added unnecessarily. "Anyhow, it was just a partitioned-off storekeeper's office that went up; lots of smoke, lots of paper ash. Put out in thirty minutes. One of the US security guys keeping the premises under routine surveillance noticed bolts of cloth and some of those big bundles of industrial cotton waste being loaded on to a truck not long before. Nothing you wouldn't expect to see going on at a warehouse, after all. And, yes, they did follow the truck. It delivered to a major retail store in downtown Denver, then to another, much smaller Colorado town in the Rocky Mountains: Leadville. The consignment of cotton waste all went there."

"I suppose there was no doubt that it was cotton waste?" said Rupert.

"Short of their applying for search warrants, there's no way of checking. The bundles were those big compressed cubes you sometimes see. Some of them were wrapped in green tarpaulins."

Jon peered across the breakfast table at Andy. "Is this all getting a bit ominous, do you think? Or is it the first stages of a raging paranoia gnawing at my cerebral cortex about Mafia goods being distributed around the United States in packs big enough to contain people?"

The other gravely smiled. "I don't think it's paranoia, Jon, but, as I say, there's nothing to indicate that the goods are Mafia or anything other than bona fide commercial merchandise."

"This Leadville drop," said Rick: "what kind of set-up took in the cotton waste? It's used in cleaning operations, isn't it? Sort of mopping up oil and such like?"

"A firm of industrial cleaners, as it happens," nodded Andy. "We're presently getting more data together about the Ciampi family. There are at least two branches, the better known one of them being in Colorado, I believe."

"There's an obvious need to go over all those premises you mentioned," decided Rupert, standing up and crossing to the coffee percolator. "Any joy in that direction from the FBI boys, Andy? And that fire: any results from the causal investigation?"

"Your second question first. It was too soon to confirm their suspicion of arson. I'll get an update from the CFD again later. As to premises searches, the authorities don't want to alarm their quarry before they can be reasonably sure of nailing some of The Light of the World's backers. But they've let it be known that anyone else with a legitimate interest would not be hindered by them. Like ourselves, Sir Rupert, they have told very few even of their own agents about Ciampi's connection with Sarah Simpson, only to look out for a kidnapped young woman, and now possibly her husband as well."

While replenishing coffee cups, Rupert addressed Jon and Rick. "You see, outside the governments concerned, only half a dozen or so people know as much as we four do. And it must remain that way at all costs until we can, some day, set a trap and spring it at exactly the right moment. It's very plausible that Signor Ciampi himself has never even heard of The Light of the World; that he was just acting as a well-paid escort when he took off from Manchester with Sarah. We certainly don't know whether she was still in his hands once they left the airport at Chicago.

"As I pointed out to you over supper last night, we've so far managed to keep the press in the dark about the security tapes. One ruse we employed was to misinform Manchester Airport Security sufficiently to make them completely discount any Chicago connection with Sarah. Naturally, they trust our Intelligence absolutely!" Rupert assembled a penitential smile at this duplicity. "But we can't take more chances than we must. Just an accidentally dropped word could put lives at risk. Sarah's and Peter's among them," he tagged on, although he privately believed that it might well be too late for them already. If Peter had indeed been snatched, his turning up couldn't but have tipped off Ciampi that he had been observed with Sarah at Manchester.

If that was the case, Rupert had yesterday confided in Andy, it could only be hoped against hope that Ciampi would flinch from informing those who hired him that he has been so careless.

"I think we should carry out our own on-the-spot investigations, Sir Rupert," advised Andy. "Precisely because we know what we're looking for."

"Volunteering?"

"Yes, I suppose I am. I need to keep my hand in, after all. Danger of getting stale – losing touch – working in this cocooning environment of Fortress Whitehall."

"Meaning I'm in danger of losing touch with reality, I suppose?" his boss acidly retorted, though radiating visible good humour solely towards his family visitors, from where he stood behind Andy.

"I can only speak for myself, Sir Rupert," his minion responded diplomatically, smiling knowingly across at Rick and Jon. Andy then thought for a moment. "Maybe I need a partner."

"I agree. In truth, Andy, you could well do with a small army. But no one else is to know about this. Hard luck, old chap. You're on your own, I'm afraid."

Unlike Jon, who'd chipped in little questions and comments during these exchanges, Rick had contributed little as he closely perused the newspapers' reports and editorials. His ears had missed nothing, however. Now he looked up.

"What kind of assistance do you need? Someone to help you breaking and entering, climbing the sides of tall buildings, swimming fast moving rivers and drawing fire away from you during gunfights? That mundane sort of thing?"

Andy grinned genially. "You missed out shooting white-water rapids. Of course. What else do secret agents get up to?"

Rupert looked at Rick seriously. "If you were contemplating enlisting yourself, forget it, my lad. Firstly, you haven't had the training and, secondly, you are too personally involved with Sarah and Peter. You need to have cold detachment as your guide when making hard judgements and decisions."

"You must also be really fit, and prepared for anything," confirmed his assistant, nevertheless appraising Rick's physique as he spoke. All of two metres tall, he'd previously assessed, huge shoulders, Rick's bare forearms indicating a well-developed musculature throughout.

Jon stared mock-offended at Andy, whose own build was sensational enough. "There's nothing wrong with old Rick's fitness. You should feel his muscles! Hey, perhaps not," he hastily retracted in the face of the assorted amused reactions from the others. Earnestly then, he took a hold of his partner's arm. "Besides, I wouldn't let you go either, Rickie, so you can trash the idea, like right now."

Big hands, Jon's, mused Andy. Feet, too. You know what they say... He's not quite as tall as Rick; more athletically built in some ways, but they're both pretty strong-looking specimens.

Rick knew better than to pursue the topic now. No way was he going to remain idle while Andy and people like him might be placing themselves in danger. If Sarah had gone wrong in some way, it was also a family matter.

The couple stayed while Andy Gregson booked his early afternoon flight and a moderately priced single room at the Centre Holiday Inn in Chicago, then they took their leave of Jon's father and Andy just after ten-thirty.

After pulling over his blue Cavalier into the car park of a Finchley Road café ten minutes later, Rick stopped the engine and sat there perfectly still, hands gripping his knees, his arms rigid. He was so incredibly tired. Jon had been right: he was in no condition to do the driving.

He'd proved them all wrong: crying was a bad way to get to sleep. Of all the tears he had nightly shed in anguish for his family, for his mum and dad at home who must be suffering a thousand deaths over their missing daughter, none gave him one iota of mind rest. Only the comfort of being held so very tightly in the loving arms of his man afforded him a few fitful hours of peace.

Jon understood well what was going through his partner's agitated mind, but said nothing. He absently watched the constant stream of northbound traffic striking aggressively towards the M1 motorway and the M25 orbital. Waiting, he was, for the inevitable pronouncement.

"I have to go after her, Jon," it came quietly. "I-I'm sorry. I know you'll take a dim view, but I can't just sit around here while Sarah might be in fear for her life. Yes," he sighed, "I know, she may be dead already." He brought Jon's right hand over to his lap and held it there between his palms. "But doing nothing – I can't hack it, not with that idea running round my head. I promise I'll be careful, and I'll come back to you safe and sound. Honest."

Jon regarded Rick's fingers distractedly kneading at his hand. "If you imagine I'll allow you to go alone, probably getting yourself into all kinds of stupid scrapes, you've really got some idiot brain in that skull of yours." He covered Rick's hands with his left. The gold rings they'd worn for nine years clinked when they touched.

"You mustn't try to stop me," insisted Rick, shutting his eyes to squeeze back the unmanly tears he didn't want to have seen by people at that moment walking past the car.

Swivelling on his hip, Jon rested his head on the back of his seat and studied the adorable profile next to him – the determination that showed on Rick's face, the pain underlying it which Jon wished from the very core of his being he could in some manner banish. If human love alone were capable of such a feat, the hurt would have gone the instant it had appeared. But the enemy was human, too, with such a destructive propensity that the only means of overcoming it was to confront it – ruthlessly, if necessary.

Jon's left hand came up to fondle his lover's far cheek. He eased Rick's head back against his seat, turning that tense face towards him as he did so. Then he leaned over and kissed away the droplets trickling perfidiously from the closed eyes, before caressing Rick's lips with his own. His fingers ran calmingly through lush hair.

"Right, you noggin," Jon murmured, "we'd better be getting to the airport if we're to catch the next flight to Chicago."

Rick's arms were instantly flung about Jon's body, and the couple embraced fervently, oblivious to the awkwardness of their confinement by the gear lever and steering wheel, and to the old car which had come to park next to theirs behind Jon's averted back. Four young football fans were getting out of it, worse for an evening of celebration followed by a lumpy night sleeping in the car before starting homeward to Tyneside.

The lads leered lasciviously when they saw what they took to be two men snogging in the neighbouring vehicle, and made bawdy noises among themselves. The two on the far side then went unconcerned towards the café entrance but, while the driver was locking his door, the friend who had alighted from the rear door on his side gave a raucous shout and slammed a fist hard against the roof of the couple's car.

Alarmed, they broke apart and stared out at the loutish face glowering down at them. Quickly, the driver grasped the other's arm raised to pound the roof again and levered it back against his own roof, causing the malefactor to follow it and crack his shaven head on the luggage rack.

"What the fuck are you doin' now, then?" the driver yelled. "Tryin' ta get us all arrested or somethin'?"

Their two companions spun round just as Rick dived out to face these adversaries. Jon was a little slower because his door opened against the driver's legs, but he managed to force himself into a standing position with his open door a barrier between himself and his antagonists. The driver instinctively began to land out ferociously at Jon's protective arm. Jon captured his wrist and took his neck in a vice-like grip, making the fellow scream to be released. Meanwhile, Rick had dashed round to the far side of the men's ancient banger and stood half crouching, fists at the ready to defend himself from the two now beginning to sprint back towards their car. They took a second glance at the formidable obstacle that was Rick, thought better of intervening and stopped dead in their tracks.

"Ouch! Stoppit. I'm on your fuckin' side, mon!" cried the panting driver. "Me mate here's what done it ta your car."

Manoeuvring his body round it, Jon shut the car door with his foot and thrust his face up to the other man's. Frequent struggles with big, recalcitrant animals provided useful training for a situation like this; a combination of knack and sheer brute force. The driver was brought to his knees, while the instigator of the incident remained where he was leaning against their car as far back as he could get from this iron avenger. Suddenly, he shot away to join the two confronted by Rick.

"Get them queer poofters!" he screeched, egging them on from behind.

Instead, the two passed a sign between them, roughly grabbed hold of his legs and shoulders and lifted him bodily to dump him, shocked and yelping, at Rick's feet.

"There y'are, mate," said one. "He's all yours. We've had nothin' but trouble with him all weekend. Spoilin' for a fight, he is."

His friend called over to Jon. "Don't hurt Paul, will you? He's the only one who can drive this jalopy, an' he's supposed ta be playin' in a big match, Wednesday."

Jon released Paul, whose gulped intake of breath caused him to cough violently as he clutched at his severely bruised neck.

"Jeezus!" Paul exclaimed at length. He stroked his friction-burnt wrist, muttering respectfully, "How d'ya get brawn like that?"

"Not by playing stupid games or picking fights," Jon flashed back disdainfully. He studied his colourful jumper for damage. There was none, though his opponent's vest was ripped where it had caught on his car's old-style door handle. Its shoulder strap was torn away, leaving his right side exposed, the material limply hanging from his opposite shoulder in two triangular flaps, front and back.

Rick briefly noted the pathetic fascist iconography tattooed on exposed parts of the still cowering skinhead's body, before retiring cautiously away towards his partner, then he strolled coolly round the car to lock it up.

"Time for tea, Jon?"

They stood by silently, each with an arm defiantly about the other's waist, as the four younger men stepped back into their vehicle. Saying nothing more, but three of them clearly signifying their regret for the incident, they drove off into the traffic.

Rick telephoned Heathrow to order their flight tickets. Andy's plane was fully booked by this time. They had a couple of hours to spare before they must make for the airport so, after a wash and tidy up, they sat down in the busy café for a snack meal. Nothing more needed to be spoken between them. Both had come to terms with their decision. Jon remarked with merited acerbity that what had just occurred outside was maybe a timely rehearsal for worse conflicts to come.

Rick, facing the entrance to the café, stiffened.

"Oh, hell, Jon. Watch out, they're back. Christ knows, we can do without this right now."

Jon turned his head and saw the same four youths bearing down on them fast. They both rose guardedly from their chairs, expecting to be attacked then and there in that crowded place.

The group stopped short of their table, however, and the one named Paul, now wearing a green sweatshirt, offered them his hand.

"We felt bad about what happened, lads. Can we talk with you about it?"

"If you think you've got anything worth saying, you may as well say it, I suppose," conceded Rick, spurning the handshake.

Paul motioned to his mates to sit at an adjacent table, which they pulled up to the couple's, its legs scraping uncouthly on the tile floor. One of the pair who had so contemptuously tossed the skinhead to Rick now went to the servery to fetch four cans of cola and Kit-Kat biscuits. Nervous smiles; chair legs shuffled noisily until they settled down.

The ensuing pregnant silence which befell the two tables was reaching its final throes of labour by the time Phil returned to his friends.

"This here is Phil," Paul felt able at last to burst out, "and his workmate, Bart."

Jon and Rick dispatched cursory nods in their approximate direction.

"I'm Paul, and this little git next ta me likes ta be called Adolf, so wes call him Winnie – Winston, get it? – whenever we wants ta get his back up."

"And that's often," averred Phil.

This met with only mild amusement from the other table, and that fit of conversation subsided prematurely, having borne no fruit for the quartet.

Following a minute of concentrated biscuit munching and swigging from cans, Paul tried another tack.

"By, we had a great night, last night," he declared, "but we didn't get really pissed, did we, boys?" as if anxious not to incur censure.

"Just light aled and furry-tongued, eh?" Jon paraphrased.

"Brown aled, y'mean, mon!" responded Phil, not relating to Jon's allusion. "Newcastle Brown Ale," he advertised that famous local product with pride. "Best brew in all the world, mon!" he loudly opined.

The two smiled forbearingly. Not having sampled all the world's beers, as credibly these guys had, they felt unqualified to comment.

"Say, do you like sports, lads?" enquired Bart.

The couple reeled off a list of their individual or shared enthusiasms.

"But we don't have time these days to do much more than climbing and caving," concluded Jon.

As that was a great deal more than any of these boys had ever attempted, or yet taken an interest in except via the tv screen, they were hugely impressed.

Jon further recalled, "Though we did get in a weekend of hang-gliding near where we live, last September."

Sullen 'Adolf's' companions leaned forward, keen to quiz these especially interesting men about their outdoor exploits. The couple truly had far more demanding concerns, but this distraction was probably harmless, after all, and took their minds off their family troubles for a while.

With a little common ground identified, a more or less free movement of chatter was finally under way. It collided with an iceberg, however, as soon as Paul announced: "There's a lot o' hang-glidin' in the Peak District, I know it. And I knew a lass once lived near you two. Northwich. Worked for ICI. But she was transferred, and went ta live in Gateshead. Wed a right plonker, too!" he grinned regretfully, but mistook the stony faces of those on his right as indicating unrecognition. "You ken Northwich, don't you? I used ta take me sister an' her ta the lassy's home weekends, and we used ta come off the motorway at Knutsford, so you must know it."

"But we haven't told you our names or where we live," said Rick coldly. "What makes you think we know either of those towns?"

Paul looked wide-eyed at Jon. "But you're the lad what's sister's scarpered. Your faces are all over the papers, mon!" He gave them both a frank smile. "We recognised you after we left you before, and thought bad of what happened when you had so much bother already. Honest, lads, your bein' gay's no problem ta us."

"Then why all that noise when you saw us in the car?" Jon challenged.

"It wasn't 'cos you was gay," Bart insisted. He lowered his eyes. "I suppose we do it sometimes ta any couple we see doin' it. Stupid really, but it's only fun. We didn't mean you no harm by it."

Paul glared at Adolf. "Exceptin' this daft sod here, an' he's only lookin' for excuses for brawls."

"One of the guys Bart an' me plays rugby with is gay," affirmed Phil, fingering his smarting neck. "Best scorer we've got."

"In both ways!" joked Bart. "An' twit-face here's older brother is gay, as well. Ain't he, Winnie!"

"He fuckin' well ain't, you bastards," growled the sorely contused skinhead.

"Aye, he is too, an' he's worth a thousand of you," Paul declared viciously.

Adolf scowled and fell silent once more.

Paul, the evident leader of the party, shot apologetic smiles at eaters nearby who surely heard Adolf's foul tongue, then he looked back at the dejected pair, and addressed Jon.

"Sorry again, Dick. We're embarrassin' you by bein' here."

"I'm Jon; he's Rick." He wasn't sure why he needed to clarify this.

"Ah, right. Sorry again, then. I'm always sayin' sorry ta you. Sorry." He covered his foolish grin with a hand. It was a disarmingly honest reaction which won him two friends.

Relenting, Rick stretched his right hand across to Paul's. "Hi. Glad to know you, too."

Paul enclosed Rick's hand between both of his. "That's cool. Cheers, Rick." He meant it.

A little more than half-an-hour later, the two cars were travelling in opposite directions, their occupants' short-term relationships happily completed. Giving Jon his works phone number, Paul had elicited one of those promises people sincerely make to comparative strangers, but rarely keep – to get in touch with him when their family problems were ironed out, to take him and his two pals hang-gliding.

Five

When the taxi carrying Rick and Jon from O'Hare Airport turned into Ohio Street and deposited them at the Holiday Inn, downtown Chicago was scintillating in the restless lights of its road traffic and poured over by innumerable floodlights magically transfiguring its imposing towers.

It was nearly midnight, but they were able to get a twin room without too much difficulty. After they had signed in, Jon asked for the number of Mr Gregson's room. Reception rang the number for him.

"Excuse me, Mr Gregson. This is your lobby receptionist speaking," she announced. "There is a gentleman here from England who wishes to speak with you: a Mr Reynolds. That is correct. *Mr* Reynolds. Very well. Thank you, sir. There you go." She handed the phone across the desk to Jon with an impersonal smile, and carried on with some paperwork.

"Hi, Andy. Yes, it's me, Jon. Why do you think?" He laughed, then: "No chance. He wouldn't let me come alone. Sure, he's here with me, where else?"

"Jon's with me, Andy," Rick called down the mouthpiece. "The bridle's on the other nag."

"And we've managed to get a room here okay," Jon carried on regardless. "Yes, in this hotel. We're just going up now. Erm, 1204. Okay, cheers. See you later."

"He's on the 17th floor," he explained to Rick. "He's going down to the 12th to meet us."

Jon gave back the phone to the receptionist with his thanks.

"You're very welcome." She put the handset back in its place. "Pardon me, have you just arrived from England, gentlemen?" On being informed that they had, she glanced round for their baggage before summoning a porter. Her alert dark brown eyes questioned the foreigners.

"Ah. You see," said Jon, "it was an impulse thing, our coming to the States. A change of mind, you know? To join our friend on his vacation. We only have these weekend bags with us. We'll need to buy some things tomorrow. I presume you have a suitable shop here in Chicago?" he teased.

The black woman looked sideways at him. "Only the trading post in Main Street, sir. Not quite what you're accustomed to, but we do what we can."

"We're sure you do," Rick condescended amid airy laughter from those standing nearby, and he was first to move away towards the elevator. "Goodnight, and thanks."

She turned to deal with the small rush of returning guests. "Goodnight, gentlemen. Sleep well, now."

Their room was a clone of the hotel chain – spacious, predictable, adequate. Its new occupants put the kettle on, removed their top clothing and threw themselves on to their nearly double-size beds. Andy's knock at the door came within a few minutes. Jon admitted him. They shook hands.

"Hello, guys," said their visitor. "That was lucky, I was just about to go out warehouse hunting when you called." He was dressed completely in blue: working denims and suede boots and a sapphire stud in the lobe of his right ear. The pony tail had gone, and his hair was cut much shorter. "Tired, Rick?" he asked as he went to shake his hand.

Rick was still lying down, the back of one hand across his forehead. "Shagged out, actually," he moaned, but extended Andy a friendly greeting.

"Not to mince words, eh?" Andy grinned, then looked accusingly at Jon. "And you've only just got here, too! Don't waste much time, do you?"

He sat down on a chair and accepted tea of the breakfast variety from Jon who, after giving the remaining cup to Rick, had to make do with one of the glass tumblers provided next to the obligatory ice bucket.

"So," Andy observed. Exhaling deeply, he leaned back and slowly stretched out his legs. "You're here, then."

"Yes, Andy," replied a rather feeble chorus.

Andy eyed Jon severely. "And does your father know where you are?"

Jon clicked his fingers. "Gosh, I knew we'd forgotten something!" he dissembled.

"Thought as much." Andy took a drink.

"'When did you last see your father?'" Rick remembered.

"It's not a very funny situation," snapped Andy.

"Of course it's not. I wasn't really joking; just picturing something. Still, we did let my parents know that we weren't going home – and cleared it at work, if that helps."

Andy was alarmed. "When you decided simply to light out like that, you didn't tell anyone where you were going, did you?"

"Why, shouldn't we have done?" asked Jon, frowning. "I'm afraid we also rang the *Sun*, the *Mirror*, the *Daily Mail*..."

"All right, all right, you can cut the sarcasm." His tone was gruff. "But a lot depends on the British interest being kept very low key. We mustn't let word of my – our presence be sent up the line to The Light of the World's backers."

"We do know that, Andy," Jon admonished him. "Good God, we're not a security risk, you know."

"No, of course not. Sorry, lads. Even so, this is a really bad idea. You've come over here against the expressed wish of Sir Rupert, making me an accessory if I don't inform him – and how the hell can I? – and, worst of all, you've dumped a ruddy great shitload of extra responsibility on me. And – did you stop to think? – there are just a few minor preliminaries which have to be gone through before engaging in Intelligence work for Her Majesty's Government, like security screening, years of training in –"

"We'll have to take a rain-check on all that," Jon interrupted.

"Geez, Andy," complained Rick, "we're not going to work for HMG, you know. We're here for Sarah and Peter, that's all."

"And to see you!" said Jon brightly, if disingenuously. "And you did tell dad that you would have liked a partner to work with on this case. Hey, now you've got two."

Rick had risen from his perch on the edge of his bed and stepped over to the single window that spanned the width of the room and reached from the ceiling to within a metre of the beige-carpeted floor. Gazing out between the curtains, he could easily discern the recognisable Wrigley Building, the Tribune Building and the twin radio masts atop Sears Tower farther away, all among the scores of resplendent landmarks to his right. And on the left, from his perspective, the Sheraton Hotel competed to proclaim its brash dignity above the blue-black inky waters of Lake Michigan. When he was showering this morning, he had had no germ of a notion that by tonight he would be overlooking such a magnificent and famous vista.

Shame they weren't here merely to savour this bewitching obverse side of the city, instead of maybe having to plumb its nether climes where a criminal underworld flourished and a large deprived and resentful underclass survived hand-to-mouth on its wits.

Rick said as much aloud.

"I'm glad you understand the enormity of what you're thinking of taking on," said Andy, critically scrutinising the clean line and motion of Jon's frame as the man crossed the room to join his partner at the window. He saw the way Jon flexed his left arm, rested it on Rick's shoulders and ran his hand through that thick brown hair in a way guaranteed to make Rick arch his neck luxuriously to meet the pressure of those big, sensuously probing fingers. Andy mentally shook himself. How he wished there was someone to do that for him.

Jon felt his eyelids drooping even as he stood with Rick admiring the magnificent view. Minutes sneaked by unnoticed. Neither man heard the faintest clunk of the door behind them closing. The background buzz of the city was having a somnolent effect on their flagging senses. Before they eventually bestirred themselves from their imagined odyssey, Andy was out on night duty. With practised stealth, he had left the room, and a scribbled note on his vacated chair. Rick picked up the slip of paper, and read out:

'I'm working. Get some kip. See you at seven. Sweet dreams. Andy.'

When their alarm clock sounded at 7am, it was Andy who switched it off. He looked down at the couple who had slept unclothed, presumably as usual, in the bed nearer to the window. How two such big men managed to be comfortable in what was, after all, a bed somewhat smaller than a standard double at home, was a wonder to Andy, but comfortable they obviously were. Probably they were accustomed to fitting snugly into each other's shape. Again he felt a pang of envy.

The room was redolent with the still warm, freshly baked bagels Andy had brought in with him from a deli two blocks away, where he'd dropped in for a bite. While he was there, and being distinctly light-headed after a virtually sleepless thirty hours followed by a night shift which had stretched both nerve and tendon, the untypically rash idea had come to him that he could fix it so that the men would wake to find their breakfast ready and waiting for them. Breakfast in bed on their first morning. A small treat, that's all. Just to compensate for his being much too harsh with them last night. Besides, he had rationalised, there were pressing new things he needed to talk over with them. They had certainly demonstrated an easy informality toward him, but now he felt qualms that they would object to him actually letting himself into their room, that he had taken his solicitousness too far so early in their acquaintanceship. Those qualms were curiously unsettling to the dispassionate Andy. It was too late to do anything about it now, however, for Jon was casting bleary eyes on him.

"Hey, you smell very tasty," he said throatily. "I suppose you got in through the usual hole in the wall?"

"You'd not pressed the deadlock in the door handle, so I used one of my keys to bring in your breakfast while it was still warm. Hope that's all right."

Jon woke Rick by breathing a kiss into his upturned ear, then gently had to restrain him.

"Whoa, hold it!" he whispered. "Room service!"

"That's nice," crooned Rick sleepily, "I'm ready."

"No, love, we have room service. We're not alone."

Jon shared comprehending grins with Andy, who mouthed, "Shall I go?" to which Jon shook his head.

Rick opened his eyes and spied their spy looming somewhere between him and the window, looking at him. Overcome with fright, he scrambled into a sitting position.

"Christ, Andy, what are you doing here? Is something wrong? Did you find something last night?"

"No, no, there's nothing wrong." Andy appeared crestfallen. "Look, I'm sorry. This was a bloody stupid idea. I wanted to make amends for my attitude last night, but I can see I've just made matters worse. I'm not very good with these things." He moved to leave.

"What's that delicious smell?" Rick enquired, calmer now. "You, Andy?"

"Not personally." Andy paused in his tracks. "But I'm responsible for it."

"It's our brekkie," said Jon, playing with Rick's gold neck-chain. "Andy's brought it for us."

Rick perked up considerably. "Great! Thanks a lot, Andy. God, I'm starving. I don't think either of us could face eating much of that air-line muck we were offered yesterday. Well, come on," he directed, rubbing his hands together, "let's get round it."

Jon shrugged another grin at Andy. "See? You did the right thing, after all." He wrinkled his nose, "But you look as though you've been chucked out of a whorehouse."

"There speaks the expert."

"I don't need to buy sexual favours," Andy drolly protested. They believed him.

Going through the motions he had mentally rehearsed, Andy draped paper napkins along the top edge of the men's duvet, then placed plastic cutlery and paper trays of sliced cheese and sweet cured ham between them, completing his arrangement with the styrene-sheet parcels containing a dozen warm pastries.

"Anyway, you can be sure that I washed my face and hands as soon as I came in," Andy said.

"I never doubted it!" replied Jon, with affected unctuousness.

Andy went to make coffee using water he'd boiled minutes earlier. Finally, he took off his filthy jacket and flopped down on the unused bed alongside Jon, first grabbing himself a couple of bagels.

"Well, this is cosy!" exclaimed Rick through a mouthful of food. "Does this mean we're forgiven, then?"

"It means I'm sorry for reacting the way I did." Andy relaxed onto his left elbow. "When you phoned me from the lobby, at first I was mad with you. I had quite enough to contend with without having the extra worry about keeping you from under my feet. You could really screw things up. Then I came down here to meet you, and after a while I began to understand you better and size you both up. You'd used enough nous not to go swanning off to try some amateur freelancing, the way Peter did. He totally ignored the advice of his own organisation. And he might well have harmed more than just himself in the process. While I was out, I felt a right shit for the lousy way I treated you. In fact – and this isn't at all like me, I've always preferred to work alone when I can – I came to realise that I was really glad to have you along with me."

"You reacted better than we imagined you would," Rick said, "under the circs. We did drop in on you out of the blue, after all." He reverted to North Country: "A bit unexpected, like."

"Well, let's call us quits, shall we?" proposed Jon, wiping melted cheese from a corner of his mouth.

"So, we're a team, then?" said Rick.

Andy's deep green eyes went from one man to the other. "I suspect that if I had been asked to choose partners from among tens of qualified men and you, I might well have finished off with you characters. It took guts for you to drop everything to come here like this. I know Sarah is close family, but you know full well how dangerous this mission may get." His demeanour became grave. "There's one thing you've got to promise me, though. You must swear, swear to avoid getting out of your depth in any gangland affairs we may encounter. Stick with me. You've had no training in intelligence gathering.

"Self-defence, for example: that's just one aspect of our training. Being hand-to-hand combat-wise can be a lifesaver if things get really hot, though in most operations matters don't get that serious. Martial arts courses: ever taken any? No? Pity. So you wouldn't know the first thing to do if you really came up against any of them who had. They'd chew even your balls off faster than you're eating this little lot."

Rick grimaced at the rolled piece of ham he'd been about to pop into his mouth. He put it down. "OK, Andy, so we're not into S&M like you. Like, what use are we going to be to you, after all?"

"Your brains and your bodies. Those are highly tuned in the right way. It's obvious that you keep yourselves in pretty fair trim. You say you remember me telling Sir Rupert that I really needed assistance for this job. Check? And even though he agreed with me, he couldn't possibly have authorised some help for me at any price?" The couple remembered that, too. "Well, to be brutally honest, you're the answer to my prayer." He'd articulated that with far more feeling than he had intended, but what the hell?

"He says the nicest things!" Jon remarked flippantly as to Rick, but his face showed what he truly thought.

Momentarily Andy hesitated, then went on in deadly earnest, "But once we are out in the field of operation, you must always take my lead without question. If you don't, we could get each other killed. Understood?"

They both readily assented. It was what they had hoped for – Andy Gregson's professional leadership.

For his part, Andy remained conscious of the couple's emotional closeness to the case. He must keep them under his strict control. It was his job to make the strategic decisions himself and use the lads essentially as extra limbs. If anything happened to them... How long had he known them? Three days or so? Seemed longer. He was intensely aware that they were having to force themselves to be mentally cool, even to have some fun to keep their distressed minds from diving into troughs of disabling despair. The fooling-around episodes were really to help them stay on an even keel.

Rick broke in to his mind-sort. "There's only one thing," he demurred.

"What's that, Rickie old son?"

"It's just that, when we're out sleuthing with you, okay, you're the boss man, but while you're in our bedchamber, we are in charge."

Andy nodded, and a half-expectant smile dimpled his cheeks. "You want more coffee?"

"Yes, ta, if it isn't too much trouble. The service has certainly deteriorated round here. And while you are about it, I want to put on my one-and-only pair of undies, and your bum's got them warmed up nicely by now!"

Jon nonchalantly yawned: "And I think you'll find mine there too, Gregson, if you please."

Andy felt under his backside and extricated two identical pairs of identically crushed white silk briefs. He separated them and suspended one in either hand for a few seconds, whimsically studying their scantiness. Suddenly, with a sustained animal growl, he flew at the other men, fiendishly buffing their faces with the garments. They yelled out, and Jon made a grab at him, but he nimbly darted back, abandoning the briefs where they were, and hopped away quickly across the room. There, with calm deliberation, he took up the kettle and refilled it, innocently, as it were, expediting their coffee orders. It tickled him to see the guys, after examining the briefs they had been left with, having to swap them over before putting them on beneath the bedcover.

Rick adjudged: "I think that as a valet, Andy, you would make a much better secret agent." He slipped out of bed in one movement.

Jon agreed. "Afraid he lacks that cultivated sense of what is proper in a gentlemen's bedroom." He gathered up the rudely scattered remains of their repast before rising himself. "It's t'breedin' what matters in t'end."

Staying by the wide shelf where the kettle was once more getting agitated, Andy in a like state stood watching them collect the crockery together. He grew noticeably nervous when they came up to him with the cups and glass ready for replenishment. He stood away, but they refrained from getting their own back.

"When you are least expecting it!" Jon warned him darkly, giving him the Evilest Eye he could muster.

The pair showered and shaved, and dressed for the most part in the same clothes they had arrived in. They were ready in fifteen minutes. Andy produced the fresh coffees and set them upon the substantial circular table near the south-facing window, where the men sat down in the spring sunshine which was beaming over the silvered waters of the lake and undercutting the fast-dispersing rain-cloud layer that was giving a final, fastidious wipe to the bemisted stone and glass forming the city's highest pinnacles. The newly adopted mentor began to relate what he had been up to during the night hours.

"I'd planned beforehand what I was going to do on my own. You needed rest last night, anyway, and I had to think what to do about you. My intention was first to suss out the warehouse where the fire had been, so I took a cab to Kingsbury Street – about a mile from here.

Just beyond it runs the North Branch of the Chicago River. It was drizzling by that time, and there weren't many street lights, but the old stone setts of the road surfaces glistened under them. I could even see the remains of the tracks where, I guess, the old goods trains and the trams used to run among the huge brick warehouses. Not that many of those still exist, and most of the survivals look deserted. So many buildings have been demolished, leaving big expanses of derelict land – but I reckon they'll get round to redeveloping them before too long...

"Anyhow, it's not a neighbourhood to hang about in. I could smell that distinctive pong of newly burnt building – it's quite unlike anything else – as I turned the corner of a block still standing. There on the far corner was Shaughnessy's Tobacco Warehouse – that's what's still painted high up on the brickwork. It's faded now. Our friend Ciampi's grandfather acquired it back in the thirties – a gambling pledge, the story goes. It's only one of several owned by Umberto in that part of town.

"I couldn't tell whether there was an official security stakeout in place at that moment. They could have been anywhere or nowhere. And I couldn't take a chance on being apprehended by them in case it got back to The Light of the World. But there are these coded body signals used by FBI agents and members of different approved organisations to sanction one another by from a distance. They are changed at short irregular intervals to foil code-breaking. Sir Rupert is in the confidence of the FBI's code initiators, so I was able to make the current signal in full view of the apparently empty premises and streets surrounding the warehouse while I looked around it. Not a sign of life anywhere. No vehicles parked anywhere I could see. I was, I suppose, the only moving thing about. Bloody conspicuous, really." Andy emitted a short laugh.

Rick stared at him. "But anyone might have attacked you, picked you off with a bullet, even."

"True, but that's one of the perks that goes with the job." The unease on his listeners' features was what had made him halt his narration.

"I told you it wouldn't be without risks, this 'sleuthing', as you call it."

Rick altered his facial expression. "No, Andy. No, it's all right. Really. Tell us, are you armed yourself? Do you have a gun or some other weapon to defend yourself with?"

"As an alien in a foreign country? That would be illegal unless I had a special permit. And the act of obtaining such a permit might itself have drawn unwelcome attention. Anyhow, in a situation like the one I was in last night, a single bullet from a modern rifle fired from a near-by building would decide the issue. You get no right of reply. Luck plays a big part in these things. All we can do is make luck's part as small as possible. I am here as an official investigator investigating unofficially. If anything more has to be done, I must leave it to the local police and other agencies. That applies to you equally."

"That's cool by me," Jon said. "I doubt if either of us would have wanted a gun anyway. Nasty things." He gave a mock shudder. "But, Christ, you mightn't have got back this morning."

Andy returned a smile of detachment. "Still want to go ahead with this? You can still back off, if you like. Only the three of us would know."

This annoyed Rick. "And what about Sarah and Peter, and what all this is doing to mum and dad and brother Mike? Just get on with the story, Andy."

"And you, Jon? Are you as committed as Rick justifiably is?"

Jon had been reflecting on how the odds were stacking so far. His fleetingly glazed eyes now came alive again, and regarded Rick steadily while he answered simply, "He knows I am, Andy." It was no more than a reaffirmation of an old understanding between them.

Some moments elapsed. "Nothing more to be said then," Andy declared.

"So, as I was about to tell you, I went round to where I'd seen the warehouse's steel fire escape. Its bottom flight was folded up to the next storey, but then I saw a rusty downspout from the roof and noticed that the fire escape steps were quite near it from second floor level, so I shinned up the wet, creaky old pipe – a bit chancy, really – until I could reach across to the hand rail and swing over on to the stairway." He demonstrated these movements with graphic arm and leg actions. "I got to the roof and slipped over the parapet, then I crawled up the tiles till I reached one of the skylights up there. I shone my torch inside, and saw there was a drop to the floor of five metres or thereabout. I had some cord rope coiled round me under my jacket, so after I had prised the window open, I tied one end to the wooden mullion and slid down to the deck.

"I spent a good four hours nosing round inside. The fire had been on the second storey, in an office area alongside a central stairwell and elevator shaft. Just as well the cops outside on the day reported the fire and got it put out so quickly, otherwise the blaze would have bolted straight up that shaft, like a chimney, and taken hold of the entire shooting match in no time flat. As it was, the office partition walls were destroyed; their broken glass crunched under my feet, making one hell of a din in that echoey black shell of a place. The two hefty filing cabinets were full of papers charred by heat, though not by direct contact with the fire. I sifted through them, drawer by drawer. I recovered lots of paper fragments and a handful of spoiled documents that were more or less legible, but I couldn't make out anything of any significance – just what looked like standard bills of lading, invoices, dispatch notes, that sort of thing.

"The building was virtually stripped bare of fittings and merchandise. There were only a few items which might conceivably hold some clues – and then, probably not. This lot, for starters."

Andy delved into a pocket of his discarded denim jacket, and took out a number of clear plastic envelopes, several containing scraps of partially burnt paper, a few with not-so-damaged printed forms and a larger one enclosing badly scorched pieces of fabric in navy blue and white. A pair of tweezers appeared in his hand.

He slid open the zip-seal of this largest envelope, and extracted its single piece of blue cloth with utmost care then, one by one, put each of the white pieces alongside it on the teak table. The trio sat inspecting the assemblage before them for quite some time. The object made out of the navy material, of which this was a remnant, had been all but melted away by the heat. The ten or more pieces of white fabric were of approximately the same shape and size as it, but their edges had tended to singe rather than melt in that mysterious fire.

"Well?" quizzed the professional, "what should we make of this lot?"

"Polyester, the blue stuff?" suggested Rick, between idly picking at a molar tooth with his tongue. "The white material seems, sort of, like the interlining they quilt into things like jackets and ski-suits for insulation. What does anyone else think?"

Jon could offer nothing better.

"And I don't suppose Sarah had anything made of that material, did she?" Andy ventured.

"I don't think so," replied Rick. "I can't answer for Peter, though. There's nothing special about articles made like this, anyway. They're seen everywhere, on the streets, in shops –"

"Positively ubiquitous," Jon confirmed. "Even things like camping and climbing gear –"

He stopped and took the tweezers from Andy. Turning over the piece of blue, he continued thoughtfully: "– especially sleeping bags, though one made of such inflammable stuff as this shouldn't be allowed on the market. Yes, Rick, do you see? One side of it looks waterproofed and strengthened, like the underside of most sleeping bags."

"Aye, it's rubberised," said Rick, "and a tad blistered. It could have been anything, quite honestly, but a strong candidate is a camper's sleeping bag, for sure."

Andy suggested, "A sleeping bag would be an odd item to discover in a warehouse office. Suppose, for example, it was just an ordinary topcoat of some kind? Where would that take us?"

"Nowhere, would it?" said Jon, surprised at the question. "It could have belonged to any member of staff or a calling truck driver, an item of lost property waiting to be claimed. Anything."

"Precisely." Andy appeared content with that, though seeing the expectancy on his companions' faces, he clarified: "Well, I think this bit of it didn't burn because the object it belonged to was lying flat on the floor at the time of the fire. There may have been more pieces I missed, 'cos I only had a hand-held flashlight to search by. But this one was right in a corner of the office area surrounded by a once molten cindery substance and, now that you've given me the idea –" he went back to his jacket and, out of a different pocket, fished another envelope from which he withdrew, in several pieces, a hundred-centimetre length of what had certainly been a heavy duty, nylon-plastic zip fastener, most of its teeth fused together, "– I'm bloody sure this would have belonged to it."

"This was in the same area?"

"Yep, it was, Rick. There was much more of it stuck firmly to the floorboards following the line of the old partition, indicating that the article had lain on the floor close up against the partition. You've got to realise that the scene was very confused. I skimmed through a great jumble of other rubbish lying on top of all this. Even so, I think that together we may have opened a little chink in our mystery already."

"So it was a sleeping bag, then," said Jon.

"In all probability. So who would be likely to need a sleeping bag in that big, draughty warehouse?"

"The night watchman-person?" Jon advanced.

"Huh, really?" rejoined Rick. "The night security guard sleeping on the job – and leaving the evidence, like, right there in the office for the guv'nor and all the world to see?"

"Well then, if the warehouse was no longer in use, maybe it was a squatter, a hobo, a homeless person – what you will."

Andy evinced a look of tacit approval for this. "But remember, goods were seen being taken out on the actual day of the fire, so at least parts of the premises were functioning as warehousing. Mind you, if the office itself was disused by that time, it probably wouldn't be too hard for a squatter to stash themselves away in there."

Nobody spoke for several minutes.

"The office wasn't disused for long, if at all, Andy," said Rick, who had been industriously messing up the ball point of his complimentary Holiday Inns biro by toying with some of the singed papers. "See? There's a document here calling itself a consignment note. It is dated up here. Look."

The three of them leaned over it. After some effort, they descried a date of two weeks earlier, when four hundred cases of an unnamed commodity were transferred in. This paper had been among those scooped up in handfuls by Andy, all from a late period in the filing system.

A further hour of meticulous perusing revealed nothing more remarkable than scant humdrum references to this and that trucking company moving goods about the country, stowing them in the warehouse and leaving them there for months on end before forwarding the merchandise on to the next links in various chains. What those goods comprised, however, was rarely specified; just quantities of outers or the weights of their contents.

"Leaving their options open for audit enquiries," declared Andy. "That's not our concern, however."

A morning report on CNN television news addressed itself to the horrendous consequences of the warring factions yesterday pulling out of the Geneva Peace Initiative following what the Bosnian government regarded as the United Nations' complicity in the bid to assassinate their President. Already, the civil war was beginning to intensify. Sieges about to be lifted from two large towns had been tightened instead, and all foreign relief aid to those trapped inside was stopped. A UN food convoy had come under heavy artillery fire, which had killed and injured a number of UN soldiers and civilians working for charity organisations.

"But that really is our concern," Andy said. "It is another reason why we must find your sister: to exonerate her and her UN employers from blame in that business. The trouble is, as a result of all that false propaganda, not every country is co-operating fully in the hunt for whoever did fire those shots at the President. Which means there are lots more hiding places for them."

"You say 'them'," noted Jon, "but isn't the balance of probabilities leaning towards that Anna Reicke, the substitute who travelled in Sarah's place, as being the culprit?"

"Yes, sure it is," answered Andy, "yet we can't just assume that unless we have some proof."

"There was the trail of blood leading from the roof where the shots were fired to a room that had been occupied by that person. Surely blood and DNA tests can be made to establish who was the marksman."

"Again, yes, Jon, so long as we have something to test the samples against. All we know about Sarah is that her blood group is O Positive. We don't even know that much about Ms Reicke. First, we must catch up with her and, even better, Sarah herself."

"What group was the blood found at the scene of the crime?" enquired Rick.

"Also O Positive, I'm afraid. That proves nothing. It's the most common Caucasian group, they say."

Jon nodded, and watched as Andy was overtaken by a splendidly eloquent yawn. "You look like we felt last night," he decided.

"It's all that night-prowling's done you in," empathised Rick.

"Not that Rick knows anything about such things," Jon said archly.

Andy yawned once more. He'd given up trying to stifle them. "Sorry, lads. It really isn't the company."

"We know when we're not wanted," cried Jon. "C'mon, Rickie, let's go shopping, shall we? We'll get us some really funky gear, and leave this fine fellow to recover his senses."

Andy stood up. "I'll go up to my room for a few hours' sleep."

"Stay here, if you want. There's a spare bed."

Jon concurred. "We'll just hang that Do Not Disturb card on the doorknob when we go out." He gave Andy a light push on the breastbone, which was not resisted. His father's assistant collapsed meekly on to the bed, and started to undress, saying nothing.

The pair sorted out their wallets, put on their jackets, wished their friend pleasant dreams and left to buy themselves clothing and other basic necessities in the seething city.

"He's even hairier than you, Rick!" Andy overheard, just as the door closed and his compatriots started to walk to the elevators.

Six

It was mid-afternoon before Rick and Jon sneaked back into their dimmed room. They were laden to the eyebrows with plastic shopping bags which rustled the more infuriatingly the more they tried to hush their noise. Thankfully, their guest remained deep in slumber as the sound accompanied him on his most daring slalom yet down that alpine slope, the firm snow fairly sizzling beneath his trusty skis. The couple were irresistibly drawn to speculating on his body's erotically swaying motion.

"Is he alone under there?" wondered Rick, putting his bags down near the curtains drawn shut across the sun-flared window.

"He evidently doesn't think so," Jon grinned, laying his impedimenta with the rest.

The graceful movements on the bed ceased as Andy reached the end of his challenging course. He breathed heavily, completely satisfied, and removed his safety helmet.

"Hi, there!" Jon greeted Andy's dishevelled head when it poked out from under the duvet.

"Oh, hi," croaked the other. "Christ, I'm aching all over!"

"I'm not a bit surprised, the way you were going at it hell for leather in there!" Rick chaffed him. "You were supposed to be sleeping to get some rest. What were you dreaming about, or would we be healthier people for not knowing?" He drew back the window drapes.

Andy heaved himself up and stretched his arms above his head. He surveyed his thoroughly tangled bed and understood. "I always seem to have exciting adventures in my sleep whenever I'm trying to solve some thorny problem or other." He didn't at all mind their overt interest in him.

"It's hard luck for your sleeping partners, then!" ventured Jon wickedly.

"The chance would be a fine thing!" Andy mumbled unguardedly almost to himself.

Rick turned away from the window. "What, a man with your personality and undoubted libidinal talents? I'll bet you're the guy with the highest score card in your office alone," he wagered, sending a wink to Jon. "The girls must flock after you."

"I get on with them okay, but scoring's not something I do, somehow. It's not without trying, I can assure you."

The kettle had been brought into the action once more, and Jon was handing round the coffees he'd made. He peered at Andy incredulously as he did so. None of this accorded with what they had previously been told about the man. "Wait, you're telling us that the females really don't fancy you? All of them? I can't believe that for one minute."

Andy shrugged. "Nevertheless, I only get so far with a woman I'm keen on before the urge dwindles. I don't know why I'm telling you this!" He sighed. "I've never told this to a living soul before, man or woman, and here I am unburdening myself on to a couple of guys I met only a few days ago! I'm definitely going off my trolley." Andy shook his head in his hopelessness.

"You were doing okay for a while, there," remarked Jon with a sardonic grin, "until you implied that confiding in us must be the mark of a madman!"

"I didn't mean it that way. You know I didn't. I-I just don't do this kind of thing. You know? – talking about myself? I prefer to be private. Besides, in my line of work, it wouldn't be fair to tie someone emotionally to me, in case something ever goes wrong."

"Any of us can fall under that proverbial bus at any time," Rick pointed out. "On the basis of what you've just said, then, no member of the fighting forces, no police officer patrolling a violent city and no one who has to drive a lot on our dangerous roads should marry or have any other kind of loving relationship lest they get killed and leave their lover grieving for them. It's just as well not many entertain the same dotty idea. D'you know what I think? I think you are hiding yourself behind that lame excuse, like, for an excuse. Besides, who's talking about affairs with strong commitments? We're talking raw nooky here, that's all, and well you know it.

"Tell me, if you want to, that is, whose urge, er, dwindles, like, first? Hers or yours?"

The purr of the air conditioning dominated the next few seconds.

"Mine is a very stressful occupation," Andy muttered uncertainly. "It's not surprising, is it?"

"Yours, then. What about before you were in Intelligence? When you were at university, for instance?"

"I need a slash," announced Andy, placing his empty cup on the bed head cabinet then throwing back his duvet to a flash of white-on-yellow polka-dot boxer shorts.

"Ouch!" Rick shielded his eyes as against the glare, and Jon made some remark about Consumer Protection laws requiring packaging to accurately reflect the nature of the goods contained.

Andy gave Jon a cuff on the cheek, put his socks on and padded in haste across the carpet to the bathroom, firing over his shoulder as he went, "If that's the case, yours and Rick's teensy-weensy knickers say that they don't have a lot to package!" He slammed the bathroom door shut before the two pillows reached him.

The duo put away their new wardrobe of items they thought might be needed during a week or so in the States. Then they reverted to pondering again over the bewildering charred papers on the table. When Andy came back into the room, he joined them sitting at the table, without getting dressed. His beard stubble was prominent. He had not shaved yesterday, either.

"We went to see the warehouse you so wantonly pillaged for these treasures last night," Jon disclosed, idly passing a little finger over flecks carbonised to nearer soot than anything else.

"You didn't let yourselves be seen, did you?" Andy was alarmed.

Rick tutted. "We could have walked – we have this street guide map given to us by the hotel, but we went by cab just to tour the area. I think we gave the driver the impression that we were foreigners looking for investment land to develop. We didn't stop anywhere, and we sat in the centre of the seat, keeping our vizogs away from the windows, just in case."

"Where did you pick up the cab?" Andy grilled him.

"Not here at the hotel," replied Rick, affecting an air of patient compliance before this invigilation. "Michigan Avenue, outside the, er –"

Jon rescued him. "Near the Hancock Building."

"Yes, that's right. And he dropped us off at the Hyatt. We went straight in as though we were guests. There's a fine shopping centre in there where we got some of our gear, then we came out of the hotel by another door, and got the rest of our stuff at various stores in the area." He reached over and gave the hirsute chest next to him a playfully vigorous rub. "There, is that being cautious enough for you?"

Reluctantly, Andy conceded that it was. "So, were you any the wiser for your experience?" His tone was still a little cold.

Jon said, "About the warehouse? No, but we didn't really expect to be. We just wished to get a sense of the neighbourhood. Well, Rick did especially."

"In case Sarah had been there, that's all," explained Rick. He didn't mention that it made him feel closer to his sister in her ordeal. Jon knew it, and that was all that mattered.

Andy, too, was perceptive enough to understand. "Did it help you, Rickie?" he asked more kindly.

"I think it did in some way, yes."

"I'm glad."

"I've been thinking through what we were discussing earlier," Andy went on. "We cannot simply presume that the supposed sleeping bag was used by a prisoner of Ciampi's, but it is the only clue we have at present. We can follow that line of thought, so long as we keep our minds open to the likelihood that it may lead us straight up shit creek, or we can keep looking for more definite evidence of her in Ciampi's other premises."

"The thing is," said Jon slowly, "that'll be all well and good if she is still in Chicago. If she isn't, if she and maybe Peter, too, were shipped off in those bales that were shadowed to Colorado – or perhaps that manoeuvre was itself a feint to mislead any onlookers –" He was characteristically thinking out loud again. If he hadn't stopped there, he could effortlessly have boxed himself into a corner.

"Hmm, it's not so easy, is it?" smiled Andy. "Tell you what, while we're thinking about it, I'll go up to my own room and get a shave."

He rapidly threw on his denims and left, saying that he would be back in half an hour. He returned in ten minutes, his tanned face several shades paler than before.

"My room's been searched," he declared indignantly. "Everything has been disturbed, just disturbed."

"Not by the room cleaners?" said Jon.

"No. My belongings have been gone through: the drawers, my cases and bags. Nothing is exactly as I left it. It's my habit of years to make a mental note of things like that and to be on the lookout for any counter-intelligence operators rumbling me."

"How'd they get in, Andy?"

"Picked the lock. A solitary, new tell-tale scratch on the lock plate."

"You don't think the scratch mark could have been put there to make you think the lock was picked, do you, when in fact a key was used?"

"It could have been, but it wasn't, because there was no purpose in doing it. They'd prefer me to believe that hotel staff carried out the break-in, should I realise in the first place that there'd been one."

"Was anything taken or damaged?" Jon asked.

"That's the point. Nothing at all, so far as I can see; just moved and put back not quite where it was before. They certainly didn't find anything to link me with the case I'm on, though, or with my department. I made sure that could not have happened."

"But they do know who you are, or they wouldn't have searched your room in the first place," Rick assumed.

Andy nodded. "I think someone wants to know why I'm here as much as anything. I dare say I'll find a listening bug in the phone or somewhere when I investigate more closely. A bit amateurish really, but I don't honestly think I was meant to know about it."

"Can you use it to your advantage, do you think?" said Rick, continuing with the task in hand at the time of Andy's revelation, putting the burnt evidence back into the appropriate plastic bags while endeavouring not to multiply the fragile parts too much.

"Meaning?" asked Jon, who had left off that fiddly job to tidy up briskly the shopping bags scattered about the room.

"I'm not sure." Nevertheless, Rick came up with an idea immediately. "For instance," he said brightly, "if they have actually bugged your room, Andy, you could lay false information. Well, like ringing up a pal in the UK, telling her or him, kind of, where you are and what for, and would they like you to take something bought for them in Chicago home with you. Sort of all matter-of-factly, you know?"

His listeners' eyes met. Both men's features registered surprise and admiration for this aspect of Rick hitherto unsuspected.

"You devious little Machiavelli, you!" pronounced Jon. "Why have I never seen this side of you before?"

Rick merely winked at Andy.

Andy sniggered. "Er, Jon, your not having noticed it before might be a measure of Rick's ability to use it convincingly. You'd perhaps, on occasions – dare I say very rare occasions? – be the very last person he intended should know when he was putting this deviousness to use!"

Jon gaped, then stuck out his lower lip in sulk. "Right. That's two I owe you, Andy. And, as for you, traitor, I'll speak to you later!"

Rick put on a frightened expression.

"There's still the important little matter of how we should take things from here," Andy reminded them. "Any ideas to contribute?" He regarded them each in turn.

"Are Ciampi's other warehouses any busier than the one you were in last night?" asked Rick.

"By all accounts." Andy took their street map and indicated where those buildings could be found in close vicinity.

His companions conferred, then Rick said, "Yes, we saw maybe three of them. There was quite a lot of life at these, when we passed. Trucks were queued up at this one." He touched the spot.

"That's what I would have anticipated," responded Andy, leaning back in his chair. "Thing is, it's unlikely he'd risk hiding a captive in such public places."

"So, you're saying that there's little or no purpose in our looking round those warehouses," said Jon.

"I am."

Rick surmised: "We are to leave the Windy City already, then?"

"If it hadn't been for the Colorado connection, I think I'd have gone for a quick shufty round his home, first. But the odds are stacked heavily against Sarah being in Chicago now, so it's not worth our staking chances on such a poor bet. I still think I might take a trip to his street, just to see who's coming and going. I may recognise somebody, or it could give some other kind of a lead, who can tell? There's no point in you two going with me, as you won't know who or what to look out for. And, oh yes, Rick, I'll first go and make that phone call you so cleverly suggested."

Jon tilted his nose in the air at that. "Oh yes, you should, you should," he said flatly, avoiding Rick's eyes. "A very good idea of Rick's, that was.".

"So I'll go up now." Andy chuckled at the quirky postures of the couple as he left them.

It was marvellous to him how these two were keeping each other's spirits up under such trying conditions. He could imagine the horrific turmoil that must be going on in Rick's head most of the time, out of his mind with worry about his sister, yet somehow the lad was able to raise smiles, even laughter, and was also capable of throwing light into the darkest corners.

He lifted the telephone handset and asked for the number of a girlfriend in Cambridge, England. Her father answered, but he fetched her.

"Hi, Andy," came a sweet and cultivated voice. "How nice to hear from you. Where are you?"

"Chicago, Illinois," he responded in a passable American accent of indeterminate statehood. "I'm just having four or five weeks' holiday here," he went on in his normal Standard English with the merest touch of Estuary. "I'm seeing an old university pal tomorrow, and we're going to where he lives with his wife and kids near Milwaukee, just north of here up the Lake. We're going to Colorado first, though. He's already here in Chicago somewhere with another British guy – a friend of his I've not met yet. We're going to drive aimlessly around the Rockies, maybe do a bit of trekking for a couple of weeks before joining his wife. She's a teacher at their kids' school. Their vacation starts then, so we'll be sailing off somewhere in their cruiser, possibly as far as Canada, who knows?"

"How lovely," said the voice. "I wish I had been to that part of the States. I've never seen the Great Lakes. But I've been skiing in Aspen. That's in Colorado."

"Yes, Sam. There were seven of us on that trip, remember?"

"Oops! We slept together, didn't we. It was you, wasn't it?" she hesitated.

It wasn't, but at least it told Andy that Dickhead Varley hadn't exactly been a memorable event in her life either. He didn't answer her. He recalled that there had been two girls and five blokes on that occasion. They had partnered up for the duration. The other two couples were still having it off, so far as he knew. And guess who had no one to sleep with for that entire month – not that Andy had been outstandingly successful in that sphere either before or since.

Without waiting for Andy's confirmation, Sam pressed on, "I'm getting engaged to Steven, did you know?"

That was the kind of opening Andy could make use of.

"Yes, Sam, you told me at Julian's party last month." She had imparted no such thing.

"Oh, did I?" She sounded not very concerned. "You and I had a few dances, didn't we? I remember that, but I got myself a bit squidgy, I'm afraid. I had a super time, though!" She giggled musically like a naughty schoolgirl.

"I want to take you something back with me as an engagement present." A pleasant enough girl, he reflected, but too superficial and fluffy. The guy, her third engagee, he didn't know at all. He would include the price of the gift on his expenses claim. "Is there anything special you'd like from Chicago?"

"Oo, that's very sweet of you, Andy darling." After a few moments, she came up with: "Bloomingdale's!"

Andy emitted a gasp. "I can't quite rise to that, Sam. But I'm sure your father could afford to buy the department store for you, plus s.a.v.!"

"No, no, silly!" she giggled once more, "a little pressie from there, that's all! You're not to spend a lot, darling."

Too right.

"I'll go there this evening," he promised. "I expect they'll be open till eight or so."

The famous store in North Michigan was indeed open at 6.45 when Andy arrived there on foot. He was not sure whether he'd been followed, but he was certain that his convoluted red herring of a trail had been convincing. To anyone eavesdropping, he was here on a private vacation, and his being spotted with the lads after tomorrow should not provide them with any problems.

He wandered from department to department searching for a suitable engagement present for a girl not yet suitable to be engaged. Samantha possessed an unassuagable passion for wild oats. She was very selective of the sowers of those seeds of bounty, and made her selections as often as she could. Safely, he had been reliably informed, as she also rejoiced in a condom fetish which she shared with her fellow activists with a singular enthusiasm.

Having chosen a piece of fine china depicting the riverside Marina Towers, and paid for it to be posted directly to Sam and Steven, Andy made his way by cab to the city's Little Italy quarter. Now confident that he was not being shadowed, he bought a copy of the *Tribune*, and located a modest little aromatic restaurant which just happened to be across the well-lighted street from a certain five-storey dwelling. He selected a window table, and passed the next two-and-a-half hours apparently luxuriating in the house's quality wines and traditional homeland foods, as well as enjoying the frenetic atmosphere of the place. Partly concealed by a red velour curtain draped from a heavy wooden pole, Andy Gregson the foreign tourist was able to observe casually what went on in that section of the street he was interested in. Between protracted courses, he read his plenitudinous newspaper and sipped his wine, careful not to over-imbibe.

Not more than a few individuals crossed Umberto Ciampi's threshold while Andy watched. He did not recognise any of them. The extended family, he knew, included the crook's wife, three sons and four daughters, his mother and his wife's parents. Of those, one son was at university and two of the daughters lived in other parts of the neighbourhood with their own families, yet he could imagine the constant, high-volume chatter that was going on in that house, if the garrulous behaviour of staff and diners in this establishment was anything to go by.

A young woman stepped out of a taxi and approached the door opposite. She had sleekly styled dark hair, and an expensive-seeming black outfit with white and grey detail was hugging her shapely figure. A female member of the household staff admitted her on sight. Some fifteen minutes later, a nattily clad man of about forty drew up driving a large, green Mercedes saloon. He went in and re-emerged with the girl a little after ten, and they drove off.

Andy pursued them in a cab. The too distinctive-looking girl was one he had noticed twice at the Holiday Inn, once in the lobby on his arrival, checking in like himself, and again only this afternoon on his floor, when she had smiled politely to him as he had passed by her in the corridor going in the opposite direction while he was making his way to his room. It had been no coincidence. Who was she? How had she learned that he was coming to Chicago and, what is more, known that he was going to stay at that particular hotel?

The Merc disappeared into the hotel's underground car park. Andy quickly paid off the cab driver, retrieved his own room key from the desk, sat down on a comfortable lobby sofa and waited behind his newspaper. At first there was no sign of the couple, then they stepped out of an ascended elevator and walked towards the desk. The man collected a key. They returned to the lifts and, as Andy could deduce from the indicator above the appropriate gate, their car halted only at the eighteenth floor before being summoned back to the ninth. Of course, by the time Andy attained their floor, they were not to be seen.

The intrusive hum of an electric motor attracted his attention. This floor's inevitable ice-storage freezer was situated in an alcove within sight of the elevators, so Andy decided to hover there for a while, as if waiting to descend in one, just in case the couple needed to get some ice for drinking water. Sure enough, after several other guests came to use the facility in the succeeding fifteen minutes, the girl's grey-suited, black-curly-haired driver rounded a corner in the corridor and made straight for the freezer. The watcher expertly mingled with the five people who had been assembling for the elevators.

Andy assessed his lithe, sinewy build as being about 170 centimetres tall. He had a thin face which made that thick moustache sit quite incongruously on his upper lip. At this closer distance, he appeared rather older than Andy had thought at first; probably more like forty. He habitually leaned back as he walked – or sauntered more like, the swing of his upper torso seeming symptomatic of the struggle his shoulders were having to keep up with the rest of him. His ancestry was almost certainly north Mediterranean. Detecting subtle indicators, the Englishman established that he was wearing a gun.

The man raised the transparent Plexiglas screen and noisily scooped out some of the irregular-shaped chips of ice and ladled them into the lidded plastic bucket he had brought with him from his room. Next, he inserted coins into the slot of the adjacent vending machine and received two cans of cold Coke in return. By the simple stratagem of shadowing him round two corners, Andy ascertained the room number he wanted.

Now to learn the couple's identities. He went down to the busy main desk and, as if he was a visitor who had entered the building only minutes before, asked to speak by telephone to his sister-in-law staying in Room 1825.

Obligingly, as the hotel's standards demanded, the duty receptionist checked his guest register, then tapped out the relevant number. "Good evening. Mr Scalfaro? This is your lobby receptionist speaking. I have a Mr Patterson here who would like to speak to Miss Connolly."

As soon as the receptionist had uttered the girl's name, however, Andy gesticulated to him that something was wrong. "Excuse me," the receptionist checked himself, "the gentleman here is telling me something."

"That's not who I want to speak to," Andy told him, inserting an apologetic tone into his Americanised voice. "There has to be some mistake. My wife is outside in the car; I'll just go and get the correct room number her sister gave her this afternoon. Kindly tell the person you have there that I'm sorry they've been disturbed. I'll be back in one minute just." Andy hurried out of the main door opening on to the covered drive-in where cars and cabs were able to set down and collect hotel guests. Ten minutes later, he re-entered by the separate door to one side of that entrance and slipped by the reception desk unrecognised.

Just in time, he darted behind a brochure display stand when he glimpsed the woman herself stepping out of one of the group of three elevators he was making for. She was carrying a small portmanteau and her tagged room key. She crossed to the desk, handed over her key and some dollar bills, waited for her receipt then made for the glass main doors. Andy followed her discreetly. Her male friend, once more in the Mercedes, drew up outside. The man held the door for her as she got in, then they drove off. Andy cursed the absence at that minute of any cabs stationed in readiness to pick up fares. He ran into the street, but the traffic lights were in the couple's favour and the big car swept away along Ohio Street, turned into Columbus and out of sight.

Room 1204 opened to his special key once more. It was unoccupied, but a table lamp had been thoughtfully left on for him. Judging from the rumpled state of their bed, the boys had kissed and made up after their 'altercation' earlier. Andy smiled to himself. Nice lads, he thought. Then he found the folded notepaper with his name on it leaning against the kettle, which was naturally his first point of call.

'Gone to North Halstead for a meal and a pint,' the note said. 'Make yourself at home. Won't be late. XX' Andy's nostrils detected the scent of aftershave on the page.

Having removed his jacket and shoes, Andy put coffee powder ready in the two cups and glass, and made up a drink for himself in the glass, then he sat down and quietly cogitated for ten minutes on the current state of play before making a lengthy phone call. Then he turned on the tv.

America's plethora of main television channels seemed, as it usually does to visiting Britons, all to consist of three-fifths' frenzied advertising slots, with much of the remaining programme time devoted to promoting overblown show-biz personalities or religious obsessives – usually with very little to distinguish between the two – selling their invariably tacky wares. What with the residual meat content too disjointed by puerile interruptions to permit for relaxed digestion, the only channel Andy considered worth devoting time to was CNN, perpetually churning out its news reports and comments thereon. As he was not a news junky, even that certainly stretched his tolerance limits.

He was snoring peacefully in his armchair in front of the illuminated box, amidst a lingering redolence of garlic and red wine, when the others came in from their night on the town.

With so much hanging in the balance, and frustrated that Andy had not yet needed their help much, Rick and Jon had not exactly been in the best of humours for really letting their hair down, but finding themselves with a little time on their hands in this great metropolis, it would have been idiotically remiss not to seek out some of the sights, flavours and sounds of the night-life for which Chicago was justifiably renowned. Even so, it was well before midnight when they returned to their room, and they were pleased to see Andy there.

Intending to waken him, Jon gave his head a passing gentle scratch with his fingertips as he went to the wardrobe.

"Hi, Andy," said Rick. No response. He switched off the tv.

Jon put away their jackets, went back to the sleeper and once again applied the massage. Both men called his name to no avail.

Jon winked at his partner and went behind the chair and started to massage Andy's scalp vigorously all over with both hands. An involuntary smirk came over the face of their 'unconscious' friend, at which Jon began lightly to pummel that bowed head from side to side.

"Come on, you fraud, we know what you're about!"

Still Andy refused to open his eyes.

Jon said to Rick: "You realise what we're going to have to do, don't you?"

"Yes, Jon. We'll have to undress him ourselves and put him to bed."

The corpse did not stir.

"Did you hear that, you lousy het guy? All the trouble you're putting us to?"

A low moan escaped those closed lips. It could have signified anything or nothing at all.

"Very well then," cried Jon, "you're asking for it!"

With no more ado, the couple heaved the limp body out of his chair and manhandled him quite roughly across the room by the shoulders and legs and threw him on to his bed. Andy grunted as he landed, but even now he steadfastly kept his eyes tightly shut.

Considerably shorter than the other two, Andy was heavily built and muscular through sports and self-defence training. Item by item, they stripped off his clothing until he was wearing only shorts, bright red ones this time. Andy co-operated not at all, but allowed his body to stay a complete dead-weight, rendering their task as difficult as it could be, making it necessary for the four strong hands to hold practically every part of him during the exercise.

"The sod's gone totally flaccid!" complained Rick, panting for breath.

"Not totally, Rickie." Jon indicated meaningfully with his eyes.

"Jesus!" stage-whispered Rick, grinning from ear to ear. "I see what you mean!"

By rolling him over both ways, they managed to get him under his duvet. Then they gazed down at his head snuggled into the soft pillows, a cat-with-a-saucer-of-cream smugness occupying that handsome face.

"Well, after that performance, this is the last time I think we should let Andy sleep in our room!" remarked Rick with mock severity. "If he's going to keep getting pissed like this... Well, he could get up to anything while we're asleep even!"

"Aye, we wouldn't ever feel safe in our bed!"

Jon couldn't help snorting raucously at the very idea, and they both fell about laughing. Andy joined in their hilarity. He raised both arms and hugged each of them down to him in turn. He was far from drunk, but he was undoubtedly under the uninhibiting influence of those excellent wines he had taken his time over during the evening.

"Don't you ever worry about that," Andy almost cackled, "It's me who should be concerned for my virginity. After all, it's two-to-one round here!"

"Yes, Andy, but we're a happily married couple," Jon averred, "so your alleged virginity's safe enough with us!"

"Ah!" chortled Andy, wagging a pedagogical finger at them, "I have it on good authority that that state is all about faithfulness in love; not necessarily about enjoying sex for its own sake. We men especially can often put those things in separate compartments."

The laughter subsided somewhat, though the feeling between the men was still companionable.

"'On good authority', you say?" Jon quizzed.

Rick intervened. "He means, from his ample experience." He grinned amiably at their friend.

"No, guys," Andy replied with deliberation, "I truthfully have never made it with anyone in my life." He lowered his eyes.

The resulting silence was palpable.

"That's twice you've said something of the sort," recalled Jon, sitting on the other bed. "I'm beginning to believe you, though I've got to say it's incomprehensible how you of all people have missed out for so long."

Andy, by this time sitting up, shrugged and smiled distantly. Was there a trace of bitterness in the corner of that mouth? "One day I hope we may discuss my problems together, but yours are much more pressing at the moment, aren't they?"

He sat forward, "Listen, and I'll tell you what I did this evening."

After Andy had recounted his activities, Rick and Jon sat looking pensive.

"Who the hell is this Connolly woman?" wondered Jon. "I suppose it was she who fitted up your room?"

"Or her boyfriend," Andy replied. "I don't know her, but she knows me, at least by sight. Still, I am sure that I wasn't followed once I left

Bloomingdale's. My phone call to Samantha seems to have bamboozled them. That was a big relief, I can tell you, because if they had known for certain that I was here on the Sarah Simpson case, the whole thing would have been blown, and the best thing I could have done then was to go straight back to England, *tout de suite*!"

"It still has to be worrying how Ciampi found out that you were here in the first place."

"That's right, Rickie. I'm going to get on to the Chief tomorrow by a neutral phone. It is, of course, entirely possible that their organisation has an efficient surveillance system of its own covering such venues as stations and airports. If that's all it is, then I'm not so concerned, because my work is based quite openly at HQ, so anyone can have pictures of me – if they're that hard up for talent, that is!" He accompanied that self-denigration with a single hearty laugh, then hastily proceeded to the conclusion of his report.

"Anyway," he underlined the word, "when I came in, I rang Amtrak, and was luckily able to book a couple of deluxe bedrooms on the California Zephyr tomorrow."

"To Denver, is it?"

"Yes, Rickie."

"I thought we'd have been going by air when we went," Jon frowned. "It'll take an age by train, won't it?"

"But when we're supposed to be on holiday, there's no hurry, is there? If 'the enemy' knew that I was jetting off to Denver as fast as I could get there, they might just have second thoughts. No, this way they're more likely to lose interest altogether in my being in this country and, moreover," Andy's eyes narrowed, "not make enquiries about who the hell you two might be. I know we want to get to Sarah quickly, but we are far more likely to find her alive and well if her captors' guard is down; if they think her trail has gone cold."

"How can we be sure that they don't know Rick's and my faces? We've been in the papers a lot lately."

"Not here in the States, you've not. But this affair tonight clearly demonstrates that we are as good as completely alone here. It's exactly as your father said, Jon, we don't know who's in the pay of these bastards who run The Light of the World. We can trust no one but each other from now on."

Seven

They were not obliged to welcome the sunrise. Their train was not scheduled to depart until 3.35 in the afternoon, so there was actually time to do some sightseeing before they left.

Nevertheless, touched as Andy was that Jon and Rick accepted his sleeping in the next bed to theirs, he did feel he should leave them early to give them some privacy. What surprised him was that it had been taken as read that he would be staying with them last night. Even he hadn't thought it through, it just happened somehow. What started out as a bit of clowning – the sort that can relieve the worst tensions at times of crisis – had led to an unexpected situation developing naturally. That consensual knockabout last night had been a lot of fun, yet no one so far as he knew, and positively not himself, contemplated that he should get dressed afterwards and return to his own room.

In fact, they had lain in their beds chatting into the smallest hours about their immediate fears and hopes, and had compared notes on their relative physical strengths in case they were going to have to call on them before many days elapsed. An essential aid to resource deployment: knowing what each was capable of. All three had talked about their families and lifestyles, though Andy had not dwelt on the darker, lonelier side of his own youth, and he had not been questioned on his chaste condition. Why should they care one way or the other whether he had ever been laid, for God's sake? To these two especially, it must surely be a matter for complete indifference. Jon had eventually been the first to drift off, which made further talk across his form between the survivors too troublesome, so they called it a night.

Again Andy jotted them a message. 'Am going to check out ahead of you. I'll leave my things at the station, and meet you at 11 in the atrium of the State of Illinois Building in LaSalle Street. We can't miss one another. It is a very public place, so, Jon, look dead fucking pleased to see your old varsity chum after so many years, and do introduce me to Rick. You don't need to eat this note, lads. Flushing it down the bog will do the trick. Andy. XX."

He had not consciously intended to put those XXs, it simply followed on after they had written the same on their note to him last night. A harmless gesture, but he had shocked himself. He surveyed the telling marks critically. What the hell, the couple would take it as another joke, anyhow. Besides, he wasn't going to write out a whole bloody new note for them now. They could like it or... whatever.

Before he closed the door, Andy glanced back at the dormant pair, lying on their right sides this time facing his bed, Rick nestled intimately against Jon's back, his left arm tucked beneath the other's so that his hand anchored easily on to his partner's right shoulder, while Jon, for his part, was gripping Rick's hand and forearm with both hands, locking that loving hold into position.

God help anyone who tries to come between those two, mused Andy, smiling grimly. And they know I'm no threat.

Forty-five minutes later, he had paid his bill and checked out of the hotel. He threw his two bags into the back seat of the leading car in the cabbies' line outside, and asked for Union Station. It took not much more than five minutes at that early hour to reach Canal Street, where the station building was on the right.

He pushed open one of the swing doors, and descended a flight of composition-marble steps into the already busy concourse and sought out the position where he was to claim his tickets and confirm the bedrooms booking. There he asked where the left luggage lockers were.

Unusually, this major terminal station had no such facilities, but there was a counter where travellers could leave their baggage.

Having rid himself of that encumbrance, he was free to fill the three hours till he was due to meet the lads just like any other tourist might. This was his second visit to Chicago which, like his first, was turning out to be all too brief.

Firstly, though, he had to phone the boss. He went to the row of telephones, entered one of the booths and closed the door after him.

"My whereabouts seems to be public property here, Sir Rupert. Exactly how they found out where I was going to stay is what I believe the department should be investigating. Even so, I don't believe they're sure why I'm here. The girl who was registered as Miss Connolly was at the hotel when I booked in there, and Carlo Scalfaro turned up, centre stage. Yes, him. And it looks as if he's still in the pay of Ciampi. They'll be wanting to know what I'm up to, even though I am apparently only here on holiday. I am certainly not taking any bets that I'm not being shadowed even as we speak. Oh, and by the way, your son and his other half are here, too!" He ought to have known better than to try to pass it off as a throw-away line. Andy winced, ready for the explosion which wasn't long in coming.

He left the station ten minutes later, his superior's stentorian rebukes still ringing in his ears, and strolled unhurriedly in the sunshine down Jackson Boulevard, which took him across the Chicago River to Sears Tower. The Observation Deck was not yet open to the public, so he walked on to Wells Street where he found one of the city's multitude of convenient diners doing a roaring trade feeding breakfasts mainly to office workers energising themselves for a further day's grind. He took a seat, and a self-possessed young waitress came up a moment later to reel off what threatened to be an unending menu of mostly unheard-of options. On realising that this foreigner could scarcely comprehend a word of her recitation, she conferred on him the smile of pity she reserved for the underprivileged and proceeded to describe each tasty-sounding offering in turn, as if there were no other customers there demanding her attention. When Andy did get his meal, not for the first time he could not but respect the efficiency of the service and the good value provided at such American establishments.

Then he sated himself on another kind of feast: the fantastic vistas to be viewed from the top of the highest of buildings, across the city and the inland sea beyond. Andy determined to take a stroll through Grant Park down to the Lake Shore.

His ensuing peregrinations led him on a four-mile trudge among those well-known sights and sounds of Chicago that any self-indulging rubbernecker would include on their itinerary, and everyone occasioning to discern that brown-leather-jacketed guy's camera-ready nerdism must have assigned him tourist status without hesitation or dubiety.

In such roving individuals, the near-triangular oddity of the State of Illinois Building unerringly excited the curiosity. Indeed, with its distinctive, tactile sculpture prominent on the adjacent sidewalk, it was altogether an obvious meeting place for locals and strangers alike.

Andy had been there before. Rick and Jon found it easily, and had even formed immediate and diametrically opposed attitudes towards it by the time their friend strode across the cavernous vastness of its crowded atrium.

Jon's welcome for his long unseen, former college roommate was far too demonstrative to be British, but then he had been resident in this country for an unspecified number of years, long enough to have absorbed some of its people's more in-your-face ways. He presented Rick to Andy as though this was their first meeting.

Their rendezvous adequately effected, the trio made their way down an escalator to the food hall where, still talking animatedly, they partook of croissants and coffee. This was the second eating place today for all of them, for Jon and Rick had left their bags and new suitcase packed ready in their room and had trotted over to North Pier, which was visible from their window. Next to the erstwhile Kraft Foods headquarters, this one-time canal-side warehouse, whose original purpose had been subverted by economic happenstance, was a tribute to the successful revamping of a large industrial property into a worthy precinct of small specialist shops, a highly popular bar and, in the iron-girdered lower ground, the food mall where the couple had breakfasted. After that, they too deposited their luggage in the left baggage department at the railroad station, and had gone sightseeing.

When the three men finished their light repast, they went up to the street.

"We should try to be at the station an hour before departure," said Andy, peering all round for hints that they might be being watched. "That gives us two or three hours to occupy. Any ideas?"

They had plenty. They stopped a cab and whizzed the hapless civil servant into the older, characterful north side of the city. There they dragged him round a few of the district's hundreds of shops, bars, restaurants, theatres and clubs which made up what was one of Chicago's most colourful cultural assets, drawing visitors from all over the world for the sheer enjoyment of it. They coped with dropping in at several rainbow bars by limiting their liquid intake, ordering bottles of beer for only two of them at a time. Andy was as awed as his companions had been the night before by the giant proportions of so many of the men they saw in the virtually all-male venues. One or two of them even made Rick seem average by comparison.

In such convivial surroundings and among all those friendly lunch time tipplers, Andy was soon into the swing of things, and with remarkable ebullience.

They were on their fourth round of drinks when, observing their friend's evident contentment, Jon whispered, "You know, Rick, that guy's a flippin' natural. You'd think he had just been rescued after spending twenty years marooned alone on a desert island."

"Perhaps, after all, he has," purred Rick. He glanced at his watch, then spoke up. "Sorry, but we're going to have to break up this merry party. It's two-thirty – time we weren't here."

They hurried from this third bar that they had patronised, accompanied by cheery good wishes for the remainder of their vacation from its regulars. As they stood on the sidewalk waiting for an available cab, Andy glimpsed the back of a familiar-looking head on the far side of the street. Its face was too dimly reflected in the smoked glass of a large bookshop window, but a vision of the man stooped over the ice making machine last evening sprang instantly to his mind.

"Don't look now," he muttered urgently through the corner of his mouth.

So Jon did. Luckily in an entirely wrong direction.

"Jon!" hissed their mentor exasperatedly, "I said, 'don't look,' and you immediately stared!"

Rick glared at his partner and tutted. "I'll send you home in a minute." Then, "What have you seen, Andy?"

"Scalfaro."

"What? O-oh, yes, Scalfaro; the girl's minder of last night?"

"That's the one, Rickie. Carlo Scalfaro, according to my microcomputer files. I'm almost sure it's him."

"There's a free taxi coming," Jon told them. "Shall I still hail it?"

"Certainly," said Andy. "We are going to Denver, and they do know about that if they were listening in to my phone conversation."

The cab drew up near them. Andy noticed that the shadowy face had a telephone held to its ear. The three jumped in to the vehicle. Jon asked for Union Station, and they sped off towards Lincoln Avenue.

Once there, they collected their bags and joined the orderly queue being boarded on to the California Zephyr, the famous, once-daily Superliner train service that, in two days, crosses seven states to San Francisco Bay, California, passing through some of the most varied and spectacular scenery anywhere. The Britons, however, were going only as far as Denver, where they were scheduled to arrive just before 9am the next day.

On the upper level of one of the huge, silver rail cars, they were shown to two neighbouring compartments, each with a single armchair facing a double seat, convertible into bunk beds. They looked comfortable enough, yet rather compact.

"You are three travelling together, gentlemen?" enquired the car attendant, after showing Jon and Rick how their private shower and toilet unit operated.

"We are," said Andy.

"In this sort of bedroom," the forty-five-ish attendant explained, grasping a handle on the wall opposite the double seat, "this partition can slide back so that the other party's room and yours become a bedroom suite. This is an option for you to consider, if you so wish. You may find it roomier for you, in any event, should you want to sit together during the daytime." He awaited a decision.

"That's fine by me," said Andy, as though doing someone a favour.

"I'm sure it is," grinned Jon.

The attendant efficiently rearranged the rooms' appointments, and in very few minutes left the men to settle down in their relatively spacious accommodation.

"So they are still interested in you, Andy," Jon remarked at last about the Scalfaro sighting.

Before Jon could go on, Andy placed a finger to his own lips and silently directed his travelling companions to help him carry out a comprehensive search of the suite's nooks and crannies, even of their own luggage. While they pulled the room apart, they carried on a lighthearted conversation about their pretended commonality of interests connected with university and sporting activities. The train had started to draw slowly out of the station by the time Andy declared an all-clear.

They began putting the room back together again as Jon went on:

"That Italian chap must have been tailing you ever since you left your room at the Holiday Inn this morning."

"I'm not really surprised," answered Andy, opening a pack of peanuts courtesy of Amtrak. "Anyhow, we've done everything according to the casual tourists' handbook, and I imagine our performance on meeting earlier was reasonably convincing, don't you? Even so, I dare say they're taking no chances. Neither will we. We'll have to shake them off, though, if they're still curious about us in Denver. I bet your dad's not come down off the wall yet, Jon," he added mischievously.

"What do you mean?"

"Well, I rang him, as I told you I would, from the station earlier."

"Ah, I see." Jon did not conceal the nervousness in his smile.

"Yes, naturally I had to tell him that you are here. Things got just a little stormy from that point, as you can guess! He was so furious that he ordered me to send you straight home."

"And without pocket money." Rick's eyes twinkled.

"I had to remind him that I could not order you to do anything. He came round to that eventually when he'd cooled down a bit. I told him that, since you were already here, and had already been helpful in one or two respects, it would be churlish of me not to enlist your aid. Unofficially, of course."

"What did he say to that?" Rick's often perverse sense of humour was being tickled. "Not to let us out of your sight, day or night?"

Andy blushed purple. "As a matter of fact, he did. But I said, 'Mission impossible'. He gave in there."

"But you still booked bedrooms which could be made into this single suite?" Rick observed.

"No!" cried Andy, "I had already done booked it!" His blush grew deeper, if anything. "I mean, I had no idea that they were convertible like this."

"Oh yeah?" crooned Jon, bestowing on Andy an amused, cynical stare.

"Yeah! I mean, yes. Well, no, I truly didn't know."

"Forget it, it's too complicated," Rick laughed. "So what did Rupert have to say about the mob's fascination with your US visit?"

Andy's features grew more serious. "It's a breach of security all right."

"The proverbial mole?"

"Something like, Jon."

"Who knew you were coming to Chicago, except us four?" asked Rick.

"No one was supposed to."

"Does that mean our talks have been bugged somewhere?"

"It's practically impossible to have one hundred per cent security even in our offices," said Andy with a slight shrug of the shoulders. "These days, you don't have to plant devices inside flower arrangements or under desks and so on. Microphone technology is now so advanced that conversations can be twitched from quite long distances. Even so, our premises are wired to muss up anything which could otherwise be picked up from outside, and with detectors to warn us of any attempted eavesdropping of that sort. But, for every advance, a new antidote is produced.

"The fact remains, these customers know only so much. I'm pretty sure they don't know the purpose for my being here. And I definitely didn't need to lose anyone when I went out to take a dekko at Ciampi's warehouse the other night, probably because I luckily left from your room rather than my own."

Jon asked, "So, if your anti-surveillance systems back home are in such bloody fine fettle, how come the enemy did discover that you were coming over here? Could Dad's flat have been bugged, do you think?"

"The same state-of-the-art systems are in place at the homes of high-ranking officials, especially those in Intelligence."

"Presumably the enemy can develop antidotes too!" observed Jon, a sardonic edge to his voice.

"Exactly. It's a dirty business."

"The original rat-race, perhaps?" Rick's mouth twisted as he spoke.

This was the same sinister world that poor old Sarah had been abducted into. And here was this Andy passing himself off as their friend, yet he must be up to the neck in all the shit he and his kind were accumulating by their disgusting activities.

"And just what kind of a rat are you, Andy?" Rick discovered himself saying. "Are you the nice, tame, white virginal sort that you've been projecting to us, or just a common-or-garden brown rodent sniffing around in the poisonous filth that vermin have been spreading all over the world since time forgotten?"

Overwhelmed at that moment, Rick turned his head away and pressed his brow to the wing of his seat. He screwed his eyes to stem the tears that he had been unsuspectingly damming back since leaving England. Jon lifted his averted gaze for long enough to witness Andy's self-respect shatter and desert him, then he moved over to console his partner, taking him in his arms and uttering soothing words in his ear. Jon motioned to Andy to make himself scarce for a while.

Needing no second bidding, Andy hastened out into the corridor and worked his way between the curtained doorways of several other bedrooms as far as the stairway leading to the coach's lower level. He remained on the stairs and looked out of the windows at the passing scene: the extensive suburbs of Chicago, both opulent and depressed. Here were scarred wastelands where once manufacturing industries had represented the life-force itself; dilapidated houses whose left-behind occupiers had seen far better days; then clean, modern, high-tech units alongside avenues of condominiums and small mansions – the dwellings of the fortunate who had, mostly by chance, found themselves in service occupations that were in the process of succeeding to the painfully vacated fast-tracks of national economic opportunity, once all the horrific pile-ups of dashed expectations and their human jetsam had been cleared out of mind and the carriageways sanitised.

It was a fact that Andy hated his life. He had never known any kind of real happiness. He felt sure very few people ever did. It was a sort of cold, hard, shiny veneer which merely cast reflections back into the smile-strained faces of all who ventured too near. It was as illusory as it was shallow. But the two northern lads had been showing him another side of humanity. Maybe there were a few decent people about, after all.

He'd just not known any properly. Perhaps all along, his detached manner had repulsed anyone who might otherwise have befriended him at a deeper level for his own sake rather than just for what they could use him for. A loveless childhood with its harsh, boarding school education had moulded him into what doubtless made him perfect raw material for his present career: a shrewd, thoroughly self-interested bastard. He was well aware of it. It was only because Jon was his boss's son that it had seemed politic, from their first meeting, to hide from the couple what he thought of as his real self.

Andy Gregson had also realised at an early stage that Jon and Rick were not exactly naive either. Perspicacity was more their level. Rick especially would be wholly capable of cool deception were the occasion to demand it. Yet both had exuded a warmth towards him such as he had never really encountered from people before, though, as he knew now, they must have understood him all along despite his barrier of self-concealment. As he stood there only half watching the accretions of numberless populations flitting by beyond the rail car's glass viewing screen, suddenly he was glad that he had let his defences become more transparent. If he could see into their lives, the reverse must have been equally true.

He could sense himself being drawn towards new possibilities that he had not identified. This job he was on was like no other. Rick's sister and brother-in-law were important to him for more than the usual reasons.

The car attendant came up the steps towards him. "Excuse me, sir, you are blocking the stairway."

"Oh, sorry. I was well away." Andy squeezed himself into the angle of the steps' turn to let the man past. "Where, did you tell my friends, are the refreshments and the viewing area?"

"The Sightseer Lounge is two coaches to the rear from here, and the Café is on the level below it."

Thanking the Afro-American, who told him he was entirely welcome then turned to the right towards the front of the train, Andy went in the direction he had been indicated. When he reached the viewing lounge with its wrap-round windows and glass roof, where dozens of passengers either sat at tables or stood around regarding the greener outskirts of the city they were just leaving, Andy pretended absently to study the people's features. No one he recognised, and he didn't seem to be an object of anyone's covert scrutiny. He stepped downstairs to the crowded refreshments bar and queued up for a cup of off-the-boil water with a tea bag and a delicious hot dog, all the while studying the noisy humanity around him for form.

He returned to the suite after what he trusted was an adequate period. He entered by the doorway to what had been his bedroom. The couple were sitting quietly on separate seats looking impassively out of the window.

Andy handed a hot dog to each of them. "A peace offering," he smiled weakly, then sat down in his own half of the room facing Rick on the opposite double seat.

"'Beware geeks bearing gifts'," Jon misquoted. "A red rose would have smelled sweeter and been more appropriate for Rick," he said breezily. "But this is very tasty, thanks."

"They were completely out of roses."

Andy sat forward. "Listen, lads, I'm not really sure what I said or did earlier to upset you, but whatever it was, I'm very sorry. I really am, Ricky. If you like, we can soon knock this suite into two rooms again."

Rick gave him a distant grin. "No, that won't be necessary. It was just that here you are, being all buddy and nice to us, when we all know that to have risen as far as you have in your department you must be among the most ruthless of your species. You called intelligence a dirty game before. I'm sure that's absolutely right, and by definition, that makes you extremely shop-soiled at the very least! And it may be because of tricky sods like you of different nationalities operating all over the world that Sarah and Peter are now in it over their heads – perhaps literally." He fearfully bit at his lower lip.

Andy gazed pensively at the carpet and said nothing.

It was not until his companions were wiping grease from their fingers with tissues that he replied, "You're dead right, Rick. But it's that vicious old circle again, isn't it? If somebody didn't keep quietly pulling the rug from under some of the wilder ambitions of other countries, we'd all be constantly at full-scale war. And that whittling process becomes a tit-for-tat condition, a feud nobody gets to hear about, barring a few diplomats and government ministers. Isn't that preferable to war, especially in these days when mass genocide can be done at the flick of a switch?"

Rick smiled ruefully. "Of course that's true, Andy. If I didn't acknowledge that that side of politics exists I'd be some kind of idiot, wouldn't I? It's just that Sarah is blameless in this affair, I'm positive of it. And she is hardly someone trained and paid to take the risks entailed, is she? God alone knows how or why, but she's been dragged into this by people like you, rotten to the flaming core, who do what they do because of people of your sort who just happen to work for another side."

"Hm, well," Jon grunted, "arguing about chickens and eggs will get us nowhere, will it? And Andy's certainly no spring chicken!"

His feeble attempt to lighten the atmosphere earned him a glare from his partner and a distracted smile from the target of Rick's current barbs. Jon decided to keep mum for the time being and let them get on with it.

However, Andy unexpectedly took up Jon's theme. "So you don't even fancy me in that way. I'm not really surprised, though. I'm pretty much of an all-round jerk where human relationships are concerned. Always have been. I dare say I'm slotted inextricably into the niche life prepared me for. I suppose I'm luckier in that way than most. Nobody can have everything, after all." He threw them a friendly enough smile and rose from his seat. "I think I'll go and take a walk, see if any of my fellow social pariahs are on board."

Leaving them to sample that nasty dose of acerbity, he got out before they had a chance to stop him.

The train was travelling fast now. The next few hours would seem interminable, offering little more to see than millions of hectares of young corn, scattered farmsteads that were almost identical and some small village settlements evidently conforming to physical, and probably communal, patterns which their conservative and isolated inhabitants dared not deviate from. Now and again, a few miles of freshly greened woodland would fill up the foreground, or an occasional small town station-stop relieve the monotony.

Lots of coach passengers chose this time to take naps in their reclining seats, or to watch video movies showing in the Lounge. This gave Andy the best possible opportunity to survey the train for potential opposition members. It was remarkable what high percentages of overweight Americans there were, and the diversity of racial types arrayed here was worthy of anybody's research, given the inclination.

Any number of individuals were on board whom the irregular dick might well have branded your stereotypical Undercover Espionage Agent, though being of a stereotypical bent would be unlikely to guarantee a person high achievement awards in any secret service. However, without any effort, Andy committed those peoples' principal features to the safe keeping of his memory. Only one person seemed, to his trained sensibilities, a likely candidate for special surveillance treatment: a shapely Hispanic girl of about twenty-two.

He was lurched towards her seat when the train hit a sharp bend unanticipated after an hour of arrow-straight motion. From the way her pupils quickly dilated within those intensely hazel irises, he presumed that he'd scared her by threatening to collapse into her lap. But, even after he checked himself by grabbing at the seat back in front of her, she continued to watch the movements of his beige-trousered lower body from beneath those long, false lashes of hers. Her blue-black hair was swept into a topknot held in position by a tortoiseshell comb, her smart black suit set off by a double necklace of good simulated pearls. She was another kind of stereotype: the Spanish señorita that every stereotypical, red-blooded male was bound to drool his tool over. Andy inwardly blenched as that awful expression learned at school somehow became dredged from the silt of his memory.

She looked up and their gazes met momentarily, she demure as her parents' culture demanded, he winsomely grinning at her and apologising in flawless Spanish.

"Think nothing of it!" she cried in a distinctively West Midlands educated accent, while she sorted out the newspaper she had inadvertently crumpled in preparing to ward off the impending collision.

The suntanned, fair-haired young man in the next seat to hers started up from his doze, understood what had happened and enquired whether she was hurt.

"No, darling. This man might easily have been, though. One of our countrymen, if I'm not too mistaken?"

Considering Andy knew beyond a doubt that his fluency in many foreign languages was nothing if not convincing even to native speakers, he was taken aback by her instant recognition that he was British. His confidence injured for a second time in less than forty minutes, he nevertheless stretched out his hand and introduced himself by his forename.

It transpired that Stephen and Mandy were newlyweds honeymooning across the United States, travelling overland alternately by train and hired car. Presumably well-enough-heeled, they had already spent three weeks in the Bahamas before taking ship to Boston where they had commenced the first leg of their US tour. Well, that accounted for their complexions, at any rate. Their travel agents had slipped up by reserving seats instead of a bedroom for them on this train, an omission coming to light only an hour before departure, by which time all the bedrooms were occupied.

He told them that he was travelling with an old college chum and another friend of his, and that they intended to rent a car once they arrived in Denver. A coincidence, for that was to be the married couple's next stopover destination before collecting their pre-booked vehicle and making for New Mexico. Stephen especially was pleased to meet this personable Englishman, and insisted that they all meet up together after dinner in the lounge. They set the hour, and Andy went on his way towards the front of the long train. On his return, he noted that their seats were vacant.

They were not to keep their after-dinner appointment, nor did Andy see them on the train again.

Eight

Back in the suite, with the final vestiges of a glorious sunset streaked in reds and golds across the slightly tinted windows, Rick was sitting in hunched contrition for what he termed his irrational behaviour.

"Andy, I'm really sorry I called you what I did. It was just all that easy talk of earwigging on people's private conversations and all that; it set up a chain of reactions inside, what with me being a bit anxious. I suppose it's to do with the way my own sister was just sort of caught up into this vortex thing, as if she was only so much insignificant dust in a whirlwind. And how coolly you spoke about your technology race, and me thinking, 'Aye, and look at how it's making ordinary, uninvolved folk like us more vulnerable.'

"You see? Rupert was correct, after all. We really are too close to your case, Andy. This has just proved it."

Andy sat down next to him. "Yes, you both are. Has there ever been any disagreement about that? But with you two, that is more than compensated for by your attributes that we've already talked about. Besides, you have been extraordinarily strong during these recent days. It was stupid and insensitive of me to go on the way I did, as though you were professional colleagues with a limited personal interest in the case. It was my fault, really.

"And I can't blame you if you've had enough of me always around you breathing down your necks. I often feel the same way about myself, but there's not a lot that I can do about it! You can. I think it would be better if we separated our rooms, so that you two can have your privacy back."

"No, there's no point in that," said Jon from his chair. "It's been done now, and after all, it's only for one night."

"And what do you say, Rick?" asked Andy.

"Me? Oh, Jon's right, as usual. It would be an empty gesture causing a lot of hassle. Besides, be honest with us, you want company, don't you?"

A voice disembodied in the ceiling began announcing passengers' dinner ticket numbers, requesting those people to take their seats in the restaurant. The three men's complimentary numbers were among them.

"That's us, I think," Andy observed, making to stand up.

He went over to his shoulder bag and took out their three vouchers issued to him by the attendant.

"I hadn't thought of it that way," he confessed in answer to Rick's assertion. "But even if that were true, it isn't right for me to foist myself on you. Anyhow, there must be scores of passengers out there only too anxious for a good old jaw. I've already been speaking to a couple from England."

While they collected their valuables together, Andy described his earlier meeting with the honeymooners. "And they wanted to spend some time with us after dinner, so we have a date with them," he finished.

"Well, that'll be nice," said Rick, "but we're not actually discussing that kind of company, are we? Your need is for closer companionship. You, Andy Gregson, are a lonely old bastard!" he pronounced. "You've got no one and, as you have let slip several times to us, you need someone. You are desperate for Love, with a capital L."

"And an S," Jon assisted.

"No, I'm not!" protested Andy vehemently, turning his back on them. "That's fucking, fucking ridiculous!" Then he bowed his head, and murmured, "Yes, I am, I bloody am." He paused before going on. "It was seeing you together, feeling what you feel for one another: it really brought home what I've been missing for all these years." Straightening up, he said, "But come on, we must go. They'll give someone else our table if we're late." He couldn't move, though. "I'm sorry, guys, you go on without me. I'll catch you up in a few minutes. Order me the soup."

Without another word, he thrust the dinner vouchers into Jon's hand, and rushed into the tiny bathroom to shut his friends out.

Ten minutes later, he entered the restaurant coach where he quickly spotted them sitting at either side of their table by the window, not touching the soups in front of them. Andy sat down where his own steaming bowl had been set next to Jon's.

"You were not waiting for me, were you?"

"Good God, no," retorted Jon. "We met this handsome marine on the way here, and invited him to take your place as we thought you weren't coming. He'll be along any minute now."

As if on cue, the waiter came up to the table. "I see that you have a free seat at your table. Would you mind sharing with that gentleman travelling alone?"

He pointed out a cropped-haired young naval officer waiting at the restaurant doorway shifting expectantly from foot to foot. When the newcomer spotted Rick's interested glance, he flashed him a brilliant, even-toothed smile, and his sideways pacings became long, loping strides following the line of his own unerring gaze.

From somewhere very deep inside Andy, rose an unambiguous growl that amounted to a "Phwoaaaar!" but was not intended to be heard.

The seated men were by now striving hard to control their mirth at the perfect timing of the seaman's appearance. Standing apart, the waiter took the young man's pre-written meal order and left them to it.

"Hiya, guys! My name's Kit." He sat down next to Rick.

When the courtesies had been exchanged, Kit exclaimed, "Say, are you fellas English or Australian or somethin'?"

"English, as it happens," said Jon slowly, eyeing Rick's body language in relation to the American. In fact, with his head tucked well down into his chest, Rick was working hard at suppressing a fit of the giggles, but it did not appear that way to those sitting opposite. Jon suspected that he was fly-watching.

"Geez! I have an aunt who lives right close to London somewhere. Maybe you know her? Her name's Mirabelle Garvey." He attacked his just-delivered grapefruit.

"I'm afraid London is quite a big place," Andy told him. "I live in London, but I know no one of that name."

"Say, that's a shame. She lives near Nottingham – you know, the Sheriff, Robin Hood, Maid Marion and all that stuff?"

All of Rick's best endeavours failed him at that moment. His face scarlet, he snorted once, twice, then spluttered explosively. His comrades immediately joined him with peals of pent-up laughter.

The whole restaurant car stared good humouredly at the trio's helpless convulsions, while the seaman's expression of innocent amazement added to the picture.

"Say," he said again, "what did I say that was so funny?" He produced some polite little sympathetic laughs of his own, before beginning to evince some embarrassment.

Andy needed to support his head on Jon's shoulder, and Rick reached a comradely beefy arm across the junior officer's neck, thus including him in their company to reassure the poor lad that they truly were not laughing at him. How to explain this joke to a stranger, though?

Between gasps and chuckles, the men eventually managed to give Kit a rather incoherent apology.

"Where about do you come from, Kit?" enquired Jon at length, wiping his eyes.

"The Naval Training Station at San Francisco is where I'm headed right now," replied the sailor, "but my home is in North Carolina, in the heart of the Bible Belt, you know?"

The Britons severally decided that they ought to avoid agitating any religious scruples the lad may have eating at him.

"Yes, I have travelled through that state," said Andy, recalling the predominance throughout the region of little white townships having little white churches with little white steeples. "Do you get back there often?" he asked guardedly.

"Hell, no! What would any right-minded, intelligent guy want to stay mixed up with that ignorant flock of sheep-brained bigots for? Shit, I left there for good five years ago. Never hankered after the place since, neither."

"It has beautiful countryside, you must admit."

"Sure, and so have plenty of other places. That's not everything. It's people who matter, not their goddammed religions! Whoops, excuse the pun!" he joked.

"What about your family?" asked Jon.

"Oh, me and my married sisters go visit mom and dad at Christmastime, you know? Reeligiously?" Kit chortled. "But most young folks leave once they've got the sense to. Leastways, that's how I see it. Say! I do hope I ain't offendin' you none."

"No, no," came the chorus.

"Say," Kit used his habitual foreword once more, "where do you other two guys come from? Do you live in London, too?" He was genuinely enthralled to be in these men's society.

"No, we live in a county called Cheshire," Rick informed him, after getting implied approval from Andy to trust this fellow. Seeing the place name denoted nothing to their friend, he added, "Chester is the county town."

"Oh, I've heard of Chester. It's Roman, isn't it, with walls all round? I've read about it somewheres, and my aunt has some relative lives round abouts. Say, do you live near there? Maybe you know my aunty's..." He grinned. "There's not a hope in hell that you know them, is there! I must sound crazy to you."

Undeterred by this self-censure, with his characteristic talkativeness boosted by the four cans of Budweiser he'd quaffed since Galesburg Kit plied them with further questions as soon as their main courses were served.

"Say," again, "are you two related someways?" He looked from Jon to Rick and back again.

"Yes, in a way," said Rick immediately. "We live near a small town called Knutsford. I teach in an agricultural college, and Jon here is a vet – a veterinary surgeon."

"And you, Andy? What do you do? I mean, you can see how I earn my crust!"

"I was a country boy, too. But now I am a civil servant; I work for the government."

Kit looked impressed.

"Just a small cog, I'm afraid," Andy dissembled.

Still intrigued by Knutsford, Kit asked, "You two ain't brothers or cousins, are you?"

They smiled and shook their heads, and went on eating.

"You share the same home, is that it? You're room-mates?"

"No, we have a house there," said Jon, smiling up at Rick.

It was beginning to dawn, at last. "You are a couple, then? Is that it?"

"That's it, Kit, old chap," Rick said.

"And how long have you been together?"

These Yanks! thought Andy. They love to delve into each others' backgrounds. Nearly always, the opening question they'll ask on a first meeting is, where are you from? He imagined that the same had been posed twenty times during the past few minutes in this restaurant alone.

"Getting on for ten years now," Rick declared offhandedly.

"Gee! Oh, ain't that marvellous? Ten years. Why, you must have met one another when you were very young."

"Flattery of that sort will win you any favours you want from those two!" chuckled Andy, jovially thumping Jon's arm.

"Careful, Andy," Jon rejoined, "We don't give everything away, you know, not even for the most lavish of compliments. We leave that kind of thing to you bachelors."

Andy grew red again. "I didn't mean it in that way." He gave Kit as sincere a look as he could manage. "I wasn't talking about sex, honestly."

Kit wasn't in the least disconcerted. He made a joke of it. "If that's the way of it, I'll just have to reserve my very best compliments for Andy here!" he cackled, then shook his head deliberately in quirky disbelief.

Rick leaned confidentially towards the seaman. "Oh, I shouldn't, if I were you," he cautioned. "We're not too sure about him, are we, Jon?"

Jon nodded his agreement from the waist, his mouth being full of pasta and fork.

Before Andy felt unfairly obliged to say something, Rick chose to divert the conversation.

"He's a very good friend, and that is more than enough for us," he pointed out. "Tomorrow, we are all going trekking in the Rockies together."

During the rest of their meal, they indulged in some small talk, and established that the American was travelling two coaches to the rear of the restaurant car, and would be quite happy to sleep the night in his comfortable reclining seat. He had travelled that way on countless previous occasions. They shook hands firmly, all too conscious that it was extremely unlikely that they would meet again in this world.

Afterwards, Jon and Rick made their way to the lounge with Andy, waited an hour, but the other English couple did not show up. They returned to their suite, cheerfully bidding the seaman goodnight as they went passed him. He pulled a hand from beneath his snug blanket, blew them a surreptitious kiss in return, and closed his eyes, his face beaming contentment.

When they arrived back at their suite, Andy went quiet once more.

"Did you mean what you said to that guy before, about me?"

"You mean, about our not knowing which way you are facing?" asked Jon.

"Well, no. I mean, about us being good friends? Earlier on, Rick was wondering what species of rat I am."

They were all still on their feet after sorting out their bags. Rick put his hands on Andy's shoulders and pulled him to himself. "Look," he said, peering at him straight in the eyes, "I was totally out of order speaking to you like that. I've tried to explain why I did it. I certainly didn't mean it. We haven't known you for very long, Andy, but you have sure made our lives easier and richer during these past few difficult days."

"Well, that makes me feel a lot better, even though you've as good as told me that neither of you fancies me in any other way."

"I don't recollect our mentioning anything to you about it," Jon insisted.

"Yes, you did, Jon. You said I was no spring chicken. I'm not that much older than you, after all. I know I've lost a little hair at the front..."

"Hardly any," Rick interposed, "and you more than make up for it in other areas!" This man had really taken Jon's banter too much to heart.

Jon gave a low whistle. "And some," he confirmed. "Grief, Andy, I only meant that you were not, mm, an adolescent; that you had worldly wisdom to your credit. I wasn't talking about your superb body and that handsome vizog," he piled it on. "And your hairline's just great, and you'd be just as nice looking even if you were to lose more of it in the years to come." Posturing like some affected couturier, he closely scrutinised Andy from this and that angle through frames he shaped with his long-fingered hands. "It's that certain – something – about those cheek and cranial bones, don't you agree, pet?"

Rick did right heartily, he too earning one of the swipes Andy landed out at them.

"Christ, I hate seeing men acting like that," he laughed, "and you didn't need to go over the top. I get the message."

At that, exaggerating their natural manliness, led by Rick, his friends rounded on him and planted a kiss on either of his cheeks.

"Hey!" he cried out, pushing them away. "I said I get the message!"

The others captured his hands, and playfully began smothering his face with more kisses, then Jon went for an ear, and they crashed on to Andy's couch in a frenzied, gurgling heap, Andy's plaintive cries for help growing weaker by the second. When they thought he'd had enough, the pair stood up, totally dishevelled. They gleefully surveyed the ragged, sweaty figure lying there panting for air, his shirt minus a button or two, his trousers seriously creased but intact – for all the agitation had been above the belt. Well, just about. He reached for tissues in his pocket, and commenced to wipe his face, his ears and all round his broad neck.

"You pair of sloppy gits!" he grumbled, "I'm covered in slobber now. Oh, Jeez," he pulled the leather belt away from his waist front, "and that's not all you've done, either. Christ!" He wriggled inside his pants, struggled to get up, and betook himself to the closet.

"You were warned that we'd get our own back on you for the other night!" laughed Jon. "And when you least expected it."

Behind their friend's back, Rick wordlessly drew Jon's attention to Andy's frantic activities involving lots of tissues at the front.

"Mind you, we didn't foresee that kind of reflex."

Comprehension alighted swiftly on Jon's countenance. He quietly pulled the door shut, and called through: "We didn't intend that to happen to you, Andy. Can we get anything for you?"

The sound of running water was his only answer.

"Say, are you the Britishers in there?" came a familiar voice beyond the curtain.

Rick pulled it back, and there stood their sailor friend from dinner, now dressed in civvies – a fashionable type of black ski-suit and sneakers favoured by devotees of American football.

"How did you know where we are?" Rick quizzed him warily.

"I didn't. It was just that I had to change out of my uniform – I dislike wearing it when I'm off duty – which I did in the washroom downstairs. Then I thought I'd take a walk along the train to stretch my legs a little, then when I came to a car with sleeping accommodation, I remembered Jon mention your bedroom on the train. I heard your English voices while I was passing just." Kit's disarmingly innocent smile washed over Rick and Jon like a warm shower.

"You'd better come in then," said Jon. Rick stood aside.

The closet door next to him opened a little, long enough for Andy's outer clothes to be ejected.

"No, no, not if you are getting ready for bed, I won't," said their visitor.

"Oh, we're not," Rick said.

"I was only looking to see if Andy wanted to go for a drink with me, he being the single guy. But he's otherwise engaged, I guess. No. I don't want to be a pest. I'll be on my way."

Passing our room, my arse, thought Jon. Where's the uniform he changed out of? That was just a ruse by Kit to get to see Andy again.

"Here, pass me some shorts out of my bag, if you want to make yourselves useful!" Andy's disgruntlement was plain to hear over the noise of the water spray. A hairy, wet arm came round the closet door, hand outstretched impatiently.

Jon rummaged in Andy's enormous fabric bag.

Said Rick, "Andy's in there, as you can tell. He had, hm, a slight accident a little while ago, hence his unaccustomed ill temper."

"Oh, he's gettin' washed up, is he?" Kit started his on-the-spot sideways pacing once more.

"Do come in, please. You're not disturbing us," Rick assured the man.

"Well, if you're sure..." Kit entered somewhat diffidently.

Jon gave him a conspiratorial wink, and passed him the flashy pair of iridescent boxer shorts he had taken from Andy's bag.

"Are you going to be all night?" Andy's brusque tone demanded.

Kit took hold of Andy's wrist and pushed the shorts into the dripping hand. "Say!" he enunciated. The hand suddenly tensed. "Great shorts, Andy, my man!"

At the sound of that unmistakable voice, the shorts were drawn inside the closet as if on a spring, and the door banged shut.

The three outside chuckled soundlessly, and frantic fumblings could be heard within the bathroom.

"You can be honest with us, Kit," said Jon. "You couldn't have just been passing our room. The corridors of these sleeper cars are only linked together at the lower deck, so you must have known our room numbers already for you to come up to this deck."

"Isn't that the truth!" grinned the visitor coyly. "Forgive me, I took a mental note from your dinner vouchers."

When the door opened again, Andy stepped out, on his best behaviour now, clad only in his shorts-of-many-colours and his very damp, very dark brown body hair. He stooped to pick his cast-off garments from the carpet.

"I can tell you don't have a desk job, either," Kit remarked appreciatively. He scanned them all. "All outdoor types, huh?"

"You could say that we each have hands-on jobs to do." Rick favoured him with an invitation to sit.

Kit sat down on the double seat recently the site of battle. Andy threw him a cordial smile and began to towel his medium-length hair dry, his every move studied by Kit. He brushed it next, then took up a comb and parted it in the shorter style he'd had cut while waiting for his flight at Heathrow. Kit stayed his arm, smiled winningly and gave an exiguous shake of the head unseen by the others. Andy wonderingly put the comb down and brushed his thick hair some more instead.

Jon, meanwhile, had been opening some individual bottles of Amtrak's best Californian white wine, pouring out four glasses which he handed round. "Kit wants to take you out, Andy."

Andy was nonplussed. "Me?"

"Yes. Not us, just you," Rick drove home.

"No, no!" mumbled the plain-clothed young officer, "I don't wish to appear rude. I just thought..."

"That's quite okay, Kit." Jon pressed his hand as he gave him his wine glass. "We truthfully couldn't be more delighted if you two want to get to know each other better."

Andy felt a glow of excitement that he had never experienced before, despite his otherwise very full lifestyle. Whenever he had dated previously, his acquired sense of anticipation had quickly and invariably evaporated out of sheer funk that it might all get beyond his control. Consequently, these days he rarely, if ever, bothered with women once he was well out of range of what he had most come to fear: the inquisitorial prurience of colleagues and friends. So what kind of a Pandora's box had he let Jon and Rickie open? Why was he only now being subjected to these stimulating emotions? Was this a truth about himself that he hadn't been remotely aware of, an essential part of his nature that he had been suppressing all along without even knowing it?

"I don't go round picking strangers up, I'll have you believe," the American was anxious for them to know. "Fact is, I never have. I'm not even doing it now – leastways, not in my book I'm not. I just liked the cut of –"

"– Andy's jib?" Rick helped him out nautically, inciting his further amusement.

"You are a great bunch of guys – chaps, I think you said earlier?" The English use of that word entertained him hugely.

Jon slapped Andy on the back. "Here, get dressed, and get that bum outa here!"

"And take dat admiral witcha, as well!" Rick remonstrated in his best Italian Brooklyn.

"That's who the bum is, twit-face!" Jon stage-whispered into his partner's ear.

"Ah," cooed the enlightened one, "I thought you meant his own bum. Still, I do think Andy has a nice, pert little –"

"Shut up, Rickie, both of you!"

"Sorry, Andy," they droned in unison, hanging their heads.

Kit immensely enjoyed this small interlude while he waited for his date to get ready, which Andy was by the time it was over, white vest and trainers sandwiching his well-fitting dark grey jeans.

"You needn't wait up," Andy lobbed high over his shoulder as he escorted the grinning Kit from the room.

Left alone, the couple couldn't get over Andy's unexpected release from what they had suspected for several days was some kind of prohibitive and punishing bondage that he had imposed upon himself. Yet the manner of that breakout would forever exercise their minds. They checked the front of Andy's soiled boxers left forgotten in the shower, and Jon finished washing them for him, hanging them up to dry on the shower curtain rail. The crumples in his trousers would fall out overnight. Afterwards, they again mulled over their fears for Sarah's safety and their personal hurt which, despite the altercation earlier, they fully understood Andy was doing his conscientious best to help them with, and they loved him for it in their own particular way.

While he pursued his admirer through the train's now dimly lit gangways, Andy was still unsteady after this evening's discovery of himself. Surely since creation itself, he had dutifully borne within his leaden heart a lifeless accumulation of repressed desires. However, during the course of the past few heady days, it had been transforming itself, almost imperceptibly to begin with, then with irresistible force, into a gushing volcano at last, making an instant Nothing of a lifetime of pointless sublimation in its first uproarious eruption of real passion. For it was the first occasion when his passion actually had someone's name on it.

He walked at first with his feet not touching the floor, yet the trembling in his knees soon brought him to a standstill, demanding that he restore his composure. He leaned against a partition screen between pairs of automatic doors where two coaches connected, gratefully inhaling some of the blast of cool fresh air that was being raucously sucked in by the train's momentum. Kit strode on till he realised that he was alone, then hurried back, frightened that Andy had had a change of mind. He found him with his hands clasped to his head, his eyes tightly shut, beads of sweat glistening on his forehead.

"Say, man, you sick or something?" He could not resist running his fingers through the wavy hair that Andy had brushed to a shine and left loose for him. This revived the patient's spirits instantaneously.

As Andy absorbed those caresses, everything looked misty through his half-open eyes. His sighs were more visible than audible in that place. A middle-aged, both-sex couple carrying cardboard trays of refreshments stole considerately past them and pleasantly bid them a good night, which was reciprocated.

"That feeling better?"

"I'm a bit freaked out, to be honest. But no, I am not ill, Kit, my boy. On the contrary, I have just seen the proverbial light, and it's showing me how fucked up I've been all my empty, useless life."

There, that heavy little speech was bound to put the easygoing American right off. How the hell was he going to get across to Kit where all that angst came from without seeming like a nutcase strictly to be avoided?

Once in the overcrowded, smoke-filled bar, they drank their bottled beers standing propped up in a corner of the swaying car while Andy elucidated so far as he could what had been done to him shortly before Kit came to their room. What was meant as a jokey reprisal after some laddish fooling around had turned into nothing less than a revelation: he'd been worked up like never before. He omitted to confide that they'd even made him come in his pants without so much as seeing or touching his dick, or he theirs.

Kit said thoughtfully, "They warned me not to try hitting on you, remember? I ain't stupid, though. I know what's what. I caught your vibes real strong from the start, Andy, whether you knew you were making them or not. And I know it wasn't just wishful thinking on my part: they were hot, like real hot, my cold and reserved Englishman. They still are. Phew, geez! I guess you've not been out of my mind for an instant since we ate together. How long have you known Rick and Jon for?"

"Only for a few days, but it seems like we met years ago." Andy's stress surfaced again. "God knows, I dearly wish we had, though!" he blurted out louder than the constant clamour of the barflies, startling his pal and two or three nearby customers. His expression mellowed. "Sorry for that. Oh, hell." He took a couple of mouthfuls of beer. "But as I was going to say, Jon's father is my boss. That is how I came to meet them."

"And already you have come to the States with them for a vacation?"

Quick on the uptake, this lad. Somehow Andy balked at the very idea of deceiving Kit about himself, so, to distract him from asking anything else regarding this 'vacation' he was on, he was compelled to spin him his whole pathetic story of self-denial. Well, he would never meet Kit again after tomorrow morning, perhaps tonight, so it was not going to harm either of them, was it? But since it was a tale about things he hadn't done, rather than what he had, it didn't take long in the telling.

"Say, you really didn't know where you were at, did you?" uttered the astonished seaman. "I've heard of this sort of thing before now."

"Have you?" Andy asked keenly.

"Well, I've read a mite about it, anyway."

"Ah." Disappointed, Andy questioned Kit about his life and naval career.

The family name was Henderson, his people residing in a town of the same name.

"So, your family are regarded as pillars of the local society," assumed Andy.

"I'm a real let-down to them, I'm sure of that," confessed Kit. "I'm their only son, and they have so-called traditional values, so the business would one day have gone to me, if I'd been able to stick it out. Farm tools and machinery."

"Sounds an interesting line. I know something about it."

"It is. But things being as they are –" Kit's voice trailed off wistfully. "Yep," he drew himself up to his full 195 centimetres, "I was destined for the big time – well, as big as it gets at home. Even got myself engaged, but I couldn't go through with it, for her sake as much as for my own. I had lots of friends I hung about with. Had some cool times, too. But most of them drifted off for the same reason's I did."

"But you joined the US Navy of all things? That's incredible."

"I fancied the life, and I knew that I would get training in a career specialty. If the big brass found out about me, I'd be able to make a living on my own anyways. I have been in the Service now for four-and-a-half years. Radio electronics is my forté. Doin' okay at it, too. There's some new European technology been developed which the navy is trying out, and I've been detailed to Oakland to learn more about it. That's where I'm goin' right now. I ain't the only one by a long stretch!" he added in answer to Andy's unspoken question, "so I don't have to go celibate – and I don't have to pick up fanciable English guys on trains to get my rocks off, neither!"

They laughed as at the very idea. Kit passed the palm of one hand over the bristly flat top of his very short fair hair.

Their talk went on for nearly two hours. They managed to get seats at the bar. The time sped by for them, and Andy was becoming childishly nervous about how they would end their evening.

"Say, just check them out," said Kit out of the blue. "See that girl over there in the corner with that, er, chap?"

Andy instinctively lowered his head and scanned the bar virtually through his eyelids.

Kit kept up the conversation, moving his own gaze indifferently around the saloon. "They seem inordinately interested in us. I've been watching them watching us for the past fifteen minutes or so. It can't be the navy keeping an eye on me, 'cos they're not so paranoid about these things as they pretend up in Washington DC!"

Andy initially expected them to be the English couple he had spoken to earlier, then he twigged that these other two were indeed keeping tabs on his movements. A couple of baggily dressed youngsters, with only the girl's eye make-up distinguishing their gender, stood smoking at the far end of the bar counter, their mousy hair outlandishly done according to one of the current fads. A veritable market stall of silverware was disfiguring their ears, eyebrows, noses and lips – as well, no doubt, as other parts. His features were pale and uninteresting, but she benefited from a suggestion of Central Asian refinement. Andy reasoned that the pair would either have boarded the train recently or they had sleeping-car accommodation, otherwise he could not have missed them during his earlier perambulations. He hadn't noticed Kit on those occasions, either.

He looked up. "Kit, where did you get on the train?"

"Why, at Galesburg. I almost missed it. It was a last-minute dash. I'd been staying in Normal with some buddies at Illinois State University for three days." Seeing Andy's face, he gave a quick laugh. "Say, Normal is just the name of the town the university is in. Those two oddballs over there boarded at Galesburg, too."

"Ah," said the Englishman. "They must be watching you, then."

"I don't think so."

Andy considered for a moment. "Tell you what, I'll leave you for a few minutes. I'll only go to a washroom in the next car, and we'll see what they do."

Thereupon, they shook hands as though saying goodnight, then Andy moved to the stairs for the upper deck. Waving cheerio to Kit, he climbed them and went rapidly through to the next car and down again to the washrooms on its lower level. He locked himself in and remained enthroned for about ten minutes before going back to the hubbub of the saloon bar, where Kit had bought in another couple of bottles for them. There was no sign of the youths. He sat down facing Kit, their knees briefly touched.

"You were away so long, I thought you had gone for good. Jesus."

"Believe me, I won't do that. Anyway, just call me Andy , don't be formal."

Kit produced another of those beaming smiles of his. "That pair fair scurried after you when you went. He left his wine behind un-drunk."

"They must still be looking for me, then. I gave them the slip easily."

Kit's smile faded, and he grew serious. His companion also lost himself in reflection. Their silence called for Kit's awkward question.

"Andy. Why?"

Andy noted the genuine concern in Kit's face. God, this kid's too bright to take any old crap from me.

"You are not being straight with me." Kit turned his head away. "You're not what you say you are. You may work for your government, but there's no way you took me in with that stupid tale of yours about being on vacation with your friends. See? those two have just come back. They sure are keeping their amphetamine eyes on you, my friend."

His choice of words was emboldened by alcohol right enough, but both men had been talking almost incessantly ever since they entered the bar, so they had not drunk so much in that space of time as to impair their judgement appreciably, or their emotions. They had not even bothered to touch these fresh bottles.

Kit could see how disconcerted Andy was. "Look, Andy," he articulated slowly, "we've only just met. Perhaps we'll never see one another again." He swallowed his remaining reticence in one gulp. "Hell, buddy, just tell me if you are in some kind of trouble, else I could find myself worrying about what might have happened to you for the rest of my days!" He had leaned forward, putting some of his weight on the hand he had placed on Andy's knee, and was peering closely into the clear green eyes of the Englishman. "Who knows? I might even be able to help some ways." He tilted his head slightly. His smile was languorous; it was caring. It was observed from the opposite end of the bar.

"Please be careful," Andy urged him, pushing the hand from his knee. "You could just be putting yourself in danger."

"Is that a promise?" The hand was put back more firmly than before.

"No, I don't mean from me; from them – I don't know. I don't know who they are, or why they should be interested in me."

Kit sat back and wagged an admonitory finger at him. "Say, don't tell me, then. I suppose I must go along with that. I accept it. I do. You don't trust me enough. But I'm no con man. What you see is what you've got." He stood up abruptly. "I'm going up to the viewing deck to watch the stars. Coming?"

"I'll be with you in a few minutes," Andy replied. "That is a promise. I just want to think by myself for a bit." In fact, he also wanted to see what happened when Kit left.

Profoundly hurt, Kit loped to the stairs, leaving his full bottle behind on the bar top, and sprang out of sight three-at-a-time. Straight away, the angular male slid from his bar stool and made for the stairs. The girl stayed where she was and lit up yet another link in her cigarette chain.

Kit was gone for only a short while before he returned. "They're following me, not you. The guy came into the lounge just after me." Then he saw the girl, and sized things up immediately. He muttered to Andy, "Both of us? Why?"

Andy pressed Kit's drink into his hand. "Here, you'd better take this. Can I really trust you, Kit?"

"Like no one else you ever have!" Kit averred. He took a swig. "Besides, I think I've fallen for you in a big, big way."

"Well, don't," Andy directed him kindly but forcefully. "I think I may already have put you at some risk simply by our being seen together."

The stalkers were once more speaking animatedly in their corner. It was ham acting.

"I can look after myself," Kit assured him. "Black Belt, crack-shooting – I've done most of it." He grinned. "Don't worry none about me."

"Be realistic. It's a question of who takes whom unawares in this game, Kit."

"Gee, tell me about it! I've been trained in my hobby by pros., then Navy combat training. I'm no pushover, Andy honey."

Nobody had ever called him anything like that, let alone a man. Preoccupied as he was by their present predicament, that phrase so tenderly put burned into his armour cladding. He felt his heart or something leap in response to it. His ability to assess people was second to none. He suspected that Kit, too, was particularly astute in that sector of his brain. Yet he dared not yield everything to this guy. For one thing, he did not want to get anyone else involved, least of all him. For another, Kit was a military man with his own loyalties and obligations. Next, there was little or no future in their striking up a meaningful relationship when their homes and ways of life were thousands of miles apart. Holiday romances, he had heard, almost never led anywhere, and this chance meeting on a train was hardly anything different. Was it?

"Let's go somewhere quieter, shall we?" he suggested.

Kit's face brightened.

"To talk," Andy qualified.

"That's what I thought you meant," laughed the other. "But those frigging weirdoes are going to try dogging us, wherever we go."

"Bartender!" called Andy.

The man came over.

"Do you see those two over there? Well, they have been making a nuisance of themselves. In what way? They keep ogling us and other people here. My friend here went to the washroom a while back, and one of them followed him there and back again. Perhaps they're just high on something, I can't tell. A man and woman standing by the window before got so annoyed that they left. We could hear what they were saying when they passed us, that's how I know. But don't you think they're probably under age to be in here? No, don't tackle them yourself. They may turn nasty, and they could be armed, couldn't they? Oh, I see what you're doing."

The bartender had pressed a button beneath the bar. A minute later, a couple of burly male staff entered the saloon, consulted with their colleague, then sauntered purposefully towards the pair. A discreet few words in their ears, and the two sullenly allowed themselves to be escorted quietly from the room through the doorway beyond the bar. The bartender winked his thanks to Andy, who was disposed to tip him a generous gratuity.

"It's real strange," remarked the bartender with a smile of regret, "Kids like that, they're usually no trouble at all, so we kind of ignore them, you know?"

"These proved to be the exceptions, didn't they?" Andy responded. At the same time, he gripped his friend's shoulder.

"Come on with me, let's go while the going's good. There may be others ready to take over."

They rose, and obediently Kit got into step behind Andy as they hurried their way along the train towards the sleeper cars.

"Say, that was three whole counts you nailed on those saddoes. You gave them no quarter at all."

"We needed to be sure we got the staff on side, didn't we?"

When they reached Andy's doorway, he drew open its curtain and went inside, pulling Kit in after him. Rick and Jon were asleep in their bunks, Rick logically occupying the slightly wider, lower one. The attendant had called on his rounds while Andy was out and had made up their beds, and the lads had left a wall light burning low at Andy's end of the suite. Andy's was to be the lower one, the upper bunk not having been pulled out.

"You'll be all right here, Kit," he whispered so as not to waken his friends. "We can pull down the other bunk bed for you, and you can get some sleep."

"The last thing I need right now is sleep," Kit told him. Then: "My gear!" he hissed, "I can't leave my bag and my coat in the other car all night. I'll have to go fetch it."

He made to leave. Andy stopped him. "Here, put this on, just in case you are spotted and followed back here."

Kit took the heavy, bottle-green jacket and put it on, covering his head with the hood in the same manner that some passengers sleeping in the seated coaches wore hoods against the inevitable draught.

"Be quick." Andy's voice sounded like a plea to Kit, who spun round and, catching Andy by the hair, pulled his mouth towards his own and kissed him deeply, then he hastened out of the room, leaving Andy bemused and shivering.

Andy flopped down on his bunk. He was extremely anxious about the way the Sarah Simpson case was shaping, yet, at the same time, incredibly comfortable about what was happening to him. In fact, being here in a darkened train speeding across a foreign continent with two beautiful people he had not even met this time last week, and waiting for someone who was turning out to be a wonderfully warm person to come back to him, he doubted if he had ever been happier, or perversely more afraid – because an essential segment of his first-ever taste of what inner well-being could feel like was going to be harshly excised in a few short hours' time. He, Rickie and Jon would be leaving the train, and this man, Kit, would be carrying on to join his training course at the Pacific coast, never to be seen by him again. In short, he was as confused as ever.

He found a large packet of roasted nuts. Its wrapper was horribly noisy as he tore its end seam apart, so he found a large, clean paper napkin and emptied the contents into it. Next, he opened two bottles of still orange juice and waited, with the softly rhythmic breathing of the sleeping couple as company.

Why his constantly alert and highly tuned ears failed to pick up, above the noises of the rushing train, those approaching footfalls, the sounds of the fabric curtain being opened and closed, and the rustling of the oncomer's clothing, he afterwards couldn't imagine.

What felt like a blanket was suddenly thrown over his head and drawn savagely down so that his arms were pinioned to his sides and he could scarcely breathe. The material was crammed into his mouth, muffling his cries of alarm, and the weight of a heavy body on top of him crushed him on to the bed. Andy knew that to go on struggling now might be the death of him at the hands of his attacker. He was absolutely helpless – apart from chancing to kick out blindly, which might only result in summary retaliation. God, have the boys been attacked simultaneously while they slept?

A pair of powerful arms hoisted him back to a sitting position, the blanket about his head was loosened, enabling him to breathe more easily. A moist, warm, tingling sensation enveloped his left ear.

"Hi, baby. I've come back!".

Those arms relaxed their hold and entered underneath the cover so that they encircled only his body, leaving his arms free. Andy raised them above his head to cast off the blanket. Immediately he was overcome once more, this time by the gentlest, most yearned-for kisses, the first that had ever filled him to the brim with joy. He was accustomed to being in control of everything in his life, now he was simply content to sanction this lover to take the responsibility off his shoulders, if only for a brief span.

It was sufficient that they merely lay alongside one another, caressing and soothing, murmuring to each other of their longings, chiefly for a companion to share their lives with.

Andy recounted how Rick and Jon had altered his entire perspective of his place in the world by helping him to find in himself, ultimately this very evening, what had always lain inert only just beneath the surface, crying out unheeded to be allowed its expression. From here on, he would be able to give significant direction and purpose to his being, perhaps even some fundamentally changed priorities. Crucially, sex had become an option.

Kit's existence had been lived to the full. He had tried everything possible that he had come across, at least once. Well, not quite everything, maybe. And one of the very few challenges he had shied away from – many, many times – was to carry out that unthinkable act: to penetrate a woman. He had even known himself, on more than one occasion when touring a red-light district of some foreign port with shipmates, actually to pay a girl for time he spent with her playing cards or some such pastime while his heterosexual friends were having it off elsewhere in the premises. Prostitute girls had told him that they came across men in his situation several times a week, and that those johns often gave them more respect and consideration than did their straight fellows. He had never had unsafe sex, he promised. Nor would he expect Andy to do so with him.

In fact, although Kit desperately wanted to go all the way with Andy, he was scared that parting from him in the morning would be made all the more painful thereby, causing its memory to languish within him for months, even years, after.

They agreed to savour these moments so that they would forever recall them with happiness for what they had each gained, rather than tinged with regret for remembrance of things so soon lost.

"So, tell me what you are all doing in the States."

They sat and nibbled the roasted nuts, drank the juice and wine, and frequently lay in each other's arms. Andy told Kit everything. Kit had heard of the recent incident when a UNESCO official allegedly attempted to assassinate that Bosnian President guy. By the time Andy concluded his story, Kit had begged him several times to suggest how he might assist them. Say, hadn't he just proved what he was capable of? And that was only for starters!

Andy warned Kit not to make a sound that would waken Rick and Jon, before he stealthily assailed Kit with a number of disabling moves that quickly held him captive. It was a mark of both men's training and self-command that neither uttered a single vocal noise during the bout. The bunk heaved and emitted one or two thuds and creaks, but luckily not quite enough to disturb those deeply asleep.

"I know you would like to help us, Kit, but there's no way that you can. You are due at your training base on Thursday. You can't conceivably go AWOL. You would be court-martialled and, with our operation being so secret, I could not guarantee to get you off the hook. Your career must come first. That's what I want for you: to carry on with your successful career, and to live to a healthy old age, perhaps thinking of tonight and me now and again."

"Say, I do love you," murmured the breathless body painfully trussed up by its own arms and legs. "Don't you ever let me loose, now!"

Nine

They had crossed the Missouri River and pulled in to the city of Omaha, Nebraska, soon after midnight. Judging by all the clangings and reverberations up the train, it seemed likely that the diesel locomotives were being changed or refuelled.

The smitten twosome idly peeped round the window drapes at the goings-on at the station, where an elderly, uniformed white woman was trundling a heavy baggage cart along the platform. Its half-open sides were constructed of upright wooden sleepers and it had solid rubber tyres, which surely made it a great deal older than she was herself. Almost empty in the outward direction, it was stacked to beyond hazard level on its return trip from the train, with the poor woman practically horizontal hauling all that weight of teetering chattels by its formidable iron T-bar designed for two men working shoulder-to-shoulder. The vision was a novel distraction to the watchers. That the indefatigable female subsequently manhandled the assorted bags and suitcases so cheerfully for the knot of waiting disembarked travellers was perhaps a measure of her stoicism. Passengers attempting to help her for their consciences' sake were given polite but decidedly short shrift. Here was a tableau entirely out of kilter with the desired image of a modern railroad system serving the world's most prosperous nation.

Andy and Kit must have dozed off, for they were disturbed a couple of hours later by a commotion outside and on board the train. They disentangled themselves, sat on the edge of the bed scarcely wide enough for them both, and again looked out of the window.

The station signs said LINCOLN NE. There were groups of police men and women outside, and an ambulance was drawn up to an opening in the wooden railings backing this section of rain-wetted platform. Lights were flashing, too, on the roofs of the police vehicles parked near to it.

Yellow-swathed paramedics could be observed bearing two stretchers out of the third car up the train. Thuds of booted feet hastening up and down coach gangways as well as the strident voices of officialdom calling for information and barking out instructions ensured that the train was reluctantly coming awake. The main lights went up along its length.

Stirring in their bunks, Rick and Jon were not surprised to see that they were now sharing the room with an extra male.

Jon rubbed his neck. "Sounds as if they've lost someone and have set up a search party!" said he archly.

"A good-looking naval officer, for instance?" rejoined Rick, squatting cross-legged on the edge of his bed.

"And why not? He's definitely worth a lifetime's searching for!" Andy cuddled the American's naked shoulders without lessening his concentration on the scene outside.

Kit pecked at Andy's cheek and nose, then looked round at the other couple. "Say, you two won't snitch on me, will you? I'm going to hang up my lanyard and go to England with Andy here."

"Christ, if only you could!" murmured his admirer wistfully.

Jon affected a sigh. "Rickie, my love, it seems we are going to have to make do with just satisfying each other, after all. Andy's already found someone else who wants to make a complete man of him."

"And it's not before time, either," Andy pronounced. "I wish we could hide him away somewhere and smuggle him home with us. Still, I hope you don't object to my bringing him back here."

"Welcome to the happy family nest, Kit," was Jon's response. He sat up and swung his strong legs over the side of his bunk.

Rick, perched below him, took a few refreshing gulps of the orange drink from the side cabinet then passed the bottle up to Jon. He held on to Jon's ankles at either side of his head. "What the hell's going on out there, anyway?" he said with a yawn, then proceeded to make love to those dangling feet by starting to take each delectable toe into his mouth in turn and washing round it with his tongue. Jon's eyes shut tight and his entire body went rigid.

Tearing himself away from that erotic vision with acute difficulty, Kit peered outside once more. "Two stretchers. Oh, and it looks as if someone's died. No," he corrected himself, then cried out. "Say, there are two body bags!"

In a trice, all four men in only their underpants lined the windows. The stretchers had been placed on trolleys and were being wheeled diagonally towards the ambulance. The black body bags denoted that there had indeed been two deaths on the train.

Andy consulted his rail timetable. "The train was running about ten minutes late when we left Omaha," he said, "so according to this, we must have been stopped here for half an hour or more. I suppose they couldn't simply take the bodies away without the police recording everything first."

Rick looked out into the passageway. The car attendant was accompanying two cops, who could be overheard interviewing a rather deaf woman in her bedroom three doorways along on the opposite side.

The attendant called down the car to the curious many who, like Rick, had poked their tousled or hairnetted heads out. "Please stay where you are, ladies and gentlemen. There has been an incident, and the police wish to interview everyone on the train. We shall resume our journey just as soon as they give us clearance to do so. Kindly have your travel documents ready for inspection."

No doubt his was a message being passed along every coach, inciting a welter of ruffled chattering among the passengers.

The four put their trousers on, then they procured their documents and sat waiting for the law to come. Andy appropriated the time to fill Jon and Rick in about what had occurred in the bar earlier. Before they could discuss the implications, the attendant hailed them.

"Yes, come in," Rick answered.

He entered with the two brawny policemen at his heels. Without looking up, he referred to his passenger list. "Here we have some more English passengers: Messrs Andrew Gregson, Jonathan Reynolds and Richard Timperley." He stopped, glanced up, accurately assessed the position, and went on without so much as batting an eyelid, "Oh, yes, and an additional passenger whose name I said I was going to get from you later." He prompted Andy with the flexing of an eyebrow. "Regrettably, I got too busy, so I was going to catch up with it in the morning."

Andy made the requisite corroborative gestures.

"Your passports, please." One of the police officers put forth a hand.

Three European Union passports were held out to him.

With laudable presence of mind, Kit spoke up for himself just as Andy was formulating a pretext on his behalf. "I am an officer in the US Navy," he announced, "travelling to Oakland. I will be reporting to the Yerba Buena US Navy Training Station on Treasure Island."

"Is that so?" remarked the attendant. "My wife's brother is a toll collector on the San Francisco-Oakland Bay Bridge, which carries the road that tunnels through that there piece of rock."

"You don't say." Kit handed over his identity papers to the cop. "I've never been there before. You make it sound most unattractive. My old friend, Andy here, told me that he was going to Denver, so I said, 'Say, why don't we travel on the same choo-choo?' And here we are, man."

The police officer perused their documents while the other, a lieutenant, asked the questions.

"Do you know of any other English people aboard this train?"

Jon and Rick shook their heads and turned expectantly to Andy.

"I did happen to come across a British couple: a young man and his wife. They are honeymooners. I almost fell across them, actually." Andy grinned, then by way of clarification, he continued, "The train lurched, and I nearly landed on top of them where they sat. We got talking for a while, then they suggested that my friends and I meet them on the viewing deck, or whatever Amtrak call it, after dinner. But they didn't show."

"Did you get their names?"

"Why, ehm, yes, I did get just their first names, as a matter of fact. Er, Mandy and Stephen. I don't know how he spells his name – with a 'v' or a 'ph', but you can ask him that."

The lieutenant turned to his naval compatriot. "And your name is...?"

"Kitchener V Henderson, officer."

Jon was hard put not to snort out loud at that bombshell. Kit was so... well... But *Kitchener*?

"And the V?"

"Victorio."

The Americans turned not a hair. Such idiosyncratic family first names were commonplace. It checked, so the cop returned Kit's pass-book without comment.

Andy had gone wide-eyed meanwhile. He actually knew so little about this man who had shown himself thoroughly adept at lying his way out of what might for him have been a tricky situation – with the ready complicity of the attendant, it must be acknowledged. In what-ever language, Discretion was indubitably the night-watchword for sleeping-car attendants everywhere.

"And you European gentlemen – are here on vacation?"

"We are indeed," Jon said. "We intend to set out on a trekking hol-iday tomorrow, in Colorado."

"A stupendous state to do it in, too," opined the interrogating offi-cer. "You will have a great time. However, I must ask you, Mr Gregson, to get dressed and go with my partner to the ambulance you see over yonder. I need you to identify, if you can, the bodies of two individuals we have just removed from your train."

This made Rick wince. "Does that mean the bodies are those of the young English couple? Oh, bloody hell, Andy, and the poor things had only just got married."

Andy shook his head. "That's what I'm being asked to help the police to determine." He tugged a sweater over his head and began to put on his trainers. His facial expression was absolutely impassive, though his brain was in turmoil.

"What are your occupations, your means of employment? Mr Timperley?" the lieutenant asked first.

The couple spelt them out in detail, but Andy merely told them that he was a civil servant.

"Oh? For which department?"

"The Foreign Office," Andy fudged.

The policeman became more deferential than ever. "Well, it is mighty nice of you all to visit our great country," he said. "I sure am sorry about this unseemly incident, and I can only assure you that such things do not happen here very often. I trust it won't spoil your vacation none." He smiled towards Kit. "But I am sure your friend here is taking very good care of you."

"Oh, he certainly is that," cried Jon rather too fervently.

Kit's eyes barely glinted.

"And the railroad staff are first rate," Rick declared quickly, favouring the car attendant with a smile of gratitude.

"The weather looks a bit rough out there," remarked Andy. He picked up the hooded jacket Kit had discarded and put it on. "OK, I'm ready to go."

The uniformed trio left the room with Andy, but the attendant and the interrogating cop went only to the next bedroom.

Rick reduced their room lighting to what it had been so that they could see out better.

Watched from their windows by the three men left behind, the first officer guided an anonymous, athletically striding hooded figure across the platform and into the ambulance. After a minute, they both climbed down the ambulance steps, and strolled in conversation to a police car. Andy got into the back seat. The cop followed, and shut the door.

"Holy shit!" exclaimed Kit under his breath which began to steam up his bit of window pane. He was wringing his hands. "They can't surely be filing some kind of rap on Andy. Can they?"

Rick and Jon studied his anxious countenance. Was it really out of fear for Andy, or was it for himself: the terminal damage that would be done to his career if his overnight *delicto,* in the illogical perception of the military establishment, were to become *flagrante*?

Kit was growing increasingly agitated. He started biting at a fingernail, his less tasty fingers being closed so tightly that his knuckles stood out white against his otherwise tanned skin. For Jon and Rick it was the ordeal of not knowing whether this affair over the corpses had any connection with them, but being sorely apprehensive that it might.

"Oh, let him not be in trouble!" prayed Kit aloud to the renounced God of his childhood. He swivelled to face the couple who were at the window in their own half of the suite. "Do you think we should go over there and help him?"

"He isn't in trouble, Kit," Rick attempted to reassure him. "He is probably just giving them a statement."

"Yes, yes, sure. That'll be it," murmured the seaman, mollified.

"If it's your job you are worried about, none of us will give you away," Jon commented sardonically.

A look of anger and disgust filled the American's eyes. "You bastard!" he growled, "is that the kind of guy you think I am? Jesus, if you weren't a buddy of Andy's I'd smash your nose for that!" He paused. "And if I weren't a buddy of his, I wouldn't give a monkey's turd what you thought of me!" He realised straight away that he had contradicted himself. "Well, you know what I mean."

Rick reasoned with him. "So, if we are all on the same side, why are we quarrelling?"

Kit's ire subsided only a little under that anodyne treatment, and he maintained his baleful glare at Jon, who had sparked it off and was evincing no hint of retraction. He was about to make a riposte when their attention was drawn to some further activity outside.

The patrol car's rear door was opened, and out stepped the cop and Andy. Another officer could be seen remaining in the car. They ambled at a steady gait back towards the train, Andy keeping his head down and his face hooded against the wind-blown, drizzling rain that had lately resumed – usefully, because it was rendering his performance the more convincing. It was unlikely that anybody could have distinguished Andy from scores of other passengers on the train that night.

Kit rose and faced the doorway, and was ready to greet Andy with a hug when he came into the room. To everyone's consternation, Andy's expression was not merely sombre – it was grim.

He let down the hood and removed his jacket. "Damn!" he expostulated, boxing his own hand. "This is bloody serious for us, not just for those poor wretches." He shook out his hair, and sat down heavily.

Rick proffered him the last of the complimentary 'house' wine. "Was it them, then?"

"It was, it was," muttered Andy into his tumbler. "On their honeymoon, too! Oh, Christ. These people will stop at nothing." He wiped the inside of his free hand across his forehead and dropped back into his seat with a deep moan. He stared at the ceiling. Kit sat down close and covered the chilled hand on the seat beside him with his own.

"Murdered?" Jon's voice cracked.

Andy answered with his eyes.

"How?" asked Rick.

"Probably an injection of poison, needle pricks in the neck."

It wouldn't have mattered much what method of dispatch was employed, they all felt the same revulsion.

"Their bodies were found dumped in one of the rest rooms."

"Murdered on a crowded train like this?" croaked Jon. "How did they pull it off? Have the police any ideas? I mean, hey, were they killed in their bedroom and then somehow spirited away, or what?"

Rick said, "They didn't have a bedroom. They only had coach seats. Don't you remember Andy saying?"

"Oh, yes."

"And that's what adds to the mystery." Andy took another slurp of wine. "It's one thing someone walking in here and bumping us off in private with a noiseless weapon – a knife or something –"

That prospect horrified his companions.

"Or lacing a drink with arsenic?" suggested Rick dully.

"– but among a coach-load of other passengers? They must have been attacked somewhere else. Their bodies were not discovered in their own coach. The cops were quite forthcoming to me, perhaps because of the Foreign Office tag. Anyhow, they say it may have happened somewhere between Galesburg and Burlington, because it was at about that time that passengers noticed the washroom was engaged. Nobody seems to have been able to use it since around 6.30. That's still the subject of inquiries, and some passengers have got off the train since then and can't be interviewed."

"Say," came the sob, "what an awesome waste of humanity!"

So rapt were they in their imaginings, that nobody had looked anyone else in the face for several minutes. These first words from Kit since Andy returned drew the Englishmen to the distressing spectacle of Kit's losing struggle for emotional self-control.

"Were they robbed or something?"

Andy clasped the trembling hand that was upon his. "Seems not, Kit. There's no motive been worked out as yet." He dispensed with his empty glass.

"Ohh, like hell, there's not." Kit's voice was low and disturbing. His glistening eyes swept the couple seated in the armchairs. "Excuse me, please," he said, then leaned over and mouthed a few words into Andy's ear, whereupon Andy's body stiffened visibly and their hands held on more firmly.

They let go as Andy stood up, his face ashen.

"What is it?" Rick demanded to know.

One hand in his jeans pocket, Andy clenched a fist to the wall and started to thump his forehead repeatedly against it. His eyes were fiercely shut.

"Jesus, what have you done now?" Jon looked witheringly at the American.

Kit ignored him.

A frigid silence ensued, which was broken by Rick.

"I don't know what's got into you two. Here you are at each other's throats, and with those two young people murdered just a few metres away from us... Isn't that enough trouble to be going on with? How can you behave so badly?"

"Your other half seems to have taken a dislike to me all of a sudden."

"It's because you are too fucking plausible to be true," complained Jon, keeping his volume down. "We have enough trouble on our plates already without you, an outsider, stirring it up. Hey, why are you so fascinated with us? Are you just looking for kicks; something spicy to tell your messmates about when you get to wherever you are going?"

Before Kit could retaliate, Andy rounded on his critic.

"You want to watch what you are saying, Jon. This man has now put himself in as much danger as have the rest of us!"

"Tcha!" Despite Jon's feistiness, there was a new undertone of uncertainty there.

"What have you told him?" asked Rick.

"Enough."

"I am terribly sorry about your sister, Rick," Kit came in.

"Bloody hell, Andy, what made you tell him about Sarah?"

Rick was astonished. Only this afternoon, theirs was deemed to be a deadly secret mission that most of the Secret Service themselves were unaware of. Tonight, an agent as senior as Andy had blabbed it out to an almost total stranger – and a foreigner. Good looks don't a trustworthy bummer make. Never did. Surely someone of Andy's professional stature hadn't permitted himself to be taken in so easily by the blandishments of a young man in uniform? That would be such an impossible cliché. But then, newly brought out, Andy's horn must be far greener than most.

Andy slowly turned to face them.

"Listen to me, you two. Those junkies in the bar had got as interested in the guy I happened to be with as in me. Kit very naturally wanted to know why he was tailed by one of them as soon as he left the bar. It hardly accorded with our story of being innocent holidaymakers, did it? So I made a carefully arrived-at decision to tell him why. I was about to let you in on that decision when the cops turned up."

"Pity you didn't," Rick grumbled. "Anyway, why did they, like, follow him? Tell us, too."

"Right, then. Kit boarded the train in his uniform at the same station they did. Let's assume that they had been detailed to keep their eyes on what I was getting up to, then they saw me a few hours later in Kit's charming and, by then, plain-clothed company, is it any wonder that they must have come to certain conclusions?"

"That Kit must be a very fast worker? Not at all!" Jon laughed sarcastically.

"This is really gross!" cried Kit, miserably starting to collect his belongings together and putting them in his bag. "I'll go get out of your hair. I'd hate for you to think I was somehow interloping, or looking for a meal ticket."

"No, no, you can't go like this!" Andy barred the doorway nearer to Kit, who straightway made for the other one.

"Are those the junkies you were talking about?" asked Rick, peering out of the window again through another gap he was making between the curtains.

As he spoke, and without altering his line of focus, he reached out his right hand and almost nonchalantly grabbed Kit's arm as he was rushing past. Sitting as Rick was, Kit's forward impetus should have broken that hold, but Rick's tremendous strength, plus a tiny grunt, were sufficient to anchor Kit practically to the spot. Kit flailed at Rick's immovable arm with his bag, but Andy came up behind him, threw his arms about him and crushed Kit's elbows to his side.

"Leggo me!" Kit directed, dropping the bag.

Instead, Andy managed to pull him down sufficiently to nip him very gently just under the right ear. Kit let out an explosive gasp and squirmed some more, but offered less resistance. His captor panted softly against his ear, "Don't go, Kit. Please. Not like this!"

Rick was ystill holding on to Kit's forearm. He jerked at it. "Just wait a minute, at least. Take a good look outside. Is that the couple who were watching you?"

Kit ceased to struggle, so Rick cautiously relaxed his grip.

Andy affirmed, "That's them all right."

"The cops must think they are the murderers," said Jon.

Andy let go of Kit. "Now look, can I trust you to stay here while I go and see what I can find out?"

Kit nodded glumly and sat down alone on Andy's ruffled bed. His eye clashed with Jon's for a second, but he gritted his teeth and remained where he was.

"And try not to fall out again while I'm away," Andy begged them, as he put his jacket back on and left the room.

He worked his way down the car until he came across the policemen who had visited their suite. They were still questioning people, but Andy was able to take on one side the officer he had given his statement to.

"I see you have detained a couple of people," he said. "Are they the ones you suspect of carrying out these dreadful murders?"

The police officer took a glimpse from the window of the nearby coach door. "Oh, them. I don't really know, sir, for sure, but I did hear that the Amtrak staff had locked them up for causing trouble in the bar saloon – or for some such reason. They had telephoned ahead for police assistance, I understand. That was only fifteen minutes prior to their making a second request after the corpses were discovered. Do you have a special reason for asking, sir?"

"Not special, no. But Kit – Mr Henderson – and I saw them in the saloon earlier, so naturally we were inquisitive when we saw them again on the platform with your colleagues."

The attendant overheard the latter part of the discussion while he waited for the other officer to round off his interview of a young lady in her room.

"Those people you talk about: we have problems sometimes," he confided to Andy. "On very rare occasions, we get no-goods come aboard to pick pockets, to break into unattended baggage, even to roll passengers when they are asleep. We have to keep real vigilant, you know. I heard that those two were seen in the saloon sizing up potential victims until passengers conveyed their suspicions to the bartender."

The police officer added: "I think you'll find, sir, that that couple were due for arrest in any case, but I'm certain that they will be closely questioned in respect of these murders, in addition."

"Yes, of course," said Andy. "And I recall you telling me in your car that theft was not thought to be a motive for the murders."

"Exactly," boomed the police lieutenant, having emerged from the bedroom. "But it is always possible that the guilty party or parties hadn't yet gotten round to reaping the profits of their crime when the bodies were discovered. We are not presuming that those two creeps are the ones we are looking for, either."

"Quite so," said Andy. "A thought has crossed my mind, though: if their strange conduct in the bar was so obvious as to alarm passengers, isn't it likely that any criminal expertise they may possess lies elsewhere than in petty theft?"

Andy had already signed a statement in the car about his encounter with the British couple. He did not wish to get involved with the police investigation of the youths as well, if it could be avoided. With his parting early assessment, therefore, he left them to do their jobs.

He re-entered the suite a few minutes later.

The atmosphere was still icy. Andy elected to ignore the fact till he had reported what he'd learned.

"Whoever did it are probably still at large, then?" said Rick. "And we still don't know the motive?"

Andy and Kit exchanged glances.

Jon contributed, "Even though they have stopped passengers getting out at this station, isn't it probably a case of shutting the stable door after the horse has bolted, since the murderer or murderers could have got off the train at an earlier station?"

He noticed Kit opening his mouth to speak, so he interjected:

"Look, everyone, I want to say how sorry I am for my treatment of you, Kit. It was unforgivable of me to jump to conclusions the way I did. It just seemed so timely, that here you were, at the precise moment when Andy was arguably at his most tender, emotionally –"

Rick flashed him a warning.

Jon switched tack. "Then, when you were so concerned at seeing Andy being put in the police car, it appeared to my jaundiced eye that you were worried not for him so much as for your own career. Well, why shouldn't you be? After all, you have only known him for a few hours, and you are a career seaman with perhaps twenty-five or more years' service to look forward to. It makes sense. What right had I to judge you?

"I truly do apologise, Kit; it was none of my business even to comment. I can't think what made me so irascible. It's not really like me, is it Rick?"

Rick tamely shook his head. This was not the right occasion for bantering remarks.

"I'm bloody glad to hear it!" declared Andy. "Just what were you about, Jon, shouting the odds like that? What did Kit do to you to deserve it?"

The object of their argument, who had shown no reaction to Jon's announcement, now upturned his face to Andy. "Leave it out, Andy.

The man's apologised, that's good enough for me. But, for the record, I honestly didn't give a shit for my career at the time I thought Andy was being arrested, whether anyone believes that or not. I was scared for you, Andy, nothing more."

Kit looked round the company. "Anyhow, you have all been friends until I came on the scene. I still think you'd be better off without me. I'll give you my address and phone number, Andy, if you like, so we can keep in touch. Who knows? I may even go to England one fine day to visit my aunt – and you, if you are still interested."

So saying, he reached inside his bag for a pen.

Andy sat down by Kit. He was in an unfamiliar, disconsolate mood. He had not known what had triggered the argument until Kit spoke of it just now.

"You know what'll happen if you go on like this, don't you?" said Rick. "You'll swap a few letters, then one of you may be unable to write for a period due to being posted away, or for some similar reason. The other will think that the silent one's had a change of heart, the old self-defence mechanism will get to work, finally preventing either of you from renewing the contact. It's an age-old story."

"So it doesn't matter whether I go now or in the morning, does it?" Kit concluded. "It's sure as hell goin' to end up the same way, ain't it? How many thousands of miles are goin' to separate us? Still," he heaved a sigh, "I'll give you my address, anyways." He wrote on the back of a printed leaflet.

"Have you forgotten what you said to me before about the murder motive?" said Andy. "I happen to agree with you. It is very possible. Stop writing, Kit, and hear what I'm saying! Haven't you considered the ramifications of it?"

"If you mean my safety," responded Kit, "I've already told you, I can look after myself. Besides, who's going to get at me while I'm sitting in the middle of a crowded railroad car?"

"Oh, sure! Like nobody got to the English couple?" Jon reminded him. Then he asked Andy, "Are you and Kit actually implying that the honeymooners were killed only because they were seen talking with you?"

Kit nodded seriously.

Andy said, "After the way Kit was followed from the saloon, we must allow for the possibility that whoever is seen in my company – including you both, of course – may automatically be regarded as likely accomplices of mine. It may seem bloody extreme to us to go around bumping people off just on suspicion, but human lives have no value to some fanatics, often not even their own."

Rick shuddered. "If this theory is correct, we are not here dealing with Umberto Ciampi's mob, then."

"Probably not – if it is correct. This would be right outside Ciampi's league."

"Who's this guy Ciampi?" queried Kit, tearing the leaflet across unevenly and giving both the written and blank parts to Andy.

Andy elucidated.

"In that case, you are being surveilled by two, maybe more organisations which are not collaborating with each other, maybe in competition, even."

"That's about the size of it, yes. So you see the predicament you are in?"

"*I'm* in! Geez, that's rich coming from a man walking your tightrope."

"It may be that this bunch don't know where our room is, or even that Jon and I are travelling with you, Andy," suggested Rick. "There might not be absolute safety in numbers but, Kit, you have no sensible option but to stay with us, at least for tonight – what's left of it," he added dryly, glimpsing his wristwatch.

"But what will Kit do after we get off at Denver in the morning?" Jon wondered, his argument with the American characteristically put behind him. "He will be on his own again, with about thirty hours further to travel. If someone has marked him out, he's as good as a dead duck. At least with us, he might stand a better chance."

Rick smiled thoughtfully. "What, with us being his Three Musketeers to him being our D'Artagnon?"

That notion restored some good humour to the proceedings.

Andy did not write his address on the piece of paper Kit intended for it. Instead he ripped up both parts very small and tossed them down the pan.

Ten

The train was well in excess of two hours overdue when it rumbled into Denver's predictably styled Union Station.

Kit had slept soundly with Andy for what remained of the night, Rick and Jon taking turns apiece to keep guard, having had a few hours' sleep earlier on. Those insubstantial curtained doorways were capable of providing no protection whatsoever from anyone harbouring murderous intent.

Morning coffee and muffins for all four had been brought unbidden by their still amiable but weary-looking attendant, who'd had no catnaps at all during that long and eventful night. Having noted mentally at the time that it was definitely no male-bonding game of strip poker he and the police had interrupted, he frankly told Andy this morning that he considered a whole night was a mighty long time for two adults to stay comfortable on one such narrow bunk bed. If he had been sensibly informed beforehand about the new arrangement, he would gladly have supplied them with an extra set of bedding, even though it was strictly against the fares regulations. The man-in-charge left a remorseful Andy feeling as if his wrist had been well and truly smacked.

They had subsequently ignored the general breakfast call, resting in bed as much as they could till after ten, while the train rushed them westward across the high rolling prairies.

"Right, then," Andy had directed, "a change of strategy is called for. I think our bit of idle speculation the other day – remember, about a possible rift in the lute between Ciampi's mob and the Light of the World organisation? – might well have been truly inspired. It looks as if Ciampi has swallowed our vacation story OK. There's been no sign of them at all."

Rick had stared at him, utterly amazed. "Like, you don't consider that last night's horror may have indicated somebody's interest in our whereabouts?"

"Don't get shirty, Rick. I don't recall implying any such thing. All I'm telling you is that, whoever was responsible for the murders, it was not Ciampi's lot. They're complete shitheads all right, but no murder charge has ever been levelled at them."

"There's always a first time," said Rick. "So what is your take on it? Do you think it was the Light of the World, then?"

"Or one of their client groups. I can't tell. The important thing is, so far as the rats on our train are concerned, you've obviously got to dissociate yourselves from me. Which may be something of a problem since, to be consistent for Ciampi's people, we still have to continue in Denver with the charade we've embarked on."

"A problem is right," breathed Jon, slumping in his chair. "And just how do we propose to perform that miraculous little feat?"

"Seems to me," drawled Kit, "if you don't mind me chipping in, well, seems that if your Ciampi faction has interests and people in Denver, all Andy wants to do is get out of the train without these killers finding out."

"Clever boy!" Andy had exclaimed. "Were you reading my mind while you were supposed to be getting a good kip? Yes, sure, it means we must leave the train separately, and I'll wait till the very last second before I do."

Rick and Jon alighted first, from the coach next to their own, and sauntered as carelessly as their baggage would allow to the brunch restaurant in the adjacent block, where they were joined a few minutes later, but at a separate table, by Kit who had gone back to his own car before leaving the train. Andy kept it to the very last possible moment prior to the train's doors rolling shut before he hopped smartly to the platform wearing, like Kit, a complete change of clothing, keeping his face averted from the train windows and walking away at ninety degrees to ask directions from a station employee felicitously standing at the right spot for his purpose. He sustained the conversation long enough for the train to depart before tipping her for her detailed information. Finally, by a tortuous route, he attained the chosen rendezvous fairly certain that he was not being tailed. He occupied a stool at the brunch bar and ate alone, a fourth pair of eyes peeled for any shitehawks hovering in their vicinity.

It looked as if their vigilance had paid off. Even so, they did not actually meet up until they had drifted into a nearby bookshop, emerging together complete with city and state road maps. Kit, however, was no stranger to the 'mile-high city'.

The cab took them on the one-way system via 19th Street to Broadway, where there was a vehicle rental depot. Their driver pointed out to Kit the location of the main post office building on 20th, so while Andy was seeing about the car with Jon, the navy man and Rick retraced on foot the last section of their route, then cut along Curtis. The teeming downtown traffic was dreadfully challenging to pedestrians, but they reached the post office in less than ten minutes.

The illness of a close relative was the only excuse Kit could think up for conveyance to both his naval base and the training centre to explain his unscheduled stopover in Denver for an indeterminable duration. He could make a clean breast of everything in due course, he assured Rick, but he would fax his tame fabrication in the expectation that doing so ought at least to allay the prospect of a court martial for desertion. He could hardly telephone the respective duty officers stating that his life had been put in jeopardy because he had taken dinner on the train with three Britishers, one of them heavily into international espionage.

"Man, I'm just going to have so much explaining to do before this day is over," he confided. "You'll never believe how much!"

He marched away to look for the service counter where he could get his faxes sent from. Rick, meantime, wandered interestedly about the bustling great hall.

Jon and Andy met up with him while Kit was still probably queuing at the fax desk somewhere in order to carry out his odious task. Andy shortly spotted that straight, military back from a distance when he went off on a necessary job of his own: Kit was by himself communicating by mobile phone. The civil servant found himself a pay phone and left a concise coded message on his boss's scrambler answering machine. It was late evening back home.

Not long after, the four were assembled to decide on their next move.

While the rental company was validating the documentation provided by Andy who had entered Kit's name as a second driver, since Jon and Rick did not have their up-to-date international driving permits with them, the holidaying quartet elected to undertake a brief jaunt round the local shopping facilities. They made their way to the 16th Street Mall – attractive and opulent, despite every fifth shop seeming to be a Vietnamese-run emporium distributing touristy Souvenirs of Colorado manufactured in Taiwan, Korea or Japan.

They enjoyed an enormous ice cream sundae at a sidewalk parlour, before resuming their stroll along the largely pedestrianised, sun-basking street. On the way, they noted the service underpass that one of Umberto Ciampi's trucks must have taken in the past few days to deliver its maybe questionable cargo to one of the big stores they were presently close to.

Once Jon had purchased a birthday card for a work colleague, they stepped into the neighbouring furniture store of their immediate concern and browsed among the room displays like regular shoppers. Unsurprisingly, nothing appeared to be amiss. Andy's professional eye could descry not the smallest hint of misdemeanour or felony. A goods entrance into the lower ground sales department was gaping wide open, as if inviting Andy to dart in to effect a good prowl round in the rear storage area and its loading bay, while his companions kept the staff busy.

"I've been looking for a washroom," Andy eventually told a carpet salesman downstairs to explain away his probable security camera appearances, "and I stupidly got myself lost in the bowels of your storeroom. Can you help me?" The willing assistant showed him to the staff toilets out of kindness and left, affording him an opportunity for a further snoop or two.

This shop visit called for another purchase to be made – a pottery figurine, exquisitely designed in modern mode, depicting genderlessly two young people in a loving embrace. Andy emerged from his poking about in time to see Kit request the assistant to gift-wrap the costly porcelain. As soon as she handed it to him, Kit presented the package to Andy, who rewarded him with an embrace all of his own, a touching diversion to those witnessing the moment.

Making use of a street plan on leaving the store, they rapidly covered the few blocks to Colfax Avenue and the busy Visitors' Bureau. There they collected some freebie leaflets and, keeping up the pretence just in case, bought a couple of illustrated books setting out national park trekking routes in order of difficulty, then they hurried back to collect their car.

After one or two formalities at the rental depot, their big Pontiac moved away across four lanes of dense, southbound traffic with Kit, who was well accustomed to such driving conditions, competently at the wheel. In the Englishmen's hearing, the Avis counter staff had commented upon Kit's advanced-standard qualification attached to his driver's licence. Kit was steadily rising in Jon's and Rick's estimation. Jon's initial caution, if understandable to a degree, had been excessive, and he was still feeling very foolish about it – and ashamed.

Having Andy sitting in the front passenger seat navigating with the aid of a map, Kit directed the car west into Colfax and, in what felt like no time at all, had negotiated a complex junction to head them north along Interstate 25. The next junction led them on to the westbound I.70, where their views ahead were dominated by the eastern flanks of the Rocky Mountains which were soon to surround them. Some of the highest peaks were not completely free of snow.

Later they left the Interstate to join Highway 91, eventually meeting Highway 25 before entering the old silver mining town of Leadville – 'elevation 10,152 feet'. Instead of steering to the right off the highway and into the town's centre, Kit pulled the car on to the parking lot of one of the several diners lining the approach.

It had been a non-stop drive. Now was the time for a romantic mountain sunset and some grub, after a well-earned pee.

They ordered four different meals and ate off one another's plates at Kit's suggestion, a consequence of having observed his friends' inevitable mealtime dilemmas. It certainly simplified the complicated choices that American menus presented to these men from overseas.

Replete once more, they motored out beyond the highway lighting zone through some gathering hill-country mist for a few hundred metres as far as the presentable-looking motel whose beckoning lights they had noticed through the crepuscular gloom and Kit said he liked the feel of. They paid for two doubles in contiguous, ranch-style wooden cabins, near the end of a row linked at the front by a covered boardwalk. Close behind the cabins, a perfumed conifer forest marched in cultivated ranks up a steep mountainside into denser haze.

Kit's plea to defer their reconnaissance of the town until dawn when they would be feeling fresher fell on deaf ears. His English companions were anxious to press on without wasting any more time.

So, as soon as they had dumped their bags, they strolled into the centre of the two-storey town, and stooged around the original log and old orange brick buildings of Main Street. For all its twentieth century excrescences and tarmacadamised roads, this was a remarkable survival of a frontier boom town as put together by its founders. A few of the shops were open this late: the bars – notably the Silver Nugget – were sure a-buzzin'.

However, they were not what these sightseers had travelled so far to discover, but a certain premises behind the west side of Main Street where the industrial cleaning firm of Shaughnessy FactoryKlenz was using bales of cotton waste delivered by truck from Chicago.

Keeping their wits alert, they wandered about the quiet, dimly-lit back streets where mostly run-down properties housed small businesses. From a number of them, humming motors and rasping machine tools were audible, and strip lights glared through wired windows. People were working late: target dates entailed by hard-won contracts needed to be met.

There, among a group of modest engineering workshops, stood the signboard of the cleaning company they were looking for. The single-floor, flat-roofed brick building was situated at the far end of its large, concreted enclosure delineated by a three metre-high chain-link fence topped by several strands of razor wire. Somebody switched off a room light in the outshot building on the left hand side, replacing it two windows away moments later. The structure may have been a toilet block or a storeroom of some sort. In any event, this unkempt joint had been cased as well as it was going to be for the present.

The men walked slowly and continuously while they talked and gestured in a relaxed way, periodically changing their pairs in the manner that foursomes do as a matter of course. The mist came and went and came back again. They soon seemed to grow bored with their mundane surroundings, and made their way back to Main Street more speedily. The supposed tourists went into the swinging Silver Dollar for a couple of drinks and some fun before retiring for the night.

But in the confines of Jon and Rick's Coke-filled room, they commenced to plan the night's operations.

"Is it really possible that Sarah and Peter are in that building?" said Rick doubtfully.

"Being realistic, Rickie, I don't think there's much likelihood of that," Andy cautioned, "but we may just get some clue there about what has happened to them. If not, I'm afraid we're back to square one, and – dare I suggest? – Chicago. For we will have been in pursuit of the legendary wild goose."

"Why didn't you stay in Chicago for longer, then?" enquired Kit, no longer as edgy as he was earlier. "Thank God you didn't – I wouldn't have met you. But this is a long ways to come if there is nothing here to help you find them."

Andy opened a can and drank from it. "This is dull, everyday detective work, Kit, where most of our time is spent – 'chasing bum steers', do you call it over here?"

"Not for the best part of a century," laughed Kit, "but Americans know what it means from watching John Wayne movies."

"We've seen the same ones then. But, yes, that's what it's about. The thing is, we had to follow up the lead – our only one – before it got too cold. We would have come to Colorado far sooner, but once we realised that my arrival in the States was no secret, it had to be dressed up as if I were here for private vacation reasons – not only for our personal safety, but so that alarm signals would not warn those who may be holding Sarah and Peter captive to move them again." Or to murder them, he might have added.

His eyes stayed on Kit. "If they are being held hereabouts, the last thing we wanted to do was let Ciampi's people think that we're on to them. At the same time, we ought to have entered those premises tonight to see what goes on there."

"I'm much more afraid, not of Ciampi's lot, but of those who killed that young couple last night," said Jon. "I keep thinking of their parents, their families and friends who must by now know about it."

His words were succeeded by a long, reflective silence. Those horrifying events were clear in their minds and would never be expunged from them.

Andy broke it finally. "It still doesn't make any sense to me at all that the Light of the World organisation would carry out such murders so blatantly. It's not been their style. I'm coming to the unpleasant conclusion that there is at least one further group closely involved in this business – possibly having no direct connection at all with the ones we know and love. Before you ask, I don't know who they might be, but we have been hounded all day."

His English friends started.

"After all that effort to throw them off our scent?" cried Rick. "How do you know?"

"Kit and I have been keeping our eyes on them, haven't we, Kit? They've got quite a team out there. I saw Kit notice a convertible staying at a discreet distance behind us when we were leaving Denver. It was still there until we joined the I.70. There I saw a couple of women standing by their car watching us intently from the parking lot of a roadside bar as we passed them. I adjusted my door's rear-view mirror and, sure enough, the convertible overtook us, the passenger on the phone, and the women's red Buick took its place behind us."

Kit played along. "The convertible peeled off at the next junction. The Buick was relieved after an hour by a blue Pontiac like ours, then that was replaced by a four-square Chevrolet when we left the I.70, and that stuck with us right up to Leadville."

"And where is that now?"

"Oh, it'll be around here somewhere, Jon, you can rely on it." Andy leaned back on his elbows. Kit was lying alongside him on the king-size bed, Jon and Rick having relegated themselves to a couple of upright chairs because the other men had done most of the work so far.

"But why the hell didn't you mention this before?" queried Rick, reserving his response until he'd heard an explanation.

"I didn't want you to act otherwise than completely naturally," said Andy, levering himself up and smiling sweetly at them. "You'd be amazed how body language – even the tilt of a head seen through the back screen of a car – can be a dead give-away, particularly to trained observers. And any extra nervousness on your parts might have shown up when we were out getting the lie of the land this evening.

"I've been trying to preserve the illusion of our being unconcerned holiday makers for as long as I can possibly get away with it, the wronged innocents," he half grinned. "This sort of unspoken stand-off may have given them a smidgen of doubt about us, just enough to have deterred someone from actually challenging us – long enough for us to identify FactoryKlenz, at any rate."

"Yes, but you've given up the idea of searching it now," Rick presumed, disappointed.

"Well," sighed Andy, "the way things are, what with the exposed location of the cleaning works and so on, it's unlikely that any of us could break in there solo without the whole of bloody Leadville getting to learn about it while the job's being done." He took in the expressions on the couple's faces. "Maybe the lovely Kit here can get us into the place."

It was the American's turn to jump. He sat up quickly. "Say, how can I get you in? You've already said it's impossible."

"For us three, yes, Kit," Andy said without altering his tone of voice. "But for you? No."

Kit was decidedly uncomfortable.

"Will you come clean with us now in your own words, Kit, or do you want me to tell them in mine?"

Uneasily glancing at each of the Britons in turn, Kit began nervously fidgeting with his fingers, then he clenched them exactly as he had the previous night when he thought that Andy was being arrested.

At last he opened his mouth. "Umberto Ciampi is my sister's father-in-law," he announced querulously.

"Shit!" Jon muttered under his breath.

Rick put his head in his hands and let out a despairing groan.

"It's not a relationship I'm exactly proud of," Kit quickly went on. "Say, it sucks, man, it really sucks!"

Nobody was convinced by his performance.

"Katy is still at the university, so is Pietro. Thing is, they got her in the family way last year and, the Italians being the way they are and Pop being what he is, they were forced into getting married. It's the twenty-first century, for Chrissakes! and there were Umberto and Pop railing at them for bringing their families into disrepute, whatever that means today! I tell you, it's like the fucking Dark Ages. Pop even agreed to her converting to Rome. His proudly vaunted Evangelical principles took second place to the honour of his name, when push came to shove!"

"And where is the baby now?" Andy's question seemed almost irrelevant. It was spoken in a voice dried of emotion, but his shoulders were trembling, showing the pain that was emptying his heart and returning it to its former void condition.

"She's in Chicago being cared for by the Ciampi family till the couple graduate next year. She's –"

From his sitting position, Andy threw a hard left punch at the side of Kit's face, drawing blood over the prominent cheekbone, then he rolled on top of him, hurling a barrage of short blows at his face and body and a tirade of verbal abuse, giving furious vent to his terrible hurt.

Yet Kit did no more to defend himself than instinctively try to cover his head with his arms. Indeed, he made no attempt to retaliate, for he too was bawling his eyes out. Then he stretched his arms wide across the bed, submitting his whole body as a sacrifice to Andy's vicious attack, which Andy intensified by kneeling up and swinging at him from there. His lifetime of arid loneliness was being avenged upon the one person he had allowed to come close to him, who had declared his love for him, who had asked for and accepted his love, while all the time escorting him and his friends into unmitigated disaster.

Appalled and numbed by Kit's revelations, Rick and Jon did nothing at first but look on while Andy mercilessly assailed the perfidious charmer's powerful body. In the end, they dragged the almost exhausted Andy away and forced him into a chair.

Kit lay where he was for a few moments then, in obvious agony, he tried to get himself up. His face was a mass of blood, and the flesh around his eyes was puffing up grotesquely. The front of his body was certain to be in a bad way. When he eventually managed to stand up, he staggered and fell back on to the bed. Nobody moved to help him. Finally, while Rick was occupied in bathing Andy's badly contused hands and Jon was getting some first aid items from Rick's bag, Kit succeeded in standing more or less upright. Without looking at any of them, he made slowly for the door, swayed a little, and opened it.

Kit stepped outside and closed the door behind him.

Jon said, "Let him go back to his mates, Andy. Screw him. Believe it or believe it not, there are millions of really nice guys out there searching high and low for someone exactly like you."

"But he's the only person I've ever got near to loving in my life." Andy was weeping. "It may have been a delusion or it may have become the real thing. I know it was only for a few hours, but I somehow managed to convince myself that, even if time and distance were to keep us apart in the future, at least we'd had something precious which we shared for a while. What a bloody fool I've been. God, how I've let you both down! But you know, we didn't do anything last night but hold one another. I thought that was all either of us wanted at the time, but for that fucking artful snake it was only calculated play-acting." Bitterly he shouted, "I'm still a virgin, lads!" at the world in general.

A gun shot cracked outside in the street, then came the sound of a heavy body crashing on to the wooden veranda.

Eleven

"Oh, Christ, no. Kit!" Andy yelled, darting for the door.

Rick intercepted him. "If that was what we think it was, it'll help no one if you get shot as well."

Andy was still breathless and shivering after the beating up he had inflicted on Kit. Even though he had seen through Kit's duplicity earlier on, that confession of his wounded him very deeply when it was articulated.

"Shit, you're right," said Andy. He wrested himself from the other's manual restraint. Instantly he regained his composure, if not his breath, letting his steely professionalism take charge.

"Douse the light!" he ordered, and crouched for the remaining distance to the door in case the cabin itself was being targeted.

Rick was already fiddling with the awkward table-lamp switch. The light clicked out. Andy carefully opened the door a couple of centimetres and peeked through the gap.

Kit was lying face down outside the next cabin, where he was probably letting himself in at the moment he was shot. Blood was oozing from beneath his body and soaking into the pine boards, but it looked to Andy as if he had been hit slightly below his right shoulder blade. Moonlight reflected coldly from the roofs of guests' cars ranged immediately in front of their drivers' cabins. Their own hired vehicle would now be shielding the fallen seaman from any further bullets.

In the purple radiance of what had become a clear mountain night, Andy glimpsed a silhouette scurrying between two darkened buildings directly across the street. It was hotly pursued by another. More figures could be discerned farther along the street to Andy's left.

A lone truck roared past.

A shot from a different weapon rang out, its echo clattering through the mountains all around. This was succeeded by more single shots, some of them recognisably from heavy types of handguns. Now came automatic fire spat from behind pallets stacked at a depot on this side of the road. Like the motel forecourt's illuminations, the few remaining interior lights burning at such a late hour in properties nearby had been extinguished at the first sounds of trouble, but that did not save scores of windows and commercial signs from being smashed to smithereens and the buildings' walls being spattered with bullets.

Andy noted that none of these shots was now aimed anywhere near their cabin. The battle raging out there was between opposing forces unknown to him. A scream of pain when someone else was hit, more people flitting from cover to cover, firing as they went.

"I'm going to bring Kit in, he's been wounded," Andy called above the din. Without listening for a response, he gingerly opened the door a little wider and crawled out on his stomach like the paratroopers who trained him.

Jon half closed the door behind Andy as he left, and gaped with mounting horror at the open warfare intensifying along the principal highway leading in and out of this hitherto peaceful settlement. Rick watched with equal foreboding from behind the venetian blind. Such scenes belonged to the previous century before the rule of law was imposed on the frontier folk, no doubt ancestors of many of today's population.

Slowly, Andy inched his way towards Kit's prone, twitching body. He reached his feet and grasped hold of the right ankle. He had begun to draw Kit to him when, zing! a bullet ricocheted off the metal decoration of a grandiose, imitation oil lamp suspended above him, sending opaque glass flying everywhere. A particularly large fragment lodged in the arm Andy was pulling Kit by, causing him to lose his grip. He struggled to regain it despite the agony of the glass dagger's point scraping at the ulna bone of his forearm. It was no use, something vital had been severed. He could partially flex his four fingers, but the power that had been there was lost. Though he changed hands, his damaged arm was useless for giving him the necessary purchase and leverage for him to drag Kit's considerable muscle weight more than a few centimetres at a time.

"Give me a hand!" he cried over the cacophony. Another stray bullet whammed into the fuel tank of a nearby car.

Jon opened the door, fell on his face and slid his lithe body forward serpent-like, as if he were rescuing a trapped fellow caver from one of his beloved Derbyshire pots. It was a faster and more efficient movement. Rick launched his huge frame after his partner in the same manner. Jon undulated past Andy to aid Kit, who was moaning incoherently and bleeding badly.

Within half a minute, the injured men were back in the comparative safety of their cabin, its door locked. Rick turned a small bedside light on and phoned to get the scared and dithering motel manager to summon ambulances for her two injured guests and for those individuals outside plainly getting hurt in the battle. Police sirens were already wailing somewhere in the town. Jon took out of his bag the first aid box they had bought in Chicago, emergency equipment he was rarely without, wherever he happened to be.

Kit had been propped against the foot of the bed. Jon cut the blood-soaked shirt away from him. Now he could see that the bullet, from a powerful weapon, may well have entered Kit's right lung from the back and re-emerged through his chest wall. He needed urgent hospital treatment before he choked or bled to death.

Andy was standing over them, his own left arm bleeding copiously onto the carpet. The heavy wedge of glass still protruded from it. He surveyed the extent of what he himself had wreaked on that fine head and body – with Kit's compliance, for God's sake: contusions, cuts, swellings – and pain. Taking firm hold of the glass, he yanked it straight out of his arm to prevent it snapping off inside his flesh. The bellow he let go as it parted with the bone made his friends wince for him.

Andy cast the bloody thing contemptuously into the trash can beside the pedestal washbasin which he needed to grab on to straight away to retain his balance. Unsteady and feeling nauseous, he sat himself on the bed, his eyes never leaving Kit's battered face, while Rick applied a tourniquet to his arm to stem the bleeding, then a sling of sorts, before cleaning the area near the injury and putting a temporary dressing on it. All Jon could do was bind sterile pads to Kit's chest and back with a broad bandage and pray that the gunfight outside would have burnt itself out by the time the ambulances arrived. He removed the duvet quilt from the bed and wrapped it about Kit's shocked and trembling body.

Kit's fitful, stertorous breathing was becoming interspersed with frightening gurgling sounds. Inaudible mutterings stumbled from between his swollen lips. Those once lively, playful eyes flickered open a little and fixed beseechingly on Jon. He tried to reach out with his hands. Jon took hold of them and bent an ear to Kit's working mouth.

Barely he could make out "... sorry... sorry... sorry..." over and over again, then "Andy... please, Andy..." the tone getting desperate.

"Come here, Andy. He's asking for you."

Andy knelt by his errant lover, whose earnest gaze into his eyes glowed for a space and pierced him like the shard of glass had done. It went out, then the eyelids drooped. But the mouth, its corners frothing bright red, kept going, "Sorry, Andy... sorry, Andy..." And stopped.

"Oh, Jesus, he's not dead is he?" Andy's face was a mask of terror.

Jon made the tests. "No, he's still managing to breathe, but with only one lung, I think. It depends now on whether those bastards outside let up soon, so that the ambulances can risk approaching the motel."

Rick peeped through chinks in the front window's blind. The first of the police had joined the fight, with reinforcements noisily on their way.

They heard a loud tapping on the rear window. Alarmed, the couple looked to Andy who waved them to duck down. He cautiously headed to the window situated above a three-drawer cabinet but, before he reached it, it was stove in by repeated blows, most of the pane tumbling behind the blind's plastic slats onto the cabinet top beneath. Andy hurled himself hard against the wall to one side of the window for protection, while his companions scrambled for the inadequate concealment offered by their bed. Chill air and the stench of gasoline invaded the room.

The blind was impatiently torn from its mounting, revealing two sinister forms wearing black balaclavas and polo-neck sweaters. Both brandished assault rifles which Andy identified as the latest types of the AKM and its smaller calibre version, the AK-74. This was the end for the four unarmed men within. They were sitting ducks. Rick and Jon tightly held hands at the last.

"Hey, you, get outa there quick before the cops get here!" instructed a gruff voice. "I said, 'quick'!" he shouted when no one moved.

"We have a badly wounded man here." Andy suddenly showed himself, taking the other speaker aback by this eyeball-to-eyeball meeting. "We can't leave him, he's bleeding to death." Andy's own voice broke as he uttered those words.

"We'll help you. Now, move!" The man motioned to someone behind him.

Feet ran over the damp grass towards the cabin, and five more people stood guard while the Britons sorted themselves out. Noticing how hampered one of the Limeys was, a member of the masked gang leaped nimbly in to the room. The four lifted Kit gently on to the stripped mattress, then carried him on it to the window, feet first, and hefted the lighter end on to the cabinet. Three willing pairs of hands, which had been painstakingly removing jagged remnants of glass from the lower half of the window frame, reached in and hauled at the mattress. By a concerted effort they managed to roll it only just small enough to squeeze its bulk through the window space, though splinters of glass in the top of the frame tore at its damask underside. Lying at the bottom of this cumbersome tunnel, its barely conscious occupant was sheltered from any bits of glass that may have dropped onto him.

It was a scary few minutes while they strove to transfer Kit's pain-racked body into the yard. The mattress was put down on the asphalt path. There was brief discussion among the armed people who huddled round the inert, bloody shape.

"Now the rest of you," rasped the voice harshly, meanwhile. "And hurry it up, will you? This man needs attention."

They did, Rick and Jon not forgetting to fling their unpacked bags out ahead of them. When they had clambered through, six people grasped the mattress handles and, led by the spokesman snapping out directions over a mobile as he went, the party jogged towards the white picket fence bordering the back of the motel grounds and away from that pervasive smell of petrol.

Appeals bawled over a loud hailer informed them that the police were still engaged in putting down the gunfight on the far side of the premises. Exactly what part these strangers, all in black, had played in it was anyone's guess.

Andy was keenly distraught about Kit being borne away from where an ambulance could pick him up, yet these people did seem to be bothered about Kit's condition, so they must be providing faster transport. Besides, they were here – the ambulance wasn't.

A big, green personnel carrier was standing alone on a dirt road that looked as if it might traverse the mountainside. Two more people jumped out of the cab and ran to open its rear doors. On Jon's advice, the bearers heaved the mattress inside with its head end first, before lowering it to the floor between the seats lining the sides. He and Rick braced that first one-third of it up against the forward-facing bench seat at the front of the vehicle so that its thickness would support and cushion the patient in a half-sitting posture to assist his breathing during the journey. Just then, a further two gang members panted up, one of them limping with a nasty knee injury. Everyone tumbled aboard the vehicle which roared into life and, without lights, took off up the bumpy road.

"Anyone missing?" demanded the rough-voiced one from the seat next to the driver.

A woman told him, "Gino took one between the eyes. Nothing we could do for him. We just made it look like he was some innocent bystander caught in the crossfire."

The company fell silent.

Back there below them, a bright flash preceded the thud of an explosion emanating from the unfortunate motel. The parked car of one of the guests was engulfed by flame. Frustratingly to the British, a small fleet of ambulances standing by could be made out, only a couple of blocks from the battleground.

"Where are you taking us?" This was Andy's voice in the darkness.

"We're rushing Kit and Mario to hospital, of course," the leader replied over his shoulder.

"Good. So you know Kit, then?"

"Of course! He is my nephew's brother-in-law. Why should I not know him?"

The speaker pulled off his balaclava. It was too dark for the British men to distinguish his features, nor those of most of his eleven companions who were also removing their knitted helmets. What this act evidenced, however, was that about four of the gang were women.

"Where has he been hit?" 'Uncle' enquired of Andy.

"In the back. Jon, here, says that the bullet went clean through his body." Seated behind the driver, Andy had been holding Kit's disfigured head steady against the bouncing of the vehicle ever since they started out.

"I think one lung is collapsed," Jon elucidated, "and he's bleeding a hell of a lot, as you can see."

More silence as the vehicle pushed higher into the mountains, now with its lights on. In approximately fifteen minutes, they began to make a steep descent into a valley. After five more, the vehicle stopped while someone went to operate a tall iron gate. They were presently on a smoother metalled drive which took them down the hillside for a couple of miles, before they encountered a second gate.

In an area bathed in light, they came to a standstill at last. Those nearest to the doors pushed them open, then hopped to the ground.

The military transporter had pulled up outside an enormous white mansion possessed of a neo-classical portico, no less. A surprise in this wild, mountainous region, the house would have been more at home in the polite company of Santa Barbara. It was itself supposedly a home, despite the garish floodlights illuminating the front of the building.

Leaving their weapons under their seats, the mini-army piled out followed by the short man with a grizzled head and an all-round paunch who was, presumably, Umberto Ciampi's brother. Enduring terrible pain, the fellow with the shattered knee was helped off the step and borne between two of his comrades, their arms linked in a chair lift hold, in the direction of plain double doors located beneath the divided grand stairway leading up to an imposing central entrance which was set behind the colonnade of that Palladian loggia. He was seen to vomit just as he was about to be taken inside.

"This is not a hospital, surely," Andy complained after 'Uncle'. "Kit needs professional surgery right away."

The man turned about, letting those still in the transporter see for the first time his flabby face, with its cold grey eyes and thick, nicotine-stained grey moustache that matched the more wiry curls of his head. He stood aside to allow Kit on his bloody mattress to be pulled out with the assistance the Englishmen.

"He will get everything he needs in my home," he declared in a manner brooking no contradiction, "so the quicker we get him inside, the better his chances."

As if synchronised to prove his point, two limousines swept down the drive that the personnel carrier had just come along and drew up in front of the opened doorway which everyone was now making for. Six men and four women stepped from the cars and hurried into the house ahead of the 'stretcher' party. These were the surgeons and theatre staff, who had been paged and primed in readiness for a summons as soon as the gunfight in town developed.

Entering this part of the house was much like walking into the casualty department of a small infirmary. Everywhere was clinically gleaming under tubular fluorescent lights. The nurses – three of them did not go through to the theatre area with the four surgeons – had only to remove their outdoor clothing and scrub up to be ready for duty.

Kit was laid on the bed in one of the five curtained-off cubicles along the wall to the left. Some of the nurses began taking off the unconscious man's clothing and to get him ready for examination by a surgeon. The other wounded man was similarly cared for in an adjacent cubicle. The small militia, comprising men and women aged from about eighteen to sixty, departed with the motel's ruined mattress and didn't return.

While the two medical teams were preparing their patients and both operating theatres, Ciampi used the respite to study the Britishers he had brought in. What he had seen so far, he liked.

He pointed them towards a door on the far side of this reception area and took them into a superbly appointed waiting or consulting room, leaving the door ajar. He held out his right hand.

"I am Giuseppe, Umberto's little brother," he said with nice self-effacement. "You know of him, I understand. Which one of you is Mr Gregson?"

Andy took the hand. "I am, Mr Ciampi. I must say, you appear to be ready for all eventualities here."

"This is a remote district, Mr Gregson. My family is large. You have just met some of them, and I feel it is my duty to look after them, just as they give their love to me and my wife." The hand gesticulations were at least as eloquent as the choice and delivery of words. "Good public medical facilities are some distance from here, so I have a resident medical staff and the best equipment available in case of emergencies." He smiled disingenuously. "Not that we ever get embroiled in shoot-outs like tonight's. I am appalled by what happened. There has been no real trouble over in Leadville for decades, yet there we were, on what I guess is your first visit, behaving so badly as soon as you arrive!

"And here I am still forgetting my manners. Do sit down, all of you."

While they selected armchairs, Ciampi crossed to the wall telephone and ordered coffee and cookies to be brought down.

"Was that one of your family who was killed?" asked Jon as the Italian came back and sat down.

"Gino was a chauffeur – Jon, was it? Yes, well, Jon, he was a very good one, too, but fighting was not what he should have been doing." He tutted sadly. "Mario, he is one of my sons-in-law. A good boy. Too pushy sometimes, gets himself needlessly into trouble. Now I dare say he will walk with a limp for a very long time. A sorrow for his papà." More tutting.

Ciampi turned to Rick. "And what is your name? I think that you have not said anything yet."

It was using up all of Rick's self-restraint not to blurt out the question he most wanted answering. Instead, he asked, "Are we your prisoners, Mr Ciampi?"

Guffaws of laughter repudiated those words. "For why would you be my prisoners, my English friend? What have you done to harm us that you should imagine such a thing?" Ciampi took a huge white handkerchief from his sleeve, wiped non-existent tears from his eyes and loudly trumpeted his nose into it.

His demeanour changed in a split second. "You can walk out of here whenever you like, and no one will try to stop you. The Ciampis never dishonour their guests." There was that allusion again: family honour. His eyes narrowed then. "But I warn you that there are people beyond my stock fences who can and will stop you! You saw what they did to poor young Kit, who I'd swear has never harmed a soul, for watching over what needs watching over."

A knock at the door presaged the arrival of two youthful housemaids carrying the required refreshments which they put down on the table between the men and then left.

Jon sat forward in his seat and leaned across to peer at Andy's left hand, which was by this time turning a very ominous shade of purple, and blood was seeping between his fingers.

"I'm sorry to interrupt this, Rick, but Andy's neglecting himself. Andy, you really must get that arm looked at right now if you don't want to lose the use of that severed tendon permanently."

Ciampi raised his bushy eyebrows. "He, too, has been wounded tonight?" He began to rise from is seat. "I had not realised that his was a new injury, and he said nothing about it. Ah, but I see he is bleeding."

"Yes, Mr Ciampi, but it was not caused by a bullet. His arm was speared by a piece of glass. His tourniquet has been on far too long. Fetch one of those trays, Rick."

Rick did as he was bidden. After Jon had helped Andy to remove his jacket, Rick placed the cleared fibreglass tray on Andy's lap as instructed. The arm was badly swollen, so Jon slackened the ligature sufficiently to let some blood flow into the starved lower arm and hand. The cold limb he rested on the tray and massaged where the restriction had been, inducing his suffering patient to hiss air in through his teeth, and blood to run into the tray from the ugly laceration.

Ciampi lumbered to the door and called for a nurse. In five minutes, Andy was occupying the third bed next to where Kit was being got ready for theatre.

The main doors to the reception were suddenly thumped open again, and in marched three men carrying some familiar-looking baggage which they were instructed to take to the Britons in the waiting room.

"Haha," spoke Ciampi, "these will be yours, I believe?"

"Why, yes, they're Kit's and Andy's. But –"

"Ask me not how or who by, Jon. Merely accept them. All part of the famous Ciampi hospitality!" he jested.

One of the newcomers spoke. "And they brought these gentlemen's Pontiac to the front, Mr Ciampi. It is undamaged. Shall we garage it?"

"*Grazie*, Paulo," their leader said, dismissing them.

"I must go say goodnight to my wife, boys. I shall be back presently." He threw back his small cup of black coffee and left.

"Christ, what do we make of all this?" cried Rick. "Do you think this is where they've got Sarah?"

"It's more likely that she's here rather than in that crap factory building. I wonder how it is that Andy didn't mention that the Ciampis had such an enormous set-up round here? He must have known, surely! Everybody else seems to."

Jon went to the large bag belonging to Kit, opened an end pocket he'd seen him use, and withdrew the leather wallet containing his papers. He examined them for a minute, then found what he was looking for.

"He's not been lying about being a seaman." There was a note of relief in Jon's utterance.

"The cops on the train would have blown that one for us if it had been a scam," Rick reminded him.

"You're not wrong. Ah, here's what I want: his blood group. I reckon we can save the medics some time." He hurried from the room.

"Rhesus O Positive, thank God," he commented on his return. "No complications there, anyway." He took his first taste of the coffee. "God, I need that!" He drank some more and lounged in his seat.

"Look, Sarah –"

"Don't, Rick," Jon cut in. "On reflection... Andy's show, yes?" Even with his eyes shut, Jon had conveyed to his partner that these walls were likely to conceal all the senses necessary for surveillance.

They finished their coffees and catnapped where they sat.

But it must have been two hours before a nurse came into the room. He coughed to waken them.

"Mr Gregson is ready now, if you would care to see him."

They both stood up and stretched muscles aching through being cramped in chairs for so long.

"That's good. How is his arm?" asked Jon.

"He won't lose it," smiled the other. "Just as I believe I heard you correctly diagnose earlier on, he severed an artery, and a tendon needed to be retrieved and reconnected, but he's all been stitched up and there's nothing broken. He'll have to keep it immobilised for a while. Your excellent first aid saved the day for him."

"And Kit? – Mr Henderson? How is he?" Rick was genuinely anxious.

"I was present during the surgeons' examination of him. He is a very seriously sick guy. He has a collapsed lung, and the chest cavity was – how shall I say? – engorged with liberated blood which restricted his breathing by the other lung, putting a huge strain on the heart. Once we had drained the fluids, his breathing got a little easier. But he's been in theatre for ninety minutes so far, and there is no indication of how matters are proceeding.

"Oh, and by the by, Mr Ciampi came down again to see you, but he found you totally crashed out, so he asked us to look after you for tonight and he would see you around ten in the morning."

The couple gladly followed the dapper, fortyish nurse through the reception area and along a wide corridor with half a dozen doorways off it. They were shown through the second of these. It was a private bedroom fitted for up-to-the-minute technology, with an adjustable bed at the far wall. Wearing a hospital shirt, a proper arm sling and a haggard countenance, Andy was reclining with his head deep in a mound of pillows. He was staring engrossed at the tiles of the room's suspended ceiling, obviously concentrating on the mysteries of this intractable case of Sarah's disappearance.

On hearing the three men's approach, he diverted his gaze and greeted his visitors with a languorous smile. "You've made me bloody lose count now," he grumbled.

"Well," cried Rick, acting as perky as a parrot, "who looks as if he's had a hard day in the orifice, then?"

Andy grimaced. "All this would have been worth it, if I had," he rejoined, his voice hoarse. "And you two look like shit," he retaliated.

His friends had to acknowledge that they probably did just then.

The nurse moved out of Andy's line of vision, mouthed to the couple the words: 'He refused an anaesthetic!', huffily plumped up the pillows and quickly absented himself.

"They say your arm will last for at least as long as the rest of you, Andy," said Jon comfortingly.

"Probably longer," Rick solemnly vouchsafed.

"Provided that you use the other arm for your more vigorous daily activities," concluded Jon.

"I'll try to keep your advice in mind, vet'nary!"

His expression became more serious. "How's Kit doing? Have they told you? I can't get anything out of them."

"That nurse chap told us that he's still undergoing surgery." Rick scrutinised Andy's face. "You still care about him, don't you? In spite of everything."

Andy nodded abstractedly.

"The fact remains –" Jon had no need to go on.

It was evident that Andy was blaming himself for Kit's present condition: if only he hadn't beaten him up like that. But Kit could so easily have put up a very effective defence if he'd wanted to. Instead, he had meekly lain back as if inviting the blows. Maybe he actually wanted the punishment being meted out. Not as in some weird masochistic orgy; rather, as Andy was coming to suspect, in a courageous act of offering himself up to assuage Andy's warranted feelings of betrayal. Or was this sheer fantasy?

"Can you tell me, lads, why Kit responded like that when I hit him? I mean, anyone else caught out and in the wrong would at least have tried to ward off the punches. It's a natural reaction. It must have been fucking difficult for him just to lie there and take that kind of treatment."

Rick answered him. "If you had been anyone else – one of us, for example, he would have protected himself as you say."

"But you were Andy Gregson," Jon continued. "He had fallen in love with the very person he'd been told to spy on, or whatever his instructions were."

"You mean, you really believe that love can make people do that kind of thing?"

"I've heard it said, yes. I reckon he was giving himself to you, that's all," Rick opined.

"All?" Andy was incredulous. "For a few minutes I wanted to kill him! And he might have let me?"

"I should think that's probably QED: what remained to be proved," murmured Jon with surprising soulfulness for one who had so recently been spitting vitriol at the American.

"I've only known the sod for five minutes. This is bloody ridiculous!" Andy pressed his face into his pillows.

Rick touched him on the shoulder and said softly, "Jon and I are to be given some sort of accommodation around here somewhere. We'll come and tell you when there's some news of Kit. OK?"

Andy nodded without turning, and the two men quietly left him to his thoughts.

They were given a larger room two doors from Andy's. It had four beds in it, and there was plenty of space on the floor for all their luggage without it causing an obstruction.

Paradoxically, they slept even less well in those comfortable beds than they had in the confining waiting-room chairs when their minds and bodies were still traumatised. Now their minds were in turmoil, going over the events of the night, trying to work out who had been trying to do what to whom, and why. Did it all have anything to do with Sarah, with international espionage, or had they simply walked into some local gangland feud of some kind, which had absolutely nothing to do with them? Yet why had Ciampi implied that they would be in peril if they left his protection? Just to keep them in fear? To control them? Why would he want to, anyway? He had known Andy's full name, yet he had evinced no indication of recognising theirs when told their first names, nor that he cared less what their surnames might be.

And what about Kit? Was he their willing entrapper, or had he been acting under some sort of duress? Come to think of it, Kit had actually done nothing to lure the Englishmen here. So he must have been in contact with the gang leader to inform him of their plans. Of course, those faxes he supposedly sent to the navy! So how much of what Kit had told them about his background was even partly true?

Andy? What of him? How much worse he looked after his arm had received treatment than before.

Jon recalled the nurse's miming antics. Andy had refused to let himself be given an anaesthetic by the medical staff. He suddenly deduced why.

"Jees-us!" His whispered exclamation in the darkness reached Rick.

"What?" mumbled his partner.

"I've just realised why Andy refused jabs from the nurses."

"So have I," Rick said. "In case they administered a truth drug or something. Is that what you're thinking?"

"Yep," said Jon. "But they can do it any time they like, can't they?"

"Probably not without him – or us, if it comes to that – being aware of it. A prick in the arse in the middle of the night is not exactly going to come unnoticed, is it?"

"I'm too tired to make you rephrase that," Jon remarked sotto voce, "but either they have no intention of playing tricks on us, or they have but in a clandestine way. Which means they don't intend to harm us. Well, not drastically, anyway. Sort of."

"I sure hope you're right about that. Sort of."

They pondered.

"My God, all that digging around in there for the two cut ends of his retracted tendon; it must have been really excruciating."

"It must. Poor old Andy."

Twelve

The nurse who seemed to have been allotted the task of being their informant knocked at their door just after dawn and entered.

"Are you awake?" he called in an undertone.

"Yes, nurse," responded Jon. "Have you any news?"

He sat out of bed as the nurse turned up the ceiling lights. They woke Rick from his shallow slumber.

"Mr Kit came out of surgery half an hour ago. It was a powerful bullet that hit him, and it did a power of damage. One of the surgeons is reporting to Mr Ciampi at this time."

"Is he going to be all right?" Rick demanded anxiously. "Will he recover?"

"Everything that can be done is being done," came the noncommittal answer. "Shall I inform Mr Gregson, or will you?"

"Oh, cheers, but I think we will," replied Jon.

"Not that we really have much to tell Andy," he went on after the nurse had departed. "I'll just nip round and tell him, if he's not asleep."

"Hi, Andy. Awake?"

"What do you think?" said Andy when the light came on. He was already sitting up, as he had been for the past two hours in the darkness. "Have you heard something?"

"Yes, from that same nurse. We're only a couple of doors from you, by the way." Jon told him what they had just learned.

"Where is he now?"

"The nurse didn't say."

Andy started to get up.

"Where do you think you're going?"

"Guess," Andy snapped resentfully. He put on a short, belted, white dressing gown which had been hanging on the side of his bed locker, and a pair of thick soled socks he had been told were in its pockets. He pressed Jon's shoulder. "Sorry." Attired like his friend, he padded into the bathroom, half shutting the door.

"I think there's someone been put in the room between yours and ours," Jon called after him. He sat on the edge of the bed.

"There's someone on either side of me, Jon."

"How's the arm feeling?"

"A bit sore, to be honest."

"I'll bet that's a big understatement."

The lavatory was flushed.

"It'll stop me beating people up for a while! Here, can you help me with this blasted sling?"

Jon went to assist. Andy was trying to wash his hands and face. Jon performed the task for him without releasing the arm from its restraint. Andy gave his thanks, and left while Jon used the toilet himself.

When Jon came out of the bathroom, he found himself alone. He practically ran to the door in time to see Andy emerging from the room between Andy's and theirs.

"Wrong one," Andy muttered, walking by him and making for the first door in the corridor. He pushed it open. There was a low light on in there, and the distinctive clicking and plopping of life-support machinery could be heard. Andy hesitated, clearly upset by the scene before him. A questioning female voice addressed the newcomer. Declining to explain his presence, Andy resolutely entered the room and closed the door behind him.

Jon waited in Andy's room for five minutes or so, then he turned out the light and returned to his own room, where Rick had at last succumbed to sleep, shortly to be accompanied by his partner, equally drained of energy.

A senior nurse rapped at the door persistently until someone bade her enter.

Rick smiled at the severe-looking woman.

"It is way past midday, gentlemen," she declared stiffly. "Mr Ciampi left instructions for you not to be disturbed before now."

Jon had woken.

"Thank you, nurse," said Rick. "How is Mr Henderson?"

She frowned a little.

Alarmed, Rick cried, "Kit! Has he –?"

"Oh, Mr Kit. He has not come round as yet, but he is stable, I have been asked to inform you."

For Andy's sake especially, their relief was heartfelt.

"He means a lot to your friend Mr Gregson," the nurse observed curiously. "He stayed up with the patient for the whole of the night. Kept up a constant flow of talk, whispering in his ear and holding his hand." She studied the men for a sign. "And showed his affection in other ways."

"Perhaps," said Rick, "he believes that speaking to people in a coma can help to keep them from wandering off too far."

"Perhaps," she initially seemed to concede. Then, "That sort of thing normally belongs to family and particularly close friends. Naturally." Her biting tone was laden with regurgitated venom of the kind she had probably been fed since infancy.

The couple held their tongues. If this had been a regular hospital, she would have been given her come-uppance, no messing.

Having not so far goaded them, she redoubled her offensive. "It is disgraceful for foreigners to be let into our state who can then go around spreading their lusts and infections among all and sundry. If he is not out of this county before next week's council meeting, I shall present a Motion for him to be blackballed – and anyone like him who happen to be with him," she added pointedly. "The pastor, my husband, will surely speak to Mr Ciampi about this affair and get him to put a stop to it before it goes any further." She spun on her heels and walked straight into the householder in question.

The saintly nurse emitted a yelp of surprise.

"I won't let 'this affair' tax your little mind any further, Mrs Patterson." He eyed her coldly. "I am sure you have had a long and tiring night, so please do not let us delay you in my house any longer. Thank you for your services."

So saying, he stepped round the woman and walked up to the men in their beds. The redoubtable Mrs Patterson stared at his pear-shaped back for a moment, then beat a swift retreat, not certain in her little mind whether she had been resoundingly commended or castigated for her vigilance. She elected to accept the compliment.

"You showed admirable restraint, both of you." Ciampi smiled broadly, moving easily despite his gross form. "That awful woman is known hereabouts as the Leadville virago."

"Your timing was impeccable, Mr Ciampi," remarked Jon.

They all knew that his arrival had not been merely fortuitous. More importantly, he understood well that they knew.

The arms began waving again. "It is good for men to get along together. All the men on my side of the family get on well together. The women? Well, that is maybe another matter!" He laughed from his belly in slow measures. His listeners' estimation of him took a drastic further tumble.

"I hope you were not too uncomfortable in here. Tonight you must have proper bedrooms. No, I insist. And you will eat with us in about an hour? Excellent! It will only be a light buffet. We always take our main meals in the early evening. You will soon grow accustomed to our ways!"

"But, Mr Ciampi," Rick said, "it is not our intention to impose on your generous hospitality for any longer than Mr Gregson needs to recover from the worst effects of his wound."

Ciampi appeared to disregard this. He smiled chiefly for his own amusement.

"When you are ready to come up, you can go through the door at the far end of this passage and up the stairs. Kit is in good hands. Try to get Mr Gregson to join you."

Ciampi left them. His incongruously light tread faded in the direction he had indicated.

The pair showered and dressed. They checked that their lockable baggage was secured, before going to Andy's room. He wasn't there, so they tapped lightly at the next following door. A small boy and a taller girl came out of the room next to their own, where the man with the injured knee was recovering from his operation. The two pairs tossed a monosyllabic greeting between them and went their separate ways, Rick and Jon entering the dense atmosphere of the sick room, where they found an exhausted-looking Andy alone with Kit, who seemed to them to be wired up to every conceivable contraption capable of substituting the functions of the body's essential organs.

Andy glanced up from his attitude of resting his head on the patient's left shoulder. He had not been roused from sleep but had been articulating into his lover's ear all his hopes for a future together, confiding in him about his so far solitary life, his yearnings for a love which had been eluding him simply because he could never identify himself with what he perceived to be the posturings and cavortings endemic in a lifestyle others had prescribed for themselves. He didn't condemn such people: their behaviour was their own business. Nevertheless, it was because he was so unlike them that he remained totally confident that he held nothing in common with them – at all.

In his shared ignorance, he had shared sincerely-held prejudices with many of his acquaintances and friends, and had presumed that his devoidness of libidinal partiality towards the opposite sex must signify that something quite unrelated was fundamentally wrong with him: Fate had consigned him to a life of abstinence. It was truly this denial of himself that had engendered his feeling that he was completely alone in his private limbo – neither in the one world nor the other.

Andy once again told Kit what he had said to him in the closeness of the train's sleeping compartment, that it was not until he had met Jon and Rick, had been with them and talked long with them that he realised that the house he had been born into had very many mansions: that it was not so much set apart from the general community as he had been misled into believing by some of its more public proponents and opponents alike. It had been a revelation to him, a veritable shower burst of self-discovery. It was in this substantial part of the world that he belonged and wanted to be.

That was what he had been telling Kit, and how Kit owed it to both of them to keep fighting for his life. So much did Andy have to impart, that he had scarcely repeated himself once during his entire vigil, except to impress upon Kit's comatose mind, over and over again, how very much he was loved and needed. It had also been Andy's beneficial opportunity to sort these unaccustomed, resurgent emotions of his into bytes of lucid thought that he himself might comprehend.

"He's rolled his eyes a few times in the past hour," Andy replied to Rick's enquiry. "Dr Trentham tells me that this could be a hopeful sign. Perhaps something of what I've been telling Kit might be getting through to that stupid, beautiful mind of his. Oh, Christ, just look at those bruises!"

"You've got to get some kip, Andy," insisted Jon. "You're looking more of a wreck than ever. You'll be no good to either of you if you go on like this."

Andy's glance darted from one man to the other. "Do you think I'm losing it, lads? Am I being emotionally immature, falling for practically the first available good-looking bloke I meet since you woke me to myself?"

Jon studied the man's face. "Is that what we did? We actually woke you to yourself?" He appraised the unconscious form in the bed. "Hey, I think maybe Kit did that, finally. Perhaps you and he have given each other something precious that relatively few people experience in a lifetime. That does not come from emotional immaturity: innocence, possibly. But that kind of innocence is no bad thing."

"That must be the first time anyone's accused me of being innocent," Andy said wearily, "but I think I know what you're getting at. So I'm not going off my trolley? Not quite?"

Said Rick, "You weren't too naive, were you, when it came to, like, sussing out what Kit had been up to all along? If anything, I was the last to cotton on that he was not all he professed to be. You didn't allow your feelings to blind you to the possibility that he was playing a double game."

Andy weighed this up. "I guessed that there was something troubling him from the outset. I still don't know whether it was that his developing feelings for me were in conflict with his assignment for the Ciampis, or whether it was the assignment itself that was fazing him so much – that holding things back from us was playing on his conscience, or whatever."

"Still, don't you start having doubts about yourself," Jon urged him. "Hold on to what you've got, 'cos, who knows? – even if you two do get separated for any reason, this could very well become a sort of, well, bedrock on which you can build and rebuild your own life almost at will. And how's that for boosting anyone's confidence?"

Andy bestowed on them a smile of gratitude that would carry the couple through the events of that day.

The nurse in charge, who had been called away for five minutes, returned to the room. The men stood back while he made routine checks of his patient and the equipment, then he sat down again at the small corner table where he jotted notes into his charts.

"Mr Ciampi wants us to join him for the family luncheon," Rick informed Andy who had resumed his post immediately the nurse finished.

Andy attentively fondled Kit's thick fair hair. They were both so surrounded by the mesh of rigging attaching Kit to his apparatus that Andy had to be extremely careful not to knock into anything vital.

"You go. I'll stay with him." He lowered his voice. "By the way, I'm now positive that we are in no danger here. Just don't say more than you absolutely have to."

More easily said than done.

It was going to be futile trying to dissuade him, so Jon and Rick left Andy as they had found him, reinforcing Kit's will to live, and strode down the passage towards the door at the far end.

At the top of some stairs was another door which opened on their left interestingly into an annexe to the kitchen. The kitchen itself was to one side of it, extending to the north side of the building which allowed for windows to open on to the walled vegetable and herb garden there. Four or five culinary staff were loquaciously engaged in producing the wonderful aromas permeating that part of the house.

Having paused for only a few seconds to take this in, the strangers passed on through a further door, up a short flight of stairs and, opening a third door, found themselves in a very large square hall opulently furnished in the grand style of the Italian Renaissance alongside what Jon identified as modern and reproduction pieces judiciously chosen to complement the impressive array of old originals. To their right were the front entrance doors leading out onto the colonnade visible through the tall windows flanking them. To the left was a fine ceremonial staircase which divided halfway up, either arm sweeping on to a three-sided gallery which was balustraded with the same delicate, maplewood-railed ironwork that dignified the stairway. Amid the florid plaster work of the ceiling was a huge stained glass depiction of Jupiter ruling the lesser divinities of the Roman world. Sunlight streamed through its glorious colours.

In its effect, this was the inner courtyard of an Italian palazzo which had been superbly roofed over. The rooms of the house would be in the four-storey building surrounding it. Both ends of the upper gallery led, by crimson curtained archways, into the front range which, supported here on deceptively slender pillars, spanned the tile-floored space where arriving visitors would normally be received. The men were to learn later that the floor they were on was at ground level at the rear of the mansion due to the rising site.

Two enormous chandeliers were suspended from the ceiling, and lustres, also of Venetian glass, hung beneath the many wall lights to flash their prismatic hues lambently about the hall and its occupants at the social functions which surely must be held here.

At present the hall was deserted, however. A buzz of activity was audible somewhere upstairs. Guided by their ears, Rick and Jon took to the right arm of the staircase when they reached it. The double doors facing them at the top had been thrown wide apart, so they could see into the big, panelled room with its voluminous window drapes and the two matching sideboards positively groaning under the weight of food laid out on them. Something like twenty-five people of both sexes were in there, standing in chattering groups or lounging about in the ample upholstery just as talkatively.

It was not any undue exertion incurred while climbing that graceful stairway that had set Rick's heart pounding. He was filled with anticipation, trepidation, an undeniable foreboding of inevitable disaster, even, concerning his sister's whereabouts. If she was at large in that great house, she would surely be here in this room, where the family was foregathered for its ritual midday meal.

Both men rapidly scanned the assembly. There was nobody remotely resembling Sarah – or her husband Peter, for that matter. It was a great disappointment.

With overwhelming *buonumore,* Giuseppe Ciampi swooped upon the hesitant Englishmen the moment he espied them.

"Haha! so you have come to join us. Welcome, welcome!"

He fussed and huffed his way round the company, introducing the newcomers to his people – most of them his family, some not, and several who had played a part after last night's fracas. It was hard to fathom why he didn't return the favour by presenting the pair using their names. Perhaps it was because he thought those unimportant, or maybe everyone was all too well aware who the two men were.

Next, Ciampi conducted the couple to one of the sideboards, where he described the fare to them just as solicitously as he had effected the personal introductions.

"Now," he said at length, "please come over here with me."

He led them to the far end of the room where four huge armchairs were arranged at a conveniently low, glass-protected table. He abruptly shooed two people away, then stuffed himself into one of their uncomplainingly vacated seats, indicating to Rick and Jon also to be seated opposite him. They put their plates, piled high at Ciampi's insistence, on the table with their wine glasses which had been filled almost to overflowing by their ebullient host himself. So much for it being 'only a light buffet' meal, as he had described it earlier.

Neither man was especially hungry, delicious though their assortments of comestibles looked and smelled. There was no sign of Sarah, Andy wasn't here to lead their side of the conversation in the way they had agreed that he would in such a contingency as this, and Ciampi's personality today was totally unnerving.

"I am sorry Mr Gregson has not made it," Ciampi commented. "How is Kit, do you know?"

"Little or no change in his condition, I'm afraid," said Jon. "We left Mr Gregson with him."

"Ah, yes," Ciampi murmured to himself, then he changed tack. "I hope you like what you have seen of the house."

"How could anyone not?" The manifest good taste of this family couldn't be faulted, notwithstanding their dubious calling. There was none of that gratuitous brashness which tends to disgrace houses of less cultured newly-rich. This was a home of genteel quality.

Rick's evident sincerity registered positively with their shrewd listener. His eyes softened towards them.

"You may think," he said, "that my biggest sin is Pride. Well, you would be right. It is. It is the one weakness that I have to confess in church every single week of the year, and twice extra at Easter!" He chuckled, then seeing that he had amused his guests, he burst into peals of laughter that turned his not too solid flesh to quivering jelly, and quite a lot of heads in the room.

"Richard Timperley and Jonathan Reynolds, are you not?"

His mood had transformed in a flicker of time. His cold eyes were directed upwards to a subject beyond their backs.

So, Kit really had told all.

The silenced room momentarily swirled round Rick's head, and Jon had a sense of falling into an abyss. Where was Andy who was supposedly trained to handle these desperate situations? Whispering sweet nothings into the ear of that perfidious creep who must have delivered them into the grip of this dangerous rogue, that's where!

It was no use gainsaying who they were. Jon looked blankly in Ciampi's general direction, then nodded meekly.

Immediately, each was shocked when a pair of hands was clasped over his eyes. What they took to be sadistic laughter sniggered among the watchers.

"Hello, Rickie," came Sarah's voice. He was kissed on the back of his head.

He swivelled round in his seat, and Jon tore the hands off his own eyes to behold his sister-in-law standing behind his partner, her face radiant with a tearful smile, and beside her, her husband.

"Sis!" Rick sprang to his feet, negotiated the chair with a bound and embraced his sister fondly. Jon and Peter, meanwhile, hugged one another before changing places.

The onlookers were delighted with the show. Hardly a dry eye, they cheered, clapped and whistled their happiness at this unscheduled reunion.

Rick's questions rushed out. "How are you? What happened to you? How long have you been here? Have they been looking after you all right?"

Ciampi stood up, looking almost as pleased with his stage

management as if he had just landed a commodities market coup. He slapped Rick heartily on the back.

"I am sure that you folks have plenty to talk about. Besides," he grinned, "you are disturbing lunch. So go in there, all of you, and talk among yourselves."

He was pointing to the connecting door to an adjoining room. They went obediently towards it, sister and brother holding one another about the waist.

"Stop," Ciampi cried, "you might as well take your food with you, boys. Ciao!"

They entered what the English would have called a drawing room, again lavishly appointed, but no more overstated than the room's proportions could stand. It was half the length of the one they had just left. Peter closed the door behind them and they crossed to a pair of sofas facing one another in front of the enormous stone fireplace, on either side of which was a door on to the gallery. Opposite their own point of entry was a further door slightly ajar. Jon went over to it, observed that it led to a landing off the gallery with a set of stairs to the higher floors, then shut it to.

Rick was still in a dream. He couldn't orientate himself. Things were changing, it seemed, by the second. Sarah squeezed his hand and gave him her umpteenth kiss.

"Rickie, you look as though you've seen a ghost!"

"Two of you, to be frank," he responded. "It's so marvellous just to know you are alive. I suppose you really are alive, aren't you?"

Peter laughed. "Oh, she's alive all right, I can promise you that!"

She pinched his unsleeved arm.

Her brother had to acknowledge that she was looking as healthy as he had ever seen her, certainly not the miserable figure she'd cut when he viewed the security tapes of her unwillingly accompanying Umberto Ciampi to the boarding gate for the Chicago flight from Manchester Airport. Her hair was more her natural light brown, not quite as dark as she had worn it when he last saw her. Her pale green suit was one he hadn't seen her in, and he noted, now that his mother had alerted him to the situation, that her slender outline was retaining its virginal shapeliness no more.

Jon strode fearlessly into the cabbage patch. "So, you couldn't wait," he asserted, sitting down in a sofa where he was joined by Rick. "I see that you two have already been working very hard to make us respectable uncles!"

"It was the only way I could think of to make you respectable!" retorted Sarah.

Peter grinned. "And she was willing to go to this length to accomplish it, too." He sighed. "Such can be sibling love!"

A man in his late twenties, he stood a little under a metre-ninety, was slim and had the complexion of one whose working life had been spent mostly under the suns of the Indies. His mid-brown hair was short. He had a generous mouth that was somehow so right with those warm brown eyes of his.

Sarah sat closely alongside him, her left arm linking his right. Her new rings sparkled proudly on that hand resting on his sporty-trousered knee.

Rick continued to stare at them. "I-I still can't believe it. How did you get here?"

"By road. How did you?"

"By road."

They laughed.

Rick grew serious. "Are we all safe here?"

"As anywhere, Rick," Peter answered. "In fact, Sarah is alive today only because Giuseppe and his brother Umberto have protected her – and now me, as well."

"I suspect Andy has been coming round to thinking of the Ciampis on those lines," Jon told Rick. "Do you remember what he told us before we came up here?"

Rick gazed at Sarah gravely. "You know, then, that there are people out there who accuse you of doing a terrible thing?"

The other two nodded.

"You mean that horrid Bosnian business," she assumed. "It was a set up, of course. I was nowhere near Switzerland on that day. I was in Chicago."

"Look," Jon intervened, "before we go on, there's another person who should be here."

"Oh, yes, this enigmatic Mr Gregson," said Peter. "Who is he, anyway? The Andy you were just mentioning?"

"He's from my father's department."

"Ah?" Sarah was pensive. "Oh yes, the MI5 1/2, or something equally fanciful."

Jon smiled. "Andy's had a Road to Damascus experience and he's down there nursing a sailor boy who may be dying."

"Who was wounded last night?"

He nodded. "Look," Jon said again, "I'll go down and tell him that we've found you." He rose. "Don't go away again!"

He went back to the infirmary the way he had come. Andy was still not in his room, so he went on to Kit's.

The scene was hardly different from when he and Rick left forty-five minutes ago. He greeted the duty nurse and approached the bed.

"Hi, Andy. Any change?"

Andy merely shook his head without looking up.

"Yes, there is, you know!"

The note of excitement in Jon's voice spurred Andy to sit up. Kit's blue eyes were open and were looking up at their faces.

"Oh, Kit, Kit! You're back! Thank God, you're back!"

Kit gave Andy a languid, loving smile. Those ravishing eyes closed. His head lolled sideways on his pillow.

Appalled, Andy shot to his feet and called out to the nurse, who was already hastening over, "Nurse! Oh, Christ! Is he dead?"

A swift scan of the instruments answered the question immediately.

The nurse felt for the pulse, and placed a hand on his patient's cooling brow. "Mr Kit has come out of his coma and is now sleeping naturally!"

Andy let his head fall on Jon's shoulder. He wept for sheer happiness and relief.

"I have to call a doctor right away, so if you wouldn't mind –"

The two men co-operatively moved to a corner of the room out of the way.

A doctor came in presently with another nurse, made a few tests, then the three of them commenced a complicated series of adjustments to the mass of equipment keeping Kit alive. One machine was disconnected altogether and wheeled to the far wall. Drips were checked once more, bottles and pouches removed and replaced. Finally, the doctor came over to the men, smiling broadly.

"Well," she told Andy, "it seems you and our technology together have saved that young man's life. Though I have to say, in view of his condition when he arrived, I didn't give him much of a chance for recovery. His prognosis was decidedly poor. I think it was you who tipped the balance, Mr Gregson. I'm sure of it. You must be very devoted to him, so I'm very pleased for the both of you."

She smiled and took his hand. "He is over the worst now. He still needs plenty of careful nursing before he will be up there batting again. Meantime, you must leave him to sleep – and you get some sleep, too, for goodness sake, else you will become seriously sick yourself. That arm dressing of yours will need changing again later. So, blow! Scram! Get outa here, man!" She gave them both a firm shove towards the door.

Glancing once more at the man whom, he recognised, he unrealistically wanted to be his future, he quietly thanked the medical staff, and permitted himself to be escorted from the room by Jon, who took him next door.

Once in his own room, he flopped down exhausted on his bed. He put his head in his one hand.

"Jon," he groaned, "Jon, Jon! he's going to be OK. Christ knows, I honestly thought I'd lost Kit almost as soon as I'd found him. I think I told him more about me than I thought I knew about myself."

"Never mind, Andy. With a bit of luck, he won't be able to recall the worst bits to his conscious memory."

"Thanks for that, mate." He grinned at him through the unstoppable tears.

"I have some more good – nay, thrilling tidings for you," Jon declared, "if you can bear to take it just now."

Andy looked at him expectantly. "Don't talk shit, man. I can take anything." He jutted out his chin. "Here, sock it to me!"

Jon playfully obliged. Andy caught Jon's hand in his own and kissed it. "Thanks for what you and Rickie have done for me, Jon. I love you both for it."

Jon smiled back. "'There is more joy in heaven over every sinner that repenteth...'!"

Andy stood up. They embraced.

"Now, will you listen to my news?" Jon persisted, nudging the other man away.

"Well, go on. Get on with it," barked Andy with mock impatience. "I'm waiting."

"Right, then. Do you think you can remember why we came to the States in the first place?"

Andy concentrated hard. "Er, yes. Something about your sister-in-law and her hubby, wasn't it?" He let forth a burst of chuckling: "They're here, aren't they!"

He laughed all the more at Jon's blank amazement. "Giuseppe told me this morning," he explained.

He sat back on the bed, Jon following suit.

"Oh, 'Giuseppe', is it?" a note of dismay slipping in. "Since when do we consort with the Mob on first-name terms?"

"In my job, Jon, you make friends wherever you can. We can't usually afford the luxury of scruples. Besides," Andy's bleary eyes met Jon's in earnest, "Giuseppe Ciampi's lot almost certainly are not part of the Mob, any more than are Umberto's. They are strictly freelance. Having said that, as the police have no record against this man, it's always been accepted by our office that, of the two, our signore runs a comparatively straight operation here and across the States."

"And what about the gunfight last night?" demanded Jon. "That was hardly an example to set for aspiring honest brokers. 'The Ciampi Business School,'" he ironically proclaimed, his right index finger 'reading' along the top line of an imaginary advertisement, and working down the poster; "'Courses include: Successful abduction techniques; How to train your own private army; Practical demonstrations on competition elimination; Private health care on command; Lots more professional advice for the independent-minded, free-wheeling entrepreneur'!" He shook his head in disgust. "I suppose we knew that yours is a dirty business: you told us as much, but this certainly puts a pinprick in the fuck-rubber."

"Tut, tut!" Andy coolly surveyed his critic. "Such eloquence sadly going to waste."

"And what was with all the theatricals, like those black balaclavas they had on?"

"Practicals, not theatricals, my friend. They made them less visible for one thing: for another, well, why tell everyone who you are unnecessarily, especially if they'd prefer not to know?"

"Why the hell didn't you mention that there was another branch of the Ciampis here, then?"

"I thought, on balance, it was better not to raise everyone's hopes too much. Just after I got to Chicago, Sir Rupert rang me. One of the things he told me was that Department data files showed that the home of the Colorado branch was near to Leadville. The cleaning business belongs to Umberto, anyhow.

"For all their championing of the family, the brothers don't get along, by all accounts. There's jealousy on Umberto's side. He's the eldest, and has been far outshone by Giuseppe in business and in his private life. Giuseppe contracted a previous marriage with one of those oil heiresses who intermittently rise out of obscurity in this country. She died less than two years after in an air accident. From our own viewpoint, he might be a well-known businessman, but how far could he be trusted, really, if our interests came into conflict with those of the Ciampi clan?

"Giuseppe told me one hell of a lot this morning. He was here for – God, I don't know – forty minutes or so? And – wait for it – Kit's mother is his wife's youngest sister. So Kit has separate connections with both main branches, his sister being the wife of Umberto's son, as he admitted to us himself before I lost my rag with him."

"Good God! And Ciampi told you all this?"

"Yes. I told you, he was very candid with me."

"Why should he be?" asked Jon suspiciously.

Andy shrugged. "I'm not too sure, to be truthful. But, by the same token, he has no reason to lie to me, has he?"

"It's funny, we didn't meet his wife upstairs just now, even though it was supposed to be the family lunch. I dare say she's been down here to see how her darling nephew is getting along?"

"Not a bit of it, no."

"So you haven't seen her either."

"No. And, incidentally, that aunt of Kit's in Nottingham: she's another sister."

"Sheesh!" Jon exclaimed. He remembered something. "Hey, what about all that crap of Kit's on the train, when he seemed so keen to be talking to real English people? I mean, that must all have been put on – an act. He had been detailed to stick to us, hadn't he! Then, after that other poor English couple were murdered, and we all feared that Kit's public association with you might put his life on the line in the same way, he became glued to us well and truly. How very opportune for him!"

"You don't like Kit, do you?"

"Oh, come on! He's just a dodgy piss-artist, a bloody sham. And, hey, it wasn't me who bashed him up. No, really, If I could trust him, I would think him a very personable and wonderful guy. If I truly thought that the persona he was portraying to us was his own, I would think him attractive in every way. But how can I, Andy, with the best will in the world?"

Andy regarded Jon steadily. It was about time he was put right once and for all.

"The man who nearly died last night, Jon, was visiting some university pals, exactly as he claimed to me he was, when his sister's father-in-law telephoned him. Umberto had set up a watch on us all right, but he had other intelligence, as well. His wasn't the only organisation interested in what I, specifically, was doing. But he fell for the yarn about me meeting friends and going on to the Rockies for a trekking vacation. I know that because he rang Giuseppe to tell him to keep a precautionary eye open, but not to worry about us being on his Colorado patch, so to speak.

"It was after that, at some stage or other I haven't determined, when his lackeys discovered that I had another shadow. Well, two others, to be precise."

"Two?!"

"Yes, Jon. More of that anon. Umberto contacted Kit, like I said, and told him how important it was to keep us under surveillance. Remember, Kit is a military man with specialised training himself. He was advised to keep his distance from us and on no account to approach us. Kit ignored that totally, so his enthusiasm when he was talking with us in the dining car was genuine enough."

"Hang on, why was it so important to trail us if Umberto believed that we had no interest in their affairs, including the little matter of Sarah?"

"Kit was detailed to protect us, Jon. To protect us," he stressed. "And, I should add, to keep the families informed of any changes in circumstances."

"It was Rick and I who kept watch the other night on the train, not Kit. So that both of you could get some sleep."

"And it was Kit who had his gun in his hand under our pillow for the remainder of the night. A top-rated Smith and Weston. He tried not to let me see it by bundling it in his shirt which he then stuck beneath the pillow, but it's difficult to hide something like that from the person you are sharing a bed with! I didn't let on to him about it, though.

"Something else, Jon – yes, Kit must have been play-acting when he was asking me who Ciampi was. He was also all too well aware of the likelihood that there were predatory espionage groups on the train. When he and I were drinking in the saloon, it was Kit who alerted me – not the other way round – to those two punks watching us. So, when you injured his feelings and he tried to leave our suite, he would afterwards have stood guard somewhere in the corridor, I know that for certain. Try to understand his frustration, Jon, when he had to put up with all that lousy diatribe from you without being able to defend himself with the truth. Giuseppe has confirmed that Kit would have known nothing about Sarah and Peter until I apprised him of our real reasons for going to Denver.

"Oh, and another thing: Kit's biggest porky was his story about being due at the Naval Training Base – today, actually," Andy calculated. "In fact, he isn't expected there until next week!" He tutted once more. "What a terrible, terrible fib!"

Jon was silent for a while, letting all this sink in.

"Andy, only Kit could have let this Giuseppe guy know we were coming to Leadville. He knew that we wanted to look round the factory premises, and he even came with us."

"That's right. One of his faxes from Denver was to inform him that Leadville was our destination, and who Rick and you were. But he also warned that we were being followed. And again, it was the watchful Kit who first noticed the sophisticated trail that had been planned to a tee: vehicles dogging us, taking over one another's lead by executing quite innocent-looking manoeuvres on the highway. Somehow, our pursuers had received advance intelligence about our rail destination so, though we probably succeeded in leaving behind those of their number on the train, some more of them were already there waiting to meet us. For all Kit could have known at the time he spoke to Guiseppe from Denver, if it hadn't been for him calling in his uncle's troops to pull us out secretly, we may very well have led that particular group of bastards straight to Sarah."

"Why, is that what they're after? To capture Sarah?"

"No, Jon. To kill her."

Thirteen

Jon dropped heavily into a chair. "Kill Sarah? Oh shit, no, Andy. That's horrendous. Did Ciampi tell you that?"

"He substantiated my own theory, yes. I put that to him, you see."

Andy sat back on to his bed. "It seems that when Umberto apparently abducted Sarah from the airport, he –"

"Stop there a sec," Jon interjected. "Just why did she allow herself to be taken like that from a busy departure lounge in broad daylight? That's a crucial question."

"But I still don't know the answer to that one. We'll have to ask Sarah herself. Have you seen her yet, by the way?"

"Certainly, I just left her and Peter talking to Rick. I came down to get you, really. I must say, though, she doesn't strike me as looking a bit like someone frightened for her life."

Andy absorbed this with fascination. "All Giuseppe could tell me was that, once Umberto got her into his custody, he was sent instructions by – guess who? – The Light of the World, of course. He had to force her to implicate herself in the planned assassination of the Bosnian president by writing that fake message on hotel notepaper, then he was to eliminate her, get her out of the way double quick.

"Now, he might have his faults – well, he does have them, but murder has never been on his agenda. Besides, I think he got a bit of a shine for our Sarah. He carried out this job personally because he owed a favour to a certain individual who, I imagine and hope, might turn out to be a link to The Light's hierarchy. Umberto also received a substantial fee for his trouble."

"He pretended to have killed her?"

"That's it in one. He hid her somewhere – Giuseppe doesn't know or care where, until Anxious Hubby turns up, having quickly done a brilliant job blowing away all Umberto's elaborate smoke screens. In order not to expose himself any further, Umberto captures Peter too, and hides him away, until The Light learns through press reports of Peter's disappearance. They begin to nose round. Umberto's near panic. Gets his brother to help him. Brings them both here. A fire to destroy the evidence – probably the fire. And now we're here, as well."

"And quite a lot of other people, by all accounts!" remarked Jon acidly. "Considering that we thought we were being so clever, so careful not to alarm anyone, getting up to all kinds of subterfuge to divert attention from ourselves, it seems instead that we've been acting like magnets attracting Christ knows how many malignant groups into our wake, with people dropping dead all round us, finding ourselves in the middle of a gun battle, Kit and you being wounded –" Jon paused for breath. "Jesus, Andy, out there baying for our blood at this very minute we may by now have the Cosa Nostra, the Black Hand, Bader-Meinhoff, the IRA – not to mention the CIA and the State Troopers!" He leaned towards Andy and lowered his voice to nearly a whisper. "Andy, do you think something went wrong somewhere?"

Andy regarded the other stonily. He grunted with pain when he attempted to move his injured arm. After the loss of so much sleep, he really was being worn down by this discussion.

"It's easy to be sarcastic, mate. As things are turning out, it's becoming obvious that we should never have set out on this mission at all."

Jon sat back.

Andy continued, "I honestly don't think this is our fault – or mine, rather. It isn't so much that we are acting as magnets: we seem to have got ourselves sucked into a situation that was going to happen anyway.

In spite of your Doomsday scenario, Giuseppe knows of just two groups who are looking for Sarah."

"Those being?"

"The Light of the World we know about, and an international, extreme right-wing religious bunch hell-bent on divine vengeance for the shooting of one of their illustrious number."

"I might have guessed religion would play a part in this débâcle somewhere," grumbled Jon contemptuously. "And who was it who did in that English couple, and who has been following us, and who was doing all the shooting last night?"

"Giuseppe tells me that his own people didn't fire a shot. They were prepared to, to defend us, Jon. Yes, us. Remember, it was Kit who suggested we take cabins at that particular motel. Do you remember, as well, that he didn't want us to go out again till morning – that is, giving Uncle Guiseppe time to pluck us from the vipers' nest. We went out anyway, not knowing any of that.

"Giuseppe's kind don't get where they do by not making sure they are fully informed at all times. He has friends everywhere. Kit was only one source of his intelligence."

"Meaning?"

"Meaning that he has known all along that Umberto's strategy was flawed. What first Peter worked out, then me, has been tumbled to by these other guys as well. Giuseppe has been anticipating trouble for days. He's more than a bit pissed-off with his dear brother about all this, as you can imagine.

"Look, Jon. Give me a chance to get some kip, will you? They're going to re-dress my arm later, so I'll go up and find you all after that. OK?" He began removing his hospital gown.

"OK. You are looking a bit shattered, to say the least." Jon grinned, and held the other's hand for a moment. "I get upset too easily sometimes. No hard feelings?"

Andy smiled at him. "Fuck you," he said softly. "And good night!" He rolled over into his bed and shut his eyes.

Jon went back upstairs to where he had left Rick and his sister. The luncheon party in the next room had long since dispersed, for all was now quiet in there.

"Hi, folks!" he called breezily. "First the good news. Andy's getting some shut-eye and won't be joining us till later on. The excellent news is that Kit has come out of his coma and is probably strolling gently through the Land of Nod hand-in-hand with Andy, even as I speak."

He sat down next to Rick. He glanced from him to Sarah to Peter and back again. The mood was sombre.

"That's great about Kit," said Rick. "But I'm surprised you are being so expansive about it."

"It's for Andy's sake. Besides, he's been clarifying a few things for me. Anyhow, don't tell me: your news is not so good. Right?"

"Have you looked outside lately?" enquired his partner.

Jon jumped up and crossed to one of the huge windows overlooking the south side of the grounds. All around, mountains soaring to enormous heights formed an awesome backdrop to the picture shaping up below. The grass and shrubberies on this side of the wire-and-post stock fence which, from Jon's outlook, looped round to the right beyond the visible part of that gravelled area at the front of the mansion where they had dismounted last night from the personnel carrier, were being patrolled by scores of armed gunmen, including a substantial contingent of uniformed police. The fence also went round the rear of the residence to the left, and presumably encircled the whole. Outside it, cattle were peacefully ruminating, occasionally sending their bovine stares of curiosity at the unaccustomed activity going on just beyond snuffling range of their wet muzzles.

"Bloody hell," breathed Jon, "is war breaking out, or something?"

"I'm afraid it did last night, Jon," Sarah told him.

Jon faced round. "But Andy has just told me that Mr Ciampi claims his people didn't fight last night."

"We didn't, Jon," said Peter. "We went down to snatch you out of the mess you got yourselves into."

"'We'? You were there? You were part of that petty militia got up like some kind of SAS force?"

Husband and wife both nodded.

"Jeez!" Jon turned away and paced to the far end of the room, where he slumped on to a chaise longue by the panelled wall.

"Then you must have been in the vehicle that brought us back here."

They were.

Rick was angry now. "Why didn't you let on to us, then?" he remonstrated. "We were sitting within feet of you, and you decided not to make yourselves known. That's not natural, Sarah. Sorry, it's not!"

"It was having those wounded men with us," Sarah tried to explain. "After all that's been happening, I wanted our reunion to be in calmer circumstances without it being spoiled – overshadowed by your worries for your friends."

"That's all very well, but you knew that we were OK. You might have had the decency to let us know that you were, as well. Our worries for you, my sister, were still infinitely greater than for anyone else just then, you know."

"What the hell have you two been up to?" Jon shouted across the room at them, leaping up again. "Do you know that there are people at home desperately worried about your safety and your very tarnished reputations? Can't you imagine, Sarah, what bloody misery you have plunged the family into? Have you made one single attempt to contact them to put their minds at ease? Don't you know what is happening out there as a consequence of what you have been accused of doing: that hundreds more people are being killed and maimed right now in Europe because of it; that an innocent young couple – on their honeymoon, damn you! – were slaughtered on the train coming here, we think just because so-called secret agent Andy Gregson accidentally bumped into them? What bloody mayhem have you started? I mean, does all this carry-on mean that you really do know who tried to kill that president; that you were implicated in some filthy conspiracy or other?" Jon rushed back to them, clenching his fists to his sides. "Were you? Were you? Were you?"

He stood there, half crouched in his fury, his eyes ablaze with indignation.

Sarah had begun to sob on her husband's shoulder halfway through Jon's angry denunciation, shaking her head in denial at each indictment aimed at her.

Peter tried to intercede. "You're terribly wrong, Jon, you really are," he muttered through clenched teeth. He knew his wife was being sapped of her characteristic firepower by the demanding twins developing in her womb. His job was not to worsen the heat just now.

Rick came over to Jon. "Don't, love. Please don't. This isn't helping."

"Well?" roared Jon, unmollified. "Why are you both standing there? Shouldn't you go and put on your balaclavas and be out there with your odious mates to defend what little is left that you can still think worth defending?"

Rick threw a hard slap at Jon's already livid face. It sent Jon to the floor, causing him to knock over the fine table that stood between the sofas.

Weeping himself now, Rick knelt down by his partner and gathered him up in his arms. All these weeks of enforced self-control with their pent-up hurt and frustration welled up within him, and he howled like his world was crashing in upon him and his beloved Jon, whom he had never seen engulfed by such rages as he had displayed just lately during all their eventful years together. He could no longer staunch the flood that had to come.

For long, long minutes they clung together. They could not bear to move from that spot where their sole compulsion was to bolster each other's love and their bond. In spite of the jovial banter and bonhomie they had managed to sustain, their relationship had undergone acute strains in recent weeks. It had never actually faltered for one moment – till now, when Jon had launched his unbridled tirade against his sister, but Rick understood that it was as much out of Jon's love for him, as for all the other reasons he had stated, that he had made that attack.

One of the doors quietly opened, and a grizzled head peered in, drawn by the raised voices and crash of furniture. Giuseppe Ciampi took in that moving scene at a glance, and left silently, comprehending all.

When Rick and Jon eventually came to their feet, they were alone. The other couple had fled, it seemed, while the men were engrossed.

They restored the table to its former position and sat down again, feeling unutterably miserable. One of the house staff knocked and entered.

"Mr and Mrs Simpson have asked me to see if there is anything you require, gentlemen. May I fetch you something? Tea, perhaps?" It was as if even she was privy to their inner conflicts and wanted to alleviate them.

Rick returned her kindly smile. "Thank you very much. That would be nice."

"Don't you go away, now. I'll be back in just a moment."

The men sat wordlessly for two or three minutes. Ridiculously, it crossed Rick's mind how totally inappropriate were their blue fashion jeans to such a sumptuous classical ambience as this veritable palace. His reflex spasms of chuckling were vindicated to Jon by explanatory gestures of the hand, and the profoundly unhappy men rediscovered the consolation of companionable mirth.

The servant returned empty-handed. "I am Eloise, gentlemen, Mr and Mrs Ciampi's housekeeper. I have instructed that your tea should be taken to your own room. Is that all right?"

Her petite figure looked well in the powder blue of her uniform, the livery colour of all the house staff: it so complemented her nut-brown complexion. Her teeth matched the spotless, white starched apron she wore. Unlike the other female members of the multi-ethnic staff, she did not wear a cap.

"That will do very well, Eloise," said Rick.

They stood and made for the nearer door to the gallery, but Eloise marched up the room to the far door onto the landing. "This way, gentlemen," she sang. "Mr Ciampi has had a room prepared for you."

They exchanged glances, then followed her compliantly up the wooden staircase. Though there was a further flight to a higher floor, she turned right at the top of the first towards the rear of the house. Plenty of light entered the broad passageway through windows on their left, the sills of which were a few metres above the roof with its stained glass centrepiece covering the great hall, or courtyard. They passed by the doors to many rooms on their right. At the end of the passage, they turned the left-hand corner and walked another fifty metres or so.

The housekeeper stopped, opened the nearest door and stepped aside to let the men go in ahead of her.

The room was a marvellous marriage of the in-built neo-classical with the ultramodern – and it worked. A single huge window admitted adequate light through this east-facing wall of the house. Its furnishings were mostly of teak, and the carpet and fabrics, in the main, an olive green warmed by rusts and golds. The whole exuded unsurpassed luxury, for their king-size bed was a four-poster such as they'd never slept in, with beautiful old-gold satin drapes to pull round the bed's privileged occupants.

Just then, a white lad and a black, both clad in the household blue, looking for all the world like hotel bellhops of a previous era, brought in their luggage on a four-wheeled trolley. They placed the cases and bags on the floor, then they checked visually with Eloise before opening the door to the room adjoining on the left and taking Andy's name-tagged baggage into it.

A housemaid arrived wheeling in a food trolley with their tea on a silver tray, which she placed on a table in the window, then left.

"Do you think everything will be to your satisfaction?" the housekeeper asked, smoothing down the already rumple-free satin bedcover.

The young men came back from the next room and closed the door. They waited for further orders.

"It is a lovely room, thank you, Eloise." Jon went over to the window. Still that paramilitary deployment outside. There must be hundreds of armed guards and police down there.

The house staff were getting on with their daily tasks as though nothing unusual were occurring.

"These are Michael and Leo. They are to be your valets during your stay. Anything you need, just ask them. Oh, and another thing, your car is downstairs in the garage. Next to Mr Gregson's room there is a service lift which you may use to reach it. The keys to your vehicle are on that table over yonder, d'you see?"

"Where is the bedroom of my sister and her husband?" enquired Rick.

"Mrs Simpson is your sister, sir? Their room is right next door to yours on this side." Eloise indicated the connecting door opposite the bed side of the room. She had known full well Rick's relationship to Sarah, but it was good manners not to presume such things without being told at first hand.

"Well, if you don't need me for the present, perhaps you will excuse me?" She left, closing the door behind her.

"May we unpack your bags for you, sirs?" enquired the slim red-haired valet who, like his colleague, was about eighteen years old.

The couple had never had such a decision to make before so, to hell with it...

"Yes, thank you, Michael," replied Rick without consulting Jon, as if they took such service for granted.

"Yes," hrrmphed Jon inaudibly.

"It won't take you long. We haven't brought a lot of things with us," remarked Rick.

The valets referred to the name tags, purposefully moved the cases about so that Leo tackled Jon's baggage and Michael Rick's, and began systematically to open them and put the clothes into the couple's respective wardrobes and chests.

While this was going on, the pair sat at the table and poured their lemon tea. They stared out of the window at that frightening sight below, saying nothing much, but thinking frantically. Was all this to protect Sarah and Peter, all of the English guests or the Ciampi family as well? They still could not comprehend how Sarah, by not denying it, had more or less confessed to complicity in the presidential assassination attempt in Geneva. It was utterly incredible.

Michael removed a plastic shopping bag from Rick's holdall. It contained their rolled-up soiled clothing destined for a laundromat somewhere, but, under the covert gaze of their owners, Michael diligently took out and unfurled each garment one by one, so that Leo could afterwards, just as carefully, put them back in again. If they derived some quirky pleasure from this unproductive occupation, they might have had the delicacy not to indulge it in the presence of the bodies responsible.

"Excuse me, sirs," called the spokesman, Michael.

"Yes, Michael?" said Jon, pivoting round as though distracted from an alternative matter.

"This laundry – may we take it away? It will be ready for you again tomorrow," he promised.

"Of course. Thank you."

Rick and Jon viewed their departing backs with some bemusement.

Left to themselves at last, they ensured that the three doors were firmly secured, then spontaneously commenced slowly to undress one another. Rick was once more able to express his heartbreak to his lover, who kissed the tears from his cheeks and the sobs from his lips, who rolled him tenderly, tenderly with himself, into their downy quilt and transported him, as only he knew how, to happier climes. There they remained for several restful and satisfying hours before fulfilling themselves amid cries of shared passion.

It was a further half hour before they rose and showered together, oiling and massaging one another all over until climaxing afresh. As it was so often with them, it felt as if they had been lovers for only a few short weeks, so inventive could their lovemaking be.

Towelling themselves, they were able to hear movements in Andy's room. Wearing only his light grey briefs, Rick went over to their friend's door and knocked at it, while Jon switched on some lamps and electronically drew the window drapes, excluding the mountain twilight.

Andy swung the door wide. He was dressed except for trousers and his bare feet.

"Hi! So you're finally awake. I've been knocking for half an hour, but the door was locked." He spied the wrecked state of their bed, and grinned salaciously. "I see you've been making up for lost time," he declared, cupping Rick's ample bulge in his hand and giving him a jiggle. Jon, coming up behind Rick, retaliated, causing Andy to squeal.

They went into his room, which was illuminated by a crystal ceiling fitment. It was just as attractively furnished as their own – its colour scheme being predominantly red and green, though the bed was not a four-poster. He offered them seats.

"Well, it makes a change for us to be in your room!" exclaimed Rick, glancing round. The luggage contents had been stowed away. "Did the peerless Leo and Michael do your unpacking for you?"

Andy frowned quizzically. "No. A manservant calling himself Jonas did it, actually."

"Bah th' 'eck!" cried Rick, reviving his north country dialect, "theer's no expense speered, is theh? We've got a lad each wot dus!"

"Wot does what?" Jon wanted to know.

"Don't let's ask them," Andy suggested wisely.

They laughed.

"How are the invalids then?" enquired Rick.

"They promise me that Kit's enjoying a natural sleep. He shows no sign of wanting to wake up, which I suppose is OK, but I do so want to talk to him, now he's conscious. But obviously I can't until he wakes by himself."

"And the arm?"

Jon interposed, "And why did you refuse to have an anaesthetic last night? They'd have had to probe about inside the wound for ages to make sure all the glass was out, then there'd have been the repair work. Afterwards, did they use staples or stitches to close it up? Either way, it must have been bloody agony for you."

Andy's face darkened at the recent memory of it. "I wouldn't have refused, had I known what I do now," he owned. "We weren't sure at the time what we had landed ourselves into, were we?"

"And we are now? I'm delighted to hear it!" Jon declared.

"How's the arm now?"

"Oh, that's nothing, Rickie. It was dressed a while ago, and doesn't need another dressing till tomorrow."

"That's really brilliant, Andy," said Rick. "I wish we had better news to meet you with, though."

"Tell me the worst."

Rick related the happenings between Jon and Sarah, and Sarah's astonishing unwillingness to repudiate any involvement in the terrorist attack. "And, of course, you'll have seen the insanity going on outside, I suppose?"

"I've been outside with Giuseppe, as it happens."

"Gosh, we are pally, aren't we!"

"In fact, Jon, yes, we are. Our Whitehall assessment of Giuseppe Ciampi is accurate enough. Doesn't the presence of the cops tell you that we are on the right side of the law here?"

"I hoped it did, yes, but we can't accept everything at face value, can we?"

"Spoken like an intelligence agent in the making!" Andy came back. "No, the thing is, Jon, Giuseppe is being brutally honest with us."

Rick came in, "Did he tell you that Sarah and Peter were among the 'commandos' who picked us up last night?"

"No. But I'm not surprised, really. Not now. You said, Jon, that we can't take everything at face value. Well, that equally applies to Sarah's reaction to you. Maybe she and Peter said nothing for a reason. I don't know."

"That has occurred to me, to be truthful," Jon admitted. "Perhaps I came on a bit heavy."

Rick gave him a lugubrious glare. "Shit, we both know you did. But, I must confess, she made even me believe there was a case for her to answer."

"We can question her later."

"OK, Andy, but how about telling us what the blazes is going on outside?" Rick had stood up and pulled the window curtains aside. In the relative darkness, he could make out knots of individuals moving about, some towards the house, others in the opposite direction. Maybe it was a duty relief.

As the trio grew accustomed to the gloom, they could spot the people huddled behind shrubs, while some were cautiously posting themselves much farther out among the rock formations of the mountainside. This was not an easy position to defend, if such was their intent, for the wild hills gave an enemy the potentially decisive advantages of elevation and surprise. Andy inferred this to the couple as a further indication of Giuseppe's normally non-violent way of doing business. It was the reason, he said, why there were so many personnel here to protect the property.

Andy had been introduced by Ciampi to the police captain in charge of the operation, it being billed only as a counter-insurgency exercise.

"Why didn't Ciampi involve us in all this imparting of information?" Rick queried a trifle tetchily.

"He says he came personally to your door at 5 o'clock, but couldn't get an answer! Need I say more?"

The couple shrugged to one another and smiled sheepishly at Andy as they returned to their chairs.

"Anyhow, lads, we have been asked to join him for dinner privately in his suite. It will be just the five of us, and him. Oh, and by the way, they dress for dinner in this establishment!"

He thought his companions' alarmed features hilarious.

"In that case," asserted Jon, "they'll have to accept us as we are, or we dine in our room."

Peering at their state of virtual undress, Andy retorted, "If you're proposing to go like that, you'd better dine in your room – attended to by your manservants!" He laughed again. "No, you plonkers, we are excused tuxedos, naturally. This will be a purely informal affair, Giuseppe assures us."

Fourteen

At seven, Eloise the housekeeper came for them. The trio trooped behind her down the passage, more or less suitably attired for a purely-informal-affair, provided there was no objection to the naked shirt sleeves resultant upon the couple's impulsive separation from their Smarter-Man-About-Cheshire outfits. Furthermore, a wretched civil servant had needed to be firmly constrained to put on his one and only necktie. Admittedly, he'd made no worse a job of the knot single handedly than of the one they had seen him behind in his chief's Whitehall office; no better either, so Jon had fixed it for him – the tie's short end still sloppy and teeth-marked – while Rick forced the recalcitrant Andy's arm behind his back.

They were shown into a modestly proportioned dining room at the front of the house. Sarah and Peter and their host were already there, standing about with drinks in their hands, prepared to take their seats at the candlelit oval dining table as soon as the three men arrived. Light orchestral music was softly filling in the background. Rick and Jon both embraced the other couple despite what had gone before. Sarah gave Jon a confidential extra hug. At last, Andy was presented to the pair he had come to America to find.

The seating arrangement divided the couples so that Andy and Sarah flanked Giuseppe, and Peter sat between Rick and Jon, who was placed next to Sarah. She appeared ravishing in a simple, smoke-grey cocktail gown that flattered her larger self. Their host and the man in her life both considerately removed their jackets before taking their seats.

"My wife is presiding over the family meal downstairs," Giuseppe advised the company. "She hopes to become acquainted with you three later in the evening," he added with an unmistakable lack of conviction. He looked at Rick and Jon. "I thought that you had decided to leave us when I couldn't raise you this afternoon. However, Eloise vouched for your being ensconced in your room. Are you all comfortable enough?"

Promised that they were extremely so, he signalled for the meal to begin. A senior manservant assisted Eloise herself in serving the first course.

"Where are the police being quartered, Giuseppe?" asked Peter.

"In the cellar next to the garage," was the reply. "Not the wine cellars, I hasten to add. That would be stretching trust too far, wouldn't it!" Those cold eyes were capable of taking on a modicum of warmth when they gleamed with good humour. "It's the one we have no regular use for. They've taken up key positions in the surrounding hills, Captain O'Connor tells me." He slurped his consommé. "I understand your cops aren't armed over there in England."

"Not usually," confirmed Andy.

"What is going on, Mr Ciampi?" asked Rick, his eyes meeting his sister's momentarily. He split and buttered a portion of Andy's roll for him.

"Merely an exercise, so far as it goes." Giuseppe wiped his mouth with his napkin. "But last night was a major incident for a peaceful little town like Leadville. Over there they don't take kindly to gun fighting. Has Andy told you anything?"

Jon answered. "Andy told me some things, which I passed on to Rick."

"They do know about some of it, but I think it would be better for you to say what you want in your own way, if you don't mind."

"I intend to, Andy."

It was finally a suitable moment for Sarah to speak. "Look, I – I want you boys to understand something first. I wanted to tell you this afternoon, but everything started to happen too fast, and I was so stung by what Jon said. I know what it looks like, but I really haven't been able to get in touch with anyone since I was abducted. I couldn't even get hold of Peter. He traced me in the end, just as you did. How do you think I've been feeling all this time, Jon? It hasn't been a bed of roses for me, you know."

Jon raised his eyebrows and gazed deliberately about the lovely room. "Yes, I can see that you have had a very hard time of it."

He avoided the glare he could sense was smouldering in Rick's eyes. What he had said earlier in the day and a moment ago was no more than he knew to be exercising his troubled partner's mind, but he was more free to express those anxieties. Rick's parental family, like many notably close ones, tended not to grasp the nettles growing up like screens around those thorny internal questions common to all families, but Jon never flinched from bearing any temporary odium that his mildly contentious words might engender within Rick's family from time to rare time, especially if they produced positive results for Rick.

Who earnestly regarded his sister across the table. "They are all frantic and broken-hearted at home, Sarah, not knowing whether you and Peter are alive or dead. Some of the press have been stirring things up as well, pointing accusing fingers at Mum and Dad – all of us, as though what you'd done was a consequence of your background."

"But I haven't done anything wrong."

"Then why don't you come out and say so? What could be more simple?"

Sarah looked helplessly at her husband.

"You've met my mother, both of you," said Peter. "Hasn't it occurred to you that there might be a connection?" He paused to give this thought fermentation time.

Andy frowned. "What about your mother, Peter?"

Rick said, "Because she's Serbian, do you mean?"

"God, yes, of course!" breathed Jon.

"And why did no one bother to mention this to me before?" Andy demanded, his annoyance roused. "There we have a civil war going on between the Bosnian Moslems and the Bosnian Serbs backed by neighbouring Serbia, and the Bosnian Croats backed by Croatia. Then the Moslem President of Bosnia is shot at, and a UNESCO official is accused of carrying it out – an official who also happens to be the daughter-in-law of a Serbian woman! God, give me strength!"

Rick and Jon looked suitably abashed.

"She's a sort of countess, isn't she?" Jon put to Peter.

"There are no inherited titles now, officially. But, yes, I suppose it's equivalent to that. But that isn't really the issue. It's my little nephew and niece in Belgrade, the Serbian capital. They were snatched from a school bus four weeks ago by a band of international terrorists, puppets of The Light of the World."

With the full, livid wrath of British Intelligence poised to explode about their heads, the conversation abruptly ceased when the door opened and the fish course was wheeled in.

"Have you been to Colorado before?" enquired Giuseppe coolly.

Andy swallowed hard and proceeded to regale the company with highlights of the skiing holiday he'd had, until the staff left them, by which time he had calmed down, mellowed by the sight and smell of the delectable thing set before him.

"Well, Peter? Giuseppe prompted, "what were you about to say?"

"Ah, it was when I rang my mother from Lake Balaton in Hungary, where Sarah and I were on our honeymoon, that she told me that my sister had phoned her from Belgrade to tell her about the dreadful thing that had happened. I should explain to Andy that my elder sister married a son of old family friends – Serbians, of course. Nice crowd."

"Peter didn't tell me anything about the kidnapping either," complained Sarah, "until the day we left Budapest."

"I didn't wish it to spoil your honeymoon," he reminded her again.

"It spoiled yours. I knew there was something wrong, but Peter blamed the fresh-water mussels, or some such thing, for making him feel out of sorts."

"It's the first time I've heard any of this, too," observed Rick, looking at his partner, who nodded in agreement.

"I thought I mentioned it over the phone after Sarah went missing," claimed Peter.

"Not to me, you didn't."

"Nor me," said Jon.

"Anyway, madam," Rick scolded her, "you could have said something about it when you were home after your honeymoon."

"Well, I didn't," Sarah declared virtuously.

"No, you kept absolutely *schtum*."

"Mum and Dad were happy for Peter and me. It was almost like a holiday for them when I came home for that fortnight. I didn't want to take that from them. I was just about to leave England again for several months, anyway, and there was nothing they could have done to help. If the kiddies hadn't been returned home soon, I'm sure that I would have told them about it then."

Jon shook his head in despair.

Said Rick, "What's just as odd is that the press don't seem to have picked that one up."

Peter considered this. "Well, I suppose – although Serbia itself isn't at war, things are far from normal there. People are going missing every day in Belgrade and elsewhere. Such matters are hardly newsworthy locally, so foreign correspondents don't necessarily hear about individual cases." He looked to Andy for endorsement.

Andy maintained an impassive front, however. He was disturbed that the British Secret Service had surely let his own department down. And, further, he wondered how it was that Interpol had not fed this extraordinarily significant information through the system. If it hadn't even reached that body's output systems, the whole thing stank of high-level entanglement.

He turned to Sarah. "Then how did you find out there was an actual link between the children's abduction and yourself?"

"Not until after I left Rick at Manchester Airport."

Rick opened his mouth to speak, but Andy nudged him with his knee.

"How old are the children?" Andy asked, as if pre-empting Rick's question. He wanted to hear Sarah's story from her alone.

"Eight and seven," said Peter.

Andy tutted his sympathy.

"Sorry, Sarah. You were saying?"

"Yes, I was sitting in the Departure Lounge, actually, waiting for the Bangkok flight to be called. It was delayed – naturally. Then this woman, about my own age, came along and sat down beside me. She said my name, told me not to look surprised, said that I was not going to Bangkok after all: she was. I told her that I was going to raise the alarm, at which she warned me that if I did not comply with her directions to the letter, Peter's niece and nephew would never be heard of again."

"What kind of an accent did she have?" asked Andy.

Sarah thought for a moment. "It was one of those indefinable transatlantic ones. Probably brought up multilingual from infancy, you know?"

"I know. Doesn't help. Go on."

"Of course, I was scared witless. She instructed me to go to the Duty Free Shop and browse round for a while, then to go to the ladies' room, where she would meet me. I did all that. In the loo, she made me change my outer clothing for hers. She looked remarkably like me when we'd finished. She even had a landing pass for Bangkok, which I had to complete there and then, doubtless for the benefit of Thai Customs when she got there. Then we went out separately. She told me to rendezvous with a fat man – sorry, Giuseppe! – in the café. I'd seen her with him in the Duty Free, so I recognised him. Mind you, I don't know how I managed to walk that far. My legs were shaking so badly I could hardly stand up. I was in a total daze after that."

Andy peered at her interrogatively. "Was there nothing at all you could have done to draw someone's attention to your plight?"

"And risk the children's lives? What would you have done in my place?"

Andy conceded the point.

"The stupid cow didn't notice that I was still wearing my hair comb," Sarah said spiritedly. "I thought of the airport's security observation tapes, though I realised that it would require someone especially bright to spot the changeover. A long shot, but it was my only hope."

When Rick opened his mouth wider this time, Andy kneed him all the harder.

Rick's contrived coughette was not enough to disguise his recoil, and Jon found it difficult to keep a straight face. "Obviously, someone did notice the comb," he said, angling to assist Rick, "otherwise we would not have known that you had left for Chicago."

"A trained eye, for sure, Andy?" cooed Sarah, attributing him with the aforesaid skills.

"And who was the fat man you had to meet?" he quizzed her as a formality.

"Why, Umberto Ciampi. He was courteous enough to me, but he could not let me go. He was being watched himself, just in case he bottled out, I suppose."

Giuseppe intervened here. "He would never have done that. Not Umberto. But he was there to usher you quietly out of England without any fuss. You knew what the consequence would have been, did you not – if you had given any trouble?"

"Why were you chosen as the scapegoat, do you think?"

"Because, Andy, I was a UN official with a passing resemblance to that woman. She was able to use my passport, and I had hers – a false one, as it turned out – to enter the States on."

"Precisely," agreed Andy, smiling for the first time since they'd sat down. "Wasn't that why the children were kidnapped, too? You know, this indicates that someone very close to you has been involved in all this, someone who knew your movements, that you were getting married to a colleague who had those family connections in Belgrade, and so on."

Giuseppe leaned back from his clean plate. "Do you know the identity of the girl who accosted Sarah at the airport?"

"I suppose you do from your brother."

"Umberto was not made privy to that, Andy. He was merely a pawn in the game, as they say. No, I have been carrying out my own research into the affair. So, do you know who she was?"

"We know the name on the passport Sarah was given," said Andy guardedly.

"That was 'Anna Reicke'," replied Giuseppe without hesitation. "No such person exists. No, I mean, do you know who the gun-totin' Annie Oakley was in all this?"

"Not by the last time I spoke to my headquarters, we didn't," Andy had to confess.

Giuseppe was visibly pleased with himself. "We learned her name only an hour ago, Andy. I'd let you in on it, but perhaps MI5 would prefer to do its own investigating," he teased.

"MI5 may," Andy parried, "but I and my department are not too proud."

"Of course, I was forgetting. Well, we did it by DNA-testing blood samples collected at the scene of the incident. The woman is a French national – Mlle Marie-Delphine Michaud."

Peter gave a start.

"What's the matter, Peter?" asked his wife. "You've heard the name before?"

"No, it can't be!" muttered Peter in disbelief, putting down his fork with a clatter. "Not her!"

"Tell us," said his brother-in-law. "How do you know her name?"

Peter looked round the table at the expectant faces, then said to Sarah, "She was just a girl I came to know before I met you. We had a thing going for a while. You know."

"You've never mentioned her to me before, have you?"

"Not by name, maybe, but she is a sister of Max's daughter-in-law."

"Our director Max?" said Sarah, aghast at the implications.

The table fell silent, then she clicked her fingers. "Ah, she's the one you said hit on you again two or three months back?"

"The same, yes. Now I come to think of it, it was immediately she saw you that time at Frankfurt. Said she couldn't wait to be introduced to you. She never was, though – introduced, I mean."

"It seems that she wasn't making another play for you, darling, after all."

"She showed an excessive interest in our wedding plans, though," he recalled. "Even wanted to know where we were going for the honeymoon."

"You didn't tell her, did you?"

Peter smiled and shook his head, then he paled. "But I did tell Max himself. He knew all our arrangements. It didn't seem unreasonable to keep the boss informed."

Once more, empty plates were collected and the diners' places endowed, this time, with a fine venison *en croute*. A different wine was uncorked and served.

"It was to Max that Umberto instructed me to address an incriminating letter," Sarah could eventually continue.

"From the Hapsburg Hotel in Vienna?" Andy grilled her.

"That's the one. You know about it?"

"Certainly. If it's any consolation to you, and so far as we have gathered, Max didn't release the contents of your letter for it to be publicly used against you. He passed it on to the Foreign Office."

Peter interjected, "Only because the letter was also damaging to UNESCO, by association. As a Project Director, he daren't have been seen as responsible for getting the Organisation embroiled any further than it already was. The Foreign Office, eh?" he murmured pensively. "When you come to think about it, by letting only the security services in on Sarah's letter, he dropped us deeper in the doo-doo with your people without jeopardising himself at all. He stayed squeaky clean."

"You're dead right about that," Andy acquiesced. "It finished up with us in Whitehall."

"Where the Civil Service are supreme masters of keeping secrets," said Jon, "especially their own! Even from themselves, sometimes," he twitted, exchanging wicked glances with Rick, who was at that moment diligently slicing up Andy's meat and vegetables for him.

Andy ignored the jibe, and spoke again to Sarah. "Where did you get the green notepaper you wrote your letter on?"

She thought for a moment. "Umberto took it from his desk at the warehouse office. Why?"

"Did he, now?" exclaimed Andy.

"Is that significant?" asked Giuseppe.

"What interest, if any, does your brother have in TransUnion Inns, Giuseppe?"

The other looked at him oddly.

"Why, none: only that his brother is Corporation President."

"You?"

Giuseppe repeated his affirmative shrug.

"Well, it did seem strange to us that a letter purporting to have been written by Sarah at the Hapsburg Hotel and posted in Vienna should have been written on a type of notepaper emanating from your exclusively North American hotels group, Giuseppe. What you've just said clears up that little conundrum for us."

Vexation showed in the Italian's plump features. "That brother of mine. I tell you, he's a thief!" The broccoli floret on the tip of his fork accentuated the fact. "Thinks he can go round the country using our hotels and pilfering the facilities we provide for guests who pay full prices for their accommodations!" The air-cooled floret went the way of its predecessors.

Whereupon he grinned unctuously, "So, your people have been studying our hotels operations, have they? I am delighted to have provided first-rate hospitality for them in such a mighty worthy cause!"

Andy affected to accept the courtesy graciously. He was tickled to hear Umberto being equated to a mere petty pilferer by his brother. His attention returned to Sarah.

"Did you gain the impression by that time that Umberto was repenting of his part in your abduction?"

"In retrospect, mm, I think maybe he was, though he didn't make it obvious till a day or two later."

"I was only wondering whether he selected that notepaper on purpose – it was an absolute dead give-away – in order to confound the aims of The Light, or whether he was just being unbelievably crass."

"Oh, the latter, most definitely!" cried his loyal brother.

Sarah smiled demurely and poked her neighbour's cuff in mild rebuke. "I now think the former, Andy. When Peter turned up that night on the fire escape of Umberto's house –"

"You were where?" ejaculated Andy, staring incredulously at the man down the table.

Peter's cheeks turned violet. "Nobody else seemed to be doing anything to find my Sarah. I couldn't bear just sitting round on my arse, so I got on with it by myself."

Andy snorted. "I tell you, Peter, if it had been the house of almost anybody else connected with The Light, you would not be here to tell the tale. Even now I can't believe anyone in their right mind... You stupid, stupid bugger. Sorry, Giuseppe, but that was so not clever. He –"

"I'm sure he knows it by this time," acknowledged their host. "It was the foolhardy action of a desperate man in love." He beamed in Sarah's direction. "Surely you know what it's like, being in love, Andy? Nothing matters but the object of your desires. Rationality flies straight out of the window."

This little homily instantly put paid to the next instalment of Andy's invective. He hesitated before saying, "That seems to be the case, yes. I apologise, Peter. That was discourteous of me. Please go on, Sarah. So, Peter was on Umberto's bloody fire escape –"

Her eyes on her shaken husband, Sarah slowly resumed, "Umberto had him taken prisoner at first, then he brought him over to where I was being held at a warehouse somewhere near the river. He still said it was for our own protection. Naturally, I had been taking that particular line of his as some kind of a sick joke. I thought he was taunting me in my lousy predicament, until Peter was brought to join me. Umberto could have had us killed. He'd been instructed to do it. Instead, he had his merchandise removed downstairs and to other warehouses, and he closed off the upper floors from his staff. Why? So that he could give us the relative freedom of his office. He alone had the key to the new door he'd had installed at the foot of the stairs, so only he could bring us food and drink. There was a washroom on that floor, but we could flush the loo only at night when the building was unoccupied.

"We were there together for only two days before he began to get really frightened. It showed in his face, didn't it, darling? I began to feel sorry for him. Imagine!"

"I said to him," Peter took over, "'if you are getting so worried, why don't you let us go?' We wouldn't squeal – isn't that what they say in Chicago?"

"Not since Eliot Ness moved on," said Giuseppe patiently. "The phrase was well and truly passé by the 1950s."

"That's another bubble of delusion burst! Anyway, Umberto insisted that he would have to make it appear as if we were both dead, otherwise not only he, but also we ourselves would be hunted down and murdered, no matter where in the world we endeavoured to hide. For one thing, The Light could not tolerate their orders being countermanded: it set a bad precedent. For another, they intended that their elaborately prepared scheme should maintain optimum results for as long as they could sustain the myth that the United Nations had been behind the plot to slay the Bosnian President. This would expose our Organisation to the charge of partiality at the very time the UN were sponsoring peace negotiations to end a civil war which has been so lucrative to The Light."

"So you've twigged all that, as well," Andy remarked, pleased. "We agree on the motives for all this, then."

"We begged to be permitted to contact our homes to put everyone's mind at rest. His only response was that, even if we wanted to endanger our families' lives as well as adding to our own perils, he did not."

"At least he was right in that," Giuseppe intervened. "No matter how hard they worked at it, your folks would, sooner or later, have stopped giving off that almost intangible scent created by their concern for your safety. The press and others would have picked that up. The Light recruits certain journalists to its ranks, too, as easily as religions convert self-centred people to self-righteousness, and, before they could yell 'Rule Britannia', members of your families would start disappearing. They would be 'persuaded' to blab about your whereabouts. Not knowing where you were would not have saved them."

Jon and Rick were beginning to regard this member of the Ciampi family with some sneaking respect. First impressions, even second and third ones, were not always blessed with certainty. Conventional notions of charm he had not. It was improbable that anybody could attain Ciampi's elevated social stature complete with unimpeachable probity, but here was a man not without a small armoury of redeeming features. There was still his other more formidable arsenal, however, and what amounted to a military hospital in his own home.

Jon spoke up. "When your friends made a DNA profile of the blood samples retrieved in Geneva, how did they know where to search for data to compare it with, Mr Ciampi? Did they have access to police files, for instance?"

Their host merely smiled inscrutably and tapped one side of his nose with a chubby forefinger.

Rick considered this an opportunity for him finally to make a useful contribution.

"Surely, if we now know who really was on that roof in Geneva, our Sarah's already been exonerated. She can go home now, can't she?"

"It helps, Rickie, sure," she answered solemnly, "but it doesn't of itself prove that I wasn't there. What about all that stuff of mine that was planted in the building?"

Peter added, "It isn't a reasonable court of law we're trying to convince, you know, but a population divided by a thousand years of racial and religious tensions, most of them imposed on the region from outside: just like the forces that build up when continents collide into each other and cause huge upheavals like those that created these mountains all round us. Perhaps understandably, such peoples often find it hard to find time to listen to reason. That's what we're up against."

Rick nodded grimly. "Well, perhaps you can tell us this, Mr Ciampi. If a sample was taken of Sarah's blood and, like, a DNA profile was constructed from it, and other forensic material could be sent, say, to the Swiss authorities, are your sources sufficiently attributable in public, or can you make them so, to prove that my sister couldn't possibly have been involved in the Bosnian President business? If you could make that a reality, it would let Sarah, the United Nations and our families off the hook in one simple exercise. Or would it?" He turned to Andy.

Andy furrowed his brow a little. "That would also really depend on who does hold the Geneva blood samples and a DNA profile record of Mlle Michaud. As you implied, Rickie, it's often the attribution of evidence which determines its acceptance. I know that the Swiss authorities are closely concerned in the affair, and that they, naturally, hold all available evidence collected from the incident scene. Who else does, is another matter." He popped a forkful of food into his mouth and shot a meaningful glance in Giuseppe's direction.

That man looked up from his plate which was now empty. "This was one of the issues I wanted to discuss with you," he said. "You see, I am not a vengeful man, but I cannot stand by, aware that my brother or any member of the family is being threatened with death. The Light is an organisation devoid of any principle whatsoever, except that of making vast fortunes from the death and maiming of hundreds of thousands of people they themselves have helped to whip up into frenzies of hatred and blood lust and genocide."

Giuseppe's eyes glowered while he dipped his greasy digits in his finger bowl and wiped them dry on the flannel provided for the purpose. "I am acquainted with at least one significant individual who would be exceedingly put out to learn that he and his particular organisation had been duped by The Light into blaming a UN official for the shooting. Now, the DNA profile I possess has been authenticated as to its source. That it matches Marie-Delphine's has also been confirmed.

"What has occurred to me is not unlike Rick's proposal, but it will require Sarah to provide her blood sample or mouth swab, and whatever else they need, at an independent laboratory of international repute, whose certification of the donor will be acceptable to those who can influence the outcome of this whole nasty affair."

"So it can be done then, and you will help us to bring it about?"

"When these miscreants chose to tangle with me and mine, Andy," he replied with menace in his gravelly voice, "they knew not what they were doing."

Andy said, "You may think this an inept question, Giuseppe, but it would be remiss of me not to put it to you: do you know the identities of any of those behind The Light of the World?"

"As I am one of their most adamant opponents, Andy, why would you expect me to be taken into their confidence about their most closely guarded secrets?"

Andy grinned and shrugged.

"But, yes," Giuseppe went on surprisingly, "I do suspect at least one high-up individual of being one of its big shots."

Thereupon Andy raised an enquiring expression.

Giuseppe laughed harshly. "And you may put that eyebrow back down where it belongs. There's no way I will divulge such information to anyone. If and when my own investigations, based on new data, expose that person as culpable, they will be dealt with in an appropriate manner, I can assure you! Now, dessert, anybody?"

He rang a little silver hand-bell in front of him. This summoned in a magnificent baked alaska topped with almonds and a variety of fresh fruits on a bed of whipped cream.

Following further small talk and the departure of the house staff, Peter announced, "I've just remembered, Rick: it was probably your father I mentioned the children's kidnapping to. Come to think of it, I don't think I actually said they'd been kidnapped –"

"Let it go, Peter," urged Rick. "We know now, and it's probably just as well mum and dad don't have that to worry them on top of everything else!"

A sharp piece of meringue glanced off Rick's nose just then, setting up a flurry of laughter. It was flack from another single-handed battle Andy was on the brink of losing.

"Oh, come here, then!" cried the stricken man, grabbing the spoon out of his neighbour's hand. Taking up the fork as well, he put a generous dollop of dessert on the spoon. "Here, open wide." Andy tamely obliged, and was fed a delicious mouthful by Rick's hand.

"Yum!" Andy spluttered, only to have his mouth roughly wiped of sugar and cream with his napkin.

"Bad breeding will out, Mr Ciampi, don't you think?" Rick uttered amidst the general amusement. He continued to break up the rest of the alaska so that Andy could manage it for himself.

The remainder of the meal progressed in that merrier vein. By coffee and brandy time, the atmosphere was thoroughly relaxed, and Giuseppe had prevailed upon the male couple to call him by his first name.

Fifteen

Retiring with his guests into his private drawing room and sitting them down, Giuseppe Ciampi stood and faced them while more drinks were served by a younger manservant, one of the many employed in the house.

Meantime, Andy excused himself and ran downstairs to see how Kit was doing. It was no use his dallying there because Kit was still asleep, though he was encouraged to learn that the patient's general stability was improving the prognosis hourly.

He returned to the dinner party just as Giuseppe was telling the others, "You see, Kit was told by Umberto not to make himself known to you unless your lives were likely to be endangered. He was to keep my brother and me advised if, instead of starting the vacation you were supposed to be taking, you seemed to have any designs on looking for Sarah and Peter. Remember, he was clued in only about Andy's identity and not that of his two travelling companions. And he was to protect you, if necessary, from those who appeared to be following you. By then, Umberto realised that someone on his own payroll must have betrayed him and he didn't want to have your deaths on his hands."

"The trouble with that," said Andy, "was that even by the time we realised certain people were showing an unhealthy interest in us, we were not aware that they, too, were seeking Sarah out. They had different motives from each other, yet the same lethal object in mind. It was

Kit who tried to put us right about them, but he daren't tell us everything he knew. In fact, he must have been able to observe those developments from his own solitary perspective, so when that English couple were killed on the train, it must have been unbelievably terrifying for him to know that only he and his gun stood between us and those murderers who might well have been aiming to kill us, too, so far as he could tell."

"And that was the very moment," recalled Jon in self-recrimination, "when I misconstrued the reasons for his nervousness, and I went for him like a bloody maddened bull rhino!"

"Note the 'bull' bit, Andy!" Rick facetiously quipped.

"Well, that's for you to know and the rest of us to wonder at!" retorted Andy, diverted by Jon's mock discomposure.

"But I don't think we can overstate Kit's courage that night," he continued seriously, "and all of yesterday, when he must have been a lot more conscious than even we were at the time about the gravity of our situation."

Giuseppe came in, "Some of my people were telling me that there were suspicious-looking strangers already in town yesterday morning. And, as I have said, Kit warned me by telephone of the extra forces about to gather right here in our midst. It was to give us some time to marshal our defences and plan to extricate you all. By the by, it was Kit who made the proposal to me that you would be staying at the motel you did."

"He made a democratic decision among himself, didn't he," said Rick, "and we just tagged along after him."

"They are known as leadership qualities, are they not?" Andy decided that was a further reason for his love for the man.

He went on, "But what we still need to be told is, if you were not fighting in the battle, Giuseppe, who really was fighting whom?"

The Italian-American regarded them steadily. "The secular and the profane were slugging it out with the religious and the more profane," was his somewhat abstruse reply.

He could see that his listeners understood his meaning, and went on: "As I said to you earlier, Andy, you were definitely not leading them here. They were coming here to strengthen their own sides while keeping tabs on you to prevent you getting to Sarah before they did. I can't be certain yet, but it will probably turn out that one or two of the religious zealots thought the honeymooners were your accomplices, and got them out of the way. Life is of no consequence to such beasts. I'm damned sure that even The Light's agents would have been more self-disciplined than to strike out at bystanders on the off-chance, in a sort of heinous crusade of blanket extermination. The point is, unbeknown to Kit when he initially faxed me and informed me that you'd actually brought members of Sarah's family along with you, both factions had been here since the previous day, awaiting their chance to get to Sarah. But they stayed lying low until last night."

"So, they definitely weren't using us to find Sarah for them," mused Andy. "They were going to try to stop us, dead."

"They could have got to us at any time last night," Jon said. "We went meandering about the town as though we were carefree tourists or something."

"I know, we saw you," chuckled Giuseppe.

"I must be losing my touch," Andy declared.

"We were using long-range night-vision equipment. At the same time, our side were keeping themselves between you and the enemy, who were just as keen to stop each other as to get you. The religious extremists see themselves as tools for divine retribution, while those working for The Light are in it just for the bounty. The one side wants Sarah dead because they have been convinced that she is guilty, The Light simply because they don't want the other side to learn that she isn't!"

"How did they discover that Sarah was here?" wondered Rick.

"The same way you did, I guess," Giuseppe said, with an easy flick of the wrist which, with anyone less practised at the mannerism, would have sent swirling across the room the costly contents of the glass he was holding in that hand.

"But we weren't certain that she and Peter were here," Rick said. "We hoped against hope that they were, that was all."

"I dare say those out there now were hoping something similar," Giuseppe deduced. "They couldn't have been really sure. We can bluff it out with them, but after last night, they must be ninety-nine per cent sure."

Andy peered curiously at Sarah. "Just how did you get here from Chicago?"

"As I said earlier, Andy, by car."

"Not by truck, then?"

Giuseppe let out a guffaw. "That was my knucklehead of a brother! Ha ha! Let me draw for you a picture of what happened: he knows that all his activities are under surveillance. It's getting too hot for him, so he has to get these two Britishers outa Chicago, right? He goes to all the trouble of convincingly disguising them as dark-haired Italian men, then he and his eldest son drive them towards Detroit. When they are purty certain they've thrown off their pursuers, they switch cars, double back and make for Leadville and me. That was fine. Then what does the idiot do? Panic takes over, he goes back to his warehouse, sends some suspicious-looking consignment or other by truck to Colorado and to his works right here in Leadville, of all places, then sets fire to his warehouse to destroy any possible evidence of this couple's previous occupancy. Of course, seemingly half the terrorists in the state of Illinois give his truck hot pursuit directly to my own front door! Sheesh! That guy needs a lobotomy, I'm sure of it!

"They sniffed around the FactoryKlenz building, presumably found nothing there to interest them, realised that Sarah and Peter were likely here with me and sent for reinforcements, some of whom you seem to have encountered on your travels."

"You are telling us," said Rick, "that the bulk cotton waste contained nothing more than cotton waste?"

"I wouldn't like to go that far," said Giuseppe, "but Sarah and Peter it certainly didn't contain. I gather you must have heard of the warehouse fire from the cops?"

That was near enough. Andy nodded his exasperation.

"I daren't think what is to become of Umberto," Giuseppe reflected. "I've offered him and his family sanctuary here awhile, but he is trying to brazen things out. He doesn't have a big enough outfit to oppose The Light. Indeed, some national governments don't, so I'm very much afraid for him. They consider that he double-crossed them, which I dare say he did. But I don't suppose he would have done their dirty work if he had realised what fate they planned for Sarah. He's like me in one respect, at least: he's not into the business of killing. Never has been."

"Excuse my directness, Giuseppe," said Jon, "but you do appear to possess what is tantamount to a private army barracked in this house."

"If you refer to my little group who grabbed you from the clutches of those who wanted to destroy you before you had the opportunity of returning to England with Sarah, then I plead guilty, Jon.

"We made a serious tactical mistake last night, you know. In order to get you outa there quickly, we almost all of us positioned ourselves too soon to get to your cabin from the rear. This left the front inadequately guarded for a few minutes, which was how Kit came to be shot from across the highway. That single shot excited the tension in the air and set the two groups at each other's throats. Of our three not behind the motel, two were shot, as you know, caught in the crossfire."

"What was the outcome of the fight once the police became involved?" asked Rick.

Andy said, "The police captain told us earlier, Giuseppe, that there were no police fatalities, so far as he had been told at that stage. Was that borne out by the facts?"

"Yes, yes, Andy, I'm glad to say. Their casualties were all relatively minor injuries. In fact, as I said to you, the terrorists melted away into the night after twenty minutes, leaving four dead. There were no wounded left behind to be arrested and questioned. Whether that means they took any wounded they had with them, no one can be sure."

"They're still at large, then?"

"Yes, Rick. Somewhere up there in the mountains all round us are two armed gangs: opposing one another, but both our enemies."

"Are the cops here now ostensibly to defend your home and family, or to help you to protect Sarah and Peter?" enquired Jon.

"Officially, neither; in fact, both. Not to mention you, as well! I should add that they don't know that Sarah is the same Sarah who is connected with the Bosnian President affair. Most of my family don't either. Not even Kit would have known until you told him, Andy. It is enough for them to believe that Sarah and Peter have information to impart to the British government and that their personal testimony will indict some terrorist leaders. So the county police are here to keep the peace without getting themselves involved in international matters."

"Your 'little group' is remarkably well-armed itself," Jon observed coolly through gossamer-veiled obloquy.

"Haha!" Giuseppe laughed rather testily. "Andy, your friend has an incisive way of getting straight to the heart of things, don't he! He'd make a mighty fine surgeon."

"That's precisely what he is: a veterinary surgeon!" Andy announced as proudly as if he had been personally responsible for Jon's vocation. "Mind you," he added, reaching over and fondling the nape of Jon's neck as a mark of gratitude, "he's not so bad at saving humans from bleeding to death when the need arises!" Rick fixed Andy with a comical sidelong glare and motioned him to keep his hand to himself, whereupon Jon closed his eyes as if in swoons of ecstasy and pressed his head against those firm, working fingers. Sarah giggled at her big brother's discomfiture.

Giuseppe was amusedly disregarding these goings-on. "In this country, Jon, we have the constitutional right to bear arms and use them in our self-defence. We are in quite a vulnerable location just here. Look around you. This house wasn't built here because of the site's military impregnability. It was well sheltered from the worst of the natural elements, that's all. My family, we are prepared to defend ourselves and what is ours."

Andy's fingers had grown tired of their exercise away from home by this time and had been returned to their rightful place.

"And the hospital?" Jon persevered, "you need it because your family normally sustains so many injuries while 'defending' itself?"

Again Giuseppe laughed sardonically. "No, no!" he insisted, "we are merciful and take lots of prisoners, most of them riddled with gunshot wounds!"

Sarah interrupted him before he could go on. "Jon – all of you, listen. Giuseppe is really something of a saviour in these parts. They don't have a national health service in America like our European ones, as you know. His small infirmary is a free hospital for hundreds of local people, especially the mountain folk eking out a poor existence up there and for his employees. It all comes out of his pocket, Peter and I have been told by one of the staff."

Said Peter, "Have you noticed what a high level of staffing there is here? Well, Giuseppe believes in employing as many people as possible to aid the local economy and population."

"Nonsense!" boomed their host, "it's in case I decide to run for Senate one day: their votes are already in the bag! That's how we run our politics round here."

"Take no notice of him," Sarah cried. "Behind that gruff exterior beats the warm heart of a poppet !"

Expressions of disbelief took Rick's and Jon's faces by surprise. "A poppet?" Jon gasped as though she had just come out with a particularly foul curse.

The poppet himself, meanwhile, had turned red and started to choke on an ill-timed swig of best Napoleon. In the attendant hilarity, Rick went to his aid, helping him to wipe down his light-coloured suit, now horribly stained, while Giuseppe dried his eyes to see once more.

"Wow!" he panted, flabbing down into a fortified armchair and mopping his brow. "Phew! Don't anyone call me such a thing again, least ways not when I can hear them and when my mouth's full!"

Rick's intimate knowledge of his sister had always impressed on him that her people-judgement was usually pretty sound and that her geese were never swans.

"You must have a fax machine here, Giuseppe."

"Ah, Andy, I think we may be able to find one lurking about somewhere. You want to use it, I suppose?"

"Well, I have to keep my boss happy, you know. Besides, there seems little point any more in their families not being told that Sarah and Peter are well and safe for the moment."

"That's what I was going to say myself," commented their host. "It will be a considerable relief for them, no doubt. I'm afraid my brother will have to take his chances."

Their own relief at this decision showed on the faces of the others present.

"We still don't want the media in on it," Andy considered, "but matters are going to be settled one way or another in a few days, anyway."

Jon piped up. "That being through DNA evidence, you mean?"

"Yes. Unless, of course, the UN or some other agency manages to dig out Mlle Michaud, meanwhile."

"Oh, so the UN are supposed to be doing something, then?" remarked Jon without conviction.

"I imagine they are pulling out all the stops," said Peter. "The UN rummage around quietly in the background when it comes to handling delicate international issues that are potentially dynamite. Consequently, they get blamed for inaction when things go wrong, and get no credit whatsoever when they are instrumental in resolving ticklish problems. But their success rating is quite high, and governments are often immensely grateful for UN intervention in such things, although they rarely, if ever, say so in public! They just continue to fund our important international development work – which I suppose is good enough," he conceded.

"Surely, by this time, the press must have homed in on all the goings-on round here," Rick assumed.

Andy looked questioningly at Giuseppe.

"TV newscasts earlier today merely reported that the police were involved in a shoot-out between rival gangs thought to be from outside the Leadville area," Giuseppe said. "As I say, the police are here now, with my consent, on an exercise. The sheriff's department is cognisant of the situation, of course, but not of who Sarah is."

"But they will be glad to be disburdened of her presence here," Andy observed. "By the way, does this house have a name or something?"

Giuseppe grinned. "For sure. *Casa Bianca*! What else?"

"What else indeed?" smiled Andy. "Just so that I can tell Sir Rupert where we are, you understand."

"If you're faxing, the paper is address-headed," Andy was told.

The expectancy pervading the ensuing pause must have seemed presumptuous.

"Well? If I may?" deferred Andy, sitting forward in his seat.

Giuseppe's countenance evinced amused puzzlement. He sat still for a moment, said teasingly, "Oh, I see!" then resumed his tiny feet with a great heave of that ungainly body. He stepped across to the right hand side of the fireplace, where there was a sort of hatch cover at chest level flush with the wall, rather like a safe's. Giuseppe slid it easily upwards, letting it disappear behind the plaster, to reveal a complex-looking console of keys and switches illuminated from behind. He perused the layout before stabbing at one of the keys.

Against the dining room wall stood a compact ebony writing desk. Its cover rolled instantaneously back, exposing a fax machine.

"There you are, *amico mio*," declared Giuseppe, "'ask and it shall be given unto you!'"

"Thanks, *amico*," Andy reciprocated, rising. He crossed the room, sat at the desk and began writing. Rick had an idea and followed him. After whispering a few words to him, he returned to his seat.

With a recondite opening reference to his having encountered here a sharp toxophilite with partner, Andy informed Sir Rupert that Sarah, whom he knew to be an archery enthusiast, and her husband were safe and well. He just as cryptically conveyed the present security position to him: that DNA evidence accused one Mlle Marie-Delphine Michaud, who could boast a significant male relative, and that further similar tests were to be done to prove no other's involvement.

Andy rationalised that to tell the boss his next move might be to invite interference in his own actions in the case at a moment when there were at last some positive prospects evolving. He'd acquitted his duty, and had given Sir Rupert plenty to get his eye teeth into. Andy fed his page into the machine and tapped out the number of a securely locked-away Whitehall counterpart which only Sir Rupert could access.

Satisfied, Andy went back to his companions who had grown comfortably somnolent with their surfeit of good foods and wines – especially the latter.

"... built by my father thirty-four years ago," Giuseppe was saying of his house. "His parents were still alive and kicking in Milano, and he brought them over here to live out their last years – in my grandmother's case, fifteen of them. Papà came to these United States as a humble chef, opened his first *ristorante* in Chicago, and in ten years was head of a giant catering corporation. My big brother would have inherited it, but he got mixed up with the wrong kind, so papà passed it all on to me.

"Umberto – well, he took it hard." The speaker shrugged. "But it was not my fault!" he protested disingenuously, as though he had striven and failed to break his parents' wills in Umberto's favour.

"My late first wife's parents were basically in oil, but my present wife's were cattle ranchers and owned a number of modest motels in Arizona and California. I put a lot of business their way, one way or another.

"Their son took over in due course, but he died tragically in a racing accident. He was a bachelor – well, legally he was. He bequeathed his own personal property to his lover, but the businesses had to remain in his blood family. My wife became the beneficiary of that particular circumstance, but you wouldn't think so to hear her berating her lovely brother. She even tried to get hold of Leo's – his terribly bereaved partner's – inheritance, on the grounds of unsuitability, undue influence, or some such fanciful reasons. Between you and me, I think she always did go to church too often and listened to too many rantings. If she ever found out that I paid for the best available lawyers to defend Leo's character against her calumnies, I think she'd sacrifice all her other Christian principles and divorce me!" He chuckled deep down in his belly.

"We won't blackmail you for being so frank with us!" Rick smilingly undertook on everyone's behalf. "Will she be joining us this evening, do you think?"

Peter covertly motioned to the others not to pursue the matter.

Giuseppe referred to his watch. "It is almost midnight. I don't think she will now. I am sorry, but she has had an overly emotional day."

"Do you often visit Britain, Giuseppe?" enquired Jon.

"I go to Europe three, maybe four times a year; to England maybe once, yes."

Jon glanced at Rick. Something they must discuss.

The door to the corridor opened and in walked a slim and erect, 60-ish blonded bombshell wearing a long blue evening gown with silver accessories. The men stood up. She paused and smiled stiffly at the company.

"This is my wife, Jessica, gentlemen."

She peremptorily came to the point.

"Giuseppe, dear, Bertha has asked me to go and stay with her until all this is over." She bestowed a less than frosty smile upon Sarah and Peter.

"Jessica," he persisted, "this is Mr Richard Timperley, Sarah's brother, and his partner Mr Jon Reynolds from England –"

She kept her distance but nodded barely politely, not offering her hand.

"– and this is Mr Andrew Gregson, who works for the Great British government."

She surveyed him critically. "Ah, so you would be the one who has 'befriended' my nephew, Kit, who has such a promising career in the US Navy?" She almost spat out the friendship part of it.

Andy cautiously indicated assent. She had meant 'corrupted' if anything at all. Strange how a word as wonderful as friend could be employed so glibly as a euphemism for something so vile. That was the real corruption round here, Andy thought. It was no use telling a person like her that it was the naval officer who had come on to him in the first instance. Besides, he wouldn't have spoken out of turn for Kit's sake.

Giuseppe viewed with concern the discomfort his wife had caused. "You would do better to stay in the house, *cara*. But go wherever you wish. Our guests have no need to feel unsafe here. Besides, Kit is going to get better, perhaps due in part to the very friendship of which you speak so fondly."

This urbane sarcasm was missed by no one. "If you say so, dear," she pouted. Nodding to Sarah, she turned on her stout heels and flounced out of the room with a rustle of expensive silk.

First indicating to the men to resume their seats, Giuseppe shrugged apologetically. "When she gets into her moral rectitude mode, there's nothing anyone can do but wait for her to tire of it. I am not always right about such things, Andy, but accurate judgement of people's characters is quite an important part of my job. One far distant day when she deems that I have at last become successful, Jessica will have to admit that one of my secrets is being able to recognise the strengths and weaknesses of others."

The twinkle in his eyes was a cue. His guests laughed. The very idea that anyone could play down this multimillionaire's success rating was utterly ludicrous.

"I'm afraid it is all part of the age-old Battle of the Sexes!" Giuseppe heaved a sigh and wordlessly flashed an open warning to Peter, then he grinned at the young wife. "Mind you," he conceded, "not everyone has such irritations to worry about in their home lives!" He peered in an avuncular manner at her brother and Jon.

"You seem to know as much about us as we know about ourselves," Jon commented, "if not more."

"It is, I fear, a habit of mine, Jon: to keep myself well informed. After all, information is money. It is part of my stock in trade. You have that expression in England?

"Fine. My wife is going to stay with that awful woman I sent packing this morning." He saw that the couple recalled the incident in their former room. "No doubt they've been jawing on about it to beat the band. If I were they, I should prefer to be rejoicing for Kit's sake – as indeed, I do."

Andy looked earnestly at him. "Look, Giuseppe, you have been marvellous to all of us – especially to Sarah and Peter – and we're more grateful than we can say. But we don't want to cause you any more problems than you have been given already. Your wife doesn't like us. I think perhaps we should take our leave of you."

"That is the first unintelligent thing I have heard you utter," Giuseppe declared. "My wife is unintelligent about human issues all the damn time – it's her religion, I've told you. They think everyone must conform to rules of their making. It's not enough for them to have created God in their own distorted image: they are determined to remould everyone else, as well! We are all accustomed to these silly ways of hers, so please do not contemplate actions which are not in the best interests of you all."

Rick said to Andy, "Should we presume some kind of a plan of campaign is forming in that noddle of yours?"

"Only that we must find someone acceptable to the various factions interested in learning the truth: someone, or an institution of some kind, who would build a DNA profile of Sarah to clear her name and the UN's reputation, so that the peace negotiations might get under way again."

"I think I know the very guy," said Giuseppe. "His grandparents hailed from Karachi via England back in the twenties. He is a professor at the Dwight Medical Center in Colorado Springs. His specialty is genetics and such. I telephoned his number earlier this evening. I was told that he is in New York at present at a world conference on some esoteric branch of medical research. I'm afraid that he won't be back home till tomorrow evening. We could get someone else sooner, no doubt, but Dev's credentials are so eminently suitable from every standpoint."

"Do you think he would do the job for us, if we waited?" asked Andy.

"Ha ha, I rang him at the Plaza Hotel number the Medical Center gave me. I simply asked him if he would be prepared to carry out such a test and certify the identity of the person it related to. He answered that he would with pleasure. I undertook to get the subject to Colorado Springs by eight tomorrow evening. Obviously, Andy and the rest of you, if you are not happy with this, I can call it off right now."

The British contingent had nothing better to propose, and readily fell in with Giuseppe's arrangements.

Andy called on Kit again before turning in himself. There was no appreciable change, so he went back up to his room, undressed and was about to go to bed when the interconnecting door was knocked. He slipped his shorts back on and answered it. Rick and Jon were standing there clad only in their briefs.

"We heard you moving about. How is he, Andy?" enquired Jon.

Andy told them.

"That's probably good news, you know," Jon reminded him. "Nature's role is crucial in all this, and nature arguably heals at its best when the patient is in soundest sleep."

Andy smiled gratefully at him for saying so. "I know what you're saying is dead right, Jon. Just the same, even with all the booze we've just had, I don't reckon I shall get all that much kip myself tonight."

Jon and Rick exchanged glances.

Rick suggested, "If you like, you can come in with us for a bit. It'll be less lonely for you, if nothing else."

"We-ell," Andy said hesitantly. He looked from one to the other. "If you're sure. I don't want to keep you awake, too."

"You don't?" Rick bridled. "Then you won't. Besides, our bed's big enough for four with room to spare."

"So's mine," insisted Andy.

"Please yourself, then," Jon carped.

Andy did. He took up a pillow from his bed, switched out the lights and tagged after them into their room.

He wasn't certain what he should be expecting. These were a couple of guys with a lifetime commitment to one another, so he ought not to be feeling this hungry anticipation. They were only being supportive and friendly towards him.

Rick got into his customary side of the bed, so Andy assumed that his mate would want to lie on Rick's right as he'd seen them before. Andy moved Jon's pillow along and put his own on the right, intent on keeping a decent space between himself and them. He was conscious that he often tussled with his bedding while he slept.

Andy lay down on his back in his side of the huge bed. The gold curtains were already drawn round two sides of it. He returned the smile Rick sent across to him. Jon had spent a minute in the loo, and could now be heard approaching over the dense carpet. The main light went out, leaving only the warm glow from the two bedside lamps.

A grinning disembodied face peeked round the bedpost, but grew indignant straight away. "And what are you doing on my side of the bed, Andrew Gregson?" it demanded. "Come on, shove over."

"I – I thought –"

"Well, don't think. Shift!"

Andy obeyed – carefully to avoid hurting his arm.

Jon pulled the remaining curtain to, enclosing the trio companionably from the world beyond. Andy could not resist once more sizing up Jon's tall athletic body which exuded so much masculine strength and concomitant sexuality. That wedge-shaped back with its narrow waist, those muscular buttocks and thighs, the definition of his calves were all a delight. As Jon turned round, Andy surveyed those powerful arms which must be so useful in his physical job and in trysts with his lover. While Andy's wayward eyes strayed down to the front, this time, of those tight black briefs, the promise of that soft, bulging pouch, though not for him, was beginning to set his own loins afire.

He hastily averted his eyes as Jon tugged back a corner of the duvet and slid himself gracefully inside. Jon's foot inadvertently slithered down the length of Andy's very hairy right shin.

The trouble for Andy was that, as soon as he'd looked away, his gaze had no alternative but to fall upon Rick's massive shoulders and pectorals liberally adorned with that silky, dark brown hair, not so plentiful as to hide any detail of the fantastic musculature that was peculiarly Rick's. His arms resting on top of the bedcover were huge too, and well up to responding to his partner's embraces in like manner.

"What's up, Andy?" asked Rick gently. "You look a bit stressed-out."

Andy regarded the mounds made by his feet. "I suppose I'm feeling in the way, lads." He thought his admission sounded pathetic once he had articulated it. "Here am I, a complete sexual novice, lying between two confident experts –"

"Hey, hey!" protested Jon, "less of the 'experts', if you please! We haven't explored all our sexual opportunities by a long way. At least," he scrutinised his partner's features, "I haven't!"

"What's that supposed to mean?"

"Nothing at all, nothing!" came the airy reply.

"If you're referring to our 'wilderness years' before we finally shacked up together, you had just as many opportunities as me. What about that –"

"Oh, shut your bloody prattling, you pair of stupid prats!" Andy blurted through his giggles at their antics.

"Ouch! ouch!" sputtered Jon, blowing on his fingers as if they were burnt.

"Feeling better after your little outburst, Andy?" Rick said with a yawn.

Better, but hardly content. "Can't you see, guys? I'm worried about my fucking virginity, really."

"That's got to be an oxymoron," Jon adjudicated.

"Ha, fucking ha!" growled Andy. "But no, honestly, it's a worry that's started to nag me lately. Especially when I think of that beautiful man downstairs. Do you see? I mean, it's one thing to fall in love: it's sustaining your lover's interest long term that's the really hard part, or so I've read somewhere."

"I don't think you'll have a lot of difficulty in that department, to be honest," Jon assured him. "You are a very interesting bloke at every level, isn't he, love?"

Rick nodded. "You've both got everything going for you – well, that is apart from the question of six thousand miles or more that will separate you once you return home."

"I'm not worried about a few miles," Andy promised them. "If we both want to get rid of those, we'll do so, one way or another. No, it's not anything like that. It's not knowing how to make love to somebody. More especially: how do I have sex with the guy? What is expected of me?"

"You mean the mechanics?" queried Rick, with a bemused grin.

"No, of course not! I mean, you must have had other experiences before you first, well, had it off with each other. Kit would be my first. I mean, he's in the ruddy navy, for Christ's sake! He must know every trick in the book."

"All the better to teach you with, Andy dear," Jon leered, squeezing the arm alongside him. "But, to be absolutely candid with you, I was certainly a whiter-than-white virgin until Rickie thankfully despoiled me in the back of his old Range Rover."

"So was I when Jon so cruelly took advantage of me," counterclaimed Rick. "He practically forced me out of the driving seat into the back."

"Oh, Jeez!"

"If you believe that, Andy, you're a bigger fool than I take you for!

Imagine anyone being capable of physically pushing this great hulk around against his will."

"Less of the 'hulk', you!" Rick snapped, giving Jon a smart thump on the chest.

"And you should have *smelled* the back of that thing," Jon went on regardless. "Sheep! I mean, it was the first night we met, and he suggested we go for a drive out of Manchester up into the Pennines in this big, stinking tank of a thing. He hadn't said anything about his living on a farm, so I thought to myself, 'Hey up, this weirdo does funny things to animals in here. Watch your step, or you'll be his next victim!'..."

"So he did," the Accused interrupted, "And look where it's got him! A job as a vet. He's the one who does the funny things to animals now! Not that I was responsible for that aberration either, you understand."

"The mountain rain was pissing down," said Jon ruefully, "and there we were in the blackness, stuck out on this bloody great moor a mile from the nearest road, and me being ravaged not once, not twice, but four fucking times on the hard metal floor."

Enthralled by this bedtime story, Andy noted during its recounting how Jon's hands were occasionally pushing down on the duvet above his groin. These were far from painful memories.

Continued the 'victim': "When I eventually got home at five o'clock in the morning, all battered and bruised from being thrown about in that tinny old thing, my hair, my clothes – everything was contaminated with sheep's wool and God knows what else!"

"Go on, tell Andy the rest," Rick goaded. "Tell him how you made me take you into the shower with us both fully dressed apart from our shoes. We stripped one another, washed each other, and then he smothered me from head to toe with some massage oil or something, and we started all over again. He still hadn't had enough, the randy bastard. I was the one who was red raw everywhere by the time he'd finished with me!

"Mind you, Andy," he added with a grin, "we could have gone back to his place right at the beginning. His parents were away for the weekend."

"I didn't know you well enough at the start to ask you back," stated Jon reasonably. "Besides, I thought going up there with you would be a nice bit of rough trade. And I was right!" Which remark earned him another punch delivered across Andy's supine body.

Rick affected righteous indignation. "We didn't even know the meaning of that term in those days when we were at the threshold of our sexual careers."

Jon put on a sneer. "Well, if we had've, I would've called it that, so there!"

"And did you stick together after that?" asked their friend.

"Not after we'd showered again," was Rick's droll riposte.

"No, idiot! I meant, is that when your partnership began?"

"Not a bit of it," said Jon. "We carried on seeing one another until we went away to our universities. We both had affairs during term time – always safely, but we always seemed to gravitate together during the vacs. By the time we graduated, I'm afraid the die was cast for us. Rick couldn't live without me, it's as straightforward as that."

Andy prepared for a further blow to be directed at Jon, but Rick was pensively nodding his agreement.

Jon felt mean then. "OK, so the sentiment was mutual, have it your way!"

"I didn't say a thing."

"No, but you were thinking it."

Andy was loathe to interrupt this loving banter, but it highlighted a major dissimilarity distinguishing their situation from his.

"But don't you see the difference between your sexual baptism and Kit's and mine? You were both inexperienced in those days. You learned together – largely from each other. Whereas Kit is surely a totally competent lover to my gauche novitiate."

Rick said quietly, "Yes, but it's really all a question of trust, Andy. It's out of trust that love between individuals grows."

"Well, perhaps so, but I'm scared he'll immediately find me dull and boring – unadventurous, after what he must be accustomed to."

His companions seemed not to be very forthcoming with their advice.

"For instance," he pressed them, "do I have to penetrate him, or does he have to do it to me? Because I'm not really sure I want either. B-but I'd do whatever he wanted. Trouble is, I still don't know how!"

"Pretty basic stuff, eh?" said Rick. "You expect us to be able to tell you what to do? We all have to learn sometime, Andy. There's a first time for everybody."

Jon looked across to Rick. "But don't fall for the popular notion that penetration is the only way gay men have sex. That is as much a heterosexist myth as anything else; like their tiresome old missionary position. Straights think we are like them in that respect, and many gays themselves fall for it, no doubt because we are brought up to think as heteros. But we aren't tied to their limited range of activities. Lots of men have no special interest in fucking. Even those who do can enjoy a huge repertoire of imaginative sex apart from that."

Rick regarded Andy's troubled face. "Don't let these things worry you overmuch, Andy. Kit loves you, and he may relish the idea of deflowering a virgin, to boot! – whether that includes shagging or not." He inclined himself towards Andy and examined his head. "Hey, Jon, he's got puce ear again! Just take a shufty at that!"

Alarmed, Andy sat up. "What the hell's 'puce ear' when it's at home?"

The couple started to chuckle infuriatingly. Andy sat tight, grimly determined. "Well? what's wrong with me now?" he cried in irritation.

"It means, old love, that you are well and truly ready for it." Rick commenced playing seductively with Andy's treacherous ear. "A bit of inside information for you: men aren't always given to volunteering their emotional states of mind, but if you are chatting a guy up and the tops of his ears start going pink, it's a sure sign that he's getting the hots for you! That's an invaluable tip, which we pass on to you at no extra charge. Jon and I call it puce ear."

Andy appeared fascinated by the very idea. "You said 'again'; that I've 'got puce ear again'. What did you mean?"

Jon answered with a beguiling grin, "Only that the last time we noticed you with it was the other night when you were with Kit. You both had it strong. Just as you have it tonight," he whispered hoarsely. He took Andy's other ear between thumb and forefinger and tweaked its lobe.

Andy's eyes began to close, and a shudder rose up through his body.

"Aah!" he moaned as his remaining inhibitions slipped away from him. He let his head fall forward.

He felt another hand caress his neck, and someone's fingers combed through his shiny hair. He sighed once more, then cried out as he sensed both his ears being licked by moist tongues and sucked at and nibbled by warm mouths. The attention on his left ear was withdrawn, then he knew Rick was carefully removing the sling from round his neck and left arm. The men eased him down on to his pillow. He winced a little when his arm was raised above his head, at the same time as Jon lifted up the corresponding arm, leaving him stretched out and thoroughly vulnerable.

Again the lapping and nibbling at his ears, his luxuriant hair being fondled and stroked. One of them was kissing his forehead, so did the other; next his eyelids were being caressed and down his cheeks to his sensitive neck. He was squirming. Each man now had a hand moving down from his shoulders through lush undergrowth to his chest. To his utter amazement, when they began to work at his strangely perked-up nipples, thrills of excitement immediately raged through him from his toes right up to his finger tips and into the roots of his hair. He could not keep his voice quiet, even when those fiendish mouths returned to his face and bore down on his open mouth, occupying it first with one tongue then the other. He so willingly jabbed and searched inside their sweet-tasting mouths with his own eager tongue, and he perceived that the couple were also earnestly kissing each another, making this one big wet, three-way smooch.

Andy could not keep himself so passive. He moved his good hand down to Jon's head, and strongly massaged his neck and scalp, next reaching for Rick's to perform the same service on him, though stretching across his own body was awkward for him. As he incidentally pulled Rick's head towards him, it suddenly took a dive into his exposed left armpit, the mouth once again sending wonderful sensations into Andy's never-so-horny brain. Immediately, his right nipple was being consumed deep inside Jon's hot mouth, the upper part of the tongue lapping away at it until Andy had to cry out for him to stop, a plea that was instantly ignored. Andy gasped and squealed for mercy, pounding with the heel of his palm on Jon's back.

While his mouth was still absorbed in its task, Rick's left hand was moving about Andy's firm stomach, his nails lightly scraping over the surface of the delicate skin there, conferring on Andy yet a further set of fresh sensations to marvel at, and prompting him to try this out on Jon's superb back. He caused his four fingernails to skim their way from the small of that back right up to his neck in one wide sweep. It was now Jon's turn to call out in the muffled way that mouths have when filled with a living pec and its proud nipple.

Rick's mouth decided it was time to seek pastures new, which happened to be Andy's other nipple. With the lightning trauma of having both nipples chewed, sucked and teased concurrently, Andy was compelled to draw in his breath and hold it there until the moment had subsided sufficiently to allow him to release the air in a huge groan. At the same time, four determined hands were groping and scratching their way about the upper parts of his tensed body.

He ventured at last to open his eyes. By God, what a vision it was to see those two magnificent creatures working at his body so assiduously and, yes, so lovingly, after all! Andy wished he possessed the mobility of both arms, the better to return some of their favours. He tried to make up for it by sharing his hand between them, feeling below Jon's arm to manipulate one of his nipples, then he'd do the same with more difficulty for Rick, who didn't seem to derive quite so much joy from that specific technique as did he and Jon. With Rick it was, yes, an extensive area around the armpit and his throat, the latter being evidenced when Jon unexpectedly assaulted the region below his partner's Adam's apple with gnawing teeth. So, that wasn't a 'razor burn' rash Rickie always seemed to suffer under there!

Andy continued to send tremors through both men by the deployment of his dextrous fingers upon their arms and upper bodies, and their kisses began to wander away from his tits, describing small circles down his stomach and back again.

They knelt up on either side of him and embraced one another, leaving Andy alone to regain his composure before renewing their attack, as they surely would. Andy glimpsed the fortunate men's love-probes coiled in readiness to spring out from the restraining pouches of their black briefs. How Andy wanted to grasp them and fondle them, but they were private property. Once again, Jon's mouth made contact with his lover's throat, causing Rick to moan and gurgle, while their hands explored familiar and well-loved nooks and crannies.

On cue, they swooped down again upon Andy's gaping mouth and treated it to further succulence. Next was the turn of the backs of his ears, and down his neck where their faces became engrossed in the wavy locks that lay upon his pillow despite being far shorter than they had been. Their mouths were working almost in unison. What one did the other immediately matched. To his mouth they returned, kissing him tenderly and savagely by turns. Always the element of surprise governed, especially where the men's four hands were operating wholly independently. When Jon vanished under the bedding and began nibbling his way back down Andy's squirming body again, Rick followed him all the way.

Sixteen

"Now there's an intriguingly familiar face," Jon announced as he inspected the landscape through Andy's binoculars.

The three men had just showered following their night together, which had started with a more than two-hour tutorial inducting Andy into some practices of the erotic arts to help him prepare for when Kit would be making demands upon him in that direction.

Andy had been a fast learner, perhaps more than ready to make up for lost time, and he had astonished the couple with a few novel ideas of his own in the exercising of creative solo performance. At one especially critical point he had breathlessly mumbled the assertion, "All wank and no foreplay makes jack-offs dull, boy", a timely remark guaranteed to trigger off chortled groans. They had each awoken on this bright spring morning from a deep slumber of unremitting arousal, and without the time to do anything more about it.

Compelled thereby to rule out his preferred boxer shorts, Andy was wearing one of the lad's briefs and a short-sleeved white shirt of his own when he rushed over to the bedroom window. Roughly he pulled Jon well back and to one side of the pane before relieving him of the powerful glasses which he put to his own eyes.

"Never make yourself such a visible target like that again," he severely reproved Jon. "That is the very best fucking way of getting yourself killed I can think of in the current situation."

"Sorry, I should have had more sense. See, over there, near the edge of that promontory," Jon instructed, standing behind him and pointing to a rocky bluff possibly a kilometre away to the south-east. "It's that thin, moustachioed gent with the curly black hair sitting on a boulder by himself. Spooky."

From the position of the house, west of the open end of the great mountain's horseshoe shape, every detail was visible in the clear, dry air of the morning.

Andy eventually located the man, who seemed about forty, wearing a pale-grey suit totally out of place and impractical in those untamed surroundings. Even so, he was complete with what appeared to be a pair of night-vision binoculars slung about his neck. It was probably a Kalashnikov rifle fitted with a laser aiming device that was leaning against a rock beside him. Secreted in a shallow recess in the cliff, the fellow was probably well concealed from prying eyes on either side of him. Presumably he was able to keep watch on activities directly ahead of his station with relative impunity. As the house was inside his field of vision, the reverse was also true to the keener-eyed of its present residents.

The Briton pondered for only a moment. "Ah, it's that increasingly ubiquitous pal of ours, Carlo Scalfaro, the bloke who was at our Chicago hotel with the female who turned my room over. He was ostensibly her driver. Then we saw him again keeping tabs on us when we were about to go to the railroad station."

"Who's he work for?"

"Umberto Ciampi, I thought, but maybe it's Giuseppe. My database describes him as a freelancer who sells his services to the highest bidder."

"What's to stop him setting one off against another?"

"Nothing. I dare say he does it all the time. I'll ask Giuseppe what he knows about him.

"Geez, these little pants of yours aren't half tight." He ran a finger under them around the top of his leg.

Jon winked at him. "With you in that state it's no wonder. Now you know why so many guys wear them."

Rick was now fully dressed in first-time-on black trousers and white shirt identical to what his partner had on, for they had purchased them hurriedly in the same store. Even their sturdy black trainers were alike. He called across, "Andy, do you propose to meet Sarah got up like that, or is it someone else you're hoping to give a treat to?"

A knock came to the door. "Come."

Michael and Leo entered, the former carrying a full, white plastic bag.

"Good morning, sirs, we have brought your laundry for you. May we put it away for you?"

"Thank you, Michael," replied Rick. He turned to Jon. "I believe that's just answered my question!" he sniggered.

Andy surveyed the young valets, a grin playing about his features. "I see what you meant yesterday," he breathed, "Someone certainly knew how to pick them!"

He was again reminded of his condition when he noticed Leo goggling in the direction of his nether region. Appalled, he hastily tugged his tunic shirt front across the hard ridge of diaphanous white silk persistently dividing it. "I'll go and finish dressing," he decided.

He threw on a pair of well-worn khaki Chinos and some heavy shoes. While yet in his room, Andy's own valet came in before he'd ruffled up his bedding to make it appear as if he had slept in it. He mumbled something about his having just made his own bed, but astute manservants were ever alert to male discomposure.

The trio left their rooms thankfully. Their valets would no doubt already be enthusiastically comparing notes. Rick knocked at Sarah's and Peter's bedroom.

Sarah opened the door. "Hello, chaps, come on in. We're nearly ready. Oh, we are ready," she amended when her husband came up behind her.

"Right now, I've really got to see how Kit is this morning," Andy told them as they made their way to the Ciampis' private apartment. "But I'll just say 'good morning' to Giuseppe first."

The door to the dining room was ajar. The housekeeper, Eloise, was there mildly ticking off one of her staff.

"Mr Ciampi's compliments, madam, sirs. He asks you to join him in his study whenever you are ready."

"Thank you, Eloise," Peter said.

She took them four doors up the corridor, knocked, and showed them in to a comparatively small, thoroughly informal room imbued with the smell of Giuseppe's favourite brand of cigar. There was no one there yet, but a side table was laid out with comestibles for a continental breakfast.

"Please take whatever you need. The coffee is over there on the Gaggia. When you need some more, please ring that bell. I imagine that Mr Ciampi will join you shortly." She departed.

Andy made a quick exit straight away, declaring, "OK, before Giuseppe gets here, I'll go and see if Kit's awake yet." Once out of the family's company, he dashed passed the surprised housekeeper headlong for the stairs, all his pent-up worries impelling him to take them too precipitately for his own good.

The English people made their breakfast selections and utilised a couple of convenient small tables, before arranging their upright chairs away from the blazing coal fire which was such a welcoming sight. The obviously worked-in room was a departure from the rest of the domestic parts of the house that Rick and Jon had seen. Its furniture was simple, practical and strikingly modern.

With an executive brown-leather swivel chair behind it and untidy with current paperwork, a fine, big wooden desk stood near the farther of the two west-facing windows whence the daylight fell on it from the left. The study was equipped with the usual high-tech electronic aids. Neutral-coloured, roll-down day blinds were fitted to these and to all the windows on the west and south sides of the mansion.

While Jon and Peter talked together, Rick and Sarah were able to continue with the brother-sister conversation they had left off the previous day.

"Even if I am cleared of complicity in this awful business," she said, "I don't see how I can be reinstated even in the behind-the-scenes work I was doing for UNESCO. The press wouldn't let me off so easily: I'd be some sort of personality."

Rick said, "At the farm, they've had it up to here with the brat pack. And Jon and I got our share of attention as well," he recalled bitterly.

"I'm so sorry, Rickie, I truly am."

"It's hardly your fault, is it? You've nothing to reproach yourself for. I suppose once the press have singled out a public-interest figure, they milk every drop of gossip about them until some other poor sods turn up to be sacrificed to the God of Circulation Figures."

"And the Organisation knows that only too well. I'd be harried by the news media to the detriment of whatever job I was doing. In short, I will be an embarrassment to them whatever comes out of this mess. I dare say, for the sake of UNESCO's valuable work throughout the world, damage limitation must be the first priority, and once the UN is exonerated from any responsibility, they and I will have to part company."

"That seems bloody unfair to me."

Sarah shrugged. "And it is, but who said life has to be fair? It wouldn't be UNESCO's fault. But the sum of its work is far more beneficial to the world than any single one of its employees. I accept that."

"Would you get any financial compensation, do you think?"

"A 'handshake' of some kind, yes, probably."

"And what about Peter? He's up to the neck in it as well, isn't he."

"Yes, and he may well find himself in the same sinking boat. We're not too sure about his position."

"Looking at it from the worst side –"

Giuseppe entered briskly at that juncture.

"Hi, everybody. Ah, you are getting tuckered out, I see. I'll be with you in a couple of shakes."

The English reciprocated his greeting, and smiled quizzically at their host's well-meant but misplaced Ozzy slang, though nobody offered to disabuse him.

While he was collecting his own food, the two conversations were carried on.

"If the worst comes to the worst," said Rick, "and you are not reinstated by UNESCO, what do you think you might do? Then there's the baby. You don't have a house, do you? Would you come home and live at Tor Farm? I'm sure there'd be plenty of room for you, and mum and dad would love to have you and Peter. Mike, too, would want to stand by you. If you are short financially, I might be able to help you a little bit."

"I hope we both would!" Jon admonished his partner. During a natural break in what Peter was telling him about his job, he had overheard the last few sentences of what Rick was saying.

"Sorry, Jon, but we say we're a democracy, so I wasn't going to speak for you without consulting you."

"That's OK then," Jon conceded cheerfully. "But if we are going to help family – your side or mine – we should do it out of our joint funds or not at all."

"Agreed."

"Not that we're exactly flush ourselves," Jon pointed out under his breath.

"Whoa, there!" cried Peter, "what's all this about? Not us, is it, Sarah?" Her expression told him it was.

Rick said to him, "We were only trying to speculate on what happens if you both lose your jobs after this lot."

"Is that really likely?" Giuseppe intervened, alarmed.

"Well, it could be on the cards, I'm afraid," replied Peter, then he explained what he and his wife had reluctantly concluded, it being more or less what she had just articulated to her brother.

"Why, this is unconscionable!" exclaimed Giuseppe vehemently. He sat down with his food and cogitated for a while, a frown creasing his flabby visage.

"I have a helicopter coming to lift all of you out this afternoon," he told them. "By the by, where's Andy? Or can I guess?" He smiled kindly. "Kit's doing fine, I'm glad to tell you."

Andy was met by a happy face as he approached Kit's bed. It was not quite up to one of those glorious beams of sunshine Andy was used to getting from him, but it was a worthy effort under the circumstances. After all, he still had a tube up his right nostril, a drainage catheter from his chest wound, drips, and goodness knew what else he was attached to besides – though the ordnance of life-support apparatus was no longer evident.

The nurse had discreetly excused herself from the room when Andy arrived, saying that she would return in ten minutes or before, if she was summoned by the buzzer. So they were thoughtfully left alone.

Andy regarded the man, smiling proudly. He took his hands between his own, leant over and kissed him tenderly on the lips. A tear fell upon Kit's right cheek. "Thank God, thank God," Andy murmured. "I love you so much, Kit. But I thought I had lost you, I really did."

Kit gazed devotedly into his eyes. "They told me what you did, Andy," he croaked in a whisper. "The surgeon told me that I might not have pulled through but for you talking me through it. Said you never left me." His handsome features contorted; it was somewhere between weeping and a cheeky grin. "Sorry, but I can't recall a solitary thing you said!"

"Perhaps that's just as well," joked Andy. "Christ, but it's so cool to have you back. Just to be near you is a tonic." He could see the life scintillating in those azure eyes, feel the pulse in his big warm hands.

Kit focused on Andy's arm dressing. The sight alarmed him. "Did they get you, too? Does it hurt bad?"

"I wasn't hit by a bullet, no. Just bad luck, really. I was stabbed by a piece of glass: nasty at the time, but it only hurts a bit now and again. Nowhere near as much as you've been put through. The nurse tells me they're controlling your pain. Is that true?"

"If that's what she said, it must be true," murmured Kit noncommittally. "Kiss me again, honey," he begged.

Andy stroked Kit's soft, bristly crew cut. How good that felt for both of them. He lowered his mouth onto Kit's, traced the tip of his tongue over the finely pronounced philtrum, and they kissed deeply and quietly and lovingly – for an age that seemed to them like a few seconds.

The nurse came in, saw her patient's arms fondly about his visitor's neck, and left without making a sound to disturb them. She shed a tear or two of her own.

Kit broke away suddenly. "Say, I'm so sorry I couldn't tell you about myself. You thought I had betrayed you, didn't you?"

"I couldn't believe what you'd done. It made me so angry and frustrated that everything I thought I knew about you was one big lie! And look what I did to you," he bemoaned.

"How can I?" retorted Kit. "All I know is that my face feels like it's been through a blender, and I bet some of the pain I think is from the bullet wound is really what you gave me." Seeing the dismay on Andy's countenance, he insisted, "But you were magnificent, baby! I deserved what you gave me and lots more. I hated myself for deceiving you of all people, and the boys. But I had to do it. You were doing a job of work; so was I. We were on the same side, but I only knew what Umberto had said. Have you spoken to Uncle Giuseppe? Do you know he is my uncle by marriage?" The fatigue was telling on him.

"Yes, I have. He explained a great deal to me."

"But you were with me yesterday?"

"I told you, I love you, no matter what."

Kit pulled Andy down to him.

The nurse entered, and saw her patient's arms were still round Andy, and made to leave once more, but she called: "Mr Kit will have to get some rest now. Don't exhaust him. You have the rest of your lives for that!"

She had departed when Andy looked round. The couple sniggered.

"Have we, Andy? The rest of our lives? Do you think we can put up with each other for the next fifty years?"

"Make that sixty, and you're on!"

Ten minutes later, Andy opened the door of Giuseppe's study, where a genial discussion was going on. The company looked up as he entered. He was patently aglow with happiness.

"My apologies, everyone. We got talking, I'm afraid." Andy went over to the coffee-maker.

"That's so wonderful, Andy," Sarah declared. "He is going to make a complete recovery, then?"

"So they assure me," said Andy. "They are on the lookout for signs of infection, as you might expect. Once past that hurdle, he should be up and about in a few weeks."

"That's what they said to me," confirmed Giuseppe. "I have asked them to inform his base that he won't be reporting for duty for a while." He looked purposefully at Andy. "You know? His navy base?"

Andy merely smiled angelically, and sat down with his coffee next to Giuseppe.

"The police made six arrests last night," Giuseppe reported. "All North African students, they tell me. Cornered them in a box canyon. They gave up without a fight."

"Does the name Scalfaro mean anything to you, Giuseppe?" Andy casually queried.

"Carlo Scalfaro works for my brother sometimes," was the surprised response. "Why do you ask about him?"

Andy outlined where they had encountered him previously. "Now he is staked out on the mountain behind our rooms. I was only wondering if he is there on your orders."

"I do not employ unrepentant criminals. I didn't even know he is in the neighbourhood. I'll phone Vinny, Umberto's right-hand man, and see what he knows. I have absolutely no notion of where Umberto might be holed up right now. Nor do I want to know," he added with acerbity. He crossed to his desk and laconically addressed a secretary by intercom.

"I get told more by Vinny than I do by Umberto, any ways," he subsequently smiled to the company as he stepped round the desk and dropped into his personalised chair to the strident protests of its hide upholstery. Presently, a buzzer sounded and the secretary put through the call.

Getting the pleasantries out of the way, Giuseppe said, "Vinny, what do you know about Carlo Scalfaro? Yes. Do you know where he is at this time?" The voice said it had no idea where he was. The man had been seen a couple of nights ago at Umberto's, but not since then. "Is he working for my brother just now?" If he were, the speaker would have known about it. Was there a problem? "Yes, Vinny. He has been spotted near here this morning, and I can't work out why he should be here at all – especially as I would have been told if he had been near the house openly. Anyhow, thanks for your assistance."

Giuseppe spoke again to his secretary.

He explained to his guests: "I must find out whether he really has been here and somebody has neglected to inform me. If there's an acceptable reason for it, I want to know what it is before putting it on the back burner. Otherwise we must assume that his presence is not friendly."

Five minutes later, a stocky, clean-shaven little man in his late thirties came into the study. Tending towards fat himself, he was introduced to Andy as Peter Ciampi, Giuseppe's second-eldest son. Jon and Rick had met him and his gorgeous-looking wife briefly the day before at the family lunch.

"I don't know, Dad," he said, preferring the American appellation for his father to the Italian, just as he chose not to be called Pietro, his baptismal name. "Nobody I spoke to has seen the guy round here for months. What he is doing here on our property today we'll have to ask him, I guess."

"See what side he's rooting for, Peter. Take a couple of guys with you.

He's a tricky customer by all accounts. He won't be alone, so take care now."

"I will go too," declared Andy. "This is fundamentally our affair, and you and your people have done more than enough to help already."

"Terrorism is the world's affair, Andy," Giuseppe reminded him, "and we have some of the resources here to help fight it."

"Yes, but it was one of our nationals who was abducted."

"And one of ours who abducted her!" averred Giuseppe. "Besides, Sarah and Peter got involved as United Nations personnel, didn't they? Not as Britishers."

"OK, you win," Andy allowed with a grin, his body language indicating his readiness to leave immediately.

Rick and Jon exchanged glances and also made to leave. Andy opened his mouth to intervene, but decided against it, though when Sarah's Peter walked over to them, Andy put his foot down.

So did Giuseppe. "I am not going to permit a United Nations official put himself at risk on my property!"

"We went with you to Leadville the other night," insisted Peter.

"That was different," stated Giuseppe without deigning to explain why, and in a voice not brooking contradiction. He turned to his son. "Get these guys some personal protection, will you? We don't want any of you hurt."

"No, we definitely don't," said Sarah, crossing to her brother and Jon and giving them a hug. "Don't you take any more chances, you two."

The four men went down into the white-painted basement maze of the house, Peter Ciampi speaking some instructions into his intercom on the way. Unlocking an elaborately secured, small steel door, he led his companions into a veritable arsenal of hand weapons suitable for every conceivable eventuality.

Off one of the wall racks he took an Israeli-made Desert Eagle Magnum – one of the world's most powerful hand guns – and offered it to Andy. "Ever used one of these?"

"I certainly have," replied Andy, grasping it with assured fingers and examining it favourably. He again took his left arm from its sling to load the gun deftly with one of the three clips he was given.

Meanwhile, his friends were presented with a pair of Smith & Wessons, which they rejected in preference for standard, semi-automatic Winchester-type rifles more approximating the kinds they had used in their university shooting clubs and, especially in Rick's case, in farm vermin control.

Two more youngish men arrived. One was a brother-in-law of Peter, the other a cousin. The three Ciampi family members selected Magnums apiece. They and Andy put on holsters, then they all donned bullet proofing, buckling the black garments round their waists. As they left the room, Rick noticed a coil of strong line hanging from a wall hook. He slung it across those broad shoulders which had just landed the party with what amounted to an unprecedented problem to them: that of finding him a protective vest large enough. A compromise solution was reached after the cousin's odd suggestion that Rick should borrow Giuseppe's met with deserved ridicule – wherever one big man was exceptionally wide, the other was narrow.

Upstairs, they emerged into the daylight at the rear of the house. The police presence close to the house was reduced here to the point of invisibility.

"They panned out through the hills to flush the bastards out," clarified Peter Ciampi as the group passed out of the gardens via a metal gate on to the gradually rising pasture beyond. "They left half a dozen of their buddies behind, that's all."

Having first established that Scalfaro no longer stood sentinel where they had observed him earlier, they initially moved to the right – away from their potential quarry's previous position, until they attained the belt of mixed woodland. In its concealment they veered to their left, climbing acutely now, skirting the enclosed valley which gave shelter to the mansion from the weather yet rendered it so exposed to any predation from the heights above.

After scrambling over an extensive area of shifting red and grey-streaked shingle eroded from the mountainside, the six began scaling a ramp of more stable igneous rock round the corner from the bluff facing the house. It was not long before they had circled with it into the opening of the horseshoe itself. Half way to the top, they could see more trees overhanging the edge of that escarpment over to their left. The group paused for a breather among some fallen boulders.

The crash of a rifle shot startled them. It had come from above where they were standing. Another followed fast behind it, resonating among the mountains and sending loose stones skittering down the slope towards them.

Darting for shelter behind the boulders, they rapidly took stock.

"Were they firing at us?" Jon gulped, looking round his fellows for signs of injury.

"It don't seem like it," drawled Peter Ciampi, scanning the hills for movement. "Might be the police cornered someone."

A further shot blasted out. A puff of what was probably gun smoke curled out of the trees to the left of those overhead.

Andy stared back at the view far below them. "Surely they're shooting at the house, Peter," he declared.

"Seems so," replied the other curtly, ducking down with the rest when three men broke cover considerably below this side of where the shots had been fired, only to disappear again into the scrub. "Damn, I reckon they spotted us!" he cried.

He was right, for a burst of automatic fire strafed the ground around them, pinning them down behind the rocks.

"We've got 'em cornered ourselves," Peter's young cousin said. "Isn't this the only way down from there?"

"It's the only easy way down for them, unless they can climb up the rock face way, way behind them which we can't see from down here." Peter had explored these hills since he was a kid.

"It goes both ways, doesn't it?" proposed Andy, pulling out his gun. "They have the height advantage and can hold us here for as long as they want. It may be a lengthy stand-off."

"Sure, except over yonder on the opposite side, just above that steep bluff, there's an easy way to get over the summit that they could use if they discovered it."

Rick was examining the topography of their surroundings. He could visualise that, long after alluvial rocks had been laid down as sediment under ancient seas, unimaginable upward pressures forming these mountains had created the cliff over to their left which Peter had just pointed out, those cataclysmic forces thrusting the horizontal layers almost to the vertical. Later in that geological period, volcanic action had sent molten lava flows, like the solidified one they were now on, gushing down between some of the series of similar, towering structures composing the mountain. Cracks had opened up in this particular mass, a fairly deep one extending laterally from about ten metres in front of the crouching men's rock fastness to where the lava had once slithered downward against the flank of that cliff.

"See that fissure just ahead of us?" Rick indicated. "If we could only get into it we could probably reach the cliff unnoticed and shin up it on the side facing the house where they can't observe us from where they've moved to."

"I see what you mean, Rick," said Andy.

"So do I," Peter captiously remarked. "That's a right fearsome bluff, and we ain't none of us rock climbers, are we!"

Rick glanced from Andy to Jon. Jon returned him a little nod.

"You get going, lads," Andy directed. "We'll give you covering fire till you get into the trench." He looked at Ciampi Junior. "You were too presumptuous, Peter. By all accounts, these two are experts at the game."

"We'll give it our best shot, any rate," Rick promised. "Right, Jon?"

"I'm ready."

Andy signalled the opening up of a fusillade of fire directed at the trees near where the gunmen were last seen. Jon and Rick began sliding on their stomachs back down the ramp to achieve maximum shelter from the boulders, then they raced for the crack in the rock floor, which they gained within a few seconds and dived into it.

By remaining hunched down, they would keep their heads below the rim and out of sight of the men above. The rock being porous, it was fairly dry under foot, but grasses and a scattering of small cacti colonised much of the crevice's meandering length. Keeping a wary eye open for poisonous snakes, Rick and Jon crept along it, its width varying from just a couple of hundred centimetres to several metres. In places, the jagged sides almost met over their heads while leaving them barely sufficient room to squeeze their bulk through what were effectively tunnels.

The gunfire had become sporadic by the time the couple hit the cliff. They tied onto the climbing rope. Without the aid of sophisticated mountaineering apparatus such as they were used to, Rick started first up the almost sheer face. The weathered nature of the stone provided the climbers with ample finger and toe holds, but the entire structure was gradually crumbling away, so it behoved them to take time and extreme care to ensure that those they selected could bear their weight. At one point, they had to backtrack due to the erosion of a whole section of cliff which looked ready to collapse at the slightest provocation. This brought them to a nasty traverse that needed to be negotiated. It was quite the most dangerous undertaking they had ever tackled. Clinging like limpets to the powdery surface, they paused for breath, and, despite being incredibly scared, took in the marvellous vista behind them and below, where the magnificent mansion nestled in its valley bottom. They could discern quite plainly the windows of the English guests' three bedrooms. Peering down past their right elbows, they were able to see their comrades staring up at them, but from here the enemy position was on their right, around the curve of the cliff out of their range of vision.

They toiled upwards for a further fifteen minutes before they heaved themselves over the rim on to more level ground. Unhesitatingly, they pushed their way into the tangled undergrowth of the trees behind. Far beyond them, the further perpendicular cliff mentioned by Peter Ciampi could be seen from here soaring up a thousand metres or more. What he had meant became obvious to the climbers when they realised that fairly close to the edge of the cliff they had just surmounted, now some one hundred metres to their left, there was a relatively easy ascent which was likely to offer the gangsters an escape route should they come this way.

The intercom that Rick was carrying chirped. It was Andy.

"You both OK?" he asked apprehensively.

"Yep, Andy," panted Rick in a low tone, "but these bloody bullet-proof whatsits – jackets – hampered us badly, and we're a bit overheated. Just give us a few minutes, will you?"

"Sure thing, guys!" chimed in Peter Ciampi's voice full of admiration. "That was some feat, you climbing the face of that bluff like that. No one's ever done it before, as I ever heard."

"No one has been that stupid, you mean!" Jon cried. "How far do you reckon we are from the gunmen?"

"Mm, about four, five hundred metres, I suppose," replied Andy.

"I guess that's about right," Peter joined in, recalling his metric from NATO exercises with Canadian infantry in British Columbia following his draft.

"The shots at the house were fired not far from where you are now," Andy gauged. "Giuseppe's just been on to us. They were directed at the house. At Sarah's bedroom window, to be precise! They were being thorough dorks, like you: she and Peter must have been watching our progress from there, when bullets smashed through the window."

"Are they hurt," gasped Rick.

"No, Rickie," Andy assured him. "One of Peter's ears was grazed either by a bullet or a flying splinter, that's all. Those were long-range shots, luckily, so not as accurate as they might have been. They were fucking idiots to have stood there on display like that! They were asking for trouble."

Jon nudged his partner and pointed at the opposite prong of cliff across the gap their companions were hiding in.

"Hey, Andy," Rick alerted him, "we can see some more blokes up here, over on the other side of you! Wait a minute. Yes, they're police, I think."

"That's great. Can they see you?"

"I doubt it. We are hidden from them."

"Well, keep it that way for now, in case they think you are on the wrong side and start shooting at you!"

"Roger."

"Peter's on his phone to them now."

From their vantage position, the couple could easily make out the police movements. There were about eight of them and two were women. They spread themselves out among the trees and rocks on the far side of the horseshoe.

A sonorous voice boomed out: "This is the police. This is the police! We have you trapped. Throw out your weapons now, and come out slowly with your hands on your heads. You cannot escape," it added hopefully, "so don't try anything!"

A barrage of automatic fire emanating from the trees at the head of the valley demonstrated the disdain those terrorists owned for the forces of law. Co-ordinating now by phone, the police and those down below immediately opened fire on the terrorists' position. Simultaneously, the same four led by Andy commenced a steady advance up the slope, rock by helpful rock, intent on pinning down the gunmen who were still concealed in the lower band of trees, rather than letting them regroup with their allies above.

Rick and Jon quickly unslung their own weapons from their shoulders.

Where the rugged upper escarpment came within two hundred densely-wooded metres of the edge of the one they had climbed, Jon posted himself on top of a tall outcrop at its base facing towards the intense rattle of gunfire, while Rick remained right at the centre of the tree belt, sprawling under a huge pine a little farther away from the current battle. They knew that these might be their final moments together, though even now neither could see the other. One or both of them might not live through the next half hour.

For they had come to the daunting conclusion that here they occupied what had to be the gang's sole way out from their predicament. The gunmen would have to pass through this gap to reach either the more gradually descending mountainside to the east or the upward alternative. The couple could try to block their way, playing the element-of-surprise card they undoubtedly possessed, or they could let them go through unchallenged, in the hope that the police might pick them up later. The latter option was rejected outright: hadn't enough uninvolved people suffered already because of this affair? They themselves must do everything they could to stop the gangsters in their tracks right now, for at least long enough to enable the cops to come up in the rear and close the trap.

Ten nerve-stretching minutes crept by. The prospect of actually having to shoot real bullets at real people was profoundly disgusting. If only the police could halt them, or make them go some other way. But a thrashing amongst the under-wood some distance away warned the trembling men of their running approach. Five or six unsuspecting figures could be glimpsed through the trees' shadows making towards the ambush set for them.

Jon briefly reflected upon the fate of the tragic honeymooners on the train, and was the first to fire. A bear of a man clutched at his head with a screech and fell as if poleaxed. Rick let go two bullets, striking one man in the midriff, another in the chest. Both went down instantly. Jon fired again, but missed his target. A bullet hit the edge of his rock, kicking up a spray of sharp stones into his face. Blood oozed over his left eye as he fired back at the man who had shot at him, hitting that killer above the ear before he had time to hide behind the nearest tree.

The surviving gunmen were shooting back in Rick's vicinity. He heard a yell of pain from his partner. Jon went cold. He slid from his rock and stole rapidly towards the sounds, scarlet blood running down his cheek. He felt sure he had lost that eye. Ahead he descried the back of the man he had observed from the house, Scalfaro, the gangster in the pay of The Light of the World who must have flown to Denver to carry out his contract to slay Sarah. He was half kneeling behind a fallen tree trunk, rifle at the ready.

Jon dropped to his left knee and raised his shaking rifle to his shoulder. "Murdering bastard!" he shrieked at the man.

Scalfaro twisted round, saw his danger, and aimed his sights at Jon's bloody head. Before he could squeeze the trigger, however, Jon's bullet struck him full in the face. He fell like a stone, just as searing pangs burst through his adversary's head. Jon saw no more, and sank to the ground with a terrible groan.

A single red-haired individual broke cover and sprinted off to his left, fleeing the many feet he could hear pounding after him. He suddenly found himself exposed in the open, a couple of metres from the precipice. A bullet fired from below hit his left thigh; a sharp ache, and he lost the use of that leg. He began to drag himself back into the wood. To his horror, the ground beneath him instantaneously split apart. Emitting a fearful screech, he threw up his arms and plummeted to oblivion amid tens of thousands of avalanching tonnes of decayed rock and living trees.

The pursuing police pulled themselves up short as the ground fell away before them, managing just in time to scamper back to safety. The roar of the landslide utterly deafened them. An entire section of that two hundred-metre high bluff had collapsed into the valley. Vast clouds of reddish-brown dust billowed across the darkened terrain.

In that choking blanket, four struggling men were continuing their steep ascent via the stone ramp. If they had stayed where they were, they would have been swept away and buried for ever along with the trio they had been after, who had taken to their heels to get away from them, straight into the jaws of the avalanche. They had to go even more swiftly now, for there was no telling what conditions awaited them up there. They had heard the second battle get under way where the escaping gangsters must have encountered Rick and Jon.

Andy was horribly afraid of what he might find. So many seasoned gunfighters against two English rookies whose only knowledge of firearms probably derived from a little recreational target practice and a spot of rabbiting on the moors. When the gunmen up there tried to escape that way, why the hell didn't they both hide themselves and wait for their friends and the cops to reinforce them? Maybe they saw the gangsters preparing to waylay the pursuing police, and decided to put a stop to it. Perhaps they were perfectly all right, and any moment they would present themselves unharmed on the ledge above him waving cheerily through the drifting dust. But time passed, and they failed to make an appearance. He had sadly lost comrades in the field prior to this, but that anything might have befallen those two lovely blokes was more than he could bear to entertain.

Still spluttering and gagging to clear their mouths and throats, the sweaty, begrimed party vaulted the final vertical metre onto the narrow ledge fronting that part of the wood. They turned to their left and strode quickly towards the forward-jutting arm of the mountain where the skirmish had apparently ended. Andy wondered whether his last bullet striking that gangster had in some perverse way brought on the catastrophe which overtook him. He asked himself grimly whether that same thug had been an instrument of hurt to Rickie or Jon.

The police were examining the casualties. Two of the gunmen were alive, but seriously wounded. Peter Ciampi found a policeman squatting by Rick's prostrate body. He called over to Andy. They had to explain to the lawman that Rick was not one of the criminals. Rick had certainly swooned with agony after at least two bullets ripped through his right shoulder. The largest available body protector was indeed too small for him.

When Andy subsequently discovered Jon's body, he nearly wept. It was lying prone, close to where the facially mutilated corpse of one whom he supposed to be Carlo Scalfaro lay half-propped against a fallen log. The brown tree litter was sponging up the blood issuing from Jon's face. Gingerly, he turned the injured head. A livid gash over the right temple indicated where he had been hit by a bullet. An unsightly wound around his left eye socket was the source of all this blood. If he lived, it was possible he would be partially blinded. Andy felt mortified and totally gutted.

A helicopter was summoned up. There was nowhere for it to land, so it took nearly an hour to winch up the wounded men and transport them to the house, two at a time. The couple were given first priority, and were met at the front of the mansion by Giuseppe and an anguished Sarah and her husband. Once again, the efficiency of the surgical team's call-out system had been tested and found not wanting.

Jon and Rick were rushed to the examination room, both still unconscious.

By the time Andy's party had descended on foot from the mountain, both theatres were scenes of feverish activity. There being no news of how the couple were, Andy went straight into Kit's sickroom.

Kit was alone. With good nursing, at least his complete recovery could be assured. He woke from another doze when Andy came in. He blinked.

"Say, you look a right mess-up!" exclaimed the patient affectionately. "What's happened to you now?"

Andy blew him a kiss and then stepped into the closet, leaving the door open. While he showered the filth from his body, Andy recounted to a distressed Kit what had occurred, though not how severely Rick and Jon might have been injured.

When he mentioned Scalfaro, Kit exclaimed, "It was after I spotted Carlo across the street that he raised his rifle and shot me."

"It was Scalfaro who shot you? Christ. I'll bet he was in the pay of The Light all the time he was supposed to be working for Umberto."

"Sure thing. I've been thinking about it a lot. His double dealing explains so much of what's been happening. Umberto trusted him too readily."

"Well, he won't be betraying anyone else, that's for certain. He got what was coming – from Jon, it looked like."

Once more clean, he donned Kit's unused short dressing gown then went to his bedside at last. He sat on the bed, taking care not to put pressure on Kit's wounded area, and kissed the agitated man tenderly on the lips, his nose and eyes.

"Hello," he whispered soothingly.

"Hi, honey."

They kissed some more, then Kit interjected.

"You ain't a Christian, are you?"

"No. I'm nothing really. I don't think you are, either."

"S'right enough. Don't hold with none of that man-made religious stuff. But, say, do you think if we meditate together in some way, think about them, try hard enough to wish those two guys well again, it may help them a mite? I know they are hurt worse than you told me."

Andy let that pass. "I don't think there is anything else you and I can usefully do for them and – who knows? – it may be very good for all of us."

"Then let's do it. But before you get too settled," said Kit with a rueful grimace, "fetch me a bottle, nurse. I'm bursting for a piss."

Seventeen

It was mid-August, ten weeks after Sarah's public exoneration, seven after the corpses of the Southern State Governor and Max Singer were discovered in adjacent Washington DC hotel rooms, shot to death by a third party. Nobody had yet found out what the prominent UNESCO man's business was with the governor, nor what he was doing in the US at all just then.

On the day Sarah and Peter had been helicoptered to Colorado Springs, they were met at the Dwight Medical Center by its internationally respected head geneticist. He took various samples from Sarah, and certified their source. No match whatsoever had been found with other microscopic traces collected from that infamous roof in Geneva. Furthermore, the DNA profile which his team subsequently built up failed to correspond with that produced from the blood of the purportedly wounded sharpshooter, so the conspiracy, falsely to sully Sarah's name and the UN's reputation for impartiality, was able to be proved. Once the Bosnian authorities accepted this evidence as irrefutable, the peace talks were immediately put back on track.

The genocide on all sides, meanwhile, continued unabated. As Sir Rupert had predicted, the deliberately misinformed populace preferred to remain that way. In war, especially civil war, myth squeezes the trigger of history.

Carol gazed affectionately across the huge farmhouse kitchen at her daughter and Peter still sitting at the breakfast table poring over the just-delivered local newspaper. The dishwasher completed its cycle, so she proceeded to unload it.

Sarah's getting quite big now, she mused. But then, the twins are due in November: the twelfth, was it? Gracious, she's been home for a month already!

It was such a shame, them deciding not to stay in England, but who could blame them for accepting that nice Mr Ciampi's generous offer? Their former careers had been compromised. Carol certainly understood that, for wasn't it bad enough for her and her family having to continue living here after all that had happened? The publicity, the filthy accusations, the villagers' and neighbours' private lives being held up to public scrutiny and criticism the way they were. The press brigades had moved on to prey on new victims, but it would take a very long time for the dust hereabouts to settle and for the resentment against her family, albeit unintended, and the hurt to subside.

Thank goodness, at least Peter's young nephew and niece were returned unharmed to their parents soon after Sarah was proved innocent. How did the story go? The police in Belgrade were given the tip-off about an address in a disused office block where the children could be found? Well...

Peter sneezed.

"Is there anything in there about Jon's operation?" Carol asked the readers.

"Yes, mum, we've just found it," replied Sarah. She read out loud: "'The well-known local veterinary surgeon, Jon Reynolds, 28, of Knutsford Road, is recovering from a third operation to save the sight of his left eye following a shooting incident in the United States three months ago, which we reported in our columns when the news was later released.

"'A splinter of stone caused by a bullet ricocheting off a rock was deeply lodged just above Mr Reynold's eyeball, severing vital muscles there. Fears were expressed that he could lose the eye altogether. But eye surgeons at Denver General Hospital succeeded in saving it, though the eye's functions were still in doubt before the operation on Tuesday of last week.

"'Latest bulletins report that Mr Reynolds is recovering well, and that the operation was expected to be a complete success.

"'Meanwhile, his live-in partner, Richard Timperley, also 28, brother of Sarah Simpson who was recently cleared of attempting to take the life of the Bosnian president, is also recovering from surgery to his right shoulder which was badly injured during the same shooting incident in the picturesque Rocky Mountains of Colorado.

"'The agricultural college principal, Mr Thomas Jenkins, 47, told our reporter that Mr Timperly is sorely missed at the college. "Rick is an invaluable member of our staff," he said, "popular among students and staff colleagues alike, and an exceedingly capable tutor. When we first heard of his injuries, we were very upset. When we afterwards learnt that he had been hurt while performing an act of such tremendous courage, we felt extremely proud of the man. All of us at the college wish him and his partner full and speedy recoveries."'

"See, mum?" Sarah said brightly, "They are saying nice things about us these days, as if to make up for the hell they put you through before."

Carol gave a smile of resignation. "It was more the national papers who did that. Besides, they can never compensate for what they did to this community, and I'm sure they were responsible for your father's stroke."

"I feel just as responsible," said her son-in-law. "If Sarah hadn't married me with my Serbian connections, she would not have been singled out for abduction by The Light of the World."

"Don't talk such rubbish, Peter!" commanded Carol. "The terrorists are the ones to blame, never their victims. Only, I'll be ever so glad when all this business has died down, and we can get back to living normally again – if ever that becomes possible. I hate going into town even now, what with people pointing me out and talking in subdued voices when I am near them. But I refuse to become a recluse," she added doggedly. "We have to face it out. And what with his road accident and now his stroke, I dare say father will have to use his wheelchair for the rest of his life. Though he is getting about in it much better," she reasoned, "and he can stand up again now, with help, so perhaps we will be able to go away for a short holiday in the autumn."

"You must both come and stay at *Casa Bianca*, mum," insisted Sarah for the umpteenth time. She was at last getting through. "Giuseppe said that to you when you went there to see Rickie and Jon. This time, dad won't be in hospital, so you can have the time of your lives. The house has a lift to all floors, as you know, and October is one of the loveliest months over there. Mike won't mind looking after the house while you're gone. He has the Platt boys to help him with the farm."

"Your amorous brother is sure to take full advantage of the situation," Peter commented archly for his wife's ears alone.

Carol's hearing was acute, however, but she enquired, "Tell me again, just what will your jobs be over there?"

"Well," said Peter, "Giuseppe is rightly concerned about the deprived underclass of people they have created in the States. He says that people without hope have no reason to behave well in a society that rejects them. He's quite the philanthropist, you know, with a genuine, old-fashioned social conscience. So he has been establishing combined educational and job-training schemes in several states, involving local businesses in providing employment initiatives. He wants Sarah and me to help his organisation set up a pilot project in uptown Denver."

"We do have some experience in that kind of thing," Sarah went on, "and Giuseppe thinks it could be useful. He's probably right. But what we will actually be doing on a day-to-day basis depends on how it develops."

"Oh, I see," her mother said lamely. She still didn't entirely. It was all so very far removed from her own bucolic world.

*

At about the same time, Andy Gregson was in the Passenger Arrivals area at Heathrow Airport. The Jumbo from Washington had landed half an hour ago, only twenty minutes late. He was beside himself with anticipation.

There! there was that familiar, loveable figure, characteristically pacing excitedly from side to side while his beautiful eyes anxiously scanned the waiting crowd. He was wearing a plain, dark-grey suit, a technicolour tie and big, clunky, black suede shoes. His luggage trolley alongside him was stacked high and wide with an assortment of bags and cases.

"Kit! Kit! Over here!" shouted Andy, pushing his way forward.

Kit distinguished Andy's voice above the clamour of the throng, spotted him and, beaming with delight from ear to ear, rushed towards the barrier.

"Andy!" he cried.

"Kit, your baggage! You've forgotten your trolley!" Andy chortled gleefully.

Slithering to a trot, Kit laughed foolishly and, without stopping, jogged comically back for it. When he did coax it through the barrier, he abandoned it once more and fell into Andy's expectant arms.

Andy had been compelled by his job to return to Britain before Kit was well enough to leave his sick room. Now Kit lifted Andy right off his feet. They hugged like lots of other men were doing but, to hell with it, they kissed one another upon the lips with all the tender passion of any loving couple reuniting after an enforced separation, oblivious to everyone and to everything going on around them – this ex-US naval officer and the British soon-to-be-ex-civil servant who meant to resign his own commission as soon as they set their plans in motion. Although Sir Rupert had become acquainted with Kit on his extended visit to his badly hurt son, naturally nothing of their project was divulged to him at that juncture.

Men kissing one another at this notoriously emotion-churning spot was not all that rare an occurrence. Two airport policemen observing the couple from afar decided they could ignore them so long as no one lodged a complaint under an antiquated public order law which was sometimes invoked mischievously by bigots. From where they were, they could see the sturdy men's joyful tears, and had no wish to spoil the moment for them. The constables sauntered away.

"C'mon, lover," said Andy at length, his eyes shining, "let's get your furniture home, shall we?"

"Gee, does it look that bad, honey? I only brought enough stuff along for the first month."

Andy shook his head in amusement. "You could have brought more? This little lot must have cost you a bomb in excess baggage charges."

Side by side, Andy's left hand resting on Kit's right, they trundled the laden trolley in the direction of the automatic doors and out into the sunlight. It was fortunate that Andy had five weeks' holiday leave owing to him which he'd started today.

They had spoken on the phone for at least half an hour every day since Andy left Kit behind, taking it turns to make the call on the dot of six o'clock BST each evening. After a couple of weeks, Kit included Rick and Jon in the developing equation, and both Rick and Andy regularly telephoned Mike at Tor Farm. Andy had driven up there to meet Rick's brother and parents, and had even stayed a couple of weekends to do some prospecting, with Mike's unstinting help.

Meantime, Kit's mother had hastened to *Casa Bianca* to see her son. He confided his intentions to her. She had never been too sanguine about his choosing a naval career, so when she learned of his business proposals, she gladly promised to discuss them with his father. With amazing graciousness, Mr Henderson actually bestirred himself to pay a call on his sister-in-law's palatial home, and there talked things over with Kit. The old sour and muddied ground that had separated them for nearly a decade was turned over, aerated and prepared for profitable cultivation.

Kit reported to his base in due course, then let it be known that he had fallen head over heels – "Ass over tip," as he'd called it – for a guy. His discharge from the Navy, though precipitate, was wholly honourable within the terms of that Service.

The bed Kit had last slept in before leaving the United States was his old one at his parents' home in Henderson, North Carolina. His father had grudgingly accepted his son's sexuality in view of the representations made by his wife, by Giuseppe and that pair of brave English stalwarts he'd met while there in Colorado. He was secretly proud of his son's conduct of his life since leaving home, and was even impressed by the company he had obviously been keeping, despite Kit's sister marrying the son of that hoodlum in Chicago, Giuseppe's brother though he was. Yet, most of all, he was gratified that Kitchener was aiming to return to the family's agricultural machinery business, even to expand it into England, Europe. He had long been seeking new markets: Europe should be big enough. Abe Henderson felt sufficiently heartened to kill the fatted calf, or rather transfer adequate company funds, even though the prodigal was not planning to live at home.

Sure, he had been greatly put out by his careless and irresponsible daughter having to marry Umberto Ciampi's son, and didn't want his own son to grow too close to that branch of the family in consequence. When Umberto's bloated body was fished out of New York's Harlem River one day, it hadn't been a cause for Henderson mourning. Much better for Kitchener to busy himself in Europe.

"So, this is England, eh?" said Kit dutifully, as Andy propelled his red Sierra GTi along the unprepossessing M4 motorway towards London.

Andy sent him a sideways glance. "As you've scarcely taken your eyes off me since you got here, I can't think you've seen much of our Sceptered Isle so far!"

Kit lowered them with a little smile of contentment. "Wherever you are is where I want to be."

"Yeah, yeah, yeah," Andy responded. "I hope we're still saying that this time next year."

"Sure we will," promised Kit, "and long after that."

Andy put his foot down harder on the accelerator.

"Say, don't everyone drive fast over here!" Kit cried, peering round at the speeding traffic, effectively for the first time. "Must be with this side of the road that does it. You are going faster, too."

"That's 'cos I can't wait to get you home," Andy punctuated with a deep-throated animal growl.

Kit stretched out his long legs and leaned back languorously in his seat, his hands folded behind his head. "Christ, honey, I'm just so chilled out. And now that I've even made it with my folks finally... We are going to be all right, you and me – so long as we get home all in one piece!" he qualified.

Andy gave him a light thump on the leg for that. "Cheeky sod. Just keep looking at the scenery, and leave the driving to me. If you are going to live and work in Great Britain, the sooner you start learning about the country the better."

"Oh, I've been learning about it for some time," declared Kit. "But mostly about agricultural practices, you know? Studying market potential an' all?"

"I'm glad to hear it," grinned Andy, who hadn't doubted Kit's inherent punchiness for a moment. "But I'm still not sure what part I am to play in the new company. I've been studying what you sent me: your catalogues and specifications and all that. It's all fascinating stuff. In fact, I'm surprising myself just how interesting I'm finding it. But even though I lived in rural Norfolk till I was nineteen, and know something about farmers and farming second-hand, I have never actually worked in agriculture."

"Why do you keep telling me that, Andy? You've got a better agricultural background than many folks who earn their crumb selling to farmers. And your present job must have taught you heaps about people. You've got a real knack for it. You're a mean judge of character."

"What makes you say that?"

Kit squinted at him and flashed his eyebrows. "Isn't that why I'm here? Out of all the guys in the world, you picked me!"

"I asked for that one," chuckled Andy. "But you were the first to come along. I couldn't be too choosy before that," he added truthfully.

"Why, thanks. So, you were ready to go with anyone who just happened along? That's not what I heard."

"No! Oh shit, you know what I mean."

Kit laughed. "You mean that you were looking in the wrong direction, don't you, sugar?"

"Did I tell you that?"

"I think you must have done, sure."

They were both frowning, trying to remember.

"Are you certain Rickie or Jon haven't said something to you?"

"Lots of things, but not that," answered Kit. "Maybe I'm wrong, but I thought I was sure about you being a virgin." He grew more pensive. "It was you. You did tell me!"

"Only once, and it was true. I was going to warn you again when we got home. Honestly. It was when you were still unconscious, and I was trying to talk you into staying alive."

"Say, I can't recall how you said it, baby, but at least I seem to have held on to something you told me, after all. Flaky, ain't it?" Kit marvelled.

"So you don't mind?"

"You being a virgin? Nope. Fact is, I think it's pretty neat, me being your first. I just hope you don't go changing your mind again afterwards."

Andy howled with laughter. "No chance of that, I promise. I've never been so comfortable with myself as I am now." He had something else to own up to. "But, well, I've got another confession to make. Honestly, I did it for you!"

Kit regarded Andy suspiciously. "Go on, tell me the rest."

"I didn't want to come to you completely green – inexperienced."

"Someone else?"

"Not quite the whole way, Kit, just enough to teach me the basics. I still want you to be the first."

"Oh, yeah?" Kit grinned amiably. "But I get your drift." He squeezed Andy's knee appreciatively. "I'm in for some wicked times, then?"

Andy reddened. "I've not even touched myself since then. I've been keeping myself for you."

"Say! ain't that cool. I've been the same!"

They exchanged a brief smile.

"Who was your teacher?" Kit persisted however. "Do I know him?"

"That's not bloody fair. How would you like me to ask you about all your lovers? How many guys have you had sex with?"

"Lots more than you, by all accounts. OK, forget it, honey."

The harmonious purring of the car's powerful engine reflected their mood as they progressed along the constantly busy highway. They left the motorway, and were soon passing Kew Gardens as they neared Richmond-on-Thames where Andy lived.

He turned into the drive of one of the large, mid-Victorian villas lining a leafy road, and parked up before a plate bearing his name, its stake planted in a narrow strip of shrubbery adorning the front of the house.

Andy inhaled deeply. "We're home," he announced, studying the American's features for his initial reaction. It was favourable.

"This is it? You live in this historic house?" gasped Kit.

"Only a flat – an apartment, I'm afraid. But it does me."

"I know that, Andy. You told me before."

"So I did."

"You are nervous, aren't you, baby?"

"I want you to like it."

"I just love it. Can we go inside?"

Andy giggled. "That's not a bad idea!"

They stepped out of the vehicle.

"Let's go straight up," Andy said. "We can come back for your bits."

"I'm never without them," Kit feebly joked, following his friend into the vestibule. "Say, you're not the only nervous one," he admitted wryly.

Andy unlocked the important-looking white wooden door, and led

Kit up wide stairs to the landing on the next floor. He opened his door and stood aside for Kit to enter.

Kit seemed aggrieved. "Aren't you overlooking somethin'?" He evinced a hopeful smile. "It's your home: aren't you going to do me the honours?"

"Sure thing, buddy!"

Without more hesitation, Andy scooped the beefy man off his feet, cradled him in his arms and transported him across the threshold. After footing the door shut behind them, he carried Kit along the passage to the end door on the right, pushed it open, and went into the colourfully furnished bedroom. Still bearing Kit's considerable weight as if he was only half the size he was, he gently kissed his man once upon the mouth.

With his arms about Andy's broad neck, Kit fiercely pulled that admired face to his own, so that their tongues could begin lusciously entwining, first in Andy's mouth, then in Kit's.

All the while, Andy was edging towards the new double bed he had purchased only last week. When his legs touched its side, he lowered Kit on to it and knelt on the rug alongside him, still engaged in that long, long kiss. He unfastened Kit's necktie and shirt buttons. He removed his own jacket, then Kit's and their shoes and socks. They took off each other's shirts and trousers. Kit got under the duvet and dragged his lover in after him.

At last, panting for breath, they broke their kiss and gazed rapturously into each other's eyes.

"If there had been a heaven, it would have been third rate compared to this," opined Kit.

Andy fingered the small scar three centimetres below Kit's erect right nipple. "If there had been a heaven, you might have gone there without ever finding that out!" He felt round to the corresponding mark on Kit's back. "Looking at my life to date, I think it's often true what they say: what you've never had, you'll never miss. But that can mean you get to live only at quarter speed, then die while still in ignorance of yourself."

Kit's steady blue eyes were piercing him: how he relished it. He kissed each in turn. "Thank God I didn't miss this," he breathed.

They commenced to explore their lusting bodies, removing each other's straining shorts to fondle the moist horniness there and the warm, soft fullness beneath. For more than an hour they lay front to front, their mobile hips locked together as they caressed, chatted about their future, chuckled at witticisms, made realistic promises they knew they would keep, spoke of their mutual friends and of those older ones they could get to know later. Andy had met three of Kit's mates when they visited Kit early on, just before Andy had needed to leave America, so he'd lost the opportunity to get to know them better. The talking ceased as the couple's breathing became more laboured, their kisses wilder. The pristine bedding rustled under their urgent movements, the intermittent grunt,the sighs first of Kit, then almost immediately of his lover as their long pent-up seed released itself and mingled copiously between their firm stomachs. Exquisite spasms were still racking their bodies minutes later while they clung together, incapable of letting go.

They lay half asleep while their skin fully absorbed their blended fluids, but it was well into the afternoon before they finally roused themselves.

"Is that what you learnt off your teacher, Andy?"

"Not really. It just happened the way it did, didn't it?"

"Sure. I never did it like that before. It seemed right for us today, honey."

They showered and symbolically dressed one another.

"Say, have you got seven hundred dollars?" Kit dropped out of the blue.

Andy was taken aback. "Run that by me again." He needed thinking space.

"Can you give me seven hundred dollars?"

"Why, I suppose so," he said curiously. "That's about five hundred quid at present."

"Yep, give or take. Let me have it."

"I – I can give you a cheque." Andy's head was whirling with the confused messages he was getting.

"That's OK, lover. That'll do fine."

Was he wrong about Kit, in spite of everything? Just because his own grandparents had married young only a few months after they met, and claimed to their dying days that they never regretted it for a moment, it didn't signify that love-at-first-itch was always a good idea; something substantial enough to base a lifelong commitment on. Their intuitions had obviously been sound in their day, but who was to say he had inherited their insightful skills intact?

"Can I ask what you want it for right now?"

"Trust me. You'll be glad you did – least ways, I hope you will." A note of uncertainty could be detected in his voice.

"This minute you want it?"

Kit smiled a trifle meekly. He nodded and sat down on the edge of the bed.

"Right, wait here."

"I ain't goin' any place."

Andy went into another room, determined to suppress those sneaking, treacherous doubts. He returned a few minutes later and presented Kit with the cheque.

"Now, what's all this about?"

Kit grinned mysteriously, stood up and went across to where his suit jacket had been hung on the back of the bedroom door after Andy had retrieved it from the floor. He took out his doeskin wallet and deposited the cheque in it. Next he went into another inside pocket. His body concealed what he was doing from Andy.

"Sit where I was and close your eyes just for a minute," came the instruction. Andy complied.

Kit came over and took hold of his hands. Andy could hear and feel what must be a set of those gauges they use in jewellers being inexpertly threaded on and off various of his fingers, leaving him guessing what kind of a ring or rings he was being measured for. "What's all this, Kit? What have you been up to?"

"Nothing, honey," came the airy response. "Be patient. Just checking something out."

Andy was disposed to keep quiet. Kit left him. Came some intriguingly sharper sounds of metal chinking against metal.

"OK, Andy. Guess you can open again."

Kit came back to him and got down on one knee at his feet. He held out two small, white-velvet pouches in a palm that was noticeably trembling. One of them he handed to Andy.

"That is what I had you pay for. If you don't want it, don't worry none. I'll give you the cheque back. No, don't open it for a second."

Tense with apprehension, Kit loosened the drawstring of the pouch he had kept and drew out a truly magnificent man's wedding ring of layered white and yellow gold. "Andy. Lover. Tell me off, yell at me, rebuke me if I have taken too much for granted. But we did say once that we would want to exchange wedding bands when we got together. I –"

"Kit! It's superb! God, you've only anticipated what I was going to say later on. I was going to suggest we go looking tomorrow for our rings."

"You don't mind that I've pre-empted it? Would you have preferred us to have gone shopping together?"

"Only to get the right sizes. I can't imagine that we'd have found any more beautiful than this one."

Plainly eased by this vindication, Kit explained, "I managed to get different sizes for you to try. I think this is the one that will fit your finger: it's the next to biggest of them."

"And I presume that this one I've bought is for me to give you, is that right?"

Kit nodded. Andy opened the bag. It was, of course, a ring identical in appearance to the first.

"Did I do the right thing, then? Are you positive you still want to go this far?"

Andy leaned forward and rested his forehead in Kit's soft crew cut. "I love you more by the minute," he tenderly averred, kissing him as he spoke. "We can go shopping whenever. Tomorrow is one hell of a long time." He sat up. "These are so tasteful and just totally fabulous. Did the lads see them?"

"I wanted to show them, but I wanted your agreement first."

"They look as if they should have set us back a damn sight more than they did."

"We got a real big discount: close friends of the family, you know? I'll show you the receipt later. They designed one pair for this year's White House wedding – remember that? – and made these four authorised copies, and no more."

They stood face to face, each holding the other's hands, and solemnly reaffirmed the promises they had articulated while in the early stages of love making: vows that need not be injuriously broken, while offering both the sense of security they craved. In all things, each would be the other's next of kin by dint of legal contract which no outsider could break; they would support and care for each other through hell and high water. The couple had already defined their ideas of sexual fidelity as questions affecting their mutual respect, and about health, rather than some crude way of shutting out the world. They couldn't, in any case, conceive of ever having it off with another guy unless they shared the occasion.

That was it: all things necessary for a fulfilled life together – constituents that would demand to be untiringly worked at to sustain and keep fresh their relationship: like any marriage, but devoid of those debilitating strictures imposed by that ancient social and economic imperative of ensuring the paternal identity of progeny.

They exchanged rings, slipping them on to the third finger of their left hands. Near perfect fits. A further embrace sealed the occasion.

"We've actually been and gone and done it!" exclaimed Andy. "We're hitched."

"Say, so we are, honey." Kit's countenance was aglow with elation and happiness. "Mated!"

"Conjugated, even!" countered Andy.

They headed for the drawing room. Andy fetched from the fridge a bottle of good champagne which he placed in an ice bucket. They toasted themselves. Andy rang his solicitor and made an appointment for the morrow to draft the documents to be drawn up. They resolved to ask Rick and Jon to witness their signatures, to make a little ceremony of it, maybe inviting family and a few friends to the celebration.

Later, they carried in Kit's baggage and unpacked some essentials. Last week, after moving what sparse bedroom furnishings he already possessed into a spare room, Andy had bought, in addition to the bed, two long, modern wardrobes and two chests of drawers – one of each for each of them – as a suite. The couple decided to open a joint bank account for household expenses: each of them would contribute equal amounts to it.

They went out for a riverside stroll, watching rowers and canoeists and picnickers enjoying their quintessentially English summer afternoon pursuits. Kit the newcomer was enthralled.

High on an overdose of happiness, they could not resist calling effusive but polite greetings to every hapless stranger they got close enough to, flashing their new rings in a 'casual' manner that was too studied to be spontaneous. From many of those who recognised their love-suffused state, they received all-knowing, indulgent grins – and, sometimes, a cheekier wink came their way.

An excellent pub meal and a couple of pints of draught beer set them up for what remained of the day. Their flat was only a few minutes' step from the river and they were home by nine. Television held their divided attention for a mere twenty-five minutes.

Twelve hours later, they were still nestled in their bed when the phone rang. Kit, just then reposing on top of his partner, reached out for the instrument and put it to Andy's ear.

"Hi, Rickie! It's bloody great to hear from you. It must be the middle of the night there. I was going to ring you later on with some news of my own. How are you both? Is Jon's eye going to be OK?"

"Yes, he's being discharged from the Denver hospital sometime in the morning."

"Bloody, fucking marvellous!"

"I know. I'm so incredibly relieved, Andy. His mum and stepfather are here at the moment. They've got the room you had."

"Does his father know about Jon? Shall I tell him?"

"No, that's OK. His mother rang Rupert earlier to tell him the good news. I think Giuseppe, on the quiet, is getting quite a kick out of the comings and goings of all these Brits. His wife is still keeping herself scarce, but he seems quite laid-back about that. My shoulder is improving bit by bit. But much more important: did Kit get there OK?"

Whereupon, Kit unleashed a disgracefully lascivious moan into the mouthpiece.

Eighteen

They drove to Tor Farm three days later, where they were welcomed with open arms and pantry by Rick's parents and brother, as well as by Sarah and Peter who were returning to the States on Wednesday of the following week. It was the first time Mike and his father had encountered Kit.

The moment those glittering new rings were espied, out came the bottles and the beer cans. Mike, emotionally matured at last by the family's traumas, first sped down to Macclesfield and collected Jill, his now regular girlfriend, from the supermarket where she worked and brought her up to the farm. Quite a merry little party was soon swinging from the hilltop.

A Carol made weepy by two goblets of sparkly telephoned her terribly missed son.

"Don't put the glasses away right at the back of the cabinet, mum," Rick advised. "Jon and I will be back home Friday next week, so we'll be expecting you to put on a right shindig."

Carol's excited squeal drew everyone's attention. More bottles were broached.

On the following day, Mike took Kit and Andy to four possibly suitable sites he had identified for them. Kit ruled out two as not having room for future expansion, another in the national park as lacking adequate road access, but the three hectares adjacent to one of the largest agricultural auction grounds in Britain, a short distance west of Macclesfield, was deemed ideal for AndiKit Agricultural Equipment Limited. It boasted at least one substantial building unit which could accommodate the proposed assembly plant, plus lots of growth potential with it being located so centrally in the British Isles and convenient to the national motorway and rail networks.

The land agents were contacted. A fruitful meeting with them next day resulted in an offer being made and, over the ensuing days, consultants were briefed, funds were transferred from the States and legal papers signed. It was Andy who negotiated almost £250,000 from the selling price of the property while Kit was keeping appointments in Manchester to sort personal finances.

The couple launched themselves on a whistle-stop tour of southern Scotland and northern England, before returning in time for Rick and Jon's homecoming. They arrived exhausted at Manchester Airport only minutes before the plane came in. Sarah and Peter were there already, having postponed their own departure for a few days.

Appearing rather gaunt, Jon was the first to turn the corner into the reception area. He was wearing special dark glasses to protect his eye from dazzling light. Rick's arm was long since unrestrained, but the shoulder was not yet entirely free of pain.

"Welcome home, boys," cried Sarah. "When you left home, I'll bet you didn't think that the next time you set foot in England it would be me saying that!"

Rick grinned back. "We didn't really intend to be away quite this long," he declared sardonically.

They were greeted vigorously, Peter alone getting not a single kiss until his wife took pity on him and plonked a gratuitous one on his cheek, prompting all the men to follow suit, much to the recipient's obvious and good-humoured confusion.

The arrivers had only two suitcases and a holdall bag between them. Andy shot Kit a meaningful glance, getting a lewd finger gesture in return.

Rick and Jon dropped off the baggage at their own Knutsford house, noting that the 'For Sale' board had gone from the unoccupied one next door. A stack of mail awaited their attention, which Mike had sorted for them in their absence, the unstated truth being that he was so weighed down with anxiety for their safety that looking after their house and being useful to them had been a necessary outlet for him. Evidently he had even done some dusting, an event practically unheard-of at the farm. It was due to Mike taking Rick's spare set of car keys and going by train to Heathrow to pick up the Cavalier that an enormous car-parking bill had not accrued. Seeing Rick and Jon walk together across the yard once more was Mike's sufficient reward when the company arrived at the farm an hour later. He sprinted out to meet them and wouldn't let them go for long minutes, until he saw his mother waiting at the kitchen door.

Their reunion with Rick's parents was tearful, particularly when Rick saw his father in his wheelchair smiling stoically up at him. Brian's was maybe the worst personal tragedy resulting locally from the whole affair.

"Oh, dad, what have they done to him?" Rick groaned under his breath. Expecting to see him like this scarcely mitigated the distress he felt when actually confronted with his father's condition.

Brian had regained most of his speech in recent weeks. "Good to have you both home, son," he uttered with a barely perceptible slur in the voice. "I'm really proud of you, really proud, and now we are all together again." He took his one sip of celebratory wine. "Long life to all of us!"

His simple toast was taken up by everyone

"Your parents are coming tomorrow, Jon," Carol informed him.

"Cheers, right," he thanked her. "Which ones?" was an afterthought.

"All of them," she said.

"Dad too?" He stared quizzically at Rick. "He said only last night he'd be coming up next weekend. What's changed his mind?" It was a rhetorical question.

"To come to the party, perhaps?" suggested his mother-in-law.

The men shook their heads dubiously.

Kit's father was flying over to see his son tomorrow, as well.

Both male couples went down to the Knutsford house for the night. At seven next morning, the doorbell rang. A bleary-eyed Rick answered it.

"Jon, it's your father!" he called up the stairs as he admitted Sir Rupert, who had left his car in the roadside because Andy had parked his vehicle blocking the driveway, not expecting callers at such an unearthly hour of a Saturday morning.

"Hi, dad!" cried Jon, tumbling downstairs in his dressing gown. "This is a very pleasant surprise."

"It's good to see you home again," said Rupert as they shook hands and hugged with the other arm. "How is the eye?" He peered closely at it when Jon took off his glasses for a moment.

"They've been wonderful at the hospital," Jon told him. "They say it'll be right as rain in a few months, but I must keep bright light out of it for now." The darkened spectacles with the blinker-like side shade were put back in place.

"Aren't you tired, Rupert?" asked Rick from the distant kitchen where he had put on the kettle.

Rupert shrugged. "Not really. I went to bed at eight o'clock last night, and left London at three-thirty. I can't stand all those interminable motorway snarl-ups, so it's the only civilised time to use the roads these days."

The couple supposed so.

Andy peeked warily between the landing banisters. There below in the square hall was his boss talking to Jon. Always alert, Rupert spotted him.

"Good morning, Andy. Enjoying your leave?"

"Very much, Sir Rupert, thank you. I'll be down in a minute."

"Don't hurry yourself, I'm not going anywhere!"

Twenty minutes later, Andy crept down, still tired and crabby after many miles of motoring and a late night. He joined the others breakfasting in the morning room, but sat apart from the table.

Almost immediately, he mistakenly perceived his Head of Department as confronting him.

"I understand from Jon's mother that you've got yourself a boyfriend: the American, Kit Henderson, whom I had the pleasure of meeting when I went over to see Jon and Rick." Andy had turned scarlet. "My ex didn't mean any harm. Just making conversation, you understand?"

Sir Rupert suddenly let out a guffaw at Andy's dumb discomfiture. "Come on, man, out with it! You're never normally lost for words. All the dangers and challenges you've overcome: now I'm not going to eat you!"

"Well," Andy began hesitantly, "I have fallen in love." He glanced round the company, his friends considerately averting their eyes and trying to pretend that they weren't there. "Oh, shit! Oh, Christ!" he shouted, "Yes, and I'm bloody glad, too." He lowered his voice, but it soon rose again to a crescendo. "I know the Service holds a dim view of these things, but that's their problem, not mine!"

Rupert leaned forward and patted the back of his assistant's hand in a fatherly manner. "Yes, I agree with you entirely," he said soothingly. "Things are changing, but perhaps not fast enough." He sat back and took some of his coffee. "Well, we have been a dark horse, haven't we! There you've been for years chatting up the females of the species in the office and everywhere else, I gather from your reputation, and all the time you've been a men's man!"

"Hey, that's a nice distinction," Jon interposed.

Rick covertly warned him to keep out of it.

"I didn't know I was until very recently," Andy tried to elucidate.

"You don't need to explain anything for my benefit. But you've certainly landed yourself quite a catch there, you know."

Andy nodded vehemently. "God, don't I just know it!" he exclaimed.

"And he's thrown up a splendid military career for you, it seems."

"He was doing well for himself, yes."

"Well? Brilliantly, you mean! Two citations for bravery and the Purple Heart – all by the age of, what, twenty-five, is he? A member of one of America's wealthiest families, all of which, according to their system, could well put him in line for the highest political office in the land one day."

The younger men stared at one another in sheer incredulity. "Geez!" they murmured almost in unison.

"*Those* Hendersons!" said Jon in awe. "It never occurred to me, not even for a second. I'd no idea it was those Hendersons he belonged to."

Andy was distinctly startled. "Why did no one say anything to me about all this? Not even the Ciampis, or his father when he wrote to me?"

"He actually wrote to you, did he?"

"Just to say thanks for helping his son."

"Kit apparently asked them to say nothing. He's a man with a very determined will so far as his family is concerned. Just like his parents, by all accounts. But his mother was glad he was intent on leaving the navy, and his father was equally pleased that you had influenced Kit to return to the family business. So you had wittingly or otherwise made powerful allies of them."

Andy was utterly dismayed. "And I simply stood by while he chucked that amazing career down the pan. Oh, bugger it! Kit! Why didn't you tell me all this?" He put his head in his hands and sighed despairingly.

"Because I didn't want to lose you, honey" came Kit's contrite appeal from the doorway.

His partner froze. Kit came to him and placed a hand on his neck and fondled it. Andy pulled away.

"We've been living a lie," he muttered querulously. "You haven't been open with me, after all we went through."

Rupert stood up and spoke to his son and Rick. "Can we go to another room, boys? I think it would be better. I'm sorry to have started all this."

"Don't you worry about that, Sir Rupert." Andy's dismal features turned to him. "It would have come out soon, anyway. Mr Henderson is coming here some time today."

"And I was intending to tell you the rest today. Honest, lover, I was!"

"You could have told me months back. After all, it's not a crime you've committed that you need to be ashamed of. It's only that you've deceived me because, fuck, you couldn't trust me. That's entirely obvious. How do you think that makes me feel, huh?"

They were alone by this time. Kit circled the chair to face Andy and squatted before him. Andy's hands were on his knees. Kit held them, but Andy released himself. Kit grasped hold of them again fiercely.

"Don't be such a dickhead, Andy. Honest, I did trust you. I do trust you. It's just that, well, I don't talk about those horrors some of us went through out there. I try to avoid even thinking about them, for Chrissakes! They can be nightmares: those beach landings, the shells exploding all round you, seeing your shipmates mangled before your eyes. All for what? So that some bum up there gets his, so we can put someone else in his place who is friendlier to our government? Shuh! That's all it amounts to. That's why I transferred to IC Technology, but even there I gotten myself involved in this search party tryin' to trace some of our guys missing in jungle country. We got most of them out. Jesus! Then when I was on shore leave and met you, I managed to get myself shot up worse than ever; for the first time, fact is!"

"Well, it's better I know late than never," grunted Andy dispiritedly. "You have tremendous physical as well as moral courage. And I knew you came from a reasonably comfortably-off family, of course I did. But not from *the* Henderson dynasty that controls so much of the food industry in the States. Does this mean that I am helping you to extend the Henderson empire into this country as well?"

"Like hell, does it! We are setting up our own enterprise, you and me. Yes, using Henderson money and know-how, but we are on the equipment side. You know all that. No way will Pop have any say in our business operation other than what relates to contracts we have with Henderson Farmtools Incorporated. We agree to assemble and distribute a certain number of Henderson machine units per annum in the UK, but there are absolutely no strings attached. You know that, too. It's strictly business between them and us. We're not even restricted like franchisees: we can deal with anybody else we choose to. I want to see if we can develop that harrow comb design of mine, too.

"Say, I ain't telling you a thing we haven't decided on already, so what's with you, buddy?"

How could Andy tell him that he felt demeaned and dishonoured; that he feared being the poor relation – or worse, some kind of lousy, sponging gold-digger, to be merely tolerated by his family simply because he was the key to Kit's change of heart about them?

"How much is your personal fortune worth, Mr Kitchener Henderson III? Don't you think I am entitled to know that?"

"Sure, honey, of course you are. I was going to talk all this out with you today. I want you to believe me, because it's the absolute God's honest truth I'm telling you. It's just crappy bad luck that your boss came and spoilt it all."

Kit suddenly leaped to his feet. "Oh, Jeezus!" he yelled out his exasperation. He yanked his unresisting partner out of his chair. "C'mon, baby, we're going upstairs. I want to show you something. God, if only we'd had time yesterday after we got to the farm."

"What do you mean?" Andy allowed himself to be led out of the room.

"You'll see in a minute."

Reaching their bay-windowed double room on the opposite side of the landing to the owners', Kit delved into his briefcase. He pulled out a bulky white envelope and slid from it a bundle of bank deposit and cheque books as well as a quantity of assorted papers.

"You'd better sit down."

Andy did, on the edge of the bed.

"These were waiting for us yesterday at the farm. See?" The envelope was shoved in front of Andy for verification. "Addressed to both of us, so you could just as easily have opened it as me. It just so happened that Mrs Timperley – Carol – handed it to me. OK? OK?"

Kit went into his case again for another, much smaller envelope which he opened. "Here is my bank statement, as you call it. This is all the money I possess here in my own name." He showed the total to Andy. "Isn't that about the same amount you told me you have in various places?"

Andy examined the sheet. "Aye, thereabouts – then I've got the flat, of course, less the mortgage outstanding on it. That's the new investment account you opened for yourself in Richmond the other week?"

"Sure thing." Calmer by this time, Kit next held up another bank statement. "Here is the opening balance of the joint household current account we opened. Right, honey?"

Andy nodded.

"Now there's this that I wanted you to see before now, but we only got it yesterday. It's what came in the big envelope while we were in Scotland. We were too tired for anything last night after we came in, so I was going to show you this morning, without any of this bad feeling." Covering up the name on the top with his hand, Kit proffered his partner a third statement form attached to a sheaf of documents. "Just the figure at the bottom; the rest is too involved to talk about right now."

"Bloody hell!" breathed Andy. "'Thirty-seven mi...'" he started to read out. "Sterling! Kit, you are a fucking multimillionaire, you bastard! How could you do this to me?" he wailed. Then he gasped as Kit revealed the two account-holders' names printed on the sheet. He gasped again.

"No strings attached here, either, baby," whispered Kit, brushing his mouth across Andy's sweating brow."

"I – I can't accept that, Kit. It's unfair of you to expect me to."

"Say, I'm not giving you something. That's a statement that summarises their portfolio of our joint holdings registered with them. Both our signatures are needed to move anything in or out of there, so I couldn't grab it back again, even if I wanted to – which I don't."

"That isn't even an ordinary high-street bank. Isn't it one the Queen deals with? Anyhow, I haven't signed anything for them, so this is all meaningless."

"Pish, just a detail we can soon put right. That's all ours, sugar. We are equal in that as in everything else. Isn't that what we agreed? It was pretty complicated, what with you being British and me American, and it has taken these weeks just to fix things the way they are. We'll need to put our minds to tax considerations shortly. We can change anything else when we're both good and ready. OK, so it's taking me a bit longer to transfer some bigger items into both our names and others into yours alone without them losing value, but what the hell, we'll get there eventually!"

"Bigger items?" Andy croaked, "I can't believe any of this. It's something you and Sir Rupert have cooked up with the lads to tease me with! Well, ha, ha; all very droll."

Kit gripped him by his quivering shoulders. "It's no joke, Andy. Y'know: 'All my worldly goods I thee endow'?"

"I don't remember our making that vow."

"No-o, but it amounted to that, didn't it?"

"Sort of. But I didn't know about your wealth then. It would have been too one-sided. I'd never have agreed."

"Either we do it this way, or we give it all away, which would be stupid just when we're setting up our lives together and our business. But this has nothing at all to do with the business capital. I couldn't just pretend my money didn't exist, could I?"

"I wish you could have done," Andy retorted, still horribly shaken. "Oh, shit! I'm really out of my depth here. Why wasn't I told any of this, Kit? Why?"

"You know why. I told you. I was scared of losing you. Just look at you now! To tell you the truth, you are the most precious thing ever to come into my life, and if it came to a choice between keeping you or the money, there's no contest. I'd scatter all of it in the streets of London or Manchester – anywhere you care to mention, rather than let it come between us. You know I really mean that, don't you!"

Andy had to admit that he did. Deeply in shock, he flung himself up the length of the bed and covered his eyes with an arm. He was instantly overwhelmed by a violent fit of sobbing and turned his face into his pillow.

Kit decided not to crowd him, so he folded his half of the duvet across and covered Andy's convulsed body with it. He quickly dressed, foregoing a shower for once, and tiptoed downstairs.

Rick and Jon had also dressed by now. The three men were sitting silently in the drawing room when Kit found them. They had been mulling over the couple's undiminished difficulties in coming to terms with their having killed people, having ended human lives and bereaving yet more who had loved them. Knowing that those men were ruthless criminals somehow did little to assuage this sense of guilt or make the deed seem more palatable. Most of them had probably become what they were because of where and when they were born, that was all. But for the grace...

Starting back to work as soon as Monday would hopefully restore some normality to the pair's interrupted lives.

"I'm sorry about that," said Rupert to Kit as he entered. "I had no idea that Andy was unaware of your situation."

"He wouldn't still have been, Sir Rupert, but for the way things worked out yesterday." Kit put the verbal stress on Rupert's title, which American mannerism never failed to exercise the knight, until today.

"My father is coming this afternoon," Kit went on. "I understand you weren't expected till next week."

"Yes, well, I was wondering what Andy was planning to do now. My ex-wife's news shook me, I can tell you! It's all right for openly gay people to hold more junior posts in the British Civil Service, but at Andy's level it becomes more of a dilemma, I'm afraid. The faintest whisper... It's a disgrace, but there we are. The old Establishment still believes homosexuals are a potential security risk, as if the notorious Mata Hari herself and the thousands of historical sirens like her were in fact transvestite men all along, seducing innocent and vulnerable, male, British secret agents to get information out of them. Fools!" he snapped with a contemptuous laugh. "But we must wait for them to shuffle off their mortal coils or retire – whichever is the earlier, to use their bureaucratic jargon – before lots of things are likely to change for the better."

Jon intervened, "I seem to remember that you weren't altogether ecstatic about me for many years."

"I was only concerned lest you got yourself into some kind of trouble. I knew nothing about what I had been brought up to believe was some kind of curable illness, except that some of its adherents were pretty odd birds. I'd no idea that most gay men were just as much men as the rest of us. It was when I met Rick and some of your friends that I realised the error of my ways. I read somewhere recently that an MP is railing against a gay organisation which is calling on every gay person to – 'come out of the closet', you call it? – because he was afraid that that would make them socially acceptable."

"That's precisely why Stonewall is making their plea," concluded Rick. "It is to defeat ignorance. Once the straight world fully realises that we have been among them all the time and are essentially no different from them in ways that really matter, the cat will be out of the bag for good."

"For a lot of you, though, it can still mean taking terrific chances," observed Rupert reflectively. "Look at you, Kit. And our young Andy, for instance." He shook his head sadly. "Such a promising career, too. With his calibre, Andy could have attained the very summit of his ambition. Even I can do nothing to save him."

Kit sat down quickly. "Sheeesh!" he gasped, "so he would have lost his job any ways," he said as to himself. "And he kept that from me."

"It seems like you both have a lot of catching up to do," Jon tactlessly commented.

Rupert had pricked up his ears. "What do mean, Kit? That 'he would have lost his job anyway'? Didn't you realise?"

But Kit had already scooted out of the room, and was flying up the stairs three at a time. He bounded into the bedroom. Andy had fallen asleep, tear runnels still shining on the side of his nose. Kit flopped himself heavily on the bed, jolting Andy into rude wakefulness.

Kit commenced to beat on Andy's chest, ignoring the twinges he was causing to his own. "Why didn't you tell me!" he cried resentfully. "You, you, you fucking hypocrite!"

Andy sat up hastily to fend off the blows. "Hell, what are you getting at?"

"You! You didn't bother to tell me you were going to have to throw in your career to live with me. You said nothing about it, either before or even after we first talked about going into business together! And now you have the brass gall to criticise me for making provision for our future! It's just as well we do have something to fall back on, otherwise we'd have both been out of work."

Andy gaped at Kit, at the look of offended righteousness on his handsome countenance. Suddenly he couldn't help himself seeing the funny side of their situation and broke into paroxysms of giggling.

"You're not laughing at me, are you?"

"No, of course I'm bloody not! I'm laughing at how fucking stupid we've been. And now here are you calling your millions 'something to fall back on'!" This brought Kit himself to snigger. "Kit, my love, you are bloody priceless! Priceless!" he iterated. "Come here!" He dragged the offender and offended down on top of him and kissed him avidly. "Oh, Jesus, Kit, I'm so very sorry I reacted like that. I forgive you for being a bloated plutocrat, if you can forgive me for not being one. Neither of us can help it, after all!"

"It's the way we were born!" Kit hooted that oft-repeated slogan, and joined in his partner's laughter.

"But you're not going to get me living like a millionaire." Andy spluttered the last word as Kit tickled his ribs. "I still want the simple life I'm used to, not cocktail parties and fashion shows at the Ritz or wherever they go. Agh! I prithee, desist!" he yelped when probing fingers found more tender spots. "I don't even like the West End, Mayfair (shit!), the Sloanes and (aagh!) all that. I live in Richmond to (uh!) get away from the (aha!) city." He emitted a hoarse scream. "Maybe I'm just a (haaah!) a booze and chips man, at heart," he finally rushed out, panting, before the next assault came.

Kit left off his attack, however. "All right, that's cool by me. We live the not-too-spartan, simple life. It's still what I want any ways," Kit assured him. "I got away from all that other stuff, and I don't want us to go down that road, neither. OK, honey bunch?"

"And we stick to our original plan."

"What else?"

"OK, it's a deal."

After a few minutes' ardent smooching, Andy came up for air to declare thoughtfully, "I'll tell you what, though: it's bloody comforting to know it's there, isn't it?" Whereupon Kit went straight for the groin to make a similar point.

Kit did eventually get his morning shower after all, but he had to share it because they were so late by then.

Their damp hair slicked down, the couple sheepishly insinuated themselves into the drawing room, where the other three had patiently taken up a game of Monopoly to while away the time.

"Well, I'm glad you finally stopped all that screaming at each other," growled Jon from Jail.

"All relationships have their teething problems," Rick remarked.

Ruefully, Rupert agreed. "You mean, when you feel your partner's sinking into your backside?"

"Or when you don't!" Kit drawled wittily.

"So you've sorted yourselves out now, have you?" said Rick.

Andy idly scratched the speaker's head with his fingertips "We certainly have, Rickie boy. Kit's promised to behave himself from now on in, haven't you, lover?"

"Not if you keep doing that to the competition, I won't!" Kit declared in a mock sulk.

Andy quickly transferred his fingers to Kit's fair hair.

"You'll get them cross-breeding, doing that."

Jon received a smart kick under the table from Rick.

Rupert drew himself up. "Well," he said counting his red £500 notes, "I think maybe I've thoroughly trounced you two, so perhaps I'd better be wending myself homeward before you demand a return bout."

"Lucky dice," Jon said grumpily. "We shall not forget," he threatened. "What time's your dad due in, Kit?"

"14.05," Andy replied for him, since he had just checked.

"Won't you stay and meet Pop, Sir Rupert? He'd be sure thrilled to make your acquaintance."

"He would?" Rupert was surprised. "I can't imagine why. I'll think about it. But I must speak to you, Andy, before I go anywhere. It's my reason for coming here today, really."

"Uh, oh," murmured Jon.

Rupert shepherded his assistant across the hall and into the dining room, shutting the door. They sat down at a corner of the table.

"You do understand that I can't help you in this situation, don't you."

"Yes, I know that."

"I mean, if you want me to try, I will. But I honestly can't see our Civil Service chiefs making an exception in your case any more than they have in countless others before you, no matter what I or anyone else says. They are totally obdurate when it comes to sexual matters, especially homosexual ones. All I could do is register my protest when the axe falls."

"I do understand. And, no, I appreciate your offer of help, but I shouldn't want you to stick your own neck out on my behalf. I might just have left it at resigning, but there is an important point of principle to be made about sick attitudes in high places."

"I shall certainly insist that my dissent be put on record, of course."

"That might help others one day. Thanks."

Rupert regarded the other man closely. "So, what are your plans for the future? I presume you must have some?"

"We are formulating some, yes."

"I asked my boys – hrrmph – Jon and his Rick, what you intended doing, but they claimed ignorance. No doubt at your direction. When Kit stormed off remonstrating about your not telling him that your own job was in jeopardy, he let slip something that clued me up to your having alternative arrangements."

"He did?"

"And I must say, I'm very relieved about it. If there is anything I can do to help you..."

"No, there really isn't. We can manage fine."

Rupert brought a hand thoughtfully to his chin. "Your flat in Richmond – do you still have a mortgage on it?"

Andy grimaced.

"Listen, Andy." Rupert leaned forward confidentially. "I would like to pay it off for you, if you will let me. By way of an apology, if you like, for the unconscionable treatment you are going to get from a country that owes you – and Kit, for that matter – so much in the affair that's just been cleared up, not to mention all those earlier cases you were on."

Andy was staring wonderingly at him. "Sir Rupert, that would be most generous of you, but really, the way things are working out... Christ! The way things are working out! I can't believe it even now. In my wildest dreams, I could never have invented a train of events like the one that's happening to me now." He started to chuckle to himself. "Lucre. It's coming at me from all directions this morning.

"You know, I have always driven myself to succeed in whatever job I was given to do, but money as such has never greatly interested me. Oh yes, what can be done with it. But acquiring vast amounts of money for its own sake? No, I was quite happy to leave that game to others."

"And now?" Rupert was intrigued.

"Well, let me just say – absolutely confidentially, you understand – that domestically, it seems we are unlikely to come across many financial shortfalls." Andy smiled secretively. "I think it will take me one hell of a long time to get used that fact, though."

"You mean you are in that enviable position of being able to say the boss, 'stuff your ruddy job where the sun don't shine'. Is that right?"

Andy couldn't help evincing a faint smirk at that notion. "Not a bit of it," he said with brazen disingenuousness.

Rupert nodded appreciatively. "I am very pleased for you. I suppose it is all legally drawn up and watertight? Good. That man of yours certainly knows what he wants, I'll give him that! I shouldn't say this to you, but I think he's getting a ruddy good deal out of it, as well, and he knows that, too. Well, even if you don't need money, don't forget that I am around if ever you need me as a friend."

Andy reached out. They shook hands on it.

"If you do have some spare cash to give away," continued Andy with some deference, "you must have noticed that Jon and Rickie have been absent sick from their jobs for a very long time. They must both have lost a lot of earnings. Need I say more?"

"Indeed not. I have thought of this, too. As it also happens, however, the Treasury have managed to scrape some meagre public funds together in recognition of their services to Britain and the international community, and the Prime Minister is minded to advise Her Majesty... I had nothing to do with it. I couldn't, being Jon's father: nepotism and all that. Ironically, Kit is about to get a Presidential award of some kind, did you know? A civilian one, of course!"

"That's great. God, that's really wonderful."

"Please say nothing to them, Andy. Let them find out in the usual way: it's far more satisfactory all round. As for surplus moneys, I truthfully am not a very wealthy man, compared to some we could mention. You probably know my salary scale. But I'm sure I can find an appropriate registered charity and perhaps a reputable campaigning group. I should want to do that. I think Rick mentioned one of them before."

"He and Jon will be able to guide you there. I'm not really well up on these things."

They rose and left the room to join the activities they could hear gathering momentum in the hall and in the driveway outside.

"We're off to the airport, Dad," Jon told him.

"Won't you go with us to meet Pop, Sir Rupert?" Kit renewed his request.

Rick added, "Then you can come straight up to the party mum and dad are putting on for us. Mike's going to be on the barby, God help us. You'll be more than welcome. There's plenty of room here for you to stay tonight."

Rupert affected a sigh of resignation. "Oh, very well," he chuckled. "How could I be so ungracious as not to succumb to such persuasiveness?"

"How indeed?" quipped his son from the car he had just reversed out of the garage.

"You and Kit can come in my car," Rupert told Andy, "and on the way, you might like to fill me in on the business ideas I presume you have got well advanced by now. I seem to be the only one left in the dark.

"And by the way, Andy," he whispered out of the corner of his mouth, "when you leave the Service, drop the 'Sir' bit, will you? If only to stop that Yankee of yours addressing me the way he does!"

"I believe you have just committed a serious political incorrectness," observed Andy, grinning widely as he went to shift his car out of Jon's way.

"This is Andrew Gregson, Pop," said Kit to his father who had arrived, amazingly, with none other than his wife's brother-in-law, Giuseppe Ciampi.

Abe Henderson imperiously eyed the Englishman with a penetrating stare through steelframed Roosevelt spectacles. "Hmm, come over here, boy," he instructed at once.

Andy glanced at his partner, whose smile was a glimmer of encouragement, and obediently followed the tall, fawn-suited man to the far side of the Club Lounge. They sat down on an unoccupied sofa, Abe talking incessantly, as the watchers could deduce from the agitated movements of that silvery, well-crowned head.

Meanwhile, Giuseppe was smiling rotundly at the welcoming party. "Surprised to see me, eh? I knew that I had some business coming up over here in the next week or two, so I thought, 'why not bring it forward and take a mini-break with those estimable, nay, awesome folks across "the pond"?', as I've heard you call it."

He and Rupert exchanged knowing grins while the younger people cast round the big lounge as if searching for the 'awesome folks' described.

"Sorry, Giuseppe," expressed Sarah, "I think they must have been delayed."

"Don't worry, though, I'll not impose on you. I'll easily find a hotel hereabouts, no problem."

"We won't hear of it: you're staying with us," Rick insisted.

They repaired to the bar. Kit carried drinks over to his father and partner, then left them to it.

Rupert took Giuseppe to one side. "I understand that you are to be congratulated."

"Me? what for?"

"The United States Attorney General happened to let me in on something the other day; something about a series of trials taking place across your country following the Federal indictment of twenty-odd prominent business people for offences ranging from sedition against friendly powers to straight murder and extortion, plus God knows how many disparate financial malpractices."

"Granville told you I was involved?"

Rupert nodded. "Which makes it three people only who know about that."

Giuseppe gave a relatively small Italianate shrug. "Well, let's wait for the outcomes, shall we? If they are all found guilty, it will constitute scarcely a flicker in the evil flame of The Light of the World. Unfortunately." His smile was philosophical. "But at least they'll know they can't always get away with their horrific activities with complete impunity."

"I was sorry to learn of the manner of your brother's death."

"Thank you. Even Sarah and the boys have been sympathetic about it, too. But you know the saying: you can't touch pitch without getting defiled? Could be whoever coined that dictum was thinking about someone like Umberto at the time."

Twenty minutes after they had entered into their conversation, Andy and Abe Henderson stood up. Andy was seen to put forth his hand, but Kit's father embraced him briefly. Was that really a smile on Pop's lips?

They strolled to the bar, Andy looking decidedly flushed but at least as triumphant as the other.

"Kit, I was just saying to Andy –" Abe was in fact referring his words to Giuseppe and the distinguished-looking individual with him "– that I consider you should have waited before exchanging wedding bands until you could benefit from the blessing of a godly pastor."

"Pop, meet Sir Rupert Reynolds, the head of Andy's department in London."

The two shook hands cordially. "So," Abe said, "they've brought you in on it, too?"

"Jon, here, is my son, Mr Henderson," announced Rupert.

"Ah, so we are both very fortunate men, despite everything."

"No, Mr Henderson. Including everything."

It was just as well that Sarah and Peter had deferred their return to Colorado, and had been around the previous day to assist Carol and Mike get things ready for the party. Not only were Carol's own family present, but also Jon's three parents, surely half the neighbourhood and those two American tycoons. What a comedown for Messrs Ciampi and

Henderson, having to put up with this simple country fare and these ordinary surroundings after what they were accustomed to!

"Why, your home is absolutely charming, Carol – might I call you that? – I am truly thrilled to be here," said Giuseppe, smiling broadly. "No doubt generations of doughty English men and women have been raised under this selfsame roof, the very stuff of nationhood!" he exclaimed. "Isn't that so, Abe?"

"You have a lovely home, Mrs Timperley. And a very interesting farm, I might add. I warrant you don't need us foreigners to tell you that. I congratulate you and your husband. Where is he, by the by?"

The sound of light applause broke from the next room. Brian was discovered there amidst a crowd of congratulatory neighbours. He had just stood up out of his wheelchair unaided for the first time since his illness, and had manoeuvred himself into a more comfortable armchair. Abe Henderson subsequently sat with him for a full hour, bending his ear, but learning quite a lot in the process from this articulate, born-to-it hill farmer.

Mike spent several hours outside in the yard struggling to keep the barbecue alive in a scant and disorientated breeze. Even at this altitude, a stiff wind couldn't be relied on. Jill would be at work until 8 o'clock. Luke and Paul Platt, who should have been helping to serve sizzling cooked steaks, sausages and cutlets, had completed the shearing only this morning, and were keeping themselves available to show the shed-full of rolled-up, unwashed fleeces to those interested. In their new, gleaming white underwear, the immaculate sheep stood out against the sun-drenched, rolling hillsides, a fraction of their former girths and rejoicing because of it. The dogs, their tongues lolling, hovered round in the afternoon heat, waiting impatiently for grilled titbits that seemed a very long time in coming.

Jon attached himself to his trio of parents for much of the time. It was good that they got on so well in recent years. His sister, Emma, telephoned to say that she and Tom would be expecting him and Rick to call on them in the next few days, or else.

Almost straight afterwards, Carol told Rick that there was someone on the line for him or Jon.

"Hi, mon! Paul here."

"Hello. Paul who?"

"You've forgotten me, haven't you? Remember the Geordie lads you met in London? At the caff. Remember us now?"

Light dawned. "Oh, that Paul. Right. I do remember you. Did you win your match the following week?"

"Wicked! You remember that after all what you've been through? Yeh, we won 'em great! But I just rung your own number first ta see how you twa are comin' on and how you're getting over it, but there was no reply. You're only just come home, ain't you?"

"That's right, a couple of days since." And they had turned off the answering machine. "It's kind of you to ring."

"I don't want to be a pest, like, you know. Sounds like you're havin' a great party. But, well, I just rung to say 'welcome home', and ta say we been thinkin' of yous both. Can I ring you again when you're not so busy?"

"Of course you can. But where did you get this number from? Ah, sure, the papers and Directory Enquiries. Well, Jon and I don't live here. Like, this is my parents' home. Yes, sorry, of course you knew that. Tell you what, though: we'll ring the number you gave us just as soon as we get ourselves sorted out. Hang gliding? Right, if you're up for it, why not? Of course I promise. Catch you later. And, Paul, thanks again for calling."

Later on, Rick recounted to Kit the unsavoury incident which had arisen just before they left England for Chicago. Jon, who was listening in, said, "Turned out they were not all skinheady types, after all: just the one, if I remember correctly – one they called Winnie, because he fancied himself as a latter-day Adolf Hitler."

"Damn nice of that guy to phone you, then," Kit concluded. "You two do hang gliding along with everything else?"

With no difficulty, Carol talked Abe Henderson into spending the night at Tor Farm after he had waxed lyrical about it being the first European farm he had ever been on. He had a childlike fascination for its, to him, ancient walls and the moorland landscape practically denuded of trees hundreds of years before. He hugely appreciated the Timperley hospitality and the taste of English country life it represented.

Mike drove him down to Rick and Jon's house late the following morning, where Giuseppe's bed had withstood his onslaught miraculously, but with the aid of two stools judiciously secreted beneath its old frame.

After he had slept well in his usual room, Rupert accompanied the other men to the site of the interesting new business venture, before embarking on his journey home.

Jon wondered, "Surely you two aren't going to commute here daily from London, are you? You'll be spending most of your time travelling."

"Oh, we'll fix something up," Andy assured him confidently, observing from a distance as Kit and his father wandered around the grounds, Abe poking inquisitively about in the various huts and better buildings. He was starting to get strong misgivings concerning the true degree of the older man's purported disinterest, but those were soon dispelled by the sight of his partner dealing his father a severe dressing-down, the sound of his words drifting towards him in the breeze. Kit was still patently in charge there, Andy was gratified to note.

"If the project makes the money it should," said Giuseppe, "and you want any additional growth capital, I may be in a position to invest a few dollars in it myself, if your terms are right."

"We'll keep that in mind, Giuseppe," Andy replied. Given the choice, he would not want more American backing coming in. Their first major goal was to make their finance base predominantly British by early profits plough-backs. That would underpin their jealously guarded legal status as a wholly-owned, independent company.

One chilly Wednesday morning two months later, shortly before AndiKits were to begin trading, Rick was backing his car out of the double garage when he noticed a large furniture removals van pull up to the empty house next door, which had just undergone 'a comprehensive programme of modernisation and refurbishment retaining the best of the original Victorian features', as estate agents' patter described such things. The vehicle belonged to a well-known London-based removals company.

Rather like their own house, the other detached dwelling was brick-built and double-fronted, with an extensive front garden placing the house a good distance from the main road, and screened from the traffic by a sturdy sandstone wall overhung by handsome trees and shrubs. The previous owners were a loveable husband and wife who had lived there for forty years, and had chosen to move to a much smaller house nearer the town, a week or so before Rick and Jon had gone to America.

Rick now reflected upon that regrettable loss of friendly neighbours, and resolved to carry out, at the weekend, their promise to get in touch with them. He wondered what kind of people the newcomers would be. He turned the car round so that he could drive forwards out of the gate onto the road. He was early for work today; there were some finishing touches to make to a mid-morning lecture he was to deliver to a fairly fresh intake of students.

Through his rear-view mirror, he saw a pair of man's arms vigorously waving at him from next door over the low dividing wall. Another pair joined them. Thinking this very odd behaviour, Rick let down his window and poked his head out.

"Hello? How can I help you?" he called. He switched off his engine.

He heard giggling, then two familiar heads popped up between the arms. "Aren't you going to give your new neighbours a welcoming kiss, then?" cried Andy. Kit's face was lit up by another of those inimitable beams of candid pleasure which so often shone out of him. "Hi, there!" he laughed. "Say, just look at Rickie's mug! He looks as if he's seen a ghost!"

"You!" Rick shouted, tumbling out of his car. "But we were speaking to you, like, only on Sunday evening and you said nothing about this.

You asked us down to Richmond to see you next Saturday, as well!"

"So now you don't need to travel so far. What're you complaining about?" retorted Andy.

Rick gave each face a hug and kiss across the wall. "God, have you been plotting this for all these months? I can't wait to tell the family!"

The pair swapped guilty looks. "Erm, I'm afraid they already know, Rickie," murmured Andy. "They've been in on it from the start. Sorry. In fact, it was your own brother who first mentioned that this house was on the market."

Rick's eyes opened yet wider. "Right! Just wait till I see them – and that interfering brother of mine!"

"Actually, he did practically all the preliminary work for us," Andy confessed.

"Say, aren't you pleased to see us, then?" Kit gave a worldly-wise smile to his partner: "I think he was secretly hoping for a family with a gorgeous son of about twenty to move in here. Now we've spoilt it for him."

"Hell, you've rumbled me!" laughed Rick. "But you two will do almost as well! Just stay there. I'll go and call the Sleeping Beauty."

He dashed into the house. Jon was, in fact, almost ready to leave for the surgery, but was just then in the greenhouse at the back of the house checking the humidity and some fairly recently struck cuttings. He had heard nothing of the minor rumpus at the front. Responding to Rick's frantic gesticulations through the kitchen window, he ran indoors and through the house in pursuit of him. Had there been an accident of some kind?

When he reached the front door, he saw two well-known figures vaulting the wall nearby.

"What the blazes are you doing here?" yelled Jon, leaping down the front steps.

"Hoping you'd be more glad to see us," mumbled Andy, breaking from Jon's mighty hug. "Because you are going to see a lot more of us from now on!"

They laughed at Jon's look of amazement.

"Oh, shit," he exclaimed. "You're moving in? It was you who've been spending all that money on the Thompsons' house?"

"It's ours now," Kit corrected him, "whether you like it or not!"

Rick told Jon, "You do realise that now we'll have to invite these two to the fortnightly orgies we organise here with our friends?"

"Huh, you needn't bother yourselves," was Andy's riposte. "We'll set up in opposition to you."

"Are all your services connected?" enquired Jon.

"What do you think?" drawled Kit with a wink to Andy.

"I'm talking about the services to your house, stupid!"

"No," Andy replied. "The electricity's off. The electric company's supposed to be switching it on after they've checked over some kitchen rewiring some time this morning."

"Well, here is my key, then," said Rick, handing Andy a bunch of house keys. "If you want to make yourselves a drink or anything, you know where everything is. We must get off to work now. See you this evening." He made for his car. "Oh, and by the way, this is one of the nicest surprises ever to have been sprung on us, isn't it, Jon?"

"The nicest, probably. I suppose we'd better put a gate in that wall: save our pants getting ripped every time we call on each other. Oh, I don't know, though!"

Nineteen

Though they were not called on to do so, Peter and Sarah quietly left their UNESCO posts to take on new employment. They were each voted a tidy severance payment, and a personal letter of commendation for their exceptional services was signed by the current President of the Security Council.

Rick and Jon had kept their promise to Paul a month after their welcome home party. The bluff Geordie brought his pals Phil and Bart with him, and on Shining Tor not far from the farm, they sampled a few of the primary thrills of hang gliding for the very first time.

On that occasion, Paul and Bart had asked their girl friends along, but they were substituted three weeks later by Mark, the skinhead Adolf's elder brother, and Carl, a rugby team-mate of Bart and Phil, because they'd been hugely anxious to meet the men from Cheshire ever since hearing the others' reports of their encounter with the couple in London, and would not be put off for a second time by the girls occupying 'their' seats in the clapped-out motor they so frequently chipped in to keep on the road.

After a chilly five hours on – and off – the windy hill, they were invited back to the house for a bite and a warming drink before setting off for home. Mark colluded with Carl to separate their hosts, then they made clumsy passes at them by the touching-up method. Both lads were gently but firmly given short shrift.

Sarah gave birth to her twins, one of each, a week early. The joyful event being registered in the States, they would benefit from dual nationality.

Paul-and-co's next visit came a fortnight after that. It was a purely social one, November being too late in the year for the novices to train in the sport which had already begun embedding itself in their memory banks of best buzzes. The two once again made awkward attempts to get into bed with Jon and Rick, but were good-naturedly put off. Having failed with them, they tried it on with the hot new pair from next door, with similar results.

At the simple naming ceremony at *Casa Bianca*, Rick, Jon and Mike were nominated as the children's sponsors. Though invited, Andy and Kit were too engrossed in that crucial week of launching their business to attend. The bonny babies were to rejoice in the family names of Richard Michael and Joanna Carol Kristina, this last being after Peter's mother who was there with his father. The parents were planning to take a lease on a cosy log cabin on Giuseppe's estate, from December. While looking after the infants for the first two or three years, before fully resuming her work with her husband, Sarah could operate from home by getting on with some of the essential clerical chores, commencing with purpose-building an integrated computer program. Their education project was only just getting off the ground.

This was the first occasion for Rick and Jon to meet Jessica Ciampi who was astonishingly relaxed in their company, considering her cold rebuttal of them only a few months before. Was it her youngest sister's change in attitude over her son, Kit? Perhaps the presence, this time, of Sarah's and Rick's parents was making the difference.

It was not long after this that Jon was allowed to discontinue wearing his protective glasses altogether. Inevitably, a small scar was left to show for his life-threatening injury, but most of it was concealed in the fold of his eyelid. Rick's boundless joy over his partner's survival with undamaged eyesight tended at times to overflow, prompting him spontaneously to smother Jon and that scar tissue with kisses, usually taking the other unawares. Jon swore that it was some kind of curative balm imparted by Rick's impulsive attacks of affection which had so much hastened his recovery. Who could disagree?

Rick still needed to do his physiotherapy exercises, but not so exhaustively as before. The pins inserted surgically in the shattered bones of his shoulder seemed to be giving no trouble now, but hang gliding, which entailed being suspended aloft from a body harness, would for him remain a no-no for several months yet. X-rays confirmed that the bones themselves had been knitting together satisfactorily and were fast consolidating their strength. The painful discomfort he had endured for those weeks after the shooting would have been far worse if his mind had not been preoccupied with Jon's parlous condition.

It became as important to them as before to pursue, so far as they were able, their various other outdoor sporting interests, so they had resumed their associations with fellow exponents soon after their return from the States. More often than not, it was those men and women contacting them as well-wishers that had revived the duo's interests very early on. Nor were their new neighbours exactly tardy in tagging themselves on whenever time allowed, and sometimes when it didn't. Mountain bikes were the next item on the list of wants, chiefly so that they could have quick, strenuous workouts on local bridle-ways when available time was restricted.

Kit and his partner were paying a seasonal call on Andy's parents near Norwich on the Saturday before Christmas, when five young men were among the hordes of supporters who descended on Manchester for the soccer match between the local United squad and Newcastle Ditto. Afterwards in the city, by prior arrangement, they met up with Jon and

Rick who'd had pressing Christmassy things to do at home in the afternoon. They insisted upon treating the pair to a slap-up Christmas dinner at a popular town-centre eatery. Later, they were introduced to some of the Village bars seething with gay abandon, before going back to Knutsford Road where they were to spend the night. Next day was for them to pay a brief first visit to Tor Farm, thence home.

Astonishingly, as soon as they reached the men's house, the Geordies went straight upstairs, three of them to sleep in one bedroom, Mark and Carl in another. Something over half an hour elapsed before Rick and Jon wandered up to their own room.

So this was why those fun-seeking lads had not wanted to go clubbing or to stay up partying into the small hours! A sizeable, flat triangle, wound in shocking-pink gift paper and scattered with rainbow glitter, had been taped right across the door frame of the couple's bedroom. In blue cut-out letters it bore the bold inscription:

'FOR RICK AND JON – A VERY MERRY XMAS FROM PHIL, BART AND PAUL.'

Smiling quizzically, the pair unwrapped their door and cautiously opened it. They switched on the soft lights within.

Whatever their large and totally unexpected Christmas present was, it had clearly been left on their king-size bed which was completely covered by that same garish gift paper. To each of the bed's brass corner posts was strung a floating Santa-shaped balloon, the faces smirking inanely, mischievously, perhaps over a secret they held in common.

Standing either side of the bed, Rick and Jon snatched off the paper then the duvet beneath, revealing the prone, butt-naked persons of Mark and Carl side by side, their contiguous wrists and ankles clamped together by police-issue handcuffs, their widely-spread opposite limbs tied securely with clothesline to the bed posts. Strands of coloured tinsel were festooned invitingly about them, and the plump testicles of both sported a well-made bow of red ribbon. Across the two lads' backs was written with a broad, indelible blue marker, !!! PLE...ASE !!!. The trussed-up boys twisted their heads round and peered up at them. Those winning smiles were unalloyed enticement.

"Please, we want you to have us!" Carl begged touchingly.

At that moment, a distant male-voice trio struck up with 'We wish you a merry Christmas' in two concurrently opposed keys. Plucking up courage, the strolling troubadours drew closer during their increasingly gusty performance to stand outside the door. Then, with Paul thankfully determining its opening note, there came their own extremely personal rendition of 'God rest ye merry, gentlemen, let nothing you dismay,' this first line being the only recognisable one, while the originality of the remaining lyrics: 'For Mark and Carl are ready there for you to have your way,' and so on in like vein, provoked the intended mirth from those they were raucously directed towards. That remarkable number was succeeded by a medley of other, relatively unharmed carols, concluding quietly with 'Silent night', sung with unaccustomed irony.

Silence did fall, however, once the retreat of bare feet tiptoeing on carpet was succeeded by the muffled closing of the would-be songsters' bedroom door.

Put thoroughly on the spot, the perplexed couple swapped bemused glances.

"Puce ear," observed Jon cryptically, indicating with a nod both submissive offerings eagerly waiting on their bed, but Rick had noticed the natural phenomenon, as well, and that the half-pair of matching gold dumb-bells piercing the upper rim of either young man's left ear was more in evidence than ever against his arousal-flushed skin.

"I suppose," Rick ventured, "that it would be churlish of us to turn down such well-packaged gifts, wouldn't it?" He appraised the burly figure of the rugger player on his side of the bed.

Their 'presents' chorused fervent assent.

"I mean, after all the trouble someone's gone to to make them look prettier," said Jon, tongue in cheek. Fanciable they definitely were; pretty, never. Try as he might, Jon could not work out how these two dark-haired rascals would have been able to package themselves up like this.

"How the hell did you manage the gift wrapping?" he asked, the unlikely mental picture of those straight guys carrying out the necessary, very intimate acts on their gay pals intriguing him immensely.

"The lads did it," was Mark's surprising, offhand reply. "Yeh, we just stripped for them. Did they do a neat job on us?"

"You could say that," said Rick, noting on his left that his was not the only riser.

Jon was surveying the well-turned back of the slender twenty-year-old. "Not a bit like his brother, is he?" he decided. "Are you absolutely sure you're both willing to go through with this?"

Cries of exasperation emanated from the two, whose pre-lubed backsides were quivering tantalisingly with anticipation.

"Shit," growled Carl, "this is really, really freaking me out." He let his head sink back on to the sheet. "Just be friendly with us, for Christ's sake. It's fucking Christmas."

"I guess that's, sort of, telling it as it is," suggested Rick, with a grin towards the pillows where plentiful choices of strong safety gear were laid out ready for use like so many fashion accessories. It was evident how these guys wanted it, too, though it wasn't what Rick and Jon normally did with one another. Gifts have to be looked after properly if they are to serve their intended purpose. So, just to oblige...

First, those fine ribbon bows, their knots super-glued solid, needed to be slipped off. Mark's had been cruelly tied so tightly that he writhed and bucked about, snorting loud oaths, while it was being forcibly removed, but he was smiling through the tears which sprang to his eyes.

"Oh, cheers, cheers," he kept gurgling into the mattress during the lengthy procedure. Carl's round face was turned towards his, and he got a broad wink for his pains.

It was not until both men had lingeringly taken turn about with them that they untied the dazed and happy lads whose charged, tingling bodies had received an all-over seeing to beyond even their wildest solo fantasies. It was a scribbled stick-it note on a mirror that divulged to Rick the hiding place of the handcuff keys.

The vigorous second and third hours were still more exhilarating for the foursome than that first one, with all their added variety and frequent changing of steeds repeatedly sending the men climbing through intensifying convulsions to erupt frenziedly out of newly discovered, multiple peaks. Perversely, it was the lively, go-getting rugby fanatic who hungered for all the kissing and loving tenderness, whereas his friend craved lots of quite severe treatment. For their part, their persistence finally paying off, the boys could scarcely believe their luck to be sharing these magnificently physical bedfellows who were proving themselves so adaptable and experienced, just as they'd hoped and astutely imagined the eight-years-older guys to be.

At ten next morning, the trio trooped in with four cooked breakfasts on trays, and were immediately confronted by a gale of banter hurled at them about their absent musical talents. However, those expressions of profound gratitude from their two satisfied and ecstatic comrades told them that their subterfuge had done the trick all right. So it had been well worth all those hours of scheming and a whole evening's preparation before they'd left home, setting their pals up to score big time: team spirit at its very best.

In the New Year's Honours List, Rick and Jon were made privately reluctant OBEs. This effectively set the Royal seal of approval upon the general vindication of their family, so it was certainly not to be declined. They also well understood the political significance of the honour, for it very publicly underlined the government's upholding of the UN's continuing role in the former Yugoslavia.

Immediately after the main Investiture ceremony at the Palace, Kit and Andy also were presented to Her Majesty. This American and the former civil servant who had, indeed, been carrying out his professional duties, were each presented with magnificent, hand-illuminated parchment scrolls marking a people's appreciation.

Kit was summoned to the White House in the February to receive his medal from the President in the course of a celebration observing the anniversary of the head of state's Inauguration. The well-briefed President, in sparkling mood, remarked that these visits to Pennsylvania Avenue were getting to be a habit with Mr Henderson. Andy and their friends accompanied him to be presented to the great man, who personally gave them Commemoration medallions engraved with their names, recording the day and the nation's thanks to these exemplary sons of an allied country. Two of the gallant police officers involved in the well-publicised Leadville engagements also received awards that afternoon.

When the four called on *Casa Bianca* next day, Jessica was positively gushing, though none of the men could find it in himself to warm to Kit's aunt.

Life in England gradually settled into new patterns for members of the twin households.

Andy's evolving job description became more like that of the company's principal ambassador to the agricultural industry as he travelled the length and breadth of the country, spearheading promotions and motivating the sales force. A trained and practised assessor of other people's strengths, foibles and weaknesses, he was the only person bewildered at how easily he fell into this novel mode of existence. As he had proved to his cost in other important respects, his self-knowledge tended towards the abysmal. He now threw himself with alacrity into the world of public speaking, fronting displays at agricultural shows, addressing landowners' and farmers' organisations and dealing with officialdom at all levels. He and Kit, as co-directors, sometimes swapped functions to see the business from various standpoints. Kit's job was more on the production and personnel sides.

During the first year of operation, the work force expanded fivefold from the twenty-seven at the outset, and orders arrived in a steady stream. The company sponsored ploughing, harrowing and harvesting competitions, and put its name to sporting trophies of diverse kinds, including a certain annual hang-gliding event in the Cheshire Pennines which AndiKit's timely intervention saved from financial insolvency. From then on, drifting above hills and valleys of many parts of Britain, the company name and eye-catching logo could clearly be discerned from the ground boldly emblazoned on the equipment of the rival clubs involved. The prototype of Kit's revolutionary harrow design received its first field trials at Rick's agricultural college. These and further tests on diverse soils in other regions of the country were spectacularly successful. The comb would be a money spinner, for sure.

The transformation to Rick's and Jon's lives was less to do with their work than with popular demands upon their time. They were constantly called upon to speak to community groups, schools and to public gatherings about their exploits, and were closely examined concerning their families' experiences with the news media at the time the crisis broke. Their own relationship was a subject which stimulated interest and open, though usually respectful, curiosity. Society was getting accustomed to the changing cultural pattern.

That new gate in the wall separating the property of the Henderson-Gregsons from that of the Timperley-Reynolds was superseded a year later by a barrel-roofed conservatory constructed, to the customers' own specification, like a glass-covered tunnel linking the two kitchens. Except at night for security, the fire doors at either end were usually left unlocked, though neither couple impinged on the other's space once Kit eventually adjusted to peculiarly British notions of privacy. Responsibility for maintaining the footway's ample flora seemed to devolve in time upon the shoulders of Andy and Jon.

From the beginning, Sarah and Peter brought the twins to England at least twice a year, sleeping at Rick and Jon's house when visiting her side of the family. Initially, this was partly to avoid adding to her mother's workload already made heavier by her desire to nurse dad back to health. It later became the custom. Besides, the men and the children grew very attached and delighted in each others' company. The neighbouring couple's slightly older children at No 30 were very good with the twins. At home in their mountain cabin, the kiddies always had to have a chat with their beloved uncles whenever there was a telephone link between the two families.

A hang-gliding section of a prestigious Newcastle sports club was formed due to the enthusiasm of some of its members. Rick and Jon were guests of honour at its first meet. Bart and his lovely, intelligent girlfriend, Teri, chose the occasion to announce their engagement. Six months later, they married. Paul was his best man, and their four friends from Cheshire were seated near the head table at the well-attended Reception afterwards. Adolf didn't show; he was remanded in custody pending trial for his part in a racial mugging.

The families and friends of the bride and groom quickly got used to these energetic men usually dancing with one another during the enormous party which ensued, though plenty of females obviously derived quite a kick out of prevailing on them to partner them on the floor. Two or three other males, their inhibitions bibulously loosened, summoned up the guts to follow suit during smoochy numbers, confirming what their friends had long since deduced anyway, and greatly enhancing their future lifestyles in the process of opening up. When a well-oiled, spaced-out and presumably straight fellow approached him for a dance, Kit had the wit to decline with a terse grin, seeing that his dodgy accoster's mates were intently watching for the outcome of their dare. Inevitably on such an ale-swilling occasion, a small fracas developed in one corner of the big hall. A glass was thrown and a girl screeched drunkenly as the two men squabbling over her flung a few punches. The spoilers were subsequently separated and sent packing home.

Shortly after, when the bride and groom took their leave of the festivities for their Costa honeymoon, their Cheshire guests with Mark and Carl left by taxi for a nearby hotel where they had reserved their stay for rest of the Bank Holiday weekend.

It was an enduring cause of casual speculation to the visitors just how completely the mates of these two insatiable guys understood them and their special preferences, especially Mark's. Could it be that the Geordies' bonds of friendship were exceedingly close, to the point of the straight guys making themselves available from time to time? It would all come out, no doubt, one day.

Brian Timperley's condition improved no further once he was able to get himself about in his chair or on crutches. The running of Tor Farm rested entirely in Mike's hands now, though at the busiest times Carol was no mean hand at most of the traditionally men's tasks when pull came to lamb dropping, shove to dipping and heave to shearing.

An unannounced visit to the north by Mirabelle Garvey had some unpredictable consequences. Kit's once errant, Nottinghamshire aunt was returning her nephew's second call of a month earlier. She, too, had married a man of the soil: a cattle farmer of the stripe Carol's mum and dad once were as tenants down in the Cheshire Plain. Both of Carol's work-hardened parents were still going strong, thank God, residing in a pensioners' bungalow in Nantwich, where she could visit them every week. Carol and Mirabelle 'got on a treat', as Rick's mother later reported to him. So much so that, after only a few weeks, Mirabelle was back, bringing her lissom younger daughter, Marcia, with her. Marcia and Mike, who was single again, were instantly smitten with one another.

"I've only once seen anything like it before," Rick recalled to Kit and Andy during a Friday evening pint at The Pheasant.

"When was that?" asked Jon.

Rick raised meaningful eyebrows at him.

"Wow, yes, of course," Jon murmured, a sweetly connotative smile on his lips.

Their friends quickly grasped the allusion. They grinned at one another.

"And the magic's still there," declared Andy, rubbing his partner's knee.

"Sure!" Kit responded. "We knew it would last and last, didn't we, honey?" He looked proudly round the company. "Y'know, I can still remember my first reaction when I saw Andy that very first time in the train dining car."

"Oh yes? And what was that?" asked Jon, interested.

A roguish gleam entered Kit's eyes. "Phwoaaaar!" he groaned, clutching Andy's arm as he did so.

Their companions laughed out loud.

"That," Rick gleefully explained, "was precisely Andy's response when you were coming up to our table!"

"Hot damn!"

"I'm bloody sure it wasn't meant for anyone's ears, though," said Jon.

The band drowned out Andy's pithy retort. It was Jazz Night at The Pheasant.

Mike and Marcia were married within the twelvemonth. They lived at the farm, their daughter, Dawn Eastre – Marcia was very much into Saxon folklore – joining them and the world two months later. The transatlantic airlines were doing very well out of this complex web of fortuitous family alliances and its occasions.

Kit had never met his cousin, Marcia, until he came to England, and already through her and Mike, family genes he had inherited were mingled with Rick's family's genes in Rick's latest niece – a concept he found oddly sexy. He felt himself to be some kind of blood brother to his true friend.

"Do you realise," he pronounced during one Sunday lunch at Tor Farm, "that if it were not for Rickie and Jon, and Andy and me, Mike and Marcia would likely never have met."

"And what a lovely little girl would not have been born!" cooed Carol, casting a fond look towards the cot near the fireside. She winked at Marcia. "I knew something good had to come from America one day."

"It was just a question of time," agreed Mike, "and waiting patiently." He gazed significantly at his wife, honeyed adoration oozing from him.

Marcia eyed him back with amused scepticism. "By all accounts you never had to wait alone!" she cried.

"Huh!" went Brian.

Mike reddened. He glanced accusingly at his chuckling brother.

"Don't look at me," Rick protested. "I've not said a word!"

An e-mail attended Jon when they reached home. It was from his father.

'I thought you might like to know that the body of Marie-Delphine Michaud, alias Anna Reicke, was found dead on the roadside near Belgrade last night. It looks as though she met with a firing squad only hours before we got to her. So much for loyalty among cannibals. Love to you all. Dad.'

"I reckon that closes another chapter," Jon muttered sourly.

They were lounging about in their neighbours' sitting room, half listening to a CD and shrinking half a bottle of Scotch. Rick absently stroked caressing fingers across the eyebrow above his partner's fading scar.

Said Andy with a doleful smile, "It's all over bar the touting for the next little conflict that The Light of the World can fart stir into flame."

"Do you ever regret leaving that life, baby? In your heart of hearts? Do you wish you were still out there using your street cred and meting it all out to 'em?"

Kit's question had snapped Andy out of his moment of pondering. "Of course not, you plonker." His tone was still subdued. "There are lots of guys out in the front line now, who I know would give it up tomorrow if they could. Trouble is, most of them have known no other life. I think we were all once wooed, like the rest of the world's great unintelligentsia, into believing that the lifestyle of the secret agent was one of glitz and daring, of uninterrupted adventure, sex and romance. Instead, we quickly discovered that it was the opposite in every particular, with buckets of blood and shit mixed in."

He brightened. "No, lover mine, I didn't believe romance even existed till I met Jon and Rick, who were my example; then you, who were my ideal. That's what did it for me. As for the daring and the making use of street cred, AndiKits is giving me a hundred times more thrills and headaches than all my years in Intelligence, I can tell you! The glitz? Well, who needs it? 'Sides, five minutes or five hours of lovemaking with you, and it's sparks and fireworks all the way – and fucking wonderful. Bliss on a stick."

Rick had started bowing a 'fiddle' accompaniment when their names were mentioned.

"Does all that boil down to your not being too sorry to be here?" enquired Jon waspishly.

Andy snuggled his head into a wing of his favourite armchair and yawned comfortably. "Oh, I think I'll hang around for a while yet." His eyelids flickered shut.

Kit sat on him heavily. "Too darned right, you will!"